Portals of Change

~The Nameless Chronicles~

Book 2

Joshua Kern

Contents

Other Books by Joshua Kern   VI

1. Prologue   1

2. Chapter 1   5

3. Chapter 2   17

4. Chapter 3   31

5. Chapter 4   43

6. Chapter 5   55

7. Chapter 6   67

8. Chapter 7   79

9. Chapter 8   91

10. Chapter 9   103

11. Chapter 10   115

12. Chapter 11   127

13. Chapter 12   141

14. Chapter 13   153

15. Chapter 14   165

16. Chapter 15   177

17. Chapter 16   191

18. Chapter 17   205

19. Chapter 18   219

20. Chapter 19   233

21. Chapter 20   247

22. Chapter 21   259

23. Chapter 22   271

24. Chapter 23   285

25. Chapter 24   297

26. Chapter 25   309

27. Chapter 26   323

28. Chapter 27   335

29. Chapter 28   349

30. Chapter 29   361

31. Chapter 30   373

32. Chapter 31   387

33. Chapter 32   399

34. Chapter 33   411

35. Chapter 34   423

36. Chapter 35   437

37. Chapter 36   449

38.	Chapter 37	463
39.	Chapter 38	475
40.	Epilogue	487
41.	Acknowledgements	491
42.	About the Author	493
	Other Books by Joshua Kern	495

Other Books by Joshua Kern

Refton & Thomas

Forgotten Spies

Forgotten Child

The Game of Gods

Arc 1 – Human

The Beginning

The Death of Champions

Arc 2 – Demi-God

Fragments

A Tower Novella

Pieces of Divinity

Arc 3 – God

Everything Ends

The Dungeon Alaria

Arc 1 – Integration

The Dungeon Alaria

The Creator's Daughter

Arc 2 – ??

The Nameless Chronicles

Portals of Albion

Portals of Change

Realms & Runes

Runic Cultivator

The Well Within

The Well Within

Stand Alone

The Ridden

Duologies & Box Sets

The Game of Gods: Arc 1 Duology Box Set

The Dungeon Alaria: The World of Alaria Arc 1 Duology Box Set

Prologue

Anna fixed her husband's tie and pushed him out the door, where Ben was waiting. He was their family's chauffeur, butler, and general everyman. He was whatever they needed him to be, because he could be trusted. And it was under his guidance that Mathew would make it to the waiting vehicle outside instead of wandering back off to his hidden lab, or to a book somewhere.

"Do you think I should take father up on his offer?" Tessa asked her mother, slipping in before the door closed.

Anna quirked a brow and pointed to her jewelry case. "Pick out a set that will match my dress, would you, dear?" Her dress was lying on the bed, all ready to be put on. It had been designed to be easily laced up from the back, and with her daughter's help, she was ready within a minute.

"Well?" Tessa asked impatiently, as her mother began putting on the azure earrings.

"I'm thinking." The older woman preened in the mirror, enjoying how the blue contrasted her red hair and emerald green dress. "It's a hard question to answer. I don't want anything to happen to you, but at the same time, if he is right, which you know he likely is, then this could give you a nice bump in the future."

She turned around and pulled her daughter close. "I can't make this choice for you, only you can do that. Now, we need to be leaving. The weekly Sonntag meeting will be starting soon, and I'll be making my retirement announcement there."

Tessa nodded mutely and opened the door for her.

"You don't have to do anything you don't want to do. If it doesn't feel right, then don't do it," Anna told her, lifting her daughter's chin gently.

"What about dad?" Tessa asked softly, not wanting to hurt her father's feelings.

"He might be disappointed, in which case all you have to do is tell him you want to see more empirical research data relating to the safety and effectiveness of the experiment on young women within your age bracket. He won't have it on hand, and it will distract him while also helping him gather useful information." Anna smiled and kissed her daughter on the cheek. "Remember, the choice is yours either way. Don't feel pressured into making a choice you don't want, or are uncomfortable making."

A maid appeared at the far end of the hall with her secondary office CryTel in hand, attached to a long trailing cord. "It's for you, madam, someone called the Major. He sounds panicky."

Anna snorted. "The Major doesn't know how to sound panicky." She accepted the device and lifted it to her ear. "Hurry up, we were just about to leave."

The maid hurried off to continue her duties in a different part of the house. It wasn't her place to linger and listen in on the madam's official calls.

"Zack and Zara are missing!" He roared into her ear. "They were taken along with Specialist McCleary from the portal after we left. The bodies of the soldiers I left with her to escort them back to the dorm safely were found just a few minutes ago. Dead inside the warehouse, with one vehicle missing. Both packs the kids had been carrying were found there as well."

Anna closed her eyes, feeling a headache instantly beginning to form behind them. "I have to ask. Could it have been her?"

"No, absolutely not. Even if she wasn't loyal to me, which you know she is! She has a soft spot for those two. She was there when we rescued them, and at this point, probably knows most of their story. She would rescue them again in a heartbeat I believe, but she wouldn't kill my own people."

Tessa looked at her mother and mimed that she would be outside, giving her some privacy for the conversation.

Anna nodded gratefully, waiting for her to disappear before growling. "I don't care what you have to do but HANDLE IT! In a couple of hours, I'm about to announce my retirement as a hidden adviser to the king before all the nobles and many of the citizens of this country. Then moments after that, I am going to make my final announcement in the role. It will be the same one I made last night, wherein I named Zara the crown's special scholarship holder and temporary royalty. Can you imagine what will happen if people find out she was kidnapped even before the announcement was made?"

"Why do you think I contacted you?" The Major ground out. "I have my people working on this already. I'm contacting you mostly as a courtesy, and to see if you might have any ideas on who might have done this?"

She tapped her nail against the back of the smooth device in thought. "The Albright brat was never captured. He might be dumb enough to try something this foolhardy."

"I had considered him," The Major hesitated. "I'll pay a visit to his parents and get some answers. You go have fun making your announcements."

The CryTel clicked off and went dark, as it lost the connection on the other side.

Anna had a vicious smile on her face as she dropped the device on a small waiting table and headed for the front. She would never begrudge anyone causing more harm to the Albright family. Not after what they had done to hers. She would make sure they paid, or none of this would have been worth it.

Tessa smiled brightly as she joined them.

Well, maybe some of it was worth the trouble.

Chapter 1

Zara clasped her hands over her cold, red ears grumpily and sat to the side. She was waiting for Zack and Jean to finish changing into the Shouvain created suits. The two had worked together to get her and Edith in them first, which she appreciated, except for one thing; it was too big for her. The excess material pooled around her legs and arms. In short, she looked like a bloated land whale. While also making every movement difficult or plain impossible.

Sure, the suits were warmer. Something she was currently enjoying. Everything not covered by the coat had begun to suffer from mild frostnipping already. The painful prickles, as fresh blood struggled to work its way through the damaged skin, constantly reminded her.

Zack found the hidden zipper on his suit and pulled it up with a relieved groan. The extreme cold had helped to dull the ache of his broken arm. The lingering numbness from its astral form being exchanged for mana had begun to fade some. Still, it was uncomfortable and cold enough that his quasi-healing ability alone could not keep him from feeling its effects.

Risking the side-effects of another healing spell would be worse than trudging over miles of frozen snow. The next spell would fix the broken bone and any other damage to the shoulder if he did it right. The cost to fuel the spell, however, could potentially leave him unable to use his legs or any other number of things. It was better to wait until later, or just let his ability fix all the damage.

Under Zara's orders, the bears had been busy gathering up everything in the area. Pieces of weapons mixed with destroyed clothing, and the bodies. Everything was brought together in a pile for them to go through.

It was true they needed to get walking, but before that, they needed to make sure they were prepared.

Of the original five available suits, they had only needed and been able to use four. The extra had a hole in its chest from Zack's element-backed attack. The body was pulled from inside it and stripped down like the rest.

Unfortunately, the spies hadn't been hiding anything under the suits. Just some thin underclothes no one wanted to wear... or touch. Dead bodies released certain *things* as they relaxed. Who knew?

Edith was given the best items they found, anything to keep her warmer. Mostly, those items had been worn by Dorn. Namely, his hat and gloves, something that none of the others had been using, as they didn't need them. The travelers had worn masks, back when they had faces, but those had all gone missing somewhere along the way. Only the two masks that the ladies who confronted Zack at the end remained. They had been set to the side for later inspection. The suits came with adjustable gloves attached to them as well. It was hard to keep the body temperature properly regulated without them.

Jean laid out the remaining clothes flat and frowned. "They brought very little in with them. Which makes sense, considering they weren't expecting to stay more than a few minutes. We have access to snow, so water shouldn't be a problem under decent circumstances. As for food..." She turned and looked around. "I'm not sure. This portal should be teeming with high-level monsters attacking us non-stop. Yet, we haven't seen one since we got inside. I can only assume that is either because of what is about to happen, or this area is desolate and barren enough to not interest them. Either way, food may be scarce."

Zara grumbled and sighed. "I was just getting used to eating good food regularly, too." She waved George over, and with difficulty, slowly reached into the small hidden pouch in his back. "I only stored four of these, but they should help." In her hand were four of the nutrition bars Jean and Rose had given Zack a week earlier.

"Okay, that will help, next then, is transporting Edith and Zara. We need to create a sled or something that we can pull with them in it. With all of this." She pointed to the heap of items the bears had gathered together.

"Not that, that's ours!" Zara shouted, pointing to the pack full of money Dorn had killed the last of their kidnappers over.

"Zara, that thing weighs almost as much as you!" Jean protested. "Besides, you don't need it anymore, remember? You were named as the crown's special scholarship holder."

Zara looked away and pouted, since she couldn't properly move her arms. "It's still ours, money should never be wasted."

"Fine, whatever, we can still use all of this to somehow create a sled."

Zack took the staff he had charred with his electrical attack and set it to the side. It would work well as a walking stick, if nothing else. Though, he had a feeling that it was likely a decent weapon even with the damage done to it. He started to toss a couple of daggers to Zelda, but stopped when he saw she had already set aside a collection of her own. Instead, he handed them to Zara, just in case she ever needed them.

Jean had two different-sized swords and a bandolier of throwing knives attached to various places on her suit.

Working together, Zack and Jean laid out the spare suit as the bottom layer of their sled. The material was tough and slicker than regular clothes. It could withstand hours of being dragged across the snow without disintegrating. Unzipping it, they made it as wide as possible before rolling back in the side with the hole in it. It was barely wider now than it had been all zipped together.

"This isn't going to work," Zack said after they had been messing with it for several minutes.

The few scraps of rope they had were the remains of what they had used to tie Jean's hands and legs together. There wasn't enough to do anything complicated with, and the clothes had already begun to freeze from residual moisture.

"Yeah, I know." Jean stood and studied the landscape, hoping to find something they could use. There was nothing. Finally, she turned to Zara, a stupid idea sparking in her mind. "What about you? Can you do something? Can you do whatever it is you did to these bears, to the bodies?"

Zack groaned and rolled his eyes. That was not something that she should have said to Zara.

Zelda picked up a dagger and charged at the experienced soldier.

"What is this bear's fixation on stabbing things?" Jean shrieked, hopping away from a furious Zelda.

"She has flat fluffy paws. Being able to hold anything is fun for her, though I think her obsession with sharp pointy objects may have come from what happened to us," Zara said dully, unwilling to stop her little protector.

"While that is interesting, and also rather disturbing. Why is she suddenly trying to poke holes in me?" Jean ran circles around the smaller bear, who was quickly growing frustrated with her larger, and much faster, opponent.

"You basically just called her a '*Necromancer*'," Zack informed her, feeling the urge to move things along faster.

"Exactly, dead bodies are not cute! They are gross. Teddy bears and other stuffed animals are cute and cuddly! I'm a puppeteer class. I can't make a puppet out of anything that was once a living body."

Jean's eyes narrowed at the name of her supposed class, flicking them thoughtfully at Zack before shaking her head. It wasn't the time to worry about any of that. They could discuss it later once they were mobile.

"Well, sorry. I guess?" She danced back from the approaching bear, nearly tripping over the spare Shouvain suit. "What about this, then? Can you make something like this into a puppet? A simple one to carry Edith."

Zara frowned thoughtfully and had the bears drag the suit over to her. "I don't know. I've never tried to make clothes into a puppet before." She began tracing mana-laced patterns into the suit, the specifics of the glowing purple imprint invisible to all but her eyes.

The process took a minute of her complete focus and adding multiple layers to the pattern. Finally, she finished and leaned back. A thoughtful look came over her face as she began pumping mana into her newest puppet. The hole in its chest changed. The jagged edges smoothing out into a circular hole that now looked as though it belonged.

The damage her brother's spell had done was too severe. That, combined with it not being her puppet at the time, meant she couldn't fix the damage entirely. She could merely mask it and make it look like something else. Maybe later she would integrate material from a coat or something else to patch the hole.

Aisha carried over the pack of money and waited for the puppet to unzip itself before stuffing it inside. Now they didn't have to make a choice. The puppet would carry the money for them, along with Edith.

"Alright, you know what, fine whatever, that works. Let's put whatever else we can fit inside the thing as well." Jean gave in with a roll of her eyes. "What about you? Are you going to do the same thing to your suit as well?"

Zara smiled and nodded. She had just discovered another use for her magic. Of course, she wanted to try it out some more.

Zack took a moment while they were busy to open his status page and review the differences.

Zackary ??	Level: 7	Exp to next Level: 58/2,210
Class: Arcane Mystic		Race: Dimensional Child
Titles: Child of the Portals, First to Second		Elemental Affinity: Space
Strength: 07.3 | 10		Intelligence: 15.1(+.2) | 13(+2)
Dexterity: 11.2(+2) | 13(+2)		Magic: 21.9(+.2) | 41(+2)
Constitution: 20.5(+2) | 25(+20)		Agility: 12.2(+.1) | 14(+1)
Abilities: Life Burner Lv. 4, Arcane Manipulation Lv. 0		SP: 23
Spells: Arcane Bolt Lv. 1, Arcane Armor Lv. 1		

He was a little surprised to see his level was seven. Getting to five had been a no-brainer. He had thought that level six might even be possible, but anything beyond that was pushing it. People just didn't give as much experience as the various forms of monsters.

Not to mention the experience jump that occurred at level five and beyond. That was always a rather severe shock to most unprepared travelers, and it would only continue to get worse. Especially when you realized the counter zeroed out with each new level. Thankfully, any extra experience you gained wasn't lost when it happened. Still, it made each new level a near monumental task of grinding out weaker enemies for experience day-in-and-day-out.

Of course, that could be fixed by simply going deeper into the portals where the stronger monsters were. Assuming whatever corporation or military group you belonged to would let you. Not something that happened very often, if ever, in Albion at least.

His eyes trailed across the various stats. Noting the natural increases in both *Intelligence* and *Magic*. Further down, he saw the new spell he had gotten at level five and shook his head.

'Arcane Armor' was... a useful spell under the right circumstances. Any other time, it was a piece of trash.

It was an instant activation spell. Which was nice, but it constantly consumed magical energy to keep it running. For someone like him with a limited amount of mana, it was a terrible spell to use. On the plus side, if you knew an attack was coming, then you could just activate it. As long as you had enough energy, then you could theoretically be safe from anything.

If a normal mage had this spell. Then, depending on how high their intelligence stat was, and thereby their mana pool, it was possible for them to instantly become unstoppable. For a little while, at least. If an attack was strong enough, then the armor could destabilize, and then even more mana was required to fix it.

He had rarely used it before, and he didn't see that changing much this time. Though, he had to admit, it might have saved him from taking that spear to the chest if he'd had it before. Maybe.

Moving on to his available status points, he grinned.

He'd already had nine points from before, and he got two extra points from his '*Child of the Portals*' title for reaching a landmark level. Then everybody also went from getting one status point per level to two when they reached level five and swapped their training class for a junior class. So, now he was getting four points for every level.

Plus, he was at an odd level, which meant he could place them wherever he wanted. The question was, what would be the best use of them?

Normally he would just dump them all into *Constitution* without a second thought. Thinking of the amount of ground they would need to cover, and the grueling pace they would need to set, had him second-guessing that. The bulk would still go towards it for sure. It was his lifeline. It was the attribute that allowed him to use more than a small handful of spells before running dry.

The question was, could he spare those points? Every time his magic stat increased, the attacks got stronger, but the energy requirement grew as well.

Gritting his teeth, he went with his gut. Two status points went to *Dexterity*, raising it to fifteen, the max his class allowed the attribute to be raised from points. One point went to *Agility*, also raising it to fifteen, though its limit was twenty.

The last twenty points went to *Constitution* raising it to forty-five. With it that high, he wasn't even sure how much damage that spear attack from before would do to him now. There were so many different variables that came into play, it was impossible for him to keep track of them. It was easier to just avoid it all and fight from afar when possible.

An intangible energy filled his body as the points came into effect, changing him in ways that only mattered on this side of the portal.

Closing his page, Zack smiled as Zara played with her bears. The suit had folded in on itself to better fit her after being turned into a puppet. It wasn't a perfect solution, by any means. However, it would allow her to walk under her own power if needed. Not that he expected that to happen.

Unlike him, she had mana for days. In some respects, her class was the opposite of his. Her intelligence attribute was high, but her magic stat was mostly average. Which made sense. Her class didn't seem to use spells to attack. It used puppets for everything, which depended on her mana to keep operating.

He snagged Zelda from behind and poked at her chest. "How are you feeling?"

Most of her fluffing had gone back to its proper places in her arms and legs.

The bear relaxed and wiggled her paw back and forth.

"You're, okay? Are you sure? You didn't seem too keen on having it inside you originally."

Zara came up beside them, puffs of air coming from her red, smiling face. "Zelda says she's gotten used to it. It's more like a stomachache at this point than an actual problem. She still wants us to remove it when we get back, but she can ignore it until then."

"Alright, but I'll carry her when we get going. I'm the one that stuck it in her, so I'll do what I can to make it easier on her."

Zelda mimed wiping away a tear, and he sighed. "I can't tell if you are being serious, or if I just got made fun of by a bear."

Zara giggled and shook her head. "I'm not telling."

Zack rolled his eyes and glanced over to where Jean was shoving the last of the items inside the other suit puppet. "What level did you get?"

"Six, and my new spell lets me modify the puppets. Like this." She motioned to her suit and the modifications that he had already noticed. "If I level it up enough, I might even be able to give Zelda and the other's proper mouths, paws, and everything!"

"Did you distribute everything already?"

She nodded.

"Good, then just keep using the spell while we run if you have the extra energy. You know how to level it up, and since we're stuck in here, you might as well make the most of the time we have."

Jean finished and called them over. "Zara, if you would have your puppet pick up Edith? Then we can get going."

Zack placed Zelda where she could hang onto the back of his neck. George jumped onto Zara's back and Aisha would run alongside them.

"Zack, how are your legs and arm?" Jean asked, taking his staff and tucking it in alongside Edith.

"They're a little shaky, but getting better. I should be able to run, I think. As for my arm..." He shrugged. "It's healing, but also still broken. Give it a few more hours and it'll be useable. By tonight, it should be completely healed."

The teacher and military woman nodded. "Alright, from here on out, no talking or joking around. We are heading into the depths of an unknown portal with what should be very strong monsters. I know the two of you can handle yourselves." She glanced at the bodies partially covered with drifting snow. "I saw that earlier, and I won't ask questions for now. However, since we have no idea what is out there or how long we'll be in here? We need to be careful. Just keep that in mind."

"Oh, one last thing." Zack tossed her one of the masks they had taken from the Shouvain travelers and gave the other to Zara. "Hopefully, these will help keep your faces and ears warm while we're running."

Jean put hers on with a grateful smile and spun around, taking off at a pace that she knew Zack could maintain. She would adjust it as needed for Zara or him, as they grew tired.

Unfortunately, they had already wasted too much time in getting ready. They needed to find another portal and get out before the invisible countdown ended and the change began. She had no idea what that entailed, but she knew being inside this particular *Dimensional Fragment* when it occurred was a bad idea.

Snow crunched underfoot as they ran, their boots digging into the top layer of the icy crust. Jean led them around the snowdrifts, the darkened portal fading into the distance behind them.

The group concentrated on maintaining their pace. Letting their thoughts fade in and out, as their minds numbed to the world around them.

Chapter 2

Jean pushed them hard for hours over an unchanging, frozen landscape. They had skipped lunch, forcing themselves to run right through their burgeoning hunger pangs. It was approaching night when they finally saw something different on the horizon. On the relatively flat terrain, it was still hours away for them, but it offered them hope.

Green aurorae with hints of purple and pink intermixed with other vibrant colors lit up the sky as night descended. The temperature dropped, and Zack felt his cheeks and ears beginning to burn. He was glad the suit had gloves, otherwise, he would have been forced to awkwardly run with his hands tucked inside the tight-fitting sleeves. His broken arm had finished stitching itself back together earlier and was now mostly healed.

They were nearing what they could now see was a large, rocky outcropping. When Edith suddenly arched her back in pain and began to thrash around. The violent actions shocked Zara, slowing her reaction time. Loud cracks and pops as the older woman flailed about, filled the air, as her body protested the movements. Coming back to herself, Zara had her puppet secure the woman before she could hurt herself more.

"Is she alright?" Zara asked Jean worriedly, as they surrounded Edith. The puppet held her tight as she continued to struggle for another minute before abruptly relaxing.

"I don't know," She replied in exasperation. "It's too dark for me to see anything clearly. I think her skin feels a little warmer than earlier, that is all I can really say. We should hurry and reach those rocks. We'll set up camp for the night there."

Zara wanted to cry in relief at those words, except that would take too much effort. The siblings had been awake and moving for nearly forty-eight hours. Both were ready to pass out as soon as the opportunity presented itself.

Zack nudged his sister. "Come on, it'll be easier to take care of her at a camp than here. The sooner-" He stopped to yawn. "The sooner we get there, the sooner I can try an examination spell and maybe even a healing spell on her."

She nodded. "I know, I'm just worried. She was nice to us... she is different from the others."

"Yeah, she is."

They started running again, only to stop a couple of minutes later as a message appeared in front of their eyes.

You have been inside this portal area for twelve hours, out of your allowed twenty-four. Would you like to stay or exit? Error, location locked. Exit from entry portal unavailable. Please find a secondary portal soon.

In front of them, Jean fell to her knees and began to gasp in pain.

Zack glanced at Edith, then at Jean, who had curled up into a ball and understood. Even if they didn't know how much time was left on the countdown that had been mentioned. They knew how long they could remain inside, and now they knew what happened to people when they couldn't leave in time.

He had a feeling they weren't going to be able to hide this from Jean. She already had a list of questions for them pertaining to what their classes actually were. Now she would have one more when she saw they weren't in any lingering pain.

He was tempted to have them both fake it, but the constant lying and hiding of the truth was exhausting. It would come out sooner or later. Why not now? At least Zara was supposedly already under the protection of the crown.

Could they trust her? Did it even matter?

"What are we going to do?" Zara implored, as they waited for Jean to come around.

"Nothing, we'll leave it up to her. She already knows too much about us anyway. She knows your class is odd, if not what it is for sure, and she's seen my different spells. Not to mention everything that message said. I'm sure she can piece those clues together. At this point, the most we could do is just not confirm anything. Which is as good as confirming it anyway, to someone like her."

Zelda climbed to the top of his head and proceeded to drum softly on his hair. Zara giggled at her actions and lifted up George so he could watch.

Zack gasped and shivered. "Your daggers are freezing!" Just having the flat of the blade resting on his hair was enough to freeze his scalp.

Zelda bopped him one more time and scurried back down to act as his neck warmer.

"Is there any way you might be able to modify a coat puppet into a hat for me later?" He begged his sister, his ears twinging painfully from frostnipping. By the time he had thought to wrap some clothes around his head earlier, they had all been frozen solid already.

"I can try, but the stupid spell refuses to level up!" She stamped her feet in a huff. "I've been modifying the suit in different ways all day and still nothing."

He shrugged. "Some spells just take more. My arcane manipulation ability started at level zero both this time and last time. I was never even able to get it above that. And Arcane Armor is almost as bad." It didn't help that both required massive amounts of mana to use, so he couldn't use them very often or efficiently.

Jean groaned and uncurled, putting a stop to their conversation.

"How do you feel?" Zack asked, helping her to her feet.

"Like I got run over by a monster horde." She bent over and ripped off her mask before raising her gloved palms to her temples and holding them there. "I got a message about the portal being locked and not being able to exit. I've never heard of anyone seeing a message like that when their time limit is up." She looked up at them with a pale face. "Why do the two of you look fine?"

Zack sniffed and scratched at a frozen cheek. "Too cold to look like anything else?"

She squeezed her temples harder and straightened, pulling back on the mask. "That is the dumbest reason I've ever heard, but I'm too cold and hurting too much to care right now. Let's just get moving or I won't be able to. I need to rest for a while soon."

Together, the group set off at a slow, shambling pace. In the beginning, Jean stumbled every few steps, her hands slapping the frozen snow to regain her balance.

Zack moved up alongside her and silently offered her his shoulder.

"This doesn't let the two of you off the hook with my questions," She muttered, leaning heavily on him for support.

"You can ask all you want. That doesn't mean we'll answer them." It was the same answer he had given her before regarding the Major questioning them.

"You're going to have to trust someone at some point." Was the soft, almost hurt reply.

"We know, but trusting the government, and trusting a person, are two separate things unless that person works for them." He responded equally quietly. "As treasonous as it sounds, I don't even know if we can properly trust the crown."

She grunted. "You're right, that does sound slightly treasonous. After what happened with the Albrights, though, I can understand the hesitation. They were nobles, after all, powerful ones at that."

Zack stared straight ahead, unwilling to say anything more about the topic. A part of him still believed that the organization behind the research institute was also related to the crown in some way. Maybe some long-forgotten portal-based operational arm that was still somehow receiving funds.

It was either that, or the crown had less control over their territory than he believed. Which was entirely possible considering the noble and corporations were apparently capable of hiding portals from them.

Either way, he couldn't mention that to her. All he knew was that for now, at least he still didn't trust anyone with power over his life or Zara's.

She sighed, but let the matter drop as they continued slowly on towards the outcropping of rocks.

A while later, the snowy crust beneath their feet changed to rock and frozen gravel. The rocks rose up in front of them and extended like a wall in both directions for as far as the eye could see. The snow and ice covering them acted as camouflage until the group had gotten closer.

"Are we stopping?" Zack asked Jean, holding her steady as their boots broke the frozen stones free beneath them.

"Let's keep going, just a little farther." She was huffing and puffing beneath the mask. The ordeal earlier had obviously sapped her stamina and strength a great deal.

George came up on her other side and helped pull her up the steeper rocks. Behind them, the larger Aisha helped Zara and the puppet suit carrying Edith up the same rocks.

"We need to rest soon," Zack told Jean when he heard Zara beginning to huff and puff behind them as well.

That could only mean that her magical energy reserves were running low, and that she had needed to kill the puppet connection to her suit.

Even for her, operating three animated bears and two puppets all day long was impressive. Her mana regeneration must have just barely been unable to keep up. It was a good thing they hadn't needed to fight all day, or that time would have been cut down by a lot. The simple act of running had probably only used a small portion of the normal amount they required for operation.

The group topped the rocky outcropping and halted in surprise.

Unknowingly, they had been running across a plateau all day, and now they had finally reached the edge. The wall of rocks was actually a short barrier before the sheer cliff face that they now saw. Far below them and across an ocean of darkness, something glittered in the distance. Unfortunately, the failing light was too dim to make out what it was.

"How far down do you think that is?" Zack wondered, backing away from the edge. He wasn't necessarily afraid of heights, but he was scared of falling.

"Doesn't matter; it's too far to jump." Jean backed up with him and slumped against a rock. "It's too dark to see the bottom." She groaned and lifted up the mask, letting the cold air wash over her face. "One of the other directions probably would have been shorter and had a better path down."

"Not to mention the mining locations." Zara gasped out. Slumping against a rock and sliding to the ground. "I didn't see any of them the entire day. Isn't that the reason the Albright's kept this portal to themselves?"

The air above them popped as the aurorae moved and shifted colors. The green faded, and the purple and pink colors became more predominant. Hints of yellow and blue shot through it in an ever-changing show of light.

The puppet carrying Edith deposited her on a flat surface near them and then collapsed as Zara cut the spell. She needed to preserve her energy as much as possible.

"If you were running so low on energy, why didn't you say anything earlier when we stopped?" Zack growled out, glaring at his sister.

She shrugged weakly, not meeting his eyes. "It wouldn't have changed anything. We're all running on fumes, and we don't have time to spare waiting on me. I decided it was better to just push through it this time."

He glared at her for a moment longer before turning away and nodding his head. She was right, and it made him happy to see her acting like this again. Zack just hoped that with enough time, it would extend beyond just the confidence she felt inside the portals. Seeing her speak up for herself in Aperra like this was one of his greatest wishes.

"What do we do for water?" He directed the question to Jean while he collapsed next to his sister.

Zelda climbed down from his neck and over to Zara. Where she began massaging the girl's legs. George came over a second later and joined in, matching his movements to Zelda's. Aisha stood above them, unsure of what to do and feeling left out.

"Eating the snow is really all we can do, though I wouldn't recommend it. Eating enough to properly rehydrate would lower your body temperature.

If we had bottles or something, then we could stuff them inside our suits and use our body heat to melt them."

Zack thought back to their packs and the bottles inside that they had been forced to leave at the school portal. With a sigh, he got back to his feet and stumbled over to Edith. The dim light and shadows from the surrounding rocks made every step a guess on his part.

Sitting down next to her, he pulled off one of her gloves along with his own and took a firm hold of her hand. He drew on everything he knew about the *'Examination'* spell. The knowledge and his recent experiences with it reinforcing his intent behind it. As long as the intent was strong enough, it would make up for his gaps in how the spell actually worked.

When Zack was ready, he tapped into his *'Arcane Manipulation'* ability and let it take over. His hands began to glow with a deep purple light. His mana drained completely in an instant, and the excess cost bled over into his astral form.

A flood of information entered his brain as he jerked back. The skin on his back had lost some feeling, was all. It wasn't too bad of a price for the spell and would be back to normal within a few minutes.

He struggled to make sense of the data the spell had given him. He had no idea what most of it meant. So, he discarded it and looked for anything obviously wrong. Something that even he could understand.

"I think," He began hesitantly, a little bit later. "She will be fine as long as she stays in the suit. I don't understand it all, but I think she is in a hypothermia-induced coma. The suit has been keeping her warm and gradually raising her internal temperature. If it doesn't get any colder, then she should be fine."

Zara nodded, "Thanks," She yawned and curled up around Aisha and the other bears. "I know healing spells are hard for you." A second later, even rhythmic breathing let them know she had fallen asleep. She had held on long enough to hear about Edith and then passed out.

Zack slipped the glove back on the older woman's hand, followed by his own, and then pulled a spare coat out of the limp suit beneath her. His face was nearly frozen.

"So, uh, does this mean that either of you is going to tell me what your real classes are now?" Jean huffed suspiciously from the side, seeing him get ready to turn in for the night as well. "I know you aren't just a mage. No training class would let its attacks be influenced by your elemental affinity that often. As it is, your affinity must be as off the chart as your compatibility rating! Not to mention what you just did. And your sister!" She whirled and pointed at Zara. "A '*Puppeteer*', really? What even is that?"

"It's an aberration class. Both of our classes are," Zack explained softly, tired of avoiding the question. He buried his face in the coat and tucked his hand into the sleeves. "Good night."

***

Zack shuddered as the four frozen nutrition bars pressed against his skin beneath his suit. He had woken up a few minutes earlier and had grabbed the bars from George's back to begin defrosting them. He doubted anyone was looking forward to eating them, least of all Zara, who thought they tasted like chalk. The nutritious bars were all they had at the moment, and if there was one thing the sibling were familiar with, it was eating what was available regardless of taste.

A part of him marveled over how great the suits were. The country of Shouvain was far ahead of anything Albion could produce in this category. To his admittedly limited knowledge, at least. He wasn't even sure what this counted as. It wasn't purely magitech, yet it also obviously didn't originate from their world. They were incredible and had kept him warm all night long despite the terrible conditions. Physical exhaustion had taken care of the rest.

A few hours of deep sleep, combined with the healing from his '*Life Burner*' ability, meant he was feeling great.

Seeing the other three were still asleep or otherwise passed out, Zack crept over to the edge and looked down. The sky was overcast with thick, mois-ture-laden clouds that hid whatever passed for a sun or light source inside this portal. Still, there was enough light for him to see by, and what he saw he didn't like.

Stretching out beneath them was a vast snow-covered forest. In the middle of it was a large lake, with a meandering river cutting through the trees to the side. All of that was close to a hundred meters below them. With a sheer, smooth-looking cliff face as their only way down.

Getting down was going to be a problem and finding a portal anywhere inside all those trees was another. Heading to the lake or the river was going to be their best option. Either one would mean constantly fighting, with them surrounded by high-level monsters.

Zack pulled back from the edge and glanced up at the clouds that appeared just out of reach. He began adding up the hours they had been inside and shook his head. The day-to-night cycle inside this portal was off. It wasn't an unheard-of phenomenon, but it was fairly rare.

He thought back to the distance between them and the lake and was overcome with a sense of urgency. What would happen if they were still inside the middle of that forest when their next time limit ran out? All four of them would be incapacitated while surrounded by whatever bloodthirsty monsters inhabited this place.

Quickly, he shook Jean and Zara awake and laid out the situation for them, along with the warmed nutrition bars.

"Well, I agree that the lake should be our destination, but I don't think we'll find a portal there. We are more likely to just get noticed somewhere like that. Up here we can make a lot of noise, but if a ruler never looks in this direction, then it makes no difference. Places of water historically have more importance placed on them and should be more closely monitored." Jean explained while peering over the ledge.

"How are we even going to get down, though?" Zara asked her. "I don't think we have the time to run around the plateau and find a better spot to climb down from."

"No, we definitely do not have the time for that." The soldier agreed with a frown.

"I might be able to get us down," Zack offered hesitantly. "But I'll be useless for a long while afterward. What I have in mind will probably burn through everything I have."

He wasn't making the offer lightly. Using everything his astral form had to give was not something he wanted to do. He had no idea what it might do to him. It could cause irreparable harm or simply extreme amounts of pain.

Unfortunately, they had an invisible countdown running against them, and every second counted. He couldn't afford to play it safe right now. Not when he might be able to keep Zara safe.

Chapter 3

"It's not much good if we have to carry you around afterward!" Jean snarked, contemplating the offer regardless.

Zara glared at him and stomped over to Edith to check on her. Next to the rocks they had slept against, Zelda was teaching the other bears how to skip rocks across the icy tundra.

Zack understood the offer was flawed, but he couldn't think of anything better.

"How much damage can one of your element-infused bolts do to the ground? Which I still haven't asked about, by the way. You originally said you didn't have one until you changing your answer when we came through the portal. What element is it?" The teacher smiled sweetly at him.

"It's, uh... nothing special." He avoided the question and twisted away from her. Then, raising his hand, he pointed at the ledge away from them.

"Why do you always point?" She asked before he could even form the spell.

"Because I haven't done this for a few years, and it helps me aim! Once I'm used to everything again, I'll be able to stop pointing." He replied, struggling not to growl. It was a sore spot for him. "Then I can start practicing how to properly control my magic. Something that no one ever taught me how to do. I had just started to make some small headway on it when we were rescued."

Jean took a surprised step back and looked at Zara for guidance.

The young girl waved her over while Zack took a few deep, calming breaths. "Pointing is just a helpful guide for him, and he can stop when he gets used to using magic again. He's more put out because until then, he can't start practicing his control. I'm sure you've noticed how powerful his attacks are?"

The woman nodded.

"That's because his class is controlling them and giving them all the energy they can handle each time. It's why he is always running out of mana. Until he learns to control it, he has no say in how much gets used each time." Zara explained to her while feeling Edith's warm cheeks.

"Can't the school help with that?"

"Maybe," Zara shrugged, putting the warm cap back on Edith's head. "I don't think they have said anything on the matter yet since they don't know what anyone's classes will be until after they go through the portal on Montag."

They were stopped from saying anything more as Zack launched his magical attack at the ground. The elementless purple bolt hit the rocks in front of the ledge and drilled partly through it. Then, with a ground shaking, thunderous crack, a section of the ledge began to separate from the rest.

The bears ran over to the girls while Zack gathered up all their loose items and joined them. None of them knew whether that was the end of it, or if more of the cliff face was going to collapse as well.

"I don't think we should try that again," Zack whispered, stuffing the various items back into the suit they were using to carry everything. He glanced at the broken section of the ledge, his sixth sense prodding him to move faster.

Zara began tracing her puppet spell onto the suit right away. "It hasn't stopped."

"What hasn't-" Jean began as the ground shuddered, and cracks began to spread out from the broken section. "Zara, hurry. We're going to have to run as fast as we can, or we'll get caught up in this!"

Zack glanced back towards the distant lake, his mind racing to come up with a workable idea. Something that had even a modicum of a chance of getting them where they needed to go. He grabbed the charred staff he had claimed and handed it to the bears. "Don't let go of this."

They waited with bated breath as Zara made the suit into a puppet again. No matter how hard she tried, it was too soon to shave any time off the spell's inscribing process. She had only started using her magic again within the last couple of days, and her old familiarity with the spell would only get her so far. As it is, it was a miracle she didn't mess up under pressure.

"Okay, here's what we are going to do." Zack took control, his mind set. It was going to be a dangerous gamble, mostly for him, but it gave them better odds of getting rescued than if they ran away. "Zara will lie on top of Edith and have the puppet pick you both up. The bears can thread the staff through its arms and hang onto that. Jean will hang onto me, and I'll be hanging onto the back of the puppet with my arms and legs wrapped around it. No time for questions, just do it!"

Zara nodded, trusting in him, and immediately laid down on Edith. The completed puppet picked them up and stood still, waiting for its next orders. The bears pushed the staff in between its arms and Edith's body, only to look back at Zack when they saw there was no space to hold on to the wood.

"Fine, forget that spot. Put it between my chest and its back." He looked back at a hesitant Jean. "You had better hold on tight for this." He climbed onto the puppet's back and was followed by the rest of them. "Zara, have the puppet jump forward when I tell you to."

Zack closed his eyes and envisioned them launching into the air. The hard part was transferring the effect of the spell from himself to the puppet, an action that would increase the cost as well. It would be his first time doing a spell like this, and he had no idea what to expect.

He gulped and opened his eyes.

His ability *'Arcane Manipulation'* read his intent and took over. It formed the proper spell and took the energy it needed from him. And take it did, endlessly. His pitiful pool of mana was drained in an instant, and his astral form began to empty at a rapid pace. Taking far more than he thought it would.

It was beginning to dawn on him how stupid this idea truly was. Unfortunately, it was too late to turn back now.

His legs went numb first, followed by his arms and hands. It was a good thing he had already locked them in place around the puppet. Since he couldn't feel them, he couldn't move them either.

The cost of using his ability was always high. It was especially extreme this time, because of all the extra weight the spell had to account for.

Finally, all he needed to do was release it.

The ground began to rumble as the cracks grew wider and spread faster. In front of them, a section of cliff face came unattached and fell away. The sound of rolling crashes echoed as loose pieces smashed against the cliff. It ended with a dull whoomph sound as it hit the layer of snow below, never even getting close to the forest tree line.

"Now!" Zack shouted, unwilling to wait any longer as the plateau crumbled around them.

The puppet angled its body towards the distant horizon and then, taking a step forward, it jumped. A burst of Zack's magic extended from its forward foot-launched them into the air and away from the increasingly fragile ground.

The force of them jumping sent a spiderweb of cracks out from the focal point where the puppet's foot had been. Within moments, that area of the cliff face was riddled with crevices upon its once smooth surface. One piece after another began to fall, taking that entire section of the plateau with it.

A cloud of dust, snow and thunderous noise rose up behind them as they escaped the danger they had wrought.

Without a second to spare, Zack began working on the second part of his plan. A '*Featherfall*' spell. With how much magical energy the first spell had taken, he was worried if he would even have enough. Unfortunately, it was too late now to second guess anything, and he would make it work no matter what. His little sister's life was depending on it, and he guessed so was his and Jean's.

They sped over the trees. With everybody holding on for all they were worth, lest they fall off and were left behind. A worry that mainly applied to the bears and Jean. Unfortunately, they wouldn't quite reach the lake. Even though they were moving fast, there was simply too much weight between all of them and the items inside the suit.

Jean watched as monsters began to appear beneath them.

Giant white-haired, long-armed, ape-like beasts that swung from one branch to the next in an effort to keep up with them. It was clear they had been spotted and were being chased, with the smarter ones just waiting for them to fall into the trees where they would be waiting. While others in the distance simply appeared to be running from the collapsing plateau.

She would be ready for them when they came. It was her duty to protect the siblings. She just hoped she was strong enough, and that the confiscated swords would hold true.

Zack felt them begin to dip down, and with a resigned sigh, cast the 'Featherfall' spell. Immediately slowing their descent. His astral form screamed as it was drained dry, and the effects began to bleed through to his physical form. Long forgotten scars started to peel open, while blood dripped from his eyes, ears, and nose.

All feeling to his physical body was cut off as his soul strained for sustenance. Instead, Zack was forced to relive every cut, slice, stab, and dissection that had ever been done to him inside the portals. Only the fact that his sight remained kept him from going insane.

It was Zelda who first noticed the blood pouring down from Zack's face. She climbed up from the charred staff and got close to him while frantically calling for Zara. Who promptly struggled to sit up without disrupting the group's delicate balance on her puppet.

Still, when she saw her brother's bleeding and increasingly pale face, she began to panic. Zara glanced around, searching for anything that might help him. There was nothing. They were over a hundred meters above the ground, with trees and monsters directly below them.

There was only one thing she could think of that might help in that situation. "Zelda, press against him as tightly as you can." Her eyes begged the bear to understand her meaning.

Zelda had the odd purple crystal inside her chest still, and while they were still inside the portal where he could heal quicker anyway, having it close to him might help. She hoped. Zara bit her lower lip and carefully reached past the puppet's empty head space to wipe the blood from her brother's face. Her mind carefully piecing the clues together as she cleaned him.

It didn't help. Fresh blood continued to dribble from the small incision scars hidden by his hair that had reopened. The streams coming from his eyes and tear-ducts had clotted and slowed, while those coming from his ears and nose continued to flow unabated.

Jean held a bloody, suit covered hand against his scarred neck. "What happened? Why did he suddenly start bleeding from everywhere?"

Zelda had snuggled herself firmly against his chest, pressing the crystal as close against him as she could.

"I think it was that last spell, the one that slowed our descent just now. It must have taken more energy than he had available." Zara ended in a whisper. "The ability he uses is called *'Life Burner'* after all, the effects can bleed through in extreme circumstances. As far as I know, he has never been forced to go this far before. I have no idea what could happen to him."

"I wouldn't worry too much, little lass. I have some people that can fix him up. Abilities that play around with astral forms, or the soul, are rare. People that can heal the damage they can cause are even rarer. He's lucky." An oddly accented voice offered from beside them. "I'd say you all are, actually. If it wasn't for that *clynt* over there falling to pieces, I never would have found you. I'd already cleared this area once before."

Zara carefully turned her head and took in the unknown speaker.

Floating beside them was a tall man with light green eyes and braided pale blonde hair that partially hid a pair of pointed ears. Woven into his hair were decorated mana crystals worn as adornments. His light green skin was streaked through with bolts of blue, grey, and ash colorings. Despite the freezing temperatures, he was only dressed in a pair of leather pants and a sleeveless vest that showed off his muscles.

"Who are you?" She asked carefully. For once, she wasn't seeing someone as a monster at their first meeting. Which could only, to her, at least, mean that he obviously wasn't human.

"I am one of several ruler class beings that are assisting in the evacuation of this dimensional fragment. You may refer to me as Alastair. Now, may I know who you are and why you did not go back through your own portal?" He followed that up by wrapping them up in a bubble of magic and began towing them away.

"Our portal was locked before we could go back through it. Our only choices were to try and find another portal, or hope we got rescued by a passing ruler. We didn't think it was likely that anyone would pass by that area, so we set out to find one ourselves." Jean explained, keeping her increasingly bloody hand on Zack's neck.

Alastair laughed. "That is probably the stupidest thing you could have done. We have been going around to every known portal, rescuing and dropping people off. You got lucky this time." He stopped talking abruptly. "Wait, you said your portal was locked? Which world or planetary fragment are you all from?"

"The one that goes to Aperra, Albion specifically." Zara stared at the man with squinted eyes, thinking.

He spun around, the braid whipping around his neck like a noose. "You are humans! Ah, that explains the ears. I was thinking you just had some unfortunate genetics. Well, in that case, no, you did the right thing. We all avoid that portal still. Until your world has fully accepted the portals, all races will continue to hide from it."

"What does that even mean to fully accept the portals?" Jean groused, glancing down as they sped over the lake and reentered the forest beyond.

"Does it matter? If you need to ask, then you aren't there yet." The ruler class being smirked back at them and then sped up with a worried look at Zack.

"Fine, whatever. Can I ask, though, and I don't mean to be rude despite how this is going to sound, but what are you?" Jean asked as they continued to pick up speed, leaving the lake far behind them.

"You would do well to learn how to phrase that particular question better in the future. Some races would take exception to it and demand a duel of honor on the spot. Luckily for you, I am not one of those. My race is called 'Snow Elves' and as such, we are particularly well suited to all things cold." They began to slow as a large clearing in the distance came into view. "Something that I notice, you seem to be well equipped for as well. I was under the impression that humans were rather weak to the cold."

"We are, but these suits are protecting us."

He peeked back at their matching outfits and shook his head. "Your world has managed to integrate the gifts of the portals well, despite not fully embracing them yet."

Below them, the clearing could be seen bustling with activity as snow elves hurried in from the forest. They would stop at a checkpoint, then rush to a healing station if they were injured. If they weren't, then they would go through the portal in the middle of the clearing. They only saw it for a second, but they could have sworn there was something revolving around on top of the portal.

"You mentioned other portals before," Zara began to say, wiping the blood from Zack's face again. She was glad to see that the trails from his ears and nose had begun to clot as well. "How many portals connect to this particular... *dimensional fragment?*" It took her a moment to remember what the message had called it.

Alastair carefully deposited them on the ground before answering. "All dimensional fragments have multiple portals connecting to them. With each one leading to a different world or planetary fragment. Some have rulers that have laid claim to them, while others have proven inhospitable or too dangerous for most species to use."

He held them back and leaned in close. "Every world, and dimensional fragment, must undergo the Change. It is your world's turn, and as such, it is the focal point of many current events and phenomena. In the future, those will switch to the next world that must undergo the change. Your world has been presented with a rare opportunity. It would behoove you all to embrace it and make the most of it while you can." He pulled back. "Now let's get your brother to the healers."

Zara rolled off Edith, while Jean helped to support Zack's weight as the bears carefully pried his legs and arms apart. Alastair picked up the charred staff with a raised brow at the bears and handed it to Zara without saying anything.

He led them into the depths of the quickly made camp and towards a healer's tent with no visitors. "He really is lucky; they weren't even supposed to be here now. We would have had to take him through the portal for his healing, which could have proven problematic."

Alastair pulled back the tent opening to reveal a well lit inside and a pair of female snow elf twins that looked distinctly like him. "Sisters, can you help this boy? He seems to have injured his soul somehow, and it's affecting his mortal form."

The twins looked up at the same time with a smile on their faces. "Good, he's here. We were waiting for him, put him on the table and we can begin."

"How could you be waiting for him?" Zara wondered doubtfully aloud, as Jean lowered Zack where they wanted.

Alastair nodded at her question, clearly wondering the same thing.

"Our tribe's Oracle told us that a male belonging to no one world would appear in need of our gifts. And judging from his... appearance, he definitely needs help." The two spoke interchangeably, seamlessly picking up the conversation from the other without pausing.

"I've asked you two to not do that," Alistair said with a sigh, settling onto a chair in the corner of the tent.

"We know, which is why we keep doing it. Who else can get away with defying one of the great and all-powerful ruler class beings?" They both giggled and turned away from him, to see Zelda sitting on his chest, still doing her best to stay close to him. "You did well, little one, but you can leave the rest up to us now."

Zelda looked to Zara for guidance, who nodded, hesitantly. The bear hopped off his chest and onto Aisha's shoulders opposite George.

Chapter 4

The twins stood on opposite sides of the table and pulled the gloves from his hands. A small stream of dark red blood gushed out as they undid the seam between the suit and the gloves. Both grabbed one of his hands, ignoring the scars that had reopened and the fresh blood.

"He's in worse shape than we thought." The one on the far side whispered.

"His soul is screaming. It's as though he is reliving each of these wounds over and over again." The other whispered in turn.

Zara whimpered and stepped closer to him. She hadn't realized how much pain he had been in until that moment.

The twins clasped their free hands together, completing the three-person circle. With the connection complete, each of them began to glow. Zack in the deep purple that was the color of his magic, and the twins in a mix of white and yellow that marked theirs.

Under their guidance, the three magical glows began to pulse together, gradually falling into a matching rhythm. With each pulse, the white and yellow aura of the twins would mix a little more with Zack's purple as their magic made its way to the core of his being. Where they would find his astral form and the cause of his current problems.

"This seems rather intimate in nature," Jean mentioned solemnly, as the twins began to cry and tremble at whatever they were seeing inside Zack's astral being. "You're not going to tell us that this is something that requires them to be married afterward, right?"

Alastair looked at her in amused amazement. "Actually, normally, yes, it is. What my sisters are doing is indeed a very intimate experience for them. However, those rules only apply among the snow elves, and certainly not to the inhabitants of a world that has yet to fully embrace the portals."

He took a long look at Zack and Zara. "Although, it would seem that may not apply to those two in any case. If my sisters were to marry the patient after doing this procedure on a snow elf, then the feelings on both sides would be stronger and built on a strong foundation of trust. The choice is ultimately up to them, of course. The feelings and trust can fade if they decide the other side is not worthy of them for any reason."

Jean winced. "I bet that is a nice slap in the face."

Alastair hesitated before responding, taking a moment to parse her words into his own native tongue. "It is indeed, more than one unworthy suitor has called for a duel of honor afterward. None have survived, as by right, all healers are protected by the entire tribe, but they managed to die with their honor intact. Supposedly." He glanced towards his sisters with a complicated expression. "Honor is important, but they dared to waste the gift of healing that was bestowed upon them by my sisters for a meaningless duel. They had no honor, even in death."

"How long will this take?" She asked, deciding to change the subject. The matter of honor was obviously a cultural difference that she was not equipped to talk about.

"It varies depending on the damage. Considering their reactions when they first started, they will probably be at it for a while." He turned away from his sisters and faced Jean. "You do not need to be leery of insulting me on matters of honor. The first thing a race learns when they embrace the portals is that your culture is your own, not someone else's. You cannot, and should not, try to force your ideals on them."

Jean took a moment to consider his words before responding. "What about races that are absolutely evil? That want nothing but war, to murder, to eat their foes, something like that. What then?"

"It doesn't matter, because of the *crìoch ùine* we can only spend a limited amount of time outside our homes."

"The time limit?" She clarified in confusion, guessing at the phrase's meaning.

He nodded. "If that is what your race calls it, then yes. When the *time limit* is up, we get automatically transported back to our homeworld, fragment, wherever we are from. That function does not work during occasions such as this, however, where the dimensional fragment is about to undergo a change. Which is why there are still so many of us here. In relation to what you were suggesting, the time limit when visiting places other than these dimensional fragments is significantly shorter. It makes no sense for them to declare war on a potential trading partner when they can simply claim a portion of a fragment such as this and sate themselves against mindless beasts."

"So, you're saying they tried and were rebuffed until they learned better?" She smirked.

He tilted his head to her and nodded. "It is as you say, some of them learn faster than others. Regardless, we do not interfere with other cultures, as long as they do not interfere with ours. We have no right to try and control those we do not understand."

Jean was silent for a long while as she absorbed the full import of his words. One of which stuck out to her especially, *trading partners*. That meant that after they embraced the portals, whatever that meant, they would be able to bring items back through the portals. Either from the other worlds or the dimensional fragments, or maybe even both.

Zelda hopped off Aisha's shoulder and ran over to Jean and Alastair, where she tapped them both on their feet.

"What is it, Zelda?" Jean asked after a moment.

The bear pointed to Edith, who lay mostly forgotten in the puppet's arms.

"What kind of magical being is that?" Alastair blurted out, unable to contain his curiosity any longer.

"I'm not even sure myself," Jean answered honestly. "She's some kind of puppet created by Zara, is all I know." She got up and walked over to Edith. "Is there anything your healers can do for her?"

Alastair followed after her thoughtfully. "The girl, she is an aberration then?" He leaned over Edith and touched her cheek.

"She is," Jean uttered slowly.

He winked at her. "She has nothing to fear from me, and remember, I could not hold her even if I desired. The most I could do is kill her. No, aberrations are rare and powerful. *If* they are raised properly, they can become the backbone of a legion, or a kingdom, maybe more." He sighed and glanced back at Zack and Zara. "Your world has much to learn still. I find it curious, though, that she can already enter the portals. She seems far too young."

"They suffered from malnourishment for years, it stunted their growth." She replied, giving the same answer she had heard them give on other occasions.

He hummed and turned back to Edith. "One of our normal healers should be able to fix this woman up in no time at all. I can take her to one of them now if you wish, or we can wait until after the boy is finished being healed?"

"Go," Zara told them from her place near the twins. "She shouldn't need to wait for healing on our account. We've made her wait long enough already, go get her taken care of. I'll stay here with Zack."

Zelda along with George and Aisha crept closer to Zara. Meanwhile, Alastair and Jean left with the suit puppet carrying Edith trailing close behind them. The pulsing light show that was a side effect of the twins healing Zack mesmerized the mentally younger bears. Only Zelda was left free of its effects and was able to climb her way onto Zara's lap.

"I know that he'll be fine, Zelda…" The girl that was her creator whispered softly in a fearful tone. "I'm just thinking about a conversation he and I had a while ago about us needing therapy. Someone that we could talk to about everything that we had experienced. A person that would help us work our way past those things."

She swallowed and looked sadly at the blood-covered form of her brother. "Now, I'm wondering if that is even possible for him. Using his *Life Burner* ability keeps him in the fight when he wouldn't otherwise be. Seeing the price now..." Zara let the sentence dangle, the meaning obvious. "He'll never be able to forget."

"Some things should never be forgotten." The twins said in unison, without turning away from Zack. "You will find that most often the things you wish to forget the most are the memories that drive and define your core values. You take those away, and you change who you are. What you truly mean is to let the memories fade, until their edges have dulled, and become less painful."

They turned to look at Zara, their eyes glowing with the color of their combined magic. "And that is something that we can help with already, at least in part. As we heal the damage done to him, we are removing the scars that have been left on his astral form. With any luck, there will be no bleeding next time he overextends himself. The damage and pain will be just as severe, just with fewer outward signs next time. The memories themselves will still have to be dealt with, however."

"How did they even manage to scar his astral form? Isn't that his soul?" Zara asked the twins softly, in a horrified tone.

The twins smiled good-naturedly at her ignorance and refocused on Zack. "Anything that is painful enough, or exciting enough, can have an effect on the astral form. It is made up of the memories that stick with us. For something to actually scar it, however, requires it to be an extreme emotion. Love, hate, loneliness, the desire to protect one's little sister, all of them can leave permanent marks on the astral form. In your brother's case, it was pain, of an unbearable level, repeated again, and again, linked with his existing physical scars that caused this."

Zara hugged Zelda tightly, wondering what scars her own form had.

"We've seen some of the memories, a hazard that comes with doing this. Don't worry, we'll forget everything but vague impressions soon enough. You should know that your world is terrifying. We've never heard of one that is willing to experiment on healthy children before. Especially not in the manner that they went about it."

The young girl was quick to notice the 'healthy' modifier. She couldn't help but wonder how brutal the conditions of those worlds must be that they would even cull the young. "You may forget the memories, but you will remember this conversation. I'm sure you'll be able to piece certain things together from that."

"Smart girl." The twins agreed. "And we're not sure if the astral form is the soul or not. Everyone and every world have their own opinion and beliefs on the matter. One last thing, and then we need to concentrate fully. What they did to both of you to get you through the portals, it has been tried before. There has never been a successful case before. So, either your world has succeeded where all others have failed, or there was something different about the two of you from the start."

Zara's grip on Zelda turned to steel as the topic of them being different reminded her of what the first ruler they had met said. The idea that they weren't from Albion or even Aperra originally kept coming up, and she was finding it harder to refute each time.

Sitting there watching the two snow elf twins heal her brother, Zara realized it didn't matter. Home was wherever her brother was. Aperra was simply the world that had tortured them. It was the world that had taken their stupid parents from them. Who cared if they didn't belong to it?

No one ever said they had to stay there for the rest of their lives. Once they were strong enough and had gotten their revenge on the organization responsible for brutalizing them. They could just... She stopped, her mind drifting to the people they had met recently. Not all of them were bad.

Zara had always known there were decent people in the world. She had just never met any before they moved to the academy. Maybe they could wait until this Great Change business was settled or something... She shook her head and dismissed those thoughts. She was getting ahead of herself there and letting her imagination get carried away with itself.

While it seemed increasingly likely that they were not from Aperra, that still didn't mean anything. They didn't have a single clue on where to look first, or how to get there. This was going to be a long-term goal at best, and one where they may never discover the truth at worst.

Sweat glistened on the brow of both twins as their magical auras began to condense and separate from Zack's. They were nearing the last step of the procedure, and despite sharing a small amount of his pain and experiencing some of his memories. They needed to continue.

Both were more grateful than could be expressed to his sister for offering them a moment's respite. Despite the horrors they had seen, and the pain the healing connection shared with them, it was the mental anguish he had gone through that brought them up short. That brief conversation had offered just enough of a distraction and rest that they were able to continue.

The yellow and white healing magic pressed on the purple of Zack's and pushed it back into his body. Slowly, and with a deft touch, it molded to his form.

"Close your eyes." The twins said in unison.

The healing light grew brighter, and Zara spun Zelda around and buried her face in the bear's chest. Even with her eyes closed and face covered, she still felt as though the world had suddenly gone white streaked with yellow.

"It is done." They announced wearily. "You can open your eye's now. We have only healed the damage to your soul. You will still need to see someone about getting your body healed, something you should do while you are still here. Our tribe's healers will take care of the scar tissue leftover inside your body. It will take away the pain you feel on a daily basis."

Zack nodded weakly. "Thank you for saving me. Having to relive all of that, was... Well, I'm sure you can imagine." He croaked through a desert-dry mouth.

They nodded, acutely aware after having experienced a small portion of it themselves.

Now that his astral form was no longer over-drawn and taking energy from his body, he felt his healing ability kick in. Along with it came the appearance of a notification.

Congratulations, your 'Life Burner' ability has leveled up. Through extreme tribulation, pain, and possibly a smidgen of masochism, you have managed to raise the level of this ability to five. This is a landmark level for a unique rated ability. As such, you will be presented with three different options on how you would like the ability to grow with subsequent levels.
1. Slight increased ratio of astral health to magical energy or mana. (Currently one astral health unit to every four mana.)

2. Decreased levels of pain and discomfort. (Note: Ratio of health to mana increases at the normal pace under this option.)
3. The healing portion of the Life Burner ability becomes fully fleshed-out and turns into a more effective sub-ability. (Note: Ratio of health to mana increases at the normal pace under this option.)

Zack immediately discounted option two. He could live with pain and discomfort. Choosing between one and three, however, was much more difficult. One gave him the potential of more future mana for less damage to his astral form. While option three would make his healing ability more powerful and turn it into an actual ability. Instead of the afterthought, it currently was.

He didn't know which to choose. Both were great options, and he depended on each of them to stay alive. More mana was always welcome, but so was more healing. Of course, if he had more mana, then he might not need more healing.

Then again, it really depended on how much it raised the ratio. Raising the ability level was much harder than raising his personal level, or even a spell's level. He couldn't depend on it going up again anytime soon.

Before he could decide otherwise, Zack made his choice and selected option one. He prayed it was the right choice.

You have chosen to slightly increase the ratio of astral health to magical energy. The new ratio is set to one astral health unit to every six energy units. The ratio will increase further with the next level. Good luck.

That was not great, but it was still decent. He could work with that. The ratio had had increased by two this time instead of the normal, one. It was too bad about the healing ability, but at least he hadn't lost what he already had.

He struggled to work up some spit and wet his mouth before speaking again. "Why did your oracle send you here?" He had to pause to wet his mouth again. "I'm grateful. I really am. But what do any of you get out of healing me?"

"A debt, honor-bound, and transferred to our Oracle."

"Why?" Zara asked suspiciously.

The twins shared a look, and after putting Zack's gloves back on to contain his bleeding, they leaned against the table. "It is what she asked of us when she sent us here to heal him. In return, all talk of us ever getting married will be halted permanently. We do not understand the idea of romantic love, nor do we wish for someone to potentially come between us." Every few words, the other twin would pick up the conversation, seamlessly continuing it as though their minds were connected.

"Do you know what she wants?" Zack asked weakly from behind them.

"We believe she merely wants to talk, and this was her way of making you feel like you owe her. The Oracle... has an odd personality at times. She sees too much at times. Not only the truth, but also possibilities, and other places. She may have seen a possibility where the debt was needed." They shrugged. "Or maybe she actually does want something from you as well. Only she can say, and she is on the other side of the portal."

"Aisha," Zara commanded. "Pick him up carefully. Let's find someone to heal him and retrieve Edith and Jean. Then we can go find your Oracle."

The twins nodded. "We will lead the way, and just in case you were wondering. She will want to meet you both."

Chapter 5

It took five different healers working together to fix Zack. They erased the scar tissue inside his body and helped mend the damage from years of malnourishment. Then they began to heal the wounds on the outside of his body. Scars that he had lived with for years scabbed over and became healthy, regular skin.

Zara absentmindedly felt at the back of her neck, and at the scars on her covered arms. She wondered if they could do the same for her, or if it was only because his had nearly all been reopened already?

Several of the healers looked shocked and slightly sick, but seemed to be handling it better than Leigha had. It still exhausted them all to heal and fix that much residual damage. Old and damaged tissue always required more energy to restore than simply repairing an open wound. Not many healers were willing to expend so much energy on a non-vital operation.

The twins had been forced to use the Oracle's authority to get them to do it at all.

Zara carefully tugged on the robes of the closest twin. "Can your healers help with scars that haven't been reopened?" She moved her hair and showed them the lines on her neck. "Mine aren't as bad as my brother's. He protected me from the worst of it, but I do have a few in other places."

They looked at her, a sad smile ghosting across their identical faces. "We can certainly ask. Our knowledge of the physical healing arts is sadly lacking. Let us wait for your brother to clean himself, and then we can ask one of the other groups."

Zara nodded gratefully and patted her bears. George was sitting on Aisha's shoulder. While Zelda was sitting on the large bear's head, occasionally rubbing her stomach where the mana crystal they had been given was hidden.

Zack returned a moment later. The blood washed from his face and the outside of the suit. The insides would need to wait until later when he wouldn't freeze just taking it off. In his hands were two steaming bottles of elven brewed tea. By this point, the siblings were rather dehydrated and needed a drink, while he also needed some liquid to replenish the blood that he had lost.

Their increased stats and a general lack of options had helped them to ignore their bodies' call for water the day before. However, presented with the bottle of sweet-smelling hot tea, they couldn't hold back any longer. In seconds, both bottles were empty, and the siblings were left with pleasantly warm throats and bellies.

The twins smiled indulgently and led them to another group of healers. Where they relayed Zara's request, once more invoking the Oracle's authority. One of them peaked outside of the tent, making sure there were no other travelers waiting before nodding to the others.

George hopped from Aisha's shoulder and onto Zara's as the healers pulled the gloves from her too-large suit. She smiled gratefully at the bear and held out her hands to them.

"Is the Oracle going to be mad that you keep using her authority like this?" Zack asked the twins softly, after grabbing another bottle of steaming tea from the side of the tent. There was a table there full of them for the patients.

"No." They shook their heads emphatically. "She would have been most displeased if we hadn't and had seen your condition." They glanced at him as the healers began their work on Zara. "Speaking of which, how do you feel?"

Zack slowly sipped the tea, carefully monitoring the healers before answering. "It doesn't feel like my body." He worried quietly. "Everything feels off, every movement feels different, but the same. There's no pain, and it's all so much easier, more fluid... but there was no adjustment phase. It's freaking me out." The last time he had been healed by Leigha, it had taken him a few minutes to get used to the changes, and that was just her removing some small scar tissue. This time, it had been his entire body.

The twins giggled. "That's a specialty of elven healing magic. Physically, there is no adjustment phase for your body. It's like how it was always supposed to be. The problem now lies with your mind and how long you were forced to live with all that damage. Only time without pain will fix that, though it shouldn't take long with your gifts."

He stilled, and took another slow sip, thinking. "How much do you remember?"

They sighed and looked at him with conflicted eyes full of pity, mixed with compassion and understanding. "Enough to understand that you and your sister are not simple orphans, and never were. Those with such a spread of... *gifts* like the two of you could never come from a simple background."

"Gifts?" He wondered softly, glancing around for anyone who might be listening.

"Don't worry, no one can hear us." They each tapped a swirl-shaped earring inlaid with a tiny rune matrix. "We're talking about your odd race, multiple titles, and odd abilities, especially yours since we didn't see your sister's."

He had no idea how they managed to make the items work, but he could guess what they were. The magi-tech researchers in Albion had tried countless ways to get runed spells to work outside of the portals. With only a few minor successes, such as the Majair weapons and a few other magi-tech items. Of course, most if not all were said to simply be a combination of repurposed tech from something else, fused with mana crystals as a power source. There were no spells of any kind involved, inside or outside the portal.

Then again, maybe that was the answer, and it was nothing. They were still inside a portal. That presented another issue entirely that the researchers hadn't been able to breach. It was a mystery he could ask them about another time.

Zack lowered the half-full bottle of tea and glared at them. "You got all of that from healing my astral form?"

"As we told your sister, the astral form is made up of strong memories, sad and happy alike. Our goal was to heal the scars and damage done to your form. Experiencing more than we initially intended was the consequence of how extensive the *destruction* was."

"How fast will the memories fade?" He brought the tea back to his lips, satisfied with their answer.

"Usually, it's after a couple of days. With you, we can already feel some of them starting to fade, taking away the sharp sting of the many scalpels you experienced." A distant look entered their eyes, and they suddenly shook their heads. "There is something greater at play here regarding you and your sister. The Oracle may have more answers for you."

"I don't care much for honor; it had no place in how we were raised. However, I do look forward to speaking with your Oracle, and a debt is a debt, regardless of honor." He finished off the rest of the tea in the bottle and grabbed another.

"It's a cultural thing." They said in understanding. "You seem thirsty?"

"We came through the portal under difficult circumstances and had no supplies or water. Then, after our portal was locked, we had to run all day in the hope that someone might find us, or we might find another portal. And lest we forget, I was bleeding inside this suit for a while as well. So, yeah, you could say I'm a little thirsty." The side of his mouth curved up in a half-grin. "Honestly, walking around in this suit feels *nasty* right now, but without it keeping my blood contained, I don't know if I would have made it."

They nodded and pointed to where the healers were finishing with Zara. It had taken them less time and energy than it had with Zack, since she had fewer scars to begin with. Some of the ones on her back, and other smaller incisions, had already faded with time and youthful healing ability. Not having to see the reminders of those days on her arms or in the mirror was another step towards leaving them behind.

"Are they gone?" She asked haltingly. Zara's eyes were glued to her brother, trusting that he would tell her the truth.

Zack brushed aside her hair and tickled the smooth skin of her neck. "They're gone from here, at least."

She spun around and threw her arms around him. "We're free."

He knocked her gently on the head, and then hugged her. "Silly, we've been free for a while, but I know what you mean. One of the biggest reminders is gone at last."

The twins coughed politely. "Shall we find Alastair and your other companions? Your next appointment with the portal's *crìoch ùine* can't be far off."

"*Crìoch ùine?*" Zack questioned, not understanding the words.

"They mean the time limit. I overheard Alastair talking with Jean about it earlier," Zara explained, pulling back from him.

Zack tried to remember how many hours they had slept for. It hadn't been long, four, maybe six at the most. Even with the time getting here and then healing him and Zara, they should still have another hour or more left. Right? He shook his head. It didn't matter. It was better to play it safe than to risk experiencing what Edith and Jean had gone through. Besides, it would undoubtedly be even worse for them, since this would be their second time experiencing it.

"Let's do it."

"Do your travelers not have to worry about the time limit?" Zara inquired, holding onto Zack with one hand and a hastily grabbed bottle of tea with another.

"They do. However, as a world that has embraced the portals, our *crìoch ùine* is longer than yours. Our *travelers,*" The twins smiled at the term. "That do not arrive back in time will simply have to suffer the effects of the portal's wrath. They will all make it back here or another portal before the countdown ends, or they will not make it back at all."

"How do you know how much time is left?"

"Above all active portals, there sits a countdown that displays it."

"Of course there is," Zack muttered. "It has to be on active portals, though not locked ones, like that piece of trash we got stuck with."

Zara elbowed him when the twins looked back at him curiously. "He's just complaining because our portal didn't have anything like that on it. At least not that we can remember. This entire time, we've been worried this place was going to collapse on us, or something. Since we didn't know how much time we had." She revealed to them.

"It started with three of our rotations on the timer," The twins told them, peeking into a healer's tent in passing.

"How many hours are there in a rotation?" Zara was quick to ask, ever curious for more information.

"It varies from world, or *fragment*, to world." Zack could feel a headache coming on. "On our world, a rotation which is a day is around twenty-seven of Aperra's hours." They willingly explained.

"So, a rotation on our world is twenty-four hours then." Zara grasped the easily understood concept right away. "You said that it started with three of your world's rotations, so that would be eighty-one hours. We've been here for maybe twenty-two or twenty-three hours. Outside of the portals' wrath trying to kill us every twelve hours, we would have had plenty of time to... potentially get eaten by beasts in the forest." She finished softly, remembering the monsters they had seen chasing them from below.

"Oh, you saw the yeti's, aren't they the cutest?" The twins squealed, pulling back the flap of another tent and finding it empty.

"No," Zara retorted. "They looked big and scary from what I saw." She held up Zelda and George and then pointed to Aisha. "They are cute and adorable and fluffy."

Zack shrugged and stayed out of it; he hadn't seen the yetis anyway.

The twins ignored George and Zelda in favor of Aisha. "The other two are too small. This one has potential."

Zara recoiled from them, aghast. "That's your requirement? That they need to be a certain size? Not cute, cuddly, easy to snuggle up to in bed when you're scared, but big?"

"Why would we be scared?" They asked without thinking. "Wouldn't a larger animal provide better protection in that case?" The two continued after an awkward cough.

Thankfully, the conversation was cut short when Zack spotted Alastair walking towards them with Jean at his side.

"There you are!" Jean called out to them in relief. "We've been looking for you everywhere."

"No, we've been looking for you." Zack retorted. "After they finished fixing my astral form, we had to go get my physical body healed as well."

"It seems that I missed a lot while I was out." Edith poked her head out from behind Alastair's large form.

"Edith!" Zara cried out in relief. "You're okay."

"Of course, I am dearie. These elven healers are much better than the ones we have back at home. Not to mention this suit you all put me in, apparently had me well on the road to recovery as it is. They just had to fix up some damage to my extremities, fingers, toes, and the like. Then patch up one or two things inside me that they didn't specify, and I was good as new." The dorm matron smiled affectionately at the siblings, her eyes twinkling at Zara.

Zack took a moment to study Alastair properly as the two groups joined together. His previous views of the large man had always been mostly blocked by Zara's head, as she tried to staunch the blood flowing from his face.

"This is where our paths must diverge. My sisters will take you through the portal. Once you are in our world, you'll have a sliver of a rotation's time before being automatically brought back to your world. Much like what would happen when your time runs out inside a portal. Now, if you'll excuse me, I have to continue my duties." With those abrupt words of parting, Alastair turned and walked away.

"That was rather odd," Zack muttered.

Zara nodded.

"He tried to flirt with Jean," Edith cackled, leaning on the suit puppet at her side. "She turned him down flat. It was gloriously brutal."

The twins sighed. "He should know better. Relationships between couples on different worlds never end well. There is no way for them to stay together in the long term. At best, it's a fling. At worst, someone becomes a single parent with a child that may not be accepted in their society. Cross-race pregnancies don't happen often, but they do occur."

Zara blushed and hid behind Zelda, holding the poor bear against her face.

Jean coughed. "I don't suppose you have a manual or a booklet full of this information that we could bring home with us? It would be most helpful if we could start preparing people for certain things now."

"Not one written in your language, I'm afraid. However, it might not be too difficult to find one you could passably understand. The only reason we and our brother can speak your language is due to the Oracle asking us to learn it. Although oddly enough, your world's language is fairly close to the standard language everyone has adopted for trading purposes. It made learning it much easier."

"How does that even happen?" Edith wondered in a shocked whisper.

The twins shrugged. "There are many things about the portals, the coming Great Change, and the other Changes that we do not understand. What we do know is that they are by design. Some of it may be random, but the overwhelming majority was put in place by some grand designer. We can only assume that there is, or at least there was a plan for all of this at some point."

"Why don't I find that comforting?" Jean asked, semi-rhetorically.

"It's not meant to be." They returned. "It just is. Now, let's get you all through the portal. The Oracle shouldn't be kept waiting."

"I'm glad you're feeling better," Zara told Edith as they tromped towards the portal. "How did you get captured?"

The matronly woman sighed. "That, I'm afraid, is a very short and boring story. I was at home, someone knocked. I opened the door and took a fist right to the side of my face. I vaguely remember waking up on a hard floor and then being shoved through a portal into this cold, icy place. Then, well, someone my age doesn't do well in the cold. My mind and body started shutting down within a minute or two of coming through. I was barely coherent enough to see you two walk through the portal. It was the last thing I saw before I gave in to the cold." She swallowed, her voice thick with emotion. "I felt for sure the two of you weren't going to make it."

Zack nudged his sister and motioned for her to hug Edith. He was less comfortable touching people that weren't family, no matter how much they were starting to grow on him. Instead, he patted her on the shoulder and gave it a gentle squeeze. He might not be as close to her as his sister was, but he was more than aware that she was coming to increasingly care for them.

It was plain enough to see that even Dorn had known to use her as a hostage against them.

There had been more opportunities for Zara to interact with the kind, almost grandmotherly, woman. Of course, he would never call her that to her face. Her hair was barely starting to grey, and she liked to joke that she was old. In reality, he didn't think she was older than her mid-fifties at most. She just carried a certain air about her that he always thought a grandmother would have.

Zack had nothing against her. He was grateful for everything that she had done for him, and especially for Zara. She had really started to come out of her shell since meeting Edith. He wanted to trust her, to care for her the same way his sister did. Yet, a part of him refused to commit, convinced that no adult could be trusted.

It was stupid and irrational, and he knew that. Emotions always were. Knowing that hadn't been helping him so far.

Zack clenched his fist and made up his mind. Zara wasn't the only one who would be talking to Edith when they got back. Assuming she agreed, of course. They hadn't even thought of how to so much as broach the subject with her.

"Look," Zara grabbed his attention and pointed at the portal ahead of them.

Directly above it was a large dodecahedron dice, showing the same count-down in each face.

Chapter 6

"Do we still have everybody?" Jean asked, stepping out of line to count heads. "How many bears do you have again?"

Zara stuck her tongue out at her. "I would never lose one of my bears. Zelda, George, Aisha, feel free to kick her as we walk past."

"Oh, come on! Not again," Jean protested weakly as Zelda hopped onto the suit puppet's neck and assumed the position of its head.

Pulling out one of her daggers, the bear pointed it at the teacher.

"Charge!" Zara giggled out. Zelda, from her perch on top of the puppet, led the charge, with the other two bears close behind.

Jean rolled her eyes and let them tackle her, groaning from the weight of the puppet. "I forgot we had so much stored in that one."

"Ooh, right, sorry about that." Zara quickly recalled them all back. It was meant to have been fun, not something that was supposed to hurt.

Jean waved her concern and smirked at her. "You forget, I'm a higher level than you. A little weight is nothing." She laughed and went to go talk to the twins for a moment before they went through the portal.

"She got you on that one," Zack smiled at his sister, glad to see she was enjoying herself. All the troubles they had faced after coming to the academy were worth it for that alone.

She mock scowled at him, her twinkling eyes betraying her. "I'll get her next time." She sighed and pulled her bear's close. Hugging each of them in turn, lingering especially long on Zelda. "I love each of you and thank you for keeping me safe. Once we go through that portal, you'll just go back to being teddy bears again. From what Zelda was telling us, though, it sounds like you may retain your awareness. I'm not sure on that. It might take a few more times, or since this was such a long one, we may be good." She sniffled and squeezed them all again.

"Let's go," Edith announced firmly, after seeing that they were all ready.

The twins went through the portal first, ensuring that anyone waiting on the other side wouldn't attack them. The puppet and Edith went next. Followed by Zack, who was carrying Aisha. Zara had her arms full with Zelda and George. Jean came last, making sure they hadn't left anything behind.

Zack felt the familiar welcoming sensation of being enveloped by the portal for a split second before it vanished, and he was in a different world. The fit of the suit loosened some with the change. Then Aisha wiggled and jumped from his arm. Against their expectations, the bears and the puppet were just fine.

A message appeared, obscuring his vision a moment later.

Congratulations, due to absorbing a portion of energy from a portal undergoing its Change, your title 'Child of the Portals' has evolved some. It has become 'Child of the Portals+'.

Zack quickly closed the simple message and pulled up the information on the title. Looking for what had changed in it.

Child of the Portals+ – A person who has taken a piece of the portal energy and made it a part of themselves. This results in a base change that makes the user more receptive to the energy of the portals. They can stay inside the portal for up to twenty-four hours at a time, in addition to their current world's limits, and are offered a choice to leave every twelve hours. It may have other undiscovered effects at this time.

It looked like the only thing that had really changed was the time they could stay inside the portals. He closed the message and moved to the side.

The twins laughed and explained, as Zara and Jean joined them. "Our world has embraced the portals; we can use magic here. Why would the spell on your bears and puppet end just because you stepped through the portal?"

"Why didn't you tell us?" Zara sulked, her eyes widening slightly and meeting Zack's in surprise as she saw her own message. He nodded his head and tapped his nose.

"There are rules for interacting with races that have yet to embrace them. We are in a grey area, due to circumstances and because our brother was the one who brought you to us. However, that doesn't mean we can just tell you everything. Somethings must first be learned on your own before we can say anything."

"Like the fact that embracing the portals means our world will have a magical energy of its own?" Zack asked, looking past them. A glimmering wall separated the portal area from a large atrium space beyond. Behind them, the portal was ringed by a giant solid onyx mana crystal, the likes of which they had never seen before.

Sure, the wall could be constructed in a similar way to the magi-tech on Aperra. The guards standing behind it, with spells held at the ready in their hands, were another matter entirely. Then of course there was what the twins had just said as well. Magic could be used here. That could only mean one thing, or at least to Zack it could, and luckily, his guess had been right.

"Let's hurry along. You don't have much time, and the Oracle will want to talk to the two of you." The twins hurried towards the glimmering wall and began tapping on it while chanting softly. Moments later, it vanished, and they were able to clearly see the guards lowering their hands and dispersing their magic spells.

The group shared a look and followed after them, the headless puppet drawing more than a few strange stares. Under the twin's guidance, they were able to skip the temporary check stations and hurry on through.

"Normally, we only have one check station at each of our portals," The twins explained, as they left the building behind and stepped into the open air. "But with the evacuation going on, we have to accept everyone, regardless of whether or not they are from our world. So, we just inspect them and make sure they don't have anything that will immediately blow up or unduly harm the facility. After that, we place them in a comfortable holding area until they are brought back to their world."

Everyone nodded, understanding the need to keep their people safe first and foremost.

Zelda tapped Zara's hand and pointed at the sky.

"You can talk, Zelda. George and Aisha do it all the time." Zara reminded her, looking up. Three moons hung overhead, two smaller ones, and one large one in the middle. "Oh, that is cool."

The twins followed her gaze. "The big one is inhabited. Magic can't be used there, so everything has to be run off of magi-tech and mana crystals. Now come along, it's better if you don't see too much until you speak with the Oracle. She can decide what you are allowed to have access to."

Despite saying that, the group still had to walk for several minutes through a snow-covered city till they reached a dome. It was large and appeared to have been cut into sections. Doors ringed the outside portion, with a staircase leading up to the lone door on the second floor.

"This is where all the most promising trainee healers live. The Oracle lives above them and offers them guidance when she is free." The twins skipped lightly up the stairs and waited patiently for them at the top before opening the door without knocking.

An open space with a wall at the back that blocked off the living area could be seen straight away as they stepped inside. Closer to the middle was a recessed sitting area full of cushions, and a small table with a steaming pot of tea on it. Hidden lights bounced off the walls and ceiling, keeping the home bright and inviting.

"Good, you have arrived." A little old lady, no taller than Zara, carrying a platter full of cups, appeared from the back. "Jay, Jade, take the other two down to get some food. I would like to spend some time alone with... the siblings." She hesitated for a brief second as though, unsure if she should call them something else.

Zack raised his brow at the twins. "Your names are Jay and Jade?"

They shrugged. "Call us what you will. We share part of our mind." A fact they continued to demonstrate with the way they talked. "A name that separates us is hardly appropriate. Only those who are unaware of the truth and the Oracle call us by those names now." They motioned Jean and Edith to follow, which they did after getting nods from the siblings.

Only the bears and puppet remained behind with them.

"Why do you call them by their names if it hurts them?" Zara asked the Oracle, releasing Zelda and George to run around the space.

"It is not good for their minds to be too closely intertwined. They have separate bodies, and sometimes they need to be reminded of it. No matter how much it pains them. Their greatest strength is also their greatest weakness. If they ever forget they are two separate beings for real, then one, or likely both of them, will die." The old snow elf lady set down the platter of cups and turned to face them. "Now come here. Let me see you."

Zack reached for Zara's hand and together they walked towards the seating area and her.

The Oracle circled around them and then took a step back, her eyes beginning to glow. "Ah, there it is. I must admit, I had my doubts. There is no reason a 'Dimensional Child' should appear and need our help. Let alone two of them."

The siblings started in surprise.

"You know what we are? Where did we come from? How can we get home?" Zack and Zara asked the questions, one on top of the other, confusing the poor woman.

The Oracle blinked, dismissing whatever spell or ability she had been using. With her brows furrowed in confusion; she began absentmindedly pouring the tea for each of them. "I don't know how to answer that. Your race is one that is older than my own. The best I can do is tell you the rumors I have heard. Some things remain hidden even from my eyes and abilities." She motioned for them to sit.

"Are we from Aperra?" Zack asked softly, accepting a cup of tea from her.

"No, your race supposedly exists in the chaos between dimensions. The ability to travel freely between worlds, fragments, and dimensions, without the use of a portal was reportedly their greatest strength." She handed a cup to Zara and picked up her own. "Of course, as I said before, these are all rumors. I know your race exists, but to my knowledge, I have never met any before the two of you."

Zara deflated at her words. "I guess we won't be going to our real home anytime soon, then."

Zack put his arm around her and pulled her close. "Don't forget, we don't know why we ended up on Aperra anyway. Maybe it was an accident and the two of us just slipped through alone and were then found by some nice people. It's also possible that our real mom and dad brought us away for a reason."

She sniffled and took a sip of the tea. "You don't believe that."

He sighed. "No, but I was hoping it might help you feel better."

Zara ran a finger around the rim of her cup, a wry smile appearing. "Oddly enough, it kind of does, but not for the reason you think." She carefully put the cup back on the table and faced the Oracle. "Why did you have us brought here? You had the twins heal my brother for a reason, and I thank you for that, but what was it?"

The Oracle nodded and set down her own cup. "You're right I did. What do you know about the Great Change?"

"Not much." Zack shared a look with his sister, who nodded. Quickly, he told the Oracle about their meeting with the strange Ruler class being in their school's portal and everything it had said. "For a while, we thought this Great Change was what was coming to Aperra, but now it sounds like you're referring to something different."

"No, the Ruler you spoke to had the right of it. The Great Change will affect everyone and everything. That is why it is called the Great Change, because it *changes* everything! However, what you are thinking about is merely called the Change, or more colloquially *'embracing the portals'*. It is a localized change that every world goes through on its own." The Oracle stood and began pacing, muttering to herself.

"I think we broke her," Zack whispered in a joking manner.

To the side, Zelda nodded. George and Aisha copied her a beat later, the two not quite understanding what was going on.

"No, I don't think it's that. I think it has more to do with the timeline the Ruler gave us. I don't think she was able to see that." Zara corrected him, watching the Oracle continue to mutter and pace.

"Another one of those things she couldn't see?" Zack snorted. "If an Oracle can't see when the Great Change is coming, how can a ruler class being?"

"I think that is what she is struggling with right now. She is trying to figure if the information we were given is real, and if so, how did it come across something that even she was unable to." Zara picked up her cup and drained it of the delicious tea inside. "I think it's safe to assume that the Oracle has fairly powerful information-gathering abilities. She wouldn't have been able to retain her position of power if she wasn't very good at what she does."

"Especially when they have access to other worlds, cultures, and people. She has to be able to match up to them as well." Zack interjected, matching her thought process.

"Exactly."

The Oracle stopped pacing and talking to herself then and walked back to the seating area. "I am unable to confirm if that timeline is correct at this time. I will need to meditate on it tonight and determine the possibilities. What I can say is that the Change for Aperra is rapidly approaching and that you can and will play a part in jumpstarting it. Unfortunately, I cannot tell you how it will turn out. There are too many variables. Some of the visions end with the world a ruined husk. While others showed it either rich in magical energy, or just like any other world with a normal amount."

"That sounds like it would be better for us not to interfere then," Zack remarked, draining his own cup of tea.

"From what I have seen, I do not believe you will have a choice in the matter. Machinations beyond your ken will force you to act. You have powerful enemies in that world."

Both siblings paused at that proclamation. "Are you sure? We're nobodies in that world. We've only offended one person, and he's dead. To my knowledge, his family has been taken care of by the local rulers. Trust me, there should be no one powerful on our enemy list. We don't run in those kinds of circles." Zack protested.

The Oracle calmly refilled their cups. "It is what I have seen. That is all I can say. That, and just know something will happen, so be prepared. How prepared you are will make all the difference for the future of that world."

"How long until we get sent back?" Zara asked her suddenly.

The Oracle sighed. "I really wish Alastair had come back with your group. You won't be getting sent back, not automatically at least. Your portal was locked. All those functions work through the originating portal. You are going to have to take the long way back, I'm afraid."

"You mean we are going to have to go back through yet another portal that connects to Aperra, and find ourselves somewhere likely far from where we want to be? A place where we will then have to make it back to the academy?" Zack clarified.

The Oracle nodded behind her teacup.

"What about the time limit for being in foreign worlds?" Zara asked her. "Will that create crippling amounts of pain as it did inside the portal?"

"I don't believe so, but you all are rather unique cases. Even if it does, it will likely only be for your two companions and not yourselves. It's hard to say, your race had a different method of transportation instead of the portals. Who can say how they interact with each other?"

They took a moment to digest that somewhat startling proclamation before moving on.

"Can we do some shopping, maybe find some things that we can bring back with us? Items that might help us in that coming fight you warned us about." Zara proposed, finally getting around to what she had really wanted all along.

"If you have something that you can trade or use as currency here." The Oracle smiled gently, as though she had been expecting the question all along.

Zara ordered the suit puppet forward and Zack removed the pack full of money and crystals from inside it. The money would be useless, but the processed magi-crystals and the regular mana crystals would hopefully be worth something.

The Oracle dismissed the mana crystals with barely a glance. She had seen them before. The processed magi-crystals, on the other hand, were of great interest to her. The snow elf people had developed something similar long ago. Like in all things, however, there was always more they could learn, especially when the item came from another world. Foreign techniques and processing methods could possibly enhance their own products.

"The mana crystals hold some value, and you will be able to use them to barter for currency or items with the twins' help. These, however," She reached for the magi-crystals. "I would like to trade for these personally."

Zack scratched the back of his head. "Would you be able to provide us with items we could use on Aperra? Something like the twin's earrings, or that can use its own mana crystal to work?" Subconsciously, he had already stopped referring to Aperra as home.

The Oracle's grin tilted slyly to one side. "Ten of these crystals for one personalized item each."

"Wait, is that ten period, or twenty, then?" Zara asked in confusion.

"Does it matter? Either way, she is asking for way too little." Zack pulled the pack away from the Oracle, suddenly wondering what her game was.

The wizened old woman nodded in approval at his action. "It is good to be distrustful and wary of those you know little about. Just know I have my reasons, and that increases the value of the items to me."

Chapter 7

"Would you mind sharing those reasons with us?" Zara asked her hesitantly.

"I wouldn't, in fact. It is information that will serve you well in the future if you use it right. My people, well, most races, in fact, have all developed our own versions of processed mana crystals over the years. The process varies wildly from world to world, as each race uses different forms of technology to achieve the same basic effect."

Zara's eyes widened in understanding. "You want to see if there is anything you can learn from them?"

"Is that even possible? I mean, it's a finished product. Can you reverse engineer something like this without knowing the technology behind it?" Zack wondered.

"My people don't need to take it apart; they just need to understand how the energy is being stored inside. Now, more than likely, we will learn nothing of value. Your world, apologies, Aperra, has yet to go through its change. That makes a difference in how things are made. You will understand more about that when you experience it firsthand."

"If you likely won't learn anything, then why pay so much for them?" Zack gathered up the processed crystals, no longer hesitating.

"The chance may be small, but it is still there. By examining these, we might get a slight increase in capacity, or a researcher might have an idea that will change the assembly process for the better." The Oracle sipped from her cup and licked her lips. "I have seen a myriad of possibilities. It's impossible to know what will happen at times. The best I can do is nudge the odds in our favor."

"And you do that by getting more of the magi-crystals, and helping us get the items we want or need as well?"

She nodded once at Zack's question.

"Is this why you helped us, then?" Zara wondered, going back to their earlier question.

The Oracle made a noise in confusion. "No, this is more of a pleasant side benefit. I knew you had information about the Great Change that I didn't. That is why I had the twins heal you and then bring you here. Some Rulers have odd abilities, beast, and monster Rulers even more so. They are more in tune with the movements of our portion of the universe than the rest of us. With how that Ruler was able to identify you both as dimensional children, it is likely it was some form of evolved beast monster."

Zack shrugged; he didn't really care why she had helped them. He was just glad that she had, being forced to relive everything they had done to him, again and again. Even with the twins' help, he was sure he would be having nightmares for weeks to come. Without their help, a regular healer would have only been able to patch him up physically. From there, the cycle would have started all over again until his astral form had regained enough energy on its own.

He would have survived, sure, but it would have been hell on him, and on the people around him. In the end, he would have made it and been little more than a shell of a person with a broken mind. It would have been Zara's turn to put him back together, and she would have tried her best. She was still healing herself, though, and he was glad that she didn't have to take up that burden.

"Regardless of the reason, thank you for helping us, and you have the information you wanted. Moving on to the business at hand," Zack laid out twenty of the processed magi-crystals, equally as confused to the number she wanted as Zara was.

Zara focused on him, noticing the haunted look hidden deep in his eyes. "Yes, thank you for having the twins there to heal him." She grabbed his hand and squeezed, refusing to let go until he squeezed back.

"I had meant ten period. For another ten, however, I'm sure I can find something else that will be worth your while."

"Done," Zack agreed, sliding the stack of crystals over to her. That one deal had depleted nearly their entire supply of them. There were only three left in the pack, along with a few mana crystals and the Albion currency.

"Would you prefer weapons, armor, items, or something else for the extra?"

"Armor, if you have it. These suits feel like they are about to fail."

She inspected his suit, pulling at the loosening material. "Some items can't handle the strain of repeated transfer between dimensions. Whoever made those would be better off just leaving them on one side of the portal at a permanently manned base. They look somewhat decent at absorbing blunt attacks, and certain non-elemental-based magic attacks. Anything with a sharp blade, or element added to the attack, however, would eat through them easily.

"Still, it's impressive enough for managing it before their world has gone through its change. And despite my dislike for these sorts of items, they are incredibly useful." She stopped speaking at their confused expressions. "Just imagine how complex all interplanetary trades become when you need to account for how many times an item has gone through the portals. Buyers generally want to know how long an item will last when they buy it."

The Oracle abruptly frowned. "That one little detail actually presents a host of problems for what I can give you and for what you can shop for."

"The Change or the repeated transfers?"

"I'm sure you all have noticed that the only things you can bring back with you through the portals are the mana crystals or sufficiently corrupted materials?"

The siblings nodded.

"That is related to the Change in some way. Once a world has gone through its Change, its inhabitants are able to bring mostly anything back. There are still a few items that won't come through the portals, no matter what. It is also how we are able to trade between worlds. The items I am going to give you are special. I mentioned before they were personalized items, and they really are almost made for you."

"I take it the problem you are talking about is with the armor?" Zack stuffed the pack back into the suit puppet and sank onto cushions beside Zara.

"Indeed."

"Well, it doesn't have to be armor then. Is there anything else that you can think of that would be able to come back with us?" Zara grabbed George as he wandered past and plopped him onto her lap. Zelda pushed him to the side a moment later. A slightly despondent Aisha looked at Zack's lap next to them hopefully, hopping on happily when he nodded.

The old woman smiled indulgently, enjoying the show. "I'll need to see what we have. In the meantime, I'll go get the two items I do have ready for you both. After that, the twins will guide you around the area while preparations are made for your upcoming journey. We have to get you from here to the portal, and then through it as quickly as possible."

"Why?" Zara had a sinking suspicion she wasn't going to like the answer.

"It depends on how much you care for your companions. I already told you, everything works through your originating portal. Your time limit doesn't reset just because you went to someone else's world. The moment your group goes through the portal again, your clock starts ticking once more. Somehow, you all managed to break something that was never meant to be broken."

Zara leaned against her brother and clutched her teddy bears tightly. "I was afraid that was going to be the answer." She muttered to him.

"Yeah, and now it makes perfect sense as to why she wanted Alastair with us. If he could transport us the same way he did before, it would have made everything so much easier. But no, he had to go and flirt with Jean." Zack threw his head back and stared at the rounded ceiling.

"You get to tell them," Zara hid her face behind both bears.

"Fine," He grunted, pulling George away from her face. "Stop hiding. It's just me here. She already left to get whatever she's giving us."

Zara nodded and placed Zelda on top of her head.

"What's going on? Why did you suddenly hide? You never hide from me, and especially not when we are inside a portal and have access to our magic."

She reached over and stroked Aisha's-stained fur. They were going to need to give all the bears a good scrubbing when they got back. "It just struck me that we really don't belong on Aperra. That we are different from them, and I don't know, it just felt like a weight was lifted from my shoulders. I didn't know how to deal with it, so I hid."

Zack gently knocked her on the head, dislodging Zelda on to the cushions. "Dummy, it doesn't matter what race we come from. They've all done terrible things at some point in their past. Maybe not to us, and maybe they have moved past it to become better people, but no one is perfect. I understand what you're saying, and I'm glad we're not Aperran's as well. Are our people any better, though? Neither of us can answer that question yet."

"You think they might be worse?"

"No, I think they'll be better overall. It sounds like they've been around long enough to work out the large problems. I don't know what it is, but something is telling me that they have problems of their own, just like everyone else." He frowned and scratched his chin. "Possibly some related to us?"

"Your sixth sense?" Zara quirked her brow and stopped Zelda from kicking him.

"No, I don't think so, but maybe. It's been acting weird ever since my magic went above forty."

"You are going to need a magic stat at least that high to use my gift, so it is good you are already there." The Oracle said, having heard the last part of his sentence as she returned. In her hands was a book, with an ordinary-looking silver bracelet sitting on top. "These are the items I have prepared especially for you. The first is a spellbook for Zack, and the second is a handy little item that I believe Zara will appreciate." A mirthful twinkle entered her eyes as she handed the items over to them.

"What do they do?" Zack accepted the spellbook readily, and Zara did the same for the silver bracelet.

"Zack's is a spell called *Blink*. Only those with the elemental affinity for Space can use the spell. Considering your race, even without my abilities, someone who knows of them would be able to guess what your affinity likely is. The spell allows you to leap through space for short distances. I believe it works with line of sight only. It is an instant cast spell, with heavy requirements on both magic and your magical energy. Use it with caution, or you may end up overdrawn again."

"Are you sure you want to give this to me?" Zack forced himself to ask. He wanted that spell, but the information they had given her wasn't worth something like this.

She smiled wryly. "It's a valuable spell in the right hands. Unfortunately, our race doesn't seem to have any affinity for the element. The book has just been gathering dust in the vault for too many years now. It's better for it to be used. It has no value otherwise."

Zara extended the bracelet back to her, almost afraid to hear what it could do now.

The Oracle laughed and shook her head. "No, this one really is perfect for you. The bracelet has two functions or abilities, if you would prefer to call them that. The first is a shield, two meters high and one wide. It can take at least as much damage as your suits plus withstand magical attacks. It lasts for..." She paused. "I don't know how you were raised to tell time, so this is hard to explain. It lasts for approximately two breaths and has a sixty-breath cooldown time before it can be used again. You must personally recharge the bracelet from your own reserves between every three uses as well."

Zara nodded along, memorizing her instructions on how to use and care for the item. "What about the second ability you mentioned?"

"Let me just say that it is related to why it will be able to go back with you and leave it at that. It is a surprise, one that I believe you will enjoy."

Zara slipped the bracelet under her suit and onto her wrist. She promptly began circulating her magic through it, binding the item to her. No one would be able to take the item from her wrist without her permission now unless they cut it off. Even then, the bracelet wouldn't work for them as long as she was alive. With how plain the item looked, she wasn't overly worried.

"One last thing, and then I'll call for the twins." The Oracle was suddenly serious. All trace of joy and mirth was gone from her aged face. "Do not spend any more of your status points before Aperra goes through its Change. And no matter what you do, you need to do your best to equalize your two stats, if at all possible. You will regret it if you don't."

"How? Why? We can't train our magic over there!" Zack wanted to tear his hair out in sudden frustration. They had both just spent all their stat points that morning. The extra constitution had even helped him stay alive earlier. Without it, when he overdrew his magic, he would have died right away.

The Oracle paused with her hand on a nearby button. "When the Change occurs on a planet, every person who has gone through the portals is equalized. Their two stats become one. Certain items are, of course, taken into consideration, such as your level and the particular stat. Magic, as you mentioned, can't be trained, so it is not equalized as heavy by whatever algorithm is used. Regardless, it is always better to have your natural stats as high as possible before the Change. You might find you instead come out ahead, instead of behind."

She winked and pushed the button.

"We're so screwed," Zara whispered.

"Yup," He agreed, feeling the pit of his stomach fall to his feet. Maybe his magic stat would be safe, but what about his constitution? It was even higher. He could be a tank mage if he wanted to be. Until he got equalized, at least.

The twins walked in and found them standing in the same place a minute later. "Are they alright?"

The Oracle had gone back to her cushions and was calmly sipping her tea. "I mentioned the equalizing to them. It seems they are worried. I need to find another item or two to complete my deal with them. While I am doing that, would you mind taking their group around for some shopping and sightseeing?"

"Their time here should almost be up?" They interjected in confusion.

"Ah, that reminds me. Make sure there are some healers on hand for their two companions. Their way back home lies through another portal. We will need someone to speedily transport them as well. Alistair would have been best, but your brother is currently otherwise engaged."

The two snow elf ladies readily agreed, not seeming to be put out by the strange requests in the slightest.

Zack picked up Zelda and placed her on top of the suit puppet, where she could act as its head. George again climbed onto Aisha's shoulder, and together, the group followed after the twins.

"We were hoping to do some shopping earlier. Then the Oracle mentioned that almost nothing would even make it back through the portal with us. If you want to just bring us back to Jean and Edith, that would be fine. Neither of us has eaten in a while either, so we could definitely use some food." Zara had lost her earlier enthusiasm towards shopping. Her feelings toward Albion had always been complicated, and now her sense of belonging was almost non-existent.

Zack nodded, agreeing silently. He was dealing with his own thoughts on the many revelations and how to deal with the upcoming equalizing of their stats. He hadn't talked with Zara about what hers looked like recently.

In the past, hers had been as badly lopsided as his were. It was a danger that came with having an aberration class.

He wasn't sure if there was anything they could do. It was a nice warning to have, but frankly, it was already causing more problems than it solved.

Zack frowned and slowed, turning around to look back at the dome behind them.

The Oracle was someone who could supposedly see possible futures and more. It was one of her abilities or spells. He had no idea which, just that she had mentioned being able to do it. Which meant she had likely known how they would react, and yet she had still told them.

Why?

She wanted them to know, and to agonize over it. Was there a secret way out of the situation she had seen, one that they would only find if they knew to look?

"Zack?" Zara called out.

"Hmm?" He asked, spinning around.

"You alright? You spaced out there for a minute and weren't responding."

"Yeah, I'm fine. I was just thinking about a few things. I'll tell you later. Now, let's get some food. I'm hungry."

The twins were watching them with an amused expression. "It would seem your time with the Oracle was fruitful. Was she able to enlighten you regarding your... *heritage*?"

"Somewhat. We still have no idea where home really is, but she was able to give us some more information, at least."

"That is good, you are one step closer than you were before." They nodded happily and continued leading them to a building only a short distance away.

A wave of delicious-smelling aromas washed over them as they stepped inside. The interior was one open space, with a dozen long tables. The wall at the back had windows that opened into the kitchen where you could order and get your food from.

The table closest to the windows was where Jean and Edith were sitting.

"If you don't mind. They will be able to help you order. We believe it would be best to fetch the healers. Your time is almost up, and they will be necessary soon."

"Go," Zack agreed, his stomach rumbling. "We'll be here for a while, regardless."

Chapter 8

T he hardest part of ordering their food turned out to be deciding what to try first. Snow Elf cuisine was different from what they were used to. The colors and shapes that they saw on the plates really drove that point home. The smell and taste, though, were divine. Thankfully, at each of the windows, they were allowed to try out the various dishes before deciding to commit to just one each.

With their plates in hand, or, in Zack's case, a bowl sitting on top of his spellbook, they finally joined Jean and Edith at their table. Zelda and the other bears had been sitting with them for several minutes by that point.

"Which one did you pick?" Jean had three empty plates in front of her, and a content, almost blissful expression on her face.

"I went with a soup; I think they called it a Peppered-Leekie. Zara went with a mix of sausages, and something called a Snow's Tablet." Zack carefully maneuvered his spellbook and bowl onto the table while answering.

"We haven't tried either of those yet. Let us know if they are any good."

Zara sat next to Edith and broke off a chunk of the Snow's Tablet. The delectable confection melted in her mouth almost instantly.

"I don't care if all this gets ripped from my stomach. It was worth it," Jean muttered, leaning against the table.

"About that," Zara glared at her brother, hinting for him to continue.

He nodded. "The good news is the food won't be getting ripped from your stomach. The bad news is we're all likely to suffer from another attack because the portal can't send us back." He dipped his spoon into the soup and began eating began.

"I don't know what that means," Edith confessed.

Jean sobered up within seconds of his announcement and cursed under her breath. "How are we getting back, then?"

"The Oracle is putting everything together right now. We'll go through another of their portals that has a connection to Aperra. Someone will transport us to the appropriate portal as quickly as possible, and that will be it. From there, we'll cross over and need to find our way back to Albion from wherever we end up." He reached over and plucked off a piece of Zara's Snow Tablet and popped it in his mouth.

"It feels like our roles have been reversed, and that you aren't telling us everything." The military woman stared at them with slitted eyes.

"It sucks, doesn't it? Not being told everything." Zack grinned and went back to eating his soup.

"How come you never told me you were a traveler?" Zara questioned Edith, biting into a spicy sausage.

"It's a painful memory mainly, and also I wasn't a traveler. I was a *Miner*. There is, or at least was, a certain stigma attached to the role. I never minded it too much while I was active, but..." She shrugged sadly, her downcast eyes staring intently at the table. "I'm not everyone. Anyway, I met my husband while inside the portal. He was a proper traveler. Eventually, I decided to retire and got a job at the academy. We wanted to start a family." She swallowed and clenched her trembling hands. "He died before that ever happened. I haven't even thought of going through a portal again since I retired."

Zelda hopped off the suit puppet and onto the table. Where she promptly hugged Edith's upper arm. Aisha and George continued to copy nearly everything that Zelda did and engulfed the older woman in their own hugs a moment later. The teddy bears were naturally caring due to Zara's influence. They just needed more time to develop their own personalities and quirks, like Zelda had.

Zara bit sadly into her sausage, sorry that she had asked the question, and dredged up old, painful memories for her. "Sorry, I didn't mean to make you sad."

"It's alright dear, you had no way of knowing it would be a sad story from such a simple question." Edith reached over the bears and tousled her dirty hair. "We need to get you in a bath soon. We all need to get into a bath soon."

They all nodded. The suits may have been keeping them warm and protected, but after going through the portal, some of the smells had started to leak through. Well, for most of them at least, Zara was still completely odorless for some reason. It wasn't too bad when they were outside, when they were inside, however, where it was warmer. That was another matter entirely.

The doors of the small cafeteria opened, and the twins stepped inside with several healers. Hurrying over to the group, they separated and pulled Jean and Edith to their feet. "We'll bring them to a separate room where the healers can watch over them. Finish eating, and when we come back, we'll bring you to your own room to be watched over."

The siblings shared an amused grin as they watched Jean get dragged from the room, whereas Edith went much more calmly.

"We should probably concentrate on eating rather than talking, even if we won't actually need any healing," Zack told his sister, already dragging another spoonful of soup to his mouth.

Unintelligible noises of agreement came back as she proceeded to stuff her face. Neither sibling was willing to pass up the opportunity to devour such good food. This place made the cafeteria back at the academy taste like the expired food they used to buy for cheap from the market.

They were both convinced they had found food heaven.

They had found it, and they hadn't even needed to die to find it.

They raced back to the windows for seconds, groaning as they quickly hit their limits. It was such a shame for them to not try all the delicious foods this wonderful place had to offer. They were willing, but the flesh was weak.

Both had been healed from the damage that years of malnourishment caused to their muscles. The other more lasting effects, unfortunately, would have required far too much energy to heal. It was unlikely that Zack's ability would even be able to help him. The damage was simply too old, and too widespread. How would it even know what to fix at this point?

The only option they had was to continue eating as well as they could and hope the rest would be healed naturally. There was only so much they could do with the limited time they had available. Considering it had only been around a month since they left that dingy government-subsidized apartment, the progress they had made was beyond amazing.

Jay and Jade came back to find Zelda prodding Zack's cheek with a sausage. Zara was next to him, with George putting pieces of a Snow's Tablet in her mouth. The delicious and sugary treat dissolved in her mouth almost instantly.

"Are you both... feeling alright?" They were clearly confused by the sibling's actions.

"It's such good food, we won't have another opportunity to eat like this again," Zack explained, chomping down on the sausage with glazed eyes.

"Ah," Their eyes lit up in understanding. Enough memories still remained from healing Zack that they could sympathize with them. "When you are ready, the Oracle believes she has something you may be interested in."

"Does she have a way for us to just store a veritable ton of your world's delicious food and bring it back with us?" Zara wondered. She wanted to bring back as many of those Snow Tablets as she could, among other things.

The twins shook their heads. "Nothing like that exists to our knowledge, and if it did, it would likely require a specialized elemental affinity to use."

Zack rolled off the table with a grunt and picked himself up off the floor. "It's fine. The information and items we gave her aren't worth something like that. It's probably not worth what she already gave us. At least not in immediate value." He corrected himself, remembering why the Oracle had wanted the processed magi-crystals.

"That's up for her to decide. She knows the true value of an item. Not its monetary worth, but what it is worth to our people. As such, she has deemed the value of your information and goods highly."

He wiped the bits of sausage from his cheek and picked up his spellbook. He still needed to read through it. The information would be transferred to him automatically as he read the book. The problem was spellbooks were single-use items. He couldn't be disturbed while learning the information inside.

Zelda dropped the half-eaten sausage on a plate and wiped her paws on a napkin. Aisha picked her and George both up and placed them on her shoulders.

Zara quickly wrapped a few of the Snow Tablet's in a cleanish shirt and then threw them into the suit puppet. "Okay, I'm ready, let's go." She said with a smile, completely unashamed of what she had just done.

They were led back to the Oracle's dome, avoiding the more crowded areas they could see in the distance. That was where the closest shopping areas were.

A message appeared when they were halfway back to the dome.

You have been visiting this world for one hour, out of your allowed three. Would you like to stay or exit?
Error, location locked. Exit from entry portal unavailable.
Please find a secondary portal soon.

It looked like their time on other worlds was affected by the same limit as the portals. They could stay inside the portals three times as long as others from Aperra. The time limit for other worlds held true as well.

They would need to figure out how their people traveled between dimensions and worlds before they would truly be free of Aperra.

"Why was the cafeteria so empty?" Zack asked them as they climbed the steps to the dome.

"That eating area is primarily for the healers learning under the Oracle and others living in the area. At the moment, all of those healers have been deployed to the portal to heal the incoming wounded. Some of them were those who worked on the two of you."

The diminutive Oracle was waiting for them inside with a fresh pot of tea. "Thank you, girls, for everything you have done. I will uphold my end of the bargain, as agreed." She glanced away regretfully. "I would suggest you move along now. The only one who can help them get home quickly enough is Skye."

Jay and Jade stopped walking and turned to look at each other.

"Are they talking with their minds?" Zara whispered.

"Remember what I said before about their minds being too closely intertwined?"

They nodded in the affirmative.

"This could be considered one of its strengths. It is how they were able to heal Zack so flawlessly. Anyone else would have required many more hours of effort, and the finished product would not have been nearly so perfect."

"Who is Skye? Do they not like each other?" Zack wondered as they waited for the twins to finish their internal conversation.

"It is not that Skye does not like them, rather it is the reverse. Skye likes everyone a little too much. I was told that Alastair flirted with Jean and her rightly refusing his advances is why he stayed behind. Well, Skye will flirt with Jean, Edith, you both, that suit puppet, little Zelda, the rug, really anything, and everything. She has an exhausting personality, frankly."

"Does it ever go beyond merely flirting?" Zara grabbed Zelda protectively.

"At times. She has her own rules, and as long as she is on the job, you will be safe."

"Will they be safe in her care?" The twins asked, suddenly finishing their shared internal conversation. "She has speed, but little actual strength."

"The portal and route I have planned for them should have little need for it. If needed, Jean has some strength, and I wouldn't underestimate the magic either of these two wields despite their low levels." The Oracle waved the two girls forward. "They'll be fine. Now say your goodbyes. Who can say when you will see them again?" She winked and went back to sipping her tea.

The twins hugged them both and patted the three bears on their heads. They had only known each other for a few short hours, but it felt longer and the emotional bond they now shared was one of old friends. Unfortunately, what the old woman had said was true.

Who could say when they would see each other again? They weren't even supposed to have met this time. Wasn't that how most stories went? The people you were never supposed to meet almost always ended up becoming some of your dearest friends.

Neither side was prepared to say that was the case here. Too short of an amount of time had passed for that to be possible. However, it was undeniable that they had left their marks on each other and that they would be remembered fondly. From there, it was only a matter of time and additional meetings for the bond to find its proper place.

The door clicked shut behind the twins, and Zara wiped at her eyes. Zack was feeling more than a little emotional himself and could feel his eyes growing hot. They had fixed him. Even more than that, they had understood him and Zara. There had been no judgment.

He knew that understanding would fade as the memories they had seen inside his astral form faded. And while he was somewhat sad to lose two people who could understand them in that way, it was also fine. The fact that they had been able to do it in the first place spoke volumes about their character and the people they were.

He sniffed, and sat down across from the Oracle, placing the spellbook on a cushion at his side. "So, they said you had something we might be interested in?"

"I do, to be more specific, I have a proposal you might be interested in instead of an item. I looked and unfortunately, I could not find anything of appropriate value that you would be able to bring back with you." She set her cup to the side. "I admit, my proposal will not sound fair to you right off hand. So, I want you to think about it for a minute before saying anything."

Intrigued, Zack and Zara agreed to her simple request.

"You must realize that this will not be your last time getting stuck inside a portal. With the Great Change approaching, it is likely that Aperra will be the last world Changed before it occurs. All the future portals that undergo their own Changes will center around Aperra. It stands to reason that the two of you will be involved in at least one or two. All portals are continually evolving, making themselves bigger, more valuable, closer to a *World Fragment*." She revealed in a whisper.

"Wait, so the world fragments we've heard mentioned before, they were once portal dimensions?" Zara asked, her eyes shining in wonder.

"Long, long ago. None have made the transition in over a dozen millennia. Several of the portals are close, now. The monsters and beasts inside would be strong, and the territory vast."

"What about the rings around the portals? Aren't those supposed to tell you how strong the monsters inside are?" Zara interrupted her, searching for more information.

"Is that what the people of Aperra think? They have so much to learn about how the portals work if that is the case. Those rings, the ones that turn black, are simply an indicator of how close the portal is to its change." She stopped to think. "I suppose, in a primitive fashion, it can also tell you how strong the monsters and beasts are going to be. The closer the portal is to its Change, the stronger the beings within a certain radius of the focal portal will become after all."

Zack tapped the table. "You were saying something about a proposal that will help us the next time this happens. Something that I agree sounds likely to occur again from your description."

He couldn't help but remember the words of the message when the portal locked behind them. It had begun its Change early because of him and Zara appearing. The odds of that happening again were high if the power bands were anywhere close to complete.

Hopefully, they could avoid those. They might not always have a choice in the matter. He could already think of two portals back home that fit that description. The one at the academy, he believed, might be getting close, but couldn't be sure, and then the one at the research facility portal. He and Zara might be able to avoid going through the school portal for a while. The Major on the other-hand would eventually force them through the research portal no matter what they tried.

"My offer is simple, any time a portal dimension undergoes its change from here on out, the ruler class beings, snow elf or otherwise, will swing by the Aperra portal. If they see you or Zara, then they will bring you back and help you get back to Aperra."

Normally, they avoided the gate from Aperra. Since as an unchanged world, one that was unable to use magical energy natively on their world, they held little value. There were established rules for interacting with them, and it was easier to pretend that they simply didn't exist.

What she was proposing would make their lives infinitely easier the next time this happened.

"What do you think?" Zack asked Zara, already knowing what his opinion of it was.

"I think this could turn out to be more valuable than an item we can use now. The Changing of Aperra is coming soon in any case, and that is going to change everything. Unless the king and queen and everyone else in charge are prepared for what is to come, it is going to be total anarchy. Especially, when they discover the equalizing." Zara grabbed Aisha as she was the closest bear and hugged her tight as she thought everything over.

Aisha was ecstatic at finally being the one chosen instead of Zelda or George. Sometimes it sucked being the biggest bear. It made her less cuddly and readily grabbable than the other two.

"Since Aperra is so close to its Change, I would think that their portal will start being monitored fairly soon in any case. We might not get much use out of this deal, only one or two times at worst. Of course, even after the Change being able to be brought back quickly would be a rather nice convenience." She nodded after sneaking a quick glance at her brother for his opinion. She extended Aisha's paw across the tea table to the Oracle. "We accept your proposal."

The Oracle laughed at the absurd action but shook the bear's paw, nonetheless. "Good, now, Zack, I suggest you use this time to read that spellbook. You won't have another chance otherwise, and I do not believe you want to show up on Aperra with such a valuable book in tow."

Chapter 9

Zack was sitting by himself, reading the spellbook, his eyes flicking from one sentence to the next. Words and information flowed uninterrupted to his brain. Their physical form vanished from the page as they were transferred from one medium to the next.

Aisha stood guard at the door, making sure no one entered the dome and interrupted him. He wouldn't get another chance to learn this spell if something went wrong.

Zara had asked if he could simply go back into the Oracle's private living space to learn the spell. The Oracle had firmly but politely refused that idea. To snow elves, their personal spaces were sacred, and only family or lovers were ever allowed to intrude upon those spaces without good reason.

He could only take the chance to learn it out here and pray that no one intruded. The Oracle didn't seem worried, which gave him a measure of confidence in accomplishing it without issue.

One page flipped after another. The sentences continued to vanish from the book as the information inside was sent directly to his brain. It was what made spellbooks so valuable, and so hard to make.

At last, he flipped to the last page and closed the book. The spellbook shuddered in a sudden contraction and began to age in front of his eyes. The magic that had been holding it together and keeping the stresses of time at bay had disappeared. The paper and material were old. In a matter of moments, the cover yellowed and lost its vibrant colors. The leather lost its supple nature and hardened with large cracks that ran through its brittle surface. MWhile the old paper inside flaked and began to fall out.

Then all at once, it broke down the middle. The age weakened leather had turned fragile and couldn't even withstand its own weight. Falling from his hands, the book fell to the ground and exploded into nothing more than a pile of leather fibers and paper dust. The spellbook was no more.

Pulling up his status page, Zack was relieved to see the spell *Blink* listed among those he had learned. He decided to forgo pulling up its information for the moment and instead just reveled in the fact that he had learned a new spell. One that could save his life, even if the energy cost was likely to be high.

That was a problem he was always going to face. All he could do was learn to control his magical energy. He stopped and groaned. Here they were among an advanced race of people who had been living with magic for who knows how long, and he hadn't even thought to ask them how he could control his magic. It was nearly a wasted opportunity.

Jumping up, he rushed over to where Zara was conversing softly with the Oracle.

"Sorry, I left a mess over there." He said in a way of opening when there was a lull in their conversation. Zack was polite and considerate enough of his little sister to not rudely interrupt a conversation she was enjoying. "I do have a question, and I can't believe I almost forgot about this. How can I control my magical energy? Right now, all my attacks go full strength and drain my magical energy or mana or whatever you want to call it. I need to learn how to control it. Can you help?"

The Oracle chuckled and winked at Zara. "The two of you are really an interesting pair. Unfortunately, Skye should be here soon, and there isn't enough time."

Zara pulled Zack down beside her. "Luckily for you, she was explaining the process to me already. You're not the only one with that problem. It just affects me less because I have a higher intelligence stat than you do."

Relieved, Zack listened in as Zara asked for clarification on a few points. He was glad she was the one who had thought to ask for the information. He would have a harder time explaining the little details to her than she would have explaining them to him.

Zara may have been the younger one, but she was smarter than him. She always had been, and he was fine with that.

Behind them, George and Zelda had found a broom and dustpan and were cleaning up the mess the spellbook had created. Aisha was still waiting at the door, though she was now sitting instead of standing. Her marble eyes were fixated on the light hitting the dangling crystal prism by the window, and creating a colorful rainbow on the floor by her feet.

They had a few more minutes of peace before there was a knock on the door. Aisha jumped to attention, now blocking the door and anyone who might enter from stepping on the rainbow.

Zara waited for the Oracle to finish speaking and to give her the okay before instructing Aisha to open the door. Zelda and George had finished cleaning up and came over to join them.

A beautiful snow elf taller than Jean by half a head stepped inside. Jean and Edith walked in behind her. Both looked physically fine, but their eyes were sunken with tired purple bruising them. Their feet dragged with every step, and their arms hung limp with no movement. They were exhausted.

"I'm not even going to ask," Jean slurred tiredly when she saw the siblings waiting for them, looking fine.

Zack nodded gratefully to her.

"Oracle," The pretty snow elf said reverently. Her fisted hand tapped her heart, then forehead, ending upright and open beside her head. It was a greeting none of them had seen before.

"Skye," The Oracle tilted her head in greeting. "The mission has been explained to you?"

"It has." Skye relaxed, letting her arms fall to her side. Her eyes took in the bears, the suit puppet, and the two siblings.

"And do you accept this task and what it entails?"

"How much time do I, or rather they, have?"

The Oracle glanced at Zack and Zara, letting them answer the question.

"I think around one hour, possibly two, if we are lucky. We weren't exactly keeping track though, so those are just my best guesstimates." Zara answered, as she was the one who had been trying to figure out how much time they had spent inside earlier. She quickly explained what the terms meant in relation to their own time system, as how she had learned it from the twins.

The snow elf woman shook her head without even needing to think it over. "I am not fast enough, not over the distance we need to cover to get to their portal."

Jean looked ill at the thought of being forced to go through the experience a third time. Edith was a little better, if only because she had only been awake for one of them.

"How much time do you need?" The Oracle questioned her.

"If we do not run into any trouble flying or otherwise, then the trip should only take a little over one of their hours. Maybe half again more on the outside. However, rarely are these runs ever done without uninvited guests showing up."

"I can probably handle some of them," Zack told her, his stomach protesting as he drew attention to himself. "My magic is rather strong, and it should be able to deter them even if it can't kill them."

Skye looked skeptical, but agreed when no one had a better idea. "Fine, but you will have to be on top."

The group paused. "Um, what do you mean on top? How exactly are you going to be transporting us?" Jean leaned against the suit puppet, while Edith rested by the door.

"I will be using a net to carry you all in while I fly." She told them, ignoring the dismayed looks.

Skye was used to it. Not everyone had access to the spells and abilities that Alastair did. He was a Ruler; they were special existences. Others, like her, were forced to make do with what they had.

In her case, that was the ability to fly fast, along with a modicum of strength. That meant she could carry passengers or goods. All she had needed to do was come up with a way to accomplish it. Sure, it wasn't the prettiest or most comfortable method, but it was effective, and that's what mattered.

It was just too bad that she would never be anything more than what she was. Her fighting strength was low, and she had always been slow to level. Skye had accepted that years ago and moved on. This was how she was making a living now. It was interesting and fun. That was all she could ask for.

"Will it be worse the second time? What is it your people call it, 'Portal's Wrath' or something like that?" Jean tried to respectfully ask the Oracle.

The Oracle nodded and put down her teacup. Zack helped her to stand and then moved to the side with Zara and the bears. "The pain will indeed get worse with each subsequent attack from the portal's wrath." Her eyes began to glow as she tapped into her ability. "I can tell you now that the longer you delay, the more trouble you will likely run into." She blinked, and the light in her eyes faded.

Jean sighed reluctantly. "Thank you for everything that you have done for us. It seems as though we should be leaving now. There's nothing we can change about the time limit; it will happen regardless. All we can do is face it as soon as possible and get it over with."

The Oracle cackled in delight. Her eyes widened in momentary madness as the glow returned to them even stronger than before. "You have no idea how true those words are, my dear. None of us can avoid our *crìoch ùine* and trust me, the greatest one of all is close at hand."

Her words left them all confused.

Skye took out a thin slate from one of her pockets and quickly wrote down what the Oracle had said. The tiny old woman had amazing powers, but she was hardly infallible. Normally, there were limits to her powers. She saw everything in possibilities. Things that could happen, but not necessarily what would.

Then there were times, such as just then, when she became almost possessed. Everything she said during those occasions held a different weight to them. They were no longer possibilities, but certainties.

The Oracle turned to Zack and Zara and simply smiled as the glow faded from her eyes. Only once she was back to normal did she say anything more. "Now, you all should hurry and leave. I need to rest. Using my ability so much takes a lot out of me." She held out an arm each to Zack and Zara. "Do be sure to visit the next time this happens. I find the two of you pleasant company."

The siblings stared at her arms, unsure of what to do with them before deciding to do different things. Zack clasped arms with her, his hand on her forearm. Zara, on the other hand, went with a different and infinitely more embarrassing tactic and hugged her arm.

Skye snorted and covered her face. "Come on, time to go. Oracle, I will report back when I return." She grabbed everyone and shoved them out the door before they could do anything else embarrassing.

"Did I just hug her arm?" Zara squeaked, her face bright red. She ordered the suit puppet over and quickly retrieved her mask. Using it to hide her face from them.

"You did," Zack chortled. "Even if what I did was wrong, at least it wasn't super embarrassing like yours."

Skye snorted again at this and shook her head. "The people of your world have so much to learn. Although what he said isn't wrong, some cultures and worlds are more closed-minded than ours. For instance, with our cousins, the *Forest Elves*, clasping the arms like that is a sign of respect. While among the *Telaur* people it is considered an intent of marriage when done among themselves. When someone from another world does it, however, it's a sign they want to fight."

"Did we ever get those primer books from the twins?" Zack asked Jean hopefully.

She nodded a patted a small bulge underneath her breasts. "I had nowhere else to store them, so I just put them in the suit for now. I figured I'd move them over to the suit puppet with everything else later."

"Will they make the trip?" Zara wondered doubtfully.

"They should. The twins said they are made from normal materials found on most worlds." Jean shrugged. "I guess we'll find out if that includes Aperra."

"Maybe we should have gone shopping then," Zara muttered wistfully.

Skye, who was listening to them talk while she laid out her net, shook her head. "It wouldn't have mattered. Most books aren't made of that material anymore." She held up the slate she had been writing on before. "Most just come on something like this. It makes their transportation easier since they take up less space and weight. I can almost guarantee something like this won't make it back through your portal."

Edith, who had been strangely quiet, spoke up then. "Could we try to get a couple of them, regardless? Ones that might help us to push our own magi-tech efforts forward if possible? Or ones with information on the portals or other worlds?"

Skye shrugged. "If you have something to buy them with, then I do not mind making the stop and running in to buy them for you. Just remember what the Oracle said. Every delay will cause us more trouble inside the portal."

"How certain are you that they wouldn't make it through our portal?" Edith pressed. She had just wanted to be helpful. She was the reason the others were all here. If she hadn't been captured and used as a hostage, then Zack, Zara, and Jean might have been able to escape.

Skye pointed up at the moons above, giving her net one final shake with her other hand. "Nothing is certain, but the odds are high. The material that these are made of is not even native to our world. It all gets mined from our two moons and a couple of asteroids close by." Portions of the net clicked together and hardened, creating a surface they could sit on.

The dorm matron deflated. "Never mind then. I guess it truly was a silly request."

Zara and her bears went over to her. "What's wrong Edith?"

"Everyone onto the net," Skye called out, letting them know she was ready.

"Nothing-" Edith stopped at Zara's glare, the young girl having already removed her mask. "Fine, I'll tell you once we get going."

"Zack," Skye called out, as they all began piling on. "Do not forget to be on top, where you can attack if something comes. How you do it does not matter to me as long as you do it. Hook your legs through the net, stand on their shoulders, just be ready when the time comes."

Zack nodded and joined the others on the net. He had until they went through the portal to get into position.

After making sure they were all inside the net, with the three bears gathered around the suit puppet for easy visibility, Skye gathered up the corners of the net and lifted them into the air. The net was clipped to a series of rings on her vest that left her hands free, while also spreading out the weight some.

Zack grabbed his charred staff from the puppet and threaded it through the loops of the net above their heads. It would give him a place to sit on later, although in all likelihood he would need to redo it after they went through the portal.

Skye kept her speed relatively slow as she carried them above and through the city.

Each person in the net kept their eyes focused on the ground. Taking what was possibly a once-in-a-lifetime opportunity to see a truly foreign city and world from the sky. It was not a sight they wanted to miss. It was also a sight they quickly grew bored with.

The snow elf world was cold. Maybe not as cold as the portal they had come from, but snow still blanketed the entire city and beyond. Everything was white or covered in traces of mud. From above, one building blended in with another.

There was no doubt that they were more advanced than the Aperran's, who hadn't even thought of heading to space yet. Everything was so well hidden from view that no one who visited would ever know that was the case. No doubt, exactly as the Oracle and their other leaders had designed.

Skye sped up as they left the city behind, drifting closer to the ground when she spotted someone ahead of them. Chuckling to herself, she skimmed the ground with the net, picking up a wake of snow behind them.

Ahead of them, the poor fellow began to yell at her, his voice lost in the approaching wave of snow. Jumping on the cart of produce he was hauling, he protected them with his body as Skye pulled up at the last second. A blast of snow-covered him and the food he had been delivering.

"Who was that?" Zack called up to Skye, who they could hear continuing to laugh.

"That was the twin's other brother, Xander. He is obsessed with potatoes and lives out on a farm near here called tall pillar or skinny rock or something like that."

"So why did you do that, then?" He wondered.

"Our last date ended badly." She told them simply, before speeding up again and heading towards the distant portal.

"That is something I can completely understand," Jean muttered, sitting down with her back against the net and stretching out her legs. "I've been on a few dates where I've wished I could do something to the guy afterward. And no, I'm not saying girls are any better." She continued when she saw Zack's expression. "But my personal experiences are with guys."

"My husband could be a real blockhead at times," Edith began wistfully. "And there were times I did want to knock some sense into him, but I always knew he was the right one for me. It makes getting through the hard parts easier when you know that the person you're with is the one you want to grow old with." She swallowed and looked away, her voice dropping off at the end.

Zara crept closer to her side and patted her on the head.

"Hold on," Skye yelled.

In front of them was a building housing the portal. After a moment, the roof began to open, and she lowered them down inside.

Chapter 10

Skye flashed the mission document she had received from the Oracle and bypassed all the questions she normally faced. It was easier to enter a portal than it was to leave.

The net settled on the ground in front of the portal and lost its rigidity as Skye gave it a shake while pulling the controlling threads.

"Everybody out. The net does not fit through the portal like this. I usually have to change the configuration when I am carrying supplies. It is easier and simpler with people."

Zack grabbed his staff and walked over to the portal. He hadn't been able to look at the last one properly and he wasn't going to miss this opportunity. The onyx mana crystal that surrounded the portal called out to him.

Reaching out, he touched the smooth black surface and closed his eyes. It had a familiar energy to it, like something from a home he no longer remembered. Pulling his hand back, he opened his eyes and shook his head. He had no idea what he was doing or what he had been expecting.

Zara had joined him while his eyes were closed and had her own hand on the dark crystal. "It feels similar to the energy inside the portals, but more familiar." She peeked up at her brother. "Do you think they had these wherever we came from?"

"Maybe. It depends on how much of what the Oracle told us is real. They wouldn't need the portals to get around, and who knows if they even have them there. The real question is, what else this mana crystal can be used for?"

She nodded. "It's too bad we can't bring some of this back with us."

Zack agreed, turning them both around as the rest of the group joined them. Zelda was once more sitting on top of the suit puppet, while George was on Aisha's shoulder. Skye was talking in a low voice to Jean and Edith at the back. The net was coiled up around her chest and shoulders.

The three ladies finished their discussion and Skye did a quick once over of the room to make sure they had everything.

"Alright, Zack and Zara, you go through first along with your bears, and that, uh... puppet thing. We will be right behind you. From there, we will do the same as we did before. I will lay out the net, and you will all get inside, except this time Zack will be somewhere near the top instead of at the bottom with the rest of you. Any questions?"

Each shook their heads in the negative.

"Good."

Zack took hold of Zara's hand, who in turn grabbed Aisha, and then the puppet with Zelda on top. Bunching up together, they walked through the portal at the same time and left the snow elf world behind.

A pungent odor hit Zack's nose moments after they walked through to the other side. The Shouvain suit he had been wearing drooped piteously from his lanky frame as the fibers tore and began to disintegrate. It had reached the max number of trips it could handle through the portals.

The smell came from the congealed blood that clung to the uniform he had been wearing underneath the suit. His blood and sweat, along with everything else that the suit had been holding inside when his scars had reopened, all of it had turned into a glistening, foul-smelling jelly.

Zack gagged and tore the ruined top off, tossing it to the side of the portal. He turned to the suit puppet to search for some of the other clothes before stopping. Zara was still dressed in her suit, and the puppet was still standing as well.

He groaned and began to laugh. "That's why you were the only one who didn't smell. Your puppet magic was maintaining your suit and this one. Keeping both in tip-top condition just like you do with Zelda, George, and Aisha."

Zara nodded. "That's what I'm thinking. If I had realized it earlier, I would have done the same for yours as well." She shrugged and pointed at the hole in the suit puppet. "But I can't fix extensive damage that was done before something became one of my puppets. I'm thinking that my current suit will become yours, and that puppet will become mine instead. With that hole and the material missing, I might have an easier time of modifying it to fit me properly."

She stopped him before he could reach the puppet. "I'll find you some clothes. You stay back. Your smell will infect the Snow Tablet's!"

He sniffed his arm and blanched, nodding in agreement. Even with the uniform top gone, the smell had seeped into his skin during the past couple of hours. Not to mention his pants and boots.

"Is there a stream nearby?" He asked Skye, as they finally dared to get close to them.

The suits Edith and Jean had been wearing had also disintegrated. Leaving each of them smelling slightly sour from the sweat clinging to their clothes. Neither of them could compare to Zack in stench, who was undisputedly in a league of his own.

She shot into the air, instead of answering, and began looking around.

Meanwhile, Zara dug out the clothes they had salvaged from Dorn and the two mercenary travelers. He would wear Dorn's clothes, since they were nice, and would fit him fairly well. The others could be used as scrubbing clothes as soon as they found a stream he could bathe in.

Skye returned with a smile on her face. "I found a stream, just a little short flight away. It looks deep enough for Zack to bathe in, but not deep enough to be hiding anything that could eat him." That comment drew some looks, as everyone began looking at their surroundings for the first time. "Is everyone willing to put off going to the portal for a little bit longer so he can get cleaned up?"

Everyone nodded emphatically, despite knowing the delay would likely mean more trouble for them.

Skye laid out the net, and everyone climbed inside. Zack was left to huddle alone in a corner, the breeze chilling his shirtless body. Zara found it hard to look away from his pale, blood-stained skin. It was flawless and smooth, without a scar in sight. It looked so different from what the bumpy, scarred skin he had before.

From above, they were provided with their first clear view of the world inside this portal. It was a swamp, for the most part, with large trees that looked as though they were weeping. Beasts slipped through the still water, snatching food and insects whenever they could.

Occasionally, those same weeping trees would reach out and snag a beast of their own. The long, tendril-like branches would wrap around them whenever they got too close. No matter how it would struggle, the beast was unable to break free, and they could only watch in interest as it was brought under the canopy and disappeared from their sight.

Ignorant of what they had seen, Skye carried them on past and to the stream she had found.

"Are you sure this is safe?" Zack asked, refusing to leave the net. Nearly all the beasts they had seen during the short flight over had inhabited the water in some fashion. He didn't mind fighting a monster or a beast, but he would rather do it with some dignity and not while taking a bath.

"There was nothing here earlier," She answered with a shrug.

"Fine," He sighed. "Zara, can you bring Dorn's clothes to the bank where I can reach them after I'm clean?" Zack grabbed the clothes he would be using to scrub his body, since he didn't care if they got dirty.

Zara nodded and followed him to the bank of the stream, Dorn's clothes in her arms.

They paused at the water's edge, both on the lookout for anything that might attack him.

"I don't see anything," Zara whispered after a minute.

"Neither do I," He agreed. "Go back and join them. I'll try to make this as quick as I can. Without soap and something to properly scrub with, it's going to be a halfway done job anyway."

She placed the clothes nearby and went back to the net.

Zack unlaced his boots and dunked them in the water. He wasn't as worried about getting them clean now, but feeling the blood between his toes was just plain unpleasant. The thick socks he had been wearing were given a quick wring as well. He did his best to ignore the discolored water that drifted downstream afterward.

He set them both to the side and jumped into the water with his pants still on. The water instantly turned dark red, and bits of jellied blood jumped to the surface. Saving the belt for later use, he peeled off the uniform pants and let them drift away.

The scrubbing clothes turned into discolored rags within moments of coming into contact with his skin. Still, they mostly did their job, and he was able to get decently clean with their aid.

A few minutes later, he was dressed, wet, and sitting on his charred wooden staff as Skye carried them towards the portal. Thankfully, there had been nothing in the water that had wanted to eat him. Although, as they flew over the downstream portions of the stream, they did see several fish floating belly up.

He might have gotten lucky and just scared them off with his foul blood.

"We have incoming!" Skye yelled out after they had been flying for several minutes, well above the reach of the dangerous trees.

Flying towards them were three of the ugliest-looking birds that Zack had ever seen. They had long necks and sharp, jagged beaks, perfect for tearing through flesh. In addition, they had large wings and bodies that would slow them down if they needed to turn.

Hitting them wouldn't pose too much of a problem with their size. He just didn't know if he could hurt them. Humans were squishy by nature. Monsters almost always had more of everything going for them but brains. Better defense, or agility, and typically more strength. Just because he had been able to wipe out those higher leveled humans didn't mean he would have such an easy time doing the same with monsters or beasts.

That was where his element came into play. It helped to even the odds. Assuming, of course, that it activated. Which it seemed to do fairly regularly. He had yet to count them out properly, to understand what the activation percentage was.

Taking careful aim, Zack pointed at the closest bird and fired off his arcane bolt. He was pleased to see the telltale signs of black clinging to his purple magic, signaling that the spell had been infused with his space element. The bolt hit the beak of the bird and ate through it to the fleshy tongue hiding somewhere inside.

The bird screamed in pain and pulled back, blood dripping from its ruined mouth. The other two awkwardly flew around it and continued on, intent on attacking the group.

Zack aimed again and fired as soon as his magic was ready. A regular bolt flew out and clipped the wing of the bird on the left. It shrieked in pain as the hollow bone broke from the bolt's attack.

He grew a little more confident as the second bird spiraled toward the ground, no longer able to remain in the air. He was able to damage them. That was all that they needed for now. Monsters that were too scared or unwilling to pursue them. Getting levels from them didn't matter.

The third bird slowed, clearly beginning to rethink its plan to attack them as it suddenly found itself alone.

Zack waited, unwilling to waste his personal supply of energy if he didn't need to. He would only get another two shots off max before he would begin burning away his astral form. After what he had experienced last time, he was a little hesitant to subject himself to that again so soon.

"I thought you were bluffing!" Skye yelled down once the last bird had turned around.

"We were lucky is all," He yelled back, keeping his eyes open for any approaching beasts. The humid swampy air was keeping his clothes from drying, and the pleasant wind was keeping him cool.

Thanks to them not needing to take any detours around and away from monsters, they were able to make better time than expected. Even with the additional two groups that Zack was forced to fight off. The second one was a much closer fight, with the birds refusing to leave until each of them had multiple wounds.

She kept up that speed until they began getting closer to the Aperran portal, and where the travelers may have roamed. At that point, Skye took them lower, skimming the tops of the trees where they would have less chance of being spotted.

"The portal should be only a little farther ahead. How much time do you have?"

Each of them shrugged, unable to answer her.

"I don't think any of us know, Skye," Zack called up to her. He was the closest, but the whistling wind still carried his voice away.

Behind them, some shouts could be heard from inside the swampy mess that made up that area.

She grunted and kept pushing. Sweat glistened from her brow, and her arms clung tiredly to the straps of her vest. She was pushing her ability as hard as she could for their sake. All so Jean and Edith didn't have to suffer through another portal's wrath episode, and so they could avoid as much trouble as possible. Something that he was convinced was impossible. Even if they avoided it inside the portal, what was waiting for them on the other side would surely make up for it.

The odds of this portal leading to Albion were slim at best. To one of their neighbors, maybe a bit better. To somewhere else in the world, where they might be held hostage as soon as they appeared? Almost guaranteed, at least in his mind.

Jean might be able to pull something out of her bag of tricks. Assuming, of course, that wherever they ended up, even bothered to listen to them.

Zack shifted uncomfortably on the staff and looked behind them. Dark clouds had begun to gather over different areas of the swampy forest. They were targeted rain-clouds, each only maybe a hundred meters in diameter. Where they were, the rain poured down, soaking everything within that space. Everything just outside those clouds only got wet from the swampy humidity.

He turned back around and kept his eyes peeled for anything that might be approaching them. Unfortunately, this time, the danger came from below.

A spear hurtled through the air on a trajectory for Skye when she spotted it from the corner of her eye. Gritting her teeth, she swerved and brought them even closer to the tops of the trees.

"I think we've been spotted," Zack informed her. Looking up, he saw her trembling arms and how pale her face was.

He didn't know if her flight ability used magical energy or some other source of energy. Regardless, it was plain to see that she was nearly to the point of running on fumes. Any longer and she may not even be able to get back to her own portal safely.

Skye glared down at him and said something in her language that sounded more than a little unfriendly.

"Is that it?" Zack pointed to the clearing just ahead of them.

The demarcation line of trees and swampy soil was easy to spot, and Skye nodded in relief.

She brought them down into the trees and dropped them where they could see the boundary line. Skye collapsed against a regular tree while they climbed out of her net.

"Are you going to be able to make it back to your portal alright?" Zara gently asked the snow elf woman who had gone above and beyond to get them here as quickly as she could.

"I just need a few minutes of rest and then I will be fine," Skye answered her between pants. Her hair was plastered to her head from a mix of sweat and hot humidity.

Zack bit his lower lip and looked at Edith and Jean. "Why don't the two of you make a run for the portal before it's too late? Zara and I'll stay here with Skye until she feels ready to head back. Someone already attacked her once. We can't let her get injured, not after what she has done for us."

Edith groaned and hurriedly grabbed a stick from the ground and jammed it into her mouth. "There, I'm ready." She garbled out around the mossy piece of wood.

Jean rolled her eyes at the older woman and began checking her weapons. Making sure that each was secure and in its proper place. Not that she was ever anything less than careful with her weapons. It never hurt to double and even triple check at times. These were not her normal swords and throwing daggers, or even scabbards and sheaths. It was all salvaged equipment taken from the Shouvain travelers.

"It would seem that we are all going to be waiting until you are ready," Jean informed the snow elf, carefully swinging the longer of her two swords.

"If I had known it would end up like this, I would have just taken it slightly slower." Skye joked, running a hand through her damp hair. Her pointed ears twitched, and she turned away from the clearing they could barely see through the trees. "We might have company in a minute. It sounds like they are the same people who threw the spear. They keep talking about the monster that was carrying off their fellow humans."

Zara giggled. "I think they thought you had captured us in that net of yours."

Jean pursed her lips and looked away, doing her best to not laugh.

Skye groaned and began to softly laugh. "At least they had a decent reason for attacking me then." She glanced at the net on the ground and began to slowly gather it up. Each section hardened together and stacked into thin layers that she could fit into the pack on her back when she was done.

Some color had returned to her face, and the trembling in her arms had stopped. The few short minutes of rest had already done her a world of good.

Skye stood and gave each of them a quick hug, not forgetting to include the three bears. "I should be fine now. I will need to take another couple of breaks, but I have enough energy to get well away from the Aperran territory. Besides, I am not exactly weak either by this portal's standards. Now go, and I will be seeing some of you again." She winked and shot straight up into the air before any of them could say anything.

Chapter 11

Jean grabbed Aisha while Zack tossed George to Zara, then they ran for the clearing. Some secrets needed to be kept as tight as possible. The bears they could hold and pass off as Zara being young and stupid. The walking suit puppet with Zelda as its head would be a harder sell if anyone noticed it. They could only hope no one would.

It really just depended on where they had their base of operations. Most places had them inside the portal, centered in the clearing where they were easily visible and controlled. The downside was they could also be easily destroyed. So other places preferred to go with a more minimal approach and keep only the bare bones inside the portal and then everything else outside.

It varied from country to country and corporation to corporation. Each had their preferred method of operation.

Luckily for them, wherever they were and whoever controlled this portal had gone with the bare bone's methodology. They wouldn't be facing any uncomfortable questions until after they went through the portal.

Edith stumbled and clenched her teeth, refusing to give in to the fire that was crawling through her veins. This was far worse than what she had experienced before, back in the snow elf world, where the healers could help her. That had hurt, and it had sapped her strength and energy, but it had been manageable.

This was a different beast entirely. Her entire body fought against her, and each step was slower than the last. They were so close to the portal, and yet, she didn't think she would be able to make it. Not under her own power, at least.

"It's started," She ground out when she could go no further.

The others had already noticed her slowing down and turned back to stay close to her.

"Why didn't you say anything sooner?" Zara huffed, ordering the puppet back to her.

The suit puppet with Zelda sitting as its head gently picked her up and ran towards the portal. They had run out of time. The only thing they could do now was push her through it first. Relieving her of seconds of pain was all they could offer her.

No one looked back as they left the swampy portal behind and stepped back into Aperra. That was a luxury none of them could afford.

Zack enjoyed the fleeting feeling of familiarity and welcoming from the portal before it vanished, and he was through.

The puppet and Edith with Zelda in her arms were laying on a smooth concrete surface in front of him. Jean was standing over her with her hands up and Aisha at her feet. Zara came through the portal a moment later and bumped into him.

Looking past their group, he saw a well-lit room filled with a military unit all armed with standard-issue Majair's aimed at them. He swallowed and raised his arms. Zara did the same a second later.

It would seem that the portal they had just used was owned by a government and under the control of the military. It was very nearly a worst-case scenario for them unless Jean had something up her sleeves.

"I would like to see your commanding officer." Jean fearlessly told the military unit. "We are envoys from a foreign country and would like to request aid in getting back to our country of origin."

The frontline shared confused looks. That was not what they had been expecting the intruders to say in the least.

Finally, someone from the back took the initiative to speak up. "What country should we tell him you are from?"

Jean glared at the person in the back. "Tell him *'Envoys From A Foreign Country!'*" She took special care to enunciate each word to its fullest.

There was silence and then a shuffling noise as someone left.

Zack shrugged mentally and lowered his arms slowly. All the while keeping his eyes trained on the people with the weapons. Carefully, he stepped forward and knelt beside Edith.

"How are you feeling?" He whispered. Taking Zelda from her and passing her back to Zara.

She groaned and rolled over with his assistance. "Like I never want to see another... portal again." Her eyes took in Zara as she resisted the urge to curse. He could feel her body trembling, and he had to keep supporting her, or she would have flopped back onto the ground. "I won't be able to walk or do anything else on my own for a while." She shuddered. "And this is the effects from only experiencing about a minute of a second portal's wrath." Edith grinned weakly up at them. "What would I be like if I had been forced to experience the entire thing?"

None of them had a good answer for that. Not to mention that it was a topic that Jean wanted to avoid since she would have been next in experiencing it.

Zara discreetly played around with her bracelet while they waited for the soldier to return. A look of thoughtful concentration would occasionally come over her face as she did so.

"Do you have any idea where we are?" Zack asked Jean as quietly as he dared.

"No, I don't recognize the uniforms at all. That just means that wherever this is, isn't a close neighbor to Albion."

Zack looked back at the portal, and the power rings around it. They still had some room before becoming completely black.

The soldier from before returned. "Stand down. The commander has given them permission to pass." He called out.

The armed formation lowered their weapons in unison and stepped to the sides. Opening a path down the middle of the room for them to walk through.

"Shall we?" Zack and Jean picked up Edith, with both supporting one side of her. Then Zara dragged the limp, item-filled suit over to Jean's other side so she could drag it along. Aisha was brought over to Zack.

Slowly, and more than a little awkwardly, the group made their way to the waiting officer. The same one who had unknowingly volunteered to be their guide.

"He seemed intrigued, so I hope for your sake that you are not lying. It would end very badly for you if you were." The officer whispered to them as he showed them from the room.

"We're not," Jean assured him. "Assuming he has a CryTel on hand, I can prove it to him easily enough."

"Good, you'll need to." The officer looked forward and led them down one hallway after another. The entire time paying attention to his speed, but also never offering to help them with their loads. It wasn't his place or his job to help them in such a manner. Besides, until they had been approved by the commander, any items they had on them could be risky.

The guards outside the commander's office would personally check them and their items before letting them inside his office. Not that he believed they were carrying a bomb of some kind, but the woman was clearly armed and trained. It was the guard's job to watch out for the commander's safety. While it was his job to not do anything more than was required of him. Something that he had failed spectacularly at today.

He led them toward an office situated well away from the portal. Four guards were waiting for them at a checkpoint about ten meters from the office door. There were two males and two females, keeping inappropriate actions to a minimum.

The officer nodded to Jean and the rest, then spun on his heel and left without another word.

Zack handed over his staff without complaint and then stretched his arms out to the side as he was patted down. Two daggers were taken from Zara, and Zelda's little belt of knives was confiscated, since she refused to leave the bear with them. Jean calmly handed over her collection of weapons and endured the pat-down from the females. They had a harder time with Edith, who was unable to stand under her own power.

The item stuffed suit initially raised some brows. However, after Zara got their rather amused word that they wouldn't steal her money or candy, which she was glad to see had survived the trip, she was fine with leaving it with them. In the rush to get Edith through the portal, she had forgotten that the Snow Tablet's might not survive the trip.

Finally, after being thoroughly patted down, they were allowed through to see the commander. Although Zara was allowed to only bring Zelda, the other two bears had to stay with them.

"You better not hurt them," Zara growled at the four intimidating guards as they walked past them to get to the office.

Four brows twitched in stunned amusement at the little girl's spunk. There were few grownups who would dare to talk to them like that over items considerably more valuable than a couple of teddy bears.

"Don't worry, little girl, we won't do anything to them." One of the female guards assured her.

Zara stamped her foot and pointed Zelda at her. "I am not a little girl! I'm almost thirteen." They already knew she had come through the portal, so there was little harm in revealing her age. Especially when it was almost guaranteed to be older than whatever, they were thinking it to be based on her looks.

Zack grabbed her arm and pulled her along. "Come on, we've had this discussion before."

Jean knocked on the commander's door and waited. Edith was being supported on one side by the other woman since Zack had to drag his sister away from the guards.

"You get so mad about being called a little girl sometimes, and other times, it doesn't even bother you."

Zara sniffed. "They took George and Aisha away. Of course, it was going to bother me."

Zack coughed, "So you mean you were really just looking for an excuse?"

She smiled.

He groaned and hugged her. "You were never this much of a pain before, but I like that you have the confidence to do it."

"I'll tell you why later." She whispered in his ear. "And don't forget to keep your mouth under control. These people can just as easily get rid of us as they can help us."

They separated as the door opened, revealing the base commander. He was a man of medium height, with peppered hair and stern eyes.

"Come in." His voice was a nice tenor, not one that commanded authority, but one that was pleasant to listen to instead.

Hanging on the wall of his office was a series of broken spears, made of progressively better materials. The last and nicest one, the one hanging above his desk within easy reach, was unbroken.

It was readily apparent that the commander was a traveler. Even without the visual aids, they could have guessed. It was a basic requirement for all higher-up military officials at this point throughout the world. The portals had become such an intrinsic part of their society and its development that everything now revolved around them. It was decided that only those who had been inside them and seen battle could be trusted to effectively lead others.

In a way, the portals had become a rite of passage, and a stepping-stone to a person's future. If you were unable to enter and cross over its shimmering horizon, then your prospects were forever limited.

In the case of the commander, he held a healthy respect for the portals and everything that came out of them. The years he had spent serving his country, all the while going inside on daily missions, watching his fellow countrymen die, had ensured that. It was that respect that had made him move the commander's office farther away from the portal when he had taken over.

He was well aware of what lived inside the portals. More importantly, he knew what other beings visited the insides of them. He had only spoken of them once to the old commander, who then ordered him to never mention them again to anyone. Now that he had more power and information, he knew why.

And it scared him.

The four visitors, envoys from a foreign country, that had somehow managed to wander through his portal. They scared him as well. Not because of their power, but because of what they represented.

There was no way they could have gotten from another portal to his without help. Which meant one of those other beings had interfered. Something that had never happened before.

He sat behind his desk, and the small plaque with the name '*Chapman*' on it and motioned for them to sit. "Now which country would dare to send envoys through the portals in such a fashion?"

Jean moved to the edge of her seat, taking the lead in the discussion. "I never said that we were envoys meant for you and your country."

The unexpected response brought the man up short and seemed to terrify him at the same time. "Are you suggesting..." His eyes flickered to Zack and Zara and the bear in her arms. He shook his head, dismissing whatever thought he had.

"Before I tell you anymore, may I know which country, kingdom, duchy, or other domain we may have ended up in?" Jean pushed him. More concerned with getting in touch with the Major back home, than whatever theory the man was concocting in his head.

The commander sat back in his chair and rubbed his eyes. "I'm giving you a lot of leeway here and being very polite, with little information to go on. So, do not make me regret this, or I will make you regret it in turn. Understood?"

He waited for them each to nod.

"Good, now we can continue. This is the kingdom of Fittrel. Now, I won't ask politely a third time, which country are you from?"

Jean frowned. "I've never even heard of the kingdom of Fittrel. Have any of you?" She looked at Zack and Zara first, before remembering that they had barely gone to school before going to the academy.

"I do," Edith said softly. "Getting home might be a bit of a trip. We are near the ocean, on the opposite side of the continent."

Jean's face fell as she turned to face the impatient Commander Chapman. "We are from the country of Albion, and if you could let us use your CryTel to get in touch with them, it would be most helpful."

Chapman rolled his fingers across his desk a couple of times. "If, and I do mean if, we can help you get back to your country in a reasonable amount of time, would you be willing to share information with us?"

Jean narrowed her eyes. "What kind of information?"

"Whatever your country knows about the current state of the portals and whatever is going on with them. Plus, what really happened to you inside the portal."

She sat back, a sole finger tapping on her knee while she thought. "I believe I can get the king and queen to agree to the first condition. It will depend on how fast your transport is, of course. As for the second condition, that will be up to their discretion and only after we have reported everything."

"Very well, that is acceptable for now. Contact your people first and get their approval. I would also like to speak with them, to ensure your identities. I'm sure you understand." They nodded. "After everything has been approved on your end, I will get the process started here. We'll find you a place to sleep and *bathe*, along with a change of clothes."

They each blushed at the extra emphasis he placed on the word and did their best to resist smelling themselves.

The commander pointed to a cabinet in the corner of his office. "My CryTel is in that if you want to use it now. I trust you know how to make such a long-distance call?"

"No, I've never needed to before." Jean corrected him. "Everything that happened this time was more by need than because we were trained for it."

He grunted in disbelief and pulled out a large card from inside his desk. "Here, this should have the code for Albion on it somewhere."

She took it from him with a smile and opened the cabinet. Inside was a sleek-looking device that looked to be based on the same model generation that was inside Edith's apartment. Jean secretly rolled her eyes and began inputting the Major's number, beginning with the prefix listed on the card.

The Fittrel designers had added a nice touch to the device with some lights that flashed as it tried to connect. Slightly distracting, but a nice touch nonetheless.

"Hello?" The Major's voice growled over the line as it connected.

"It's me," Jean said simply. "I have both of them with me, along with Edith from their dorm. We're all healthy and in one piece, somewhat miraculously considering everything that's happened."

He coughed. "Not on this line. Now, where are you?"

"I know. I wasn't going to. We're in a kingdom called Fittrel."

There was a muffled curse as the Major moved the receiver away from his mouth. "How did you all get over there so quickly?"

"We went through the portals. The Albright's had a personal one outside the city."

"Yeah, we found it and the vehicle, along with a dead body inside. Your work I presume?"

"Yes, sir."

"Good, the portal was locked down like the one at the research facility. We had no way of going inside, or even knowing if you were still in there."

"We were, and it's a long story, sir, one best held in person. I just wanted to let you know that we are back and safe. Right now, I'm standing in the office of a Commander Chapman, who has a proposition for you." Jean extended the handset to Chapman. "The Major is the man to talk to if you want that information, and he can also verify our identities."

Jean sat back down as he took over and began talking quietly to the Major.

"Do you think this is all going to work out?" Edith asked her, struggling to sit up on her own.

"That is up to Chapman, and how much authority he actually has. I know the Major can back up everything he says. I'm not sure if the base commander for a portal can do the same."

Zara, who had been hugging Zelda the entire time, suddenly squeezed her tight and frowned. "She feels smaller." She said softly, looking at Zack.

He leaned closer. "Smaller? How much smaller?"

"I'm not sure, but she feels different."

"Let me try."

Zara passed her treasured bear over to her brother and watched as he carefully hugged her.

"I can't say for sure, but I think she feels denser, like someone put more fluffing inside her." He frowned and hugged her again, concentrating on her middle this time. "The crystal, I think it has shrunk in size somehow. That was probably the initial size difference you were feeling."

Chapter 12

C ommander Chapman finished writing down the communication details for the third time. The previous two tries had been completely illegible. They were for the man he had been speaking with and closed the cabinet doors with shaking hands. That man had been terrifying in an understated way, that he couldn't quite place. It was like every word was a threat, but not at the same time. He couldn't react to them, but he knew the consequences of betraying his trust all the same.

"Well?" Jean asked, somewhat impatiently.

He turned to stare at the group of people, or rather the envoys, sitting in his office. "He confirmed your identities. I need to set up a meeting with myself and a few others for a conference call later to sort out the details of our deal." He blinked and blanched. "What am I doing just standing here? There is so much that needs to be done to set something like this up in time!"

Jean stood and helped Edith to do the same. "I trust all of our items will be returned to us?"

He nodded absently and walked over to the door. "RETURN ALL OF THEIR ITEMS AND THEN SHOW THEM TO SOME NICE ROOMS! MAKE SURE THE LADIES ROOM HAS A CRYTEL

AVAILABLE FOR THEIR USE! THEY ARE OUR GUESTS!" His face was a pallid color when he closed the door. "There, that should take care of that for you."

"I look forward to hearing the details of whatever deal you work out when you are finished later." Jean helped Edith to the door while speaking to him.

"Of course, now if you'll excuse me, I really must begin making preparations for this meeting."

Zack and Zara were the last to walk out of the office. Both were wondering why the commander had suddenly become so helpful. It was almost as though he were afraid of them for some reason. Could the Major have threatened him while they were talking? That didn't seem like his style.

Shaking their heads, they walked out of the office and hurried to get the items they had left with the guards.

A little while later, they were situated in adjoining rooms and relaxing.

Zack stepped out of a long, hot shower and put on the uniform that had been set out for him. His skin was pink from several rounds of intense scrubbing, but the last of the bloodstains had finally been erased. It had been unsettling at first, feeling how smooth his skin was without the countless scars that had riddled its surface. He hadn't had the chance to appreciate it when he was washing in the stream before.

The change was refreshing, both mentally and emotionally. Even if remembering everything that had led up to it, *had* put him on the floor of the shower in tears for several minutes. What the twins had done to him and for him, and then Zara with her healing, was something he could never thank them enough for. Frankly, it made him feel ungrateful that he hadn't thanked them even more emphatically before they had left.

Zara was sitting on one of the beds when he stepped out of the bathroom. She was dressed in a uniform that matched his own, though several sizes smaller. The two remaining Shouvain suits had been turned inside out and were draped over a chair drying. She had taken them with her earlier into her own shower and cleaned them.

"How are you feeling?" He asked, noticing how she was picking at Zelda's dripping back seam.

"Fine, I was just waiting for you to get out of the shower so we could take the crystal out of her."

"It seems like you have something else on your mind, even if that may be true." He picked up one of her daggers and sat on the edge of the bed next to her.

She handed Zelda to him before replying. "I do, but I want to see what this crystal did to Zelda before we get to any of those things."

He paused with the blade pressed against the seam. "That's fine, but you do realize we don't have any needle and thread to fix her, right? We'll have to ask for them, which means she'll be like this for a few hours at least."

"It'll be fine. Go ahead."

Seeing her set on moving forward with the operation on Zelda, he continued. As carefully as he could, he slid the blade up the seam, slicing through the sopping wet threads and not the bear. Zara had done her best to wash the favored bear during her shower, and while she smelled cleaner, the stains would have to wait until they got back home.

When he had finished, he handed Zelda to his sister and let her do the rest. Gingerly she pulled apart Zelda's wet back and revealed her soaked fluffing, or rather what should have been her stuffing.

"What in the-" Zara elbowed him when he tried to grab the bear, sending him into a coughing fit and cutting him off.

The fluffing inside of Zelda hadn't been white in years. Too many trips through the portal and being soaked in various fluids had ensured it had a nice, mottled coloring. Now, though, it was a deep purple that almost matched the color of his and Zara's magic. Or, more likely, the crystal that the bear had somehow been cannibalizing without realizing it.

The purple fluffing was a denser, and stronger material than the normal cotton she had been made with. It required both of them working together to tear it apart enough to retrieve the crystal buried in the middle. It was indeed smaller now than when they had first put it in her, not by a lot, but it did explain why Zelda had stopped complaining about it.

There was another item inside her as well that surprised them both.

"Is that a... seed?" Zara asked softly, plucking it gently from where it had been stuck beside the crystal.

"Yeah." Zack got close to her hand and saw that it had sprouted while inside the bear. "It must have gotten in there with some dirt from my hand."

"How did it survive the trip?"

Zack pulled back and studied where it had been inside Zelda. "It was pressed against the crystal and judging from what this thing did to Zelda, it's not a normal mana crystal. Maybe it was the cause of both." He could only scratch at his head in confusion. "If the seed survived, though, why didn't the scale needle and sinew I used to secure the crystal in place?"

None of those things was normal.

"Maybe," Zara began hesitantly, dropping the seed on the nearby nightstand. "The crystal reacted to my magic inside, Zelda? They were parts of a monster, and the seed wasn't. Maybe?"

Zack wanted to refute her idea, but it was no less ridiculous than what had obviously happened to the bear. He stopped and considered it in that light. "You could be on to something there. That might even be why that ruler gave us the crystal in the first place. It may be one that reacts especially well with our arcane magic."

In the end, they just didn't know.

"What should we do with it?"

Zack tossed the crystal into the air a couple of times while he thought it over. His eyes drifted from Zelda's purple fluffing to the two Shouvain suits drying on a chair.

"How about we put it in one of those? After I sew up Zelda, I'll sew this into the crotch area of yours. Next time we go through a portal, and you make it into a puppet, you can make some more changes so that it'll be more comfortable. Then when we come back, we can check to see if the inside has changed colors and density at all. If it has, then we'll do the same to mine after a while, and then the bears until it's gone. What do you think?"

"I like it except for one thing." She played with her bracelet and leaned closer to him. "We don't have to wait until we go through the portal. I can make the suit into a puppet now. You remember that other function of the bracelet that the Oracle mentioned? The one that was a surprise, and all that."

Zack nodded, remembering the conversation from hours before.

"It lets me use my magic here," She scowled. "But I can't regenerate anything I use. So, I can turn the suit, or Zelda and the others into puppets, but I can only maintain them for a set amount of time."

He almost dropped the crystal when he heard that, and a spark of understanding came into his eyes. "That's why you were so confident before with the guards, because you knew you had magic now."

She smiled. "Yup."

Zack gave her a quick, relieved hug and yawned. "Well, it's up to you then. You know the limits of your magic better than I do. If you decide to do it, just make sure to save some for an emergency."

Zara rolled her eyes. "Of course, now go ask for a needle and thread so we can take a nap. I don't know about you, but sleeping inside that portal was not exactly comfortable." She yawned and pushed him. "See, you've got me started doing it already." She rubbed her eyes and pointed to the door.

Zack stuffed the purple crystal in his pocket and opened the door of their room. Standing a few feet away was a guard, watching both of the rooms they had been assigned. Jean and Edith were in the other room.

"Hi, do you think we could get a needle and some thread? My sister's bear is coming apart at the seams and needs some repairs." Zack asked the guard as politely as he could.

There was a moment's pause. "That shouldn't be a problem. I'll ask someone to have a kit with an assortment of thread colors brought over."

Zack thanked him for the consideration and closed the door, retreating back inside the room.

Zara had managed to fall asleep during his short talk with the guard outside. She was above the bedcovers and clutching Zelda. Carefully, he worked the wet bear loose from her arms, replacing her with George. Then he moved her under the covers and began tidying up the room.

All the items that had been inside the suit puppet were moved to a corner of the room and sorted. Picking up the purple mana crystal, he decided to temporarily store it in the pack with all the Albright money and the other mana crystals. He assumed the guards had already checked everything in the bag during their time speaking with Commander Chapman.

With any luck, it wouldn't matter in any case, and he would be able to sew it into Zara's suit before it became an issue.

It was a struggle for Zack to stay awake until there was a knock at their door. A soldier was standing outside with a wooden tailor's box filled with everything he would need and more to get the job done.

"Thanks, I'm just sewing up a teddy bear though." He told the soldier, while gingerly accepting the hefty box.

The soldier smirked. "This is what we had on hand."

It took Zack's tired mind a moment to understood that they were messing with him and being slightly petty. The inside of a tailor's box would be complicated, with specialized needles and other tools he didn't know how to use. He wasn't sure why they were doing this for such a simple request, but he wasn't going to let it bother him.

Zack closed and locked the door and placed the tailor's box on the floor by the drying suits. He plopped Zelda on top of the box and then laid down to sleep. He had probably almost undoubtedly slept better than his sister, but it had been a long and very eventful day for them both and he was wiped.

Everything they had gone through that day had been exhausting. There had been so many reveals and emotional moments. Sleep was all he could think about at the moment. Sewing Zelda and the suits could come later when his mind was clearer.

***

Jean finished her extended call with the Major and looked over at Edith, who was standing in the open bathroom doorway.

"You didn't tell him everything," The older woman stated, steam billowing out behind her.

"No, I didn't. I don't trust these knock-off whatever crap brand CryTel's to not be bugged. And a lot of it needs to be told in person, where it's secure." She looked away and sighed. "Plus, I don't feel like I should tell them everything about the kids, either. I know I should. I have a duty to, I know that, I do. But after the things they have been through, those two have trust issues a dozen kilometers high. I just don't want to be another person that has used them and then betrayed them."

"Then don't," Edith wrapped her hair in a towel and sat on the bed. "Let me ask you, why did you enter the military? Was it to protect people like Zack and Zara? Or was it to turn them over to the government, and the crown, where they might be subjected to even more experiments yet again?"

"How much do you know about their past?"

"I've pieced things together, little details from conversations that didn't fit. Odd comments that Zack or Zara would say. I don't know everything, and I'm not going to ask. If they want to tell me, that is up to them." Edith inhaled and pressed her tongue against her lower teeth, fighting for control.

Jean let her talk, not saying anything. Instead, just waiting for her to continue.

"From what I do know, or at least suspect, the two of them have a very good reason for those trust issues. You seem to me like a nice woman, and you've done them both right so far. Take it from someone with a little more life experience than you and don't screw this up. You'll regret it for the rest of your life otherwise."

***

Zack was feeling much better after a short nap. Situating himself on the floor, he promptly opened the tailor's box to begin work and groaned softly. Being poor had truly limited his imagination.

There was a vast array of items inside that he had never even seen before, let alone knew what they were for. There were dozens of needles in different shapes and size. Some were designed with the hole at the end like he was used to. While others had them near the tip instead, on those the rear shafts had been shaped into an oblong cube.

Finally, he managed to find some needles that fit his needs, and the color of thread that matched Zelda. The box included scissors and everything else he had ever wanted or needed to do more than a passable sewing job. He ignored roughly ninety percent of the items in the box and concentrated on those he recognized and knew how to use.

In the end, he was glad the soldier had brought this tailor's box. Sewing Zelda shut was no longer the easy task it had once been. The fluffing inside her was not the only thing that had grown stronger and denser. Her outer fur had as well, though thankfully it hadn't changed colors. The box had come with a pair of pliers that he ended up putting to thorough use.

Sewing the purple mana crystal to the inside of his sister's suit with a piece of spare cloth was around the same difficulty. The material was hard to work with, and each poke of the needle was a slow and laborious affair. Even outside the portals, the suits were exceptional in their ability to withstand damage.

"You don't need to do a great job with that," Zara said with a yawn. She rolled to the edge of the bed and picked up Zelda. "Once I turn the suit back into a puppet and use the modifying spell on it, I can fix the stitches easily enough. Thanks for fixing Zelda." She held her close to her chest alongside George.

Zack smiled up at her and ruffled her messy hair. "Of course, always, although it was a lot harder to get the needle in her this time than it was before. The crystal didn't only change her insides, it changed all of her."

He turned back to the suit and showed her the large hole in its chest. "Speaking of your modifying spell, do you want me to add some cloth here? Something with some color that you can spread around the suit?"

"Maybe when we get back," She decided after a moment's thought. "None of the remaining clothes are pretty enough for that, and I wouldn't want their clothes on my suit, anyway."

"That's fine with me." Zack pulled out a couple of rolls of colored thread, along with a few needles. He stabbed the needles into the thread rolls and set them to the side before closing up the tailor's box. He was tempted to swipe everything inside the box. Unfortunately, they didn't have enough room.

"Here, help me out with this." Zack dumped the pack full of money and mana crystals onto the bed.

"What are you doing?"

"Rearranging everything." He carefully rolled up both suits and stored them at the bottom of the pack. Next went in the stacks of money, with the mana crystals, thread rolls, the seed from inside Zelda, and the Snow Tablet's at the top.

It was a slightly tight fit, but they managed to get almost everything inside. Only their weapons and the clothes they had taken from the dead bodies were left out.

"I think we can just throw out the clothes. We have some more money now and can afford to buy some... new ones." A dreamy look came over Zara's face as she spoke.

"Don't forget, you're also supposedly a princess." Zack nudged her.

She snorted and muttered. "The poorest princess there ever was, maybe."

"Not anymore. You made sure of that."

She hugged the pack, and that dreamy look came back. "I did, didn't I? I guess that means you won't object when I buy some clothes for Zelda and the others then."

Zack rolled his eyes. "Sure, why not? Buy the ultra stabby bear, a pair of nice clothes. That makes perfect sense."

"Easily washable, and non-stainable clothes?" She asked hesitantly.

He nodded.

"Fine, what do we do about the weapons then and Dorn's clothes? Those were fairly nice."

"The weapons we can just strap to the outside of the pack. As for his clothes..." Zack took a second to remember the spoiled brat of a teen who had caused them so many problems. "Let's just get rid of them with the rest. The only reminder I want of him is his money as we spend it."

Chapter 13

A knock at the door startled Zack and Zara out of their quiet discussion. They had finished putting everything together over an hour ago and had just been relaxing ever since. Of course, Zara had needed Aisha to join them on the bed as well, and she looked happy, surrounded by her three favorite bears and protectors.

Zack opened the door to find Jean and Edith waiting for them on the other side. "Come on, the meeting is about to start."

"I didn't realize we were all invited?" Zack looked back at Zara and the bears.

"We weren't initially, but the king and queen insisted that all of us be present during the meeting."

Edith stood behind the military woman and temporary teacher. Her eyes roved over the two kids, making sure they were alright. Her body visibly relaxed when she confirmed they were fine.

Zack hesitated for a moment. "Alright, whatever." He picked up the fully loaded and heavy pack from the floor, taking a moment to remove the weapons from it. "I'll carry this. If one of you wants to carry Aisha, then we can go."

Edith volunteered and grabbed the large bear from the bed, taking the opportunity to talk with Zara.

"You know, you could have just left all of that in the room," Jean told him, as they followed their guide to the meeting room.

He snorted. "This pack has the suits and the money in it. Do you really think Zara would let it out of her sight?"

She laughed. "Not likely. That girl has the makings of a first-rate money-grubber." Jean edged closer to him. "Speaking of the suits, do you think the crown could have one of them?" She asked softly, mindful to not let their guide overhear.

"Have one of them, no." It was a question he didn't even need to think about. "A piece of one, maybe. I'll have to talk to Zara on that one and knowing her even if she agrees it'll come at a price."

"Like I said, first-rate money-grubber. Talk to her. I'll mention the idea to the crown when I get your response. Otherwise, I'll just forget to mention that any made it back." She winked at him and stepped away.

The room where the meeting was being held was a large conference room. An oval-shaped table with individual CryTel transmitters placed in front of every seat took up the middle of the room. Commander Chapman and several other important-looking men and women were already sitting at the table.

"You're here. Good, we can get this meeting started." Chapman effused readily, a drop of nervous sweat rolling down his face. He nodded to the technician in the corner who would be in charge of operating the CryTel during the conference call.

The four quickly took their seats, with Zack leaving the pack near the far end of the table. Less than a quarter of the chairs were filled, leaving plenty of them open for him to choose from.

Introductions were made as the technician connected with the group in Albion. The group consisted of the Fittrel Prime Minister, and then several of their ranking military members. Zack didn't bother remembering any of their names.

Jean leaned over to Zack, while covering her transmitter, and motioned for him to do the same. "I spoke with the Major some more earlier while in my room with Edith. I didn't tell him everything that happened for two reasons. First, I don't trust their equipment, and..." She sighed. "Second, I didn't know what to tell him in regard to you and your sister. So, while we are making our way back to Albion, decide how much you want them to know."

"I appreciate that, especially since I know you still have a lot of questions." He glanced over at his sister. "I think we are fine with the Major and the crown knowing that we are aberrations. That information is too hard to hide from anyone who sees us fight inside the portals. I think anything more than that is best left buried for now though. We have some information of our own, which we will be giving the crown on our terms later."

He and Zara had already decided to warn the Crown along with Anna and the Major about the coming *Change*. They needed to know and prepare, if they could, for the equalizing. That said, the information was valuable, and the pair of poor orphans intended to profit as much as they could from it.

The meeting was boring, with everyone on the Albion side first wanting to ensure that the two kids were alright. Privately, Zack thought that they were more concerned with Zara's safety than his own, not that he minded. It made sense. She was the princess, not him. Terms were discussed, and an agreement was made. Only then was the method of transportation revealed.

It was Fittrel's pride and joy, something they called a dirigible. It was an airship that could float using a gas created through a chemical reaction process they had pioneered in conjunction with the mana crystals. It had a current top speed around double that of a high-end Vortex carriage or automobile.

Finally, the people from Albion understood why they were demanding so much for their help. This technology would change the face of their world. It would open up new trade routes and possibly change the way countries did war if it fell into the wrong hands. And it would do it on a global level.

All that depended, of course, on them understanding what was going on with the portals.

Information that Zack, Zara, and to a much lesser extent Jean, had. Not that the people from Fittrel knew that.

After over an hour and a half of back-and-forth negotiations, they settled on terms that both sides could be happy with. They would be leaving the next day early in the morning and would be taking the dirigible on its maiden voyage outside of its homeland. Every flight it had done up to that point had been done secretly inside the country of Fittrel.

They would be accompanied by a diplomatic envoy and a unit of soldiers. The soldiers would serve as both the envoy's guards, and perhaps more importantly, the protectors of the airship.

A little while later, Jean and Edith followed them back into their room. Zack passed the tailor's box out to the guard with a word of thanks and flipped the lock shut behind him.

"You really shouldn't go to sleep with damp hair. It makes your hair get all tangled." Edith was running her fingers through Zara's hair while gently unknotting the worst offenders.

Zack felt a pang of unknown emotion in his chest at the sight. It was one of the things he had always done for Zara, because it had always been just the two of them. Now suddenly there was this third person, and he didn't know how to feel about the intrusion. He had known, or at least thought it was coming. Zara was already rather attached to her.

They were even thinking of talking to her as their therapist. Her spot in their lives was becoming ever larger. However, knowing all of that and seeing it in action were two entirely different emotional conundrums.

He stared at Zara for a second and shook his head. It didn't matter; she was happy. There had been precious little of that in her short life, and she deserved as much of it as she could handle.

Did it really matter if that happiness came from him, Edith, or even from other friends that she might eventually make? He settled on to the bed with them, pulling Zelda into his lap. No, he decided, no, it didn't.

"Now, why did you both follow us in here?" He asked as Jean finished dragging one of the chairs closer to the bed.

Jean shrugged and yawned. "I didn't feel like going to the room alone, and Edith was coming here."

Edith looked up as her name was mentioned, her hands stilling their work in Zara's hair. "I wanted to talk to the both of you. It has become increasingly apparent to me that you both have... How can I put this delicately? Massive issues with authority, mixed with a well-earned belief that others all want to hurt you in some way."

She looked back down, afraid to meet their eyes. "In my completely non-expert opinion, you should talk to someone soon about what happened to you back then. I know this is a tall order, but find someone you can trust and let it all out. I'm afraid that if you don't that it will develop into a near soul-crushing stumbling block you can't move past later on."

Zara shot her brother a pointed look.

Zack cleared his throat, understanding the hint. "That is something Zara and I have actually been discussing recently as well. We had heard the academy had someone who specialized in matters such as this. However, for secrecy, personal, and just plain general trust reasons, we can't use someone like that." He scratched the back of his head. "But, the idea intrigued us both, and we agreed that we probably should talk to someone."

"Who did you decide on?" Jean asked. She had placed a towel on the bed before placing her booted feet on it. That way, she could recline in her chair and not get their bed dirty.

"Edith, if she'll agree to it." Zara piped in, tilting her head to look at the woman fixing her hair.

The woman in question froze completely, her eyes wide open in shock.

"I think you broke her," Zack told his sister dryly as he began delicately untangling her hair from Edith's unmoving fingers.

"I'm curious. Why did you choose her?" Jean wondered, straightening in her chair.

"It's because we think we can trust her," Zack responded, showing a rare hint of vulnerability. "She's been good to us and hasn't mistreated Zara while I was away at classes. She even teaches her some when she can."

Jean groaned and covered her face. "That's it? Those are normal things! Most people would do the same in her situation."

"To most people, those might be." Zack shook his head. "But, trust me, they aren't normal to us. You may think those are normal, and maybe to you and people with money and a good upbringing they are. To us, however, to people from the slums, and the orphanages, we get treated differently. Even after we've left all of those places behind, we still get treated as lesser than those with money, especially the nobles."

"Outside of our first interaction, Edith didn't really do that. She got to know us and helped us understand the academy." Zara took up the reins of the conversation, explaining their reasoning to her. "It was like she actually began to care about us." The young girl's face twisted as she described something that was to her unbelievable.

A finger came down and flicked her on the head.

"Don't make that face," Edith sighed and relaxed against the backboard of the bed. "I did, or rather have come to care for the two of you. I never had kids of my own. My husband died before that happened. I've told you that story before, if only briefly."

Zara rubbed her forehead while nodding.

"Well, the reason I stayed at the academy was to fill the void his death left behind. All the kids, coming through each year, even though they weren't mine, and I couldn't treat them as mine, helped. Then the two of you arrived, and I initially didn't know what to expect. I'd already heard a few negative rumors by then about you. Fortunately, they were nothing like what the two of you were actually like."

A lone tear slid down Edith's face as she told them everything. "I think it was just before school started, after you had been there for a week or two already, that I began thinking, *fantasizing* about what it would like to have more. You couldn't be my kids. There is too much of an age gap for that, but what if you were my grandkids?" She shook her head, dispelling the notion. "I started teaching Zara with purely selfish intentions. I wanted you both to view me as something more. I'm sorry!" She broke down completely into sobs.

Zara pulled away from her. A conflicted expression on her face as she tried to process what she had just been told. "So, was it fake then? Was it all a lie put together so we would like you more?"

"No, sweetie," Edith hiccupped out tearfully. "I really do like and care for you both. I'm just trying to say, albeit badly is that I tried to manipulate you into liking me more."

"Oh." A light of understanding entered Zara's hurt eyes. "Is that all?"

"Wait, hold on." Jean butted in incredulously. "So, what you're saying is that you tried to manipulate their feelings for you by treating them nicely and teaching Zara? Do I have that right?"

Edith sniffled. "That's basically it. I was trying to treat them like they were already my family, without it being obvious."

Jean blinked slowly and palmed her face again. "Does that even count as manipulating someone? If it does, I want to be manipulated like that."

"What do you think?" Zara whispered to her brother.

"I think we've gotten away from the original point of our discussion. As for what Edith did..." Zack wasn't sure how he felt about it himself. Her phrasing of the actions had done more to damage his trust in her than the actions themselves. He knew what people were like. This was completely normal. "I don't know. Part of me feels like this is a betrayal of our trust, while a larger portion understands that what she did is completely normal. I don't know that either Zara or I can make a sound decision on the matter right now."

"I understand." Edith quickly ran her fingers through Zara's hair one last time and slid out from behind her. "It is because I know that the two of you have trust issues that I needed to tell you the truth. Whether we move forward or not is up to you now. Just know the bond we could form with this now in the open is stronger than if I had decided to hide it." She sniffed again and wiped the tears from her red eyes.

"We'll be leaving early tomorrow morning, so be ready," Jean warned them, before leaving behind the kind older woman.

Zack closed the door behind them and stared at his sister. "What do you really think?"

She played with Zelda's paws as she thought the matter over. "What she said at the end is true. Any bond we make with her now would be stronger as a result."

"Or this could be another manipulation tactic." Zack sighed as he flopped onto the bed next to her.

"Or there is that. I want to believe in her, but why did she have to go and phrase it the way she did? She could have said it in any number of different ways, and we probably wouldn't have even blinked."

"That phrasing definitely shook our trust in her more than I think the actions did." He agreed.

Zara nodded. "What you said before was right. It is something completely normal. We even already experienced it with Tessa. Granted, what she did was at her mother's orders, and she did tell us everything afterward..." She rolled over, hugging the bear tight. "Maybe that wasn't such a good example."

"I used to experience it at work on the job sites all the time. The point is, I never trusted those people. I was beginning to trust Edith, and I know you trusted her more than I did. So, the question remains. What do you really think and what do you want to do?"

"I think... that I want to go to sleep." She whispered softly. "Everything is too fresh and emotional right now; we'll be able to think more clearly in the morning."

He nodded and removed his boots, turning off the lights before slipping into the bed. Aisha's giant form separated them from each other.

"Zack?" Zara asked the darkness a little while later.

"Yeah?"

"Do you think that we just don't understand people anymore? That because of what happened to us, we removed ourselves from society in general and held ourselves apart from our peers?"

Zack groaned and turned over. "Simplify the question for me, please."

"I'm asking if we stunted our social skills by staying away from people because we were scared? Well, me more than you, I guess." She finished timidly.

He reached over the large teddy bear and found her hand. Gripping it tightly while he considered how best to answer her question. "No, I don't think we did, or at least not to the extent that you are imagining. Don't forget that we did go to school for a while there, and I was always working and around people. You might have an excuse, but I certainly don't. If even I don't understand these things, then it must be something else."

"Something they broke in the research facility?" She asked softly.

Zack yawned. "Perhaps, or maybe, it was some lesson everyone gets taught as a child that we missed. Who knows?"

Zara snuggled up to his hand, refusing to let go. He could feel the soft freshly cleaned fur of Zelda wrapped in her other arm. "At least we have each other. Night Zack."

"Yup, night Z."

***

"Answer the door," Zara grumbled, kicking Zack over the side of the bed early the next morning.

The annoying knocking morphed into a loud thumping that shook the door. "Wake up Zack, Zara, we need to leave in just a bit! Can't you guards just unlock the door from this side?"

Flipping the lock, Zack swung the door open and glared at Jean. "Is this what they meant by early in the morning? We might as well have simply slept on the ship at this point!"

"Well, you're not wrong, but that's military life for you." Jean replied lightly.

"We are not in the military though!" He growled at her, tempted to just slam the door shut in her face and be done with it.

"No, but the ones who own and operate the airship are."

"Right, we're operating on their schedule. Fine, give us just a moment to gather our things, and then we'll be out."

Zara was already putting on her boots when he turned around and had his ready for him. All they needed to do after that was gather up the bears and the pack full of their items.

Jean ended up carrying Aisha while explaining to them that Edith had already been transported to the ship. She had wanted to give them as much time as possible to clear their minds before they saw each other again.

The trip from the portal base to the airship's facility would take them a little over an hour.

Chapter 14

Z ack and Zara went back up to the top deck of the airship after stowing the pack, along with Aisha and George. Zelda had rarely left Zara's side in the last couple of days, and that wasn't about to change now.

Currently, the airship was in a partially underground facility. The above-ground portion belonged to a warehouse with a roof that could swing open down the middle. They would fly out through that.

It was a sight that the siblings didn't want to miss. They had flown through two different portal dimensions, and one world at this point. All three times, they hadn't truly been able to appreciate the experience. This time, however, they intended to remedy that and fully enjoy the experience and sights.

It was a while longer before the dirigible lifted into the air.

Behind them, crewmen ran about running countless last-minute checks and making sure everything was in order.

"All pre-flight checks have been completed. We are preparing to release all anchor lines. All non-crew personnel on the flight deck strap in. No one will be able to rescue you if you go overboard." A voice they assumed to be the captain's announced over the ship's messaging system.

A crewmember ran up to Zack and Zara and handed them each a long sturdy belt with a clip on one end. The clip was meant to attach to the underside of the railing and could slide along underneath it.

Zara stuffed Zelda into her shirt as the airship rose with a jerk. Above them, the dark warehouse ceiling spread open, revealing the oncoming light of dawn.

They zoned out the bustling commotion going on behind them and concentrated fully on the slow, gentle rise of the airship. Aperra's red and orange horizon gradually came into view as they left the ground far behind. A series of propellers on each side of the ship kicked into gear and began moving the behemoth forward.

A cold wind cut through their uniforms, reminding them of how they had endured the cold temperatures before.

"Should we go change?" Zack asked his sister, rubbing his arms. He didn't want to miss the sights, but he also wanted to enjoy it and not freeze.

She nodded. "I'll need to turn mine into a puppet, and then modify it though, to get it to fit right."

"You'll have to do that at some point regardless, and it's better to do it sooner rather than later." He conceded readily. "Also, Jean was wondering if she could have a piece of the suit material to give to the Major or the crown for research purposes. I told her it would be up to you, but that it would likely cost them something if you agreed."

"Let's go inside," Zara shivered and unclipped from the railing.

Safely inside their room, they pulled out the suits from the bottom of the pack.

"If I was to give them a piece then, it could make it even easier to modify it to fit me properly." Zara began while Zack stripped in the corner. "It would mean slightly less material that I have to deal with after all."

"Plus," He grunted, beginning to pull on the Shouvain suit. "If the Albion magi-tech researchers are any good, then they might be able to replicate these. Just think, they could give us upgrades when we grow, or they might make even better ones."

"Do you really think you're going to grow anymore?" Zara asked him. Behind her, he was already putting the uniform on over the suit.

His hands paused on the buttons. "I hope so. I'm already one of the shortest people in my class. You weren't the only one who had their growth stunted. I wouldn't mind a dozen centimeters or more. I've got another year or two at least of normal growing time in me. You should have around three, I think."

Zara grabbed one of her daggers while she thought that over. "The snow elves healed us, and we've been eating better. Do you think it'll happen soon?"

Zack turned around and grabbed his boots. "How would I know? I don't even know if our growth cycles are the same as normal humans. I'm just hoping they are."

"That's true, I keep forgetting." Her dagger slowly cut into the chest of the suit and removed a chunk of material.

Her forehead creased in concentration as she began tracing her puppet spell into the suit. The mana-laced pattern created one layer after another.

The specific spell she was imprinting was invisible to all but her eyes, but the purple glow of her arcane magic visibly suffused the suit.

A minute passed and still, she continued, a drop of sweat falling from her forehead to the floor. Another thirty seconds passed before she finished the spell with a groan and collapsed onto her back.

"I just leveled up my puppet spell," Zara told Zack weakly. "The new version takes longer to activate and has more layers, but uses less magical energy to maintain. It couldn't have come at a better time."

"Congratulations! Don't rest on the floor, it's dirty." Zack picked her up and put her on the bed after brushing off her back. "Well, you have used it a bunch in the past. It was honestly due for a level up."

She nodded. "I know. I just think it's funny. My puppet spell got up to level two, before any of the spells that you use far more often did."

He stumbled. "Wait." A look of dawning understanding came over his face as he leaned over to pick up the scrap of material.

"Yup, I guess my compatibility or comprehension might be even higher than yours." She grinned, enjoying his look of dismay.

"That's true, what the- OUCH!" He had nicked his finger on the edge of her dagger during a moment of inattention. Since they didn't want anyone not already in the know asking questions about the suits, he had left the gloves off.

"Are you alright?" She asked, sitting up in a rush. Her vision swam as the blood rushed to her head, and she collapsed weakly back onto the bed.

"Yeah, I'll be fine," Zack mumbled while sucking on his finger. "Still, that's great news! That means you can have Zelda activated for longer over here before you run out of energy."

She nodded. "I just wish there was a way I could regenerate my mana while we're over here."

He pulled the finger from his mouth and opened the pack for one of the smaller mana crystals. "You could try holding one of these, or we could stuff a regular one in Zelda and see if that works."

She snorted at his evil expression. "I don't think she would appreciate that. Besides, that works for you as part of your ability."

"No, it heals me as part of my ability." He corrected her as his finger slowly scabbed over. "But I have to first have magical energy to heal, which I don't have access to over here without these." He shrugged and tossed her the crystal. "Just saying, hold on to it. Best case it works, worst case it does nothing and you've been holding on to a mana crystal all day for no reason. Besides, when you first became a traveler again, didn't you say you might be able to use them the same way?"

She nodded, remembering. "Fine, now turn around so I can change. Then I'll need your help modifying this suit to better fit me."

He turned around as the suit puppet stood and unzipped itself for her. A minute later, the room lit up with a purple glow as she began modifying the suit on her own.

"You can turn around now," Zara told him, as the glow flickered out and died.

The hole in the chest area of her suit had closed up and joined together, additionally the suit legs and arms had shrunk to properly fit her now. Where to put the excess material remained the issue, as currently, it was all around her belly and hips. It made her look ridiculous.

"I don't think I should let you eat any more of those Snow Tablet's. They are clearly far too unhealthy for your body." Zack joked, poking at her round middle.

"Ha, ha, you're very funny. Now, where can I put it all, that won't be obvious?"

"I'd first put some in the crotch area where we put the crystal, some extra padding to prevent any chaffing." He thought for a moment and walked around her. "You could put some on your knees, just thicken that area up some, and maybe do the same for your elbows. I suppose you could thicken up the material on your back and chest a little as well. More protection never hurts. That shouldn't hurt your mobility too much, and if it does, then you can tweak it more. Any extra after that, we can just sell to Jean, I guess."

Zara's hands began to glow, and the puppet began to modify itself before his eyes. The suit wriggled and gained a little extra thickness all around. Creases formed around the joints and any other stress areas, ensuring that her movements would remain uninhibited.

"Yeah, I suppose you can just do that as well," Zack muttered in surprise.

"I got the idea from you." She looked down at the small amount of remaining excess with a frown. "Now that I've managed to use this much, I want to use the rest!" She stamped her foot in frustration.

"Well, have you thickened the soles of your feet? How about raising the neckline a little?" Zack tossed a couple of random ideas out there for her.

"I did the soles, but I suppose I could do something with the neckline."

"You should probably walk around a little as well, make sure everything is comfortable. Especially where the crystal is. You won't be able to make modifications after we leave the room."

She took a few tentative steps and grimaced. "Yeah, that crystal is way too big for where it is."

When they had first gotten the purple mana crystal, it had been around the size of Zack's fist. Now it was a little smaller than that.

"Where are you going to put it, then?"

She glanced down at her flat chest. "Never mind, I'll make it work."

Zara modified her suit a couple of more times. Making minute adjustments before she was finally happy with how it fit and moved.

Zack grabbed Zelda and the spare piece of suit material for Jean while she got dressed in her uniform. With them on, if anyone other than Jean or Edith saw glimpses of the suits peeking through, they would assume it was just another layer of clothes for warmth. Which they were, in a sense.

Zara grabbed the mana crystal from the bed and stuffed it into her sleeve where it could touch her skin. "Alright, I'm ready. Let's go back up."

He handed her Zelda and opened the door. "Then let's head back up. I want to see what Aperra looks like from the sky." His eyes had an interesting twinkle to them, as though he expected the world to suddenly turn magical from above.

The wind had gotten worse on the top deck, and Zelda was once more secured inside Zara's shirt. Each step was harder than the last as they approached the railing and attached themselves to it.

The view, however, was worth it, every face and ear-numbing second of it. They got to see a Fittrel city from above, as its inhabitants began their day. They were able to witness farmers reaping their fields. Then, as they continued to drift higher, they were able to make out distant mountains.

Zara sighed suddenly and stepped back from the railing. "Let's go back inside. My face is numb."

"What's wrong?" Zack asked once they were back inside the safety of their room.

She hugged Zelda, burying her face in the bear's chest. "I'm not sure. Everything was great. It looked incredible and magical. Then suddenly, it didn't. It was making me sad instead."

Zack pushed off the door he had been leaning against and pulled her from the bed. "I think it's time we talked to Edith. She didn't mean any harm with what she did, and she has been really good to us. That hasn't changed. Our close proximity to the portals is only going to rile our emotions up even more. I mean, let's face it, we're both unstable enough as it is."

She laughed against his chest. "We're not even going to bother pretending that we're normal when alone, huh?" She sniffed and pushed away. "I'm afraid. What if we scare her off? The entire point of these therapy sessions is to help us deal with our issues. Not to push them onto another person."

"We'll just have to ask her then if she thinks she can handle it, and if she can't then we'll find someone else. It would be better to use someone else than to scare her off and potentially lose her."

"Alright, but before we go," She handed him Zelda and then hurried over to Aisha and George. Placing the big bear on the bed closest to the window, she placed George on her head where they both could look outside. "There, now they won't be bored."

Zack rolled his eyes and kissed the top of her head. "You can be so considerate to them sometimes."

"What do you mean sometimes? I'm always considerate!"

The two went down the hall to where Jean and Edith were again sharing a room. Space inside the airship was at a premium and all the spare rooms had been taken by the military, acting as the ship and envoy's protective detail.

On the plus side, each room was surrounded by a storage locker, which guaranteed their privacy. It was the reason they hadn't needed to worry about being overheard by someone in another room. There was enough wind noise from above in the hallways to keep anyone from listening in at the doorway as well.

"You aren't going to hang out on deck for the rest of the day?" Jean asked with a grin when she opened their door.

"Nope, we decided it was time to talk to Edith and ask if she even thinks she can handle talking to us about our past." Zack nodded solemnly to Edith, who was sitting on her bed reading a book. "Is that even something you are interested in, or willing to do?" He asked Edith when she looked up.

Edith lowered her book with a look of consternation. "I don't know enough about your history to say either way. I didn't want to encroach on your privacy without permission. How, um, how bad is it exactly?"

"It's bad," Jean answered for them, all hints of joviality gone from her demeanor. "A few days ago..." She stopped. "Wow, was it really only that short of a time ago? Anyway, a few days ago, I took Zack through the portal for some specialized healing. I was later told that the military healer almost had a breakdown because of what she saw inside him. Damage that was done when they were kids. That's how bad it is."

"Gee, thanks for that glowing endorsement on my body, besides it got better." Zack smiled, reminding them. "The snow elves healed us both, so there are no more physical scars left. Just the emotional and mental ones left to deal with."

"That might just be the most terrifyingly self-aware sentence that I have ever heard." Edith sympathized.

Zack glanced at Jean, wondering what he had said wrong.

She shrugged.

Zara was squeezing Zelda tight as she walked towards Edith. "What do you think? Is that something you can handle hearing us talk about in detail?"

Edith paled. "I don't know, but I'm going to do my best, regardless."

Zack's opinion of the kind older woman went up a couple more notches. She was clearly scared, but was willing to work past it for their sake. He just hoped she wouldn't regret it. "Just let us know if it becomes too much for you. We can stop for the day or find someone else, period. There's no point in scarring you just to fix us."

Edith gulped and nodded. "I understand." Her voice was soft and weak.

They had managed to scare her, and they hadn't even started the therapy sessions yet.

"Have you been up on the top deck yet? Being able to see everything from up there is incredible!" Zara pointed towards the circular window. "These just don't give you the same view as up there."

"What are we going to do during the rest of the trip back to Albion?" Zack asked, sitting on the edge of Jean's bed.

"Well, it should only take us a couple of days to get back. So, we can either relax and enjoy the time off, or you two can start your therapy sessions? When you aren't doing that, you'll be training with me. Staff for Zack, and daggers for Zara. Which option do you want to go with?"

Zara bit her lower lip and gazed at Edith. "Would you be willing to start talking with us that soon?"

Edith nodded. "You both need to understand that I'm not a professional in this field. I understand the basics, having gone through it after I lost my husband. However, that's all I know. Much of what we'll be doing is talking and trying to exorcise the control the memories have over you. We'll have to work together and figure things out as we do this."

Zack and Zara nodded. "That's fine. The reason we chose you was because we could trust you, not because you were a professional."

Zack agreed with what his sister had said. "Sounds like we're all on the same page, then. Does this airship even have an open place where we can train? The top deck is far too windy, and everywhere else is packed with supplies or soldiers."

"They do have a space. I wouldn't say it's optimal, but it'll work if we schedule our times right. When the galley isn't in use, the tables can be cleared away to open up a space for us to use. There won't be any mats or padding, so we'll need to be careful."

There were a few mana crystals in the pack stored in their room if Zack needed to heal himself. He wasn't worried about that; he just didn't want to keep being unprepared every time something happened.

"Can we also do some unarmed combat training? I won't always have the staff by my side at school."

The location specific request initially shook Jean. Until she quickly re-membered how he had been attacked by Dorn and the others at the school. "Alright."

Chapter 15

The trip back to Albion took a total of three days. With each of those days busy, and filled with the siblings constantly on the move and draining themselves physically and emotionally.

Their sessions with Edith had begun that first day, with a tentative explanation of how they had found themselves in the orphanage. From there, they moved on to the research facility and the facility's goal.

Zack separated from Zara at that point to go train with Jean. That was how the following days went. They would take turns talking to Edith and then get some intensive training in. Often times, their sessions would end with Edith in tears and hugging them. For Zack, that emotional and sympathetic connection helped far more than the talking did. Knowing that someone outside of his sister actually cared enough to cry for him was eye-opening in a way.

Any time they had left over in the day, Edith would use to tutor them in the various subjects they were behind on. Which was, namely, all of them. They had a full schedule that kept them each busy, and with little time to themselves.

All too soon, the trip came to an end, and the airship landed in front of the Albion royal castle.

A procession of armed military acting as guards soon emerged from the castle, followed by the king and queen. The Major, Second, and Anna appeared moments later. The airship and its guests had been expected.

It was several more minutes before a door slid open on its side and a ramp was extended out to the ground. Edith led the group carrying Aisha, with Jean by her side. Zack and Zara were behind them, carrying the pack and the other bears.

They stood off to the side and waited for the Fittrel envoy to appear. They had been warned beforehand about how to act and what to do. This would be their first time meeting the envoy, who had remained hidden inside their cabin the entire trip.

A woman flanked by armed soldiers appeared at the top of the ramp. She wore a wide-brimmed sunhat that shaded her face and kept her identity hidden for a while longer. With slow deliberate steps, she made her way down the ramp and then, ignoring protocol, she walked past the king and queen and stopped in front of Second.

"Father, I've returned, just like I said I would." She swept off her hat and glared at the man in front of her.

Second's face stiffened. "Is this really how you want to begin your duty as an envoy by introducing our family's issues to everyone here? Fine, then I'll play along. I told you never to call me father again, not after you decided to follow that woman after she betrayed me."

The envoy shook with rage, and the brim of her hat crumpled in her fisted hands. "We'll continue this later!" She hissed coldly, taking a moment to regain control before turning to face the monarchs she had rudely ignored.

The king and queen watched with interest as the young teenage girl they had once known returned to them as an envoy. "Envoy Nivean, it has been years since last we heard from you. We're glad to see that you are alright."

Nivean had the grace to look abashed. "I apologize for my indiscretion, your royal Highness King Orlandris, your Majesty Queen Caroline. I was caught up in the moment and didn't expect to see him this early on." She curtsied gracefully and maintained it until they allowed her to stand.

Orlo glanced past her to Zack and Zara. "Let us take this inside, where there is some shade. I have a feeling there is much we need to discuss. Frankly, I think we can do away with the rest of the traditional greetings and pomp at this meeting. Do you agree?"

The envoy, who was easily in her late twenties to early thirties, blushed in embarrassment. "I do."

Nivean turned to her guards. "Stay out here with the rest. I'm in no danger from the crown of Albion."

The guards appeared as though they wanted to protest, but knew better than to do so in public. "Yes ma'am. Please be back inside the airship before nightfall or warn us of any dinner activities."

She nodded and was left to face them alone.

"I assume you were chosen as the envoy for this mission because of our shared history?" The queen asked her kindly.

"It helped," She replied with a backward glance, noticing Jean and the other moving towards them. "I had already been in training for it, however. Ever since they began developing the airship, Fittrel realized the importance of having closer ties with other countries. I was one of several envoys chosen because we had experience outside their borders."

"That seems odd." The Major commented as Zack and Zara stopped behind her. "I would have thought they would want people who were born there. Someone with guaranteed loyalty."

Nivean shook her head. "You don't want someone with absolute loyalty. Those people are unwilling to bend or to make deals. They turn into zealots or make situations worse. It was easier for them to just pick people like me, who are grateful to the country that took us in.

"We view it as a job and will do our best to accomplish what has been asked of us." She shrugged as they began walking towards the castle. "I don't get access to truly classified information, but that's fine. No one has a reason to kill me then, either."

Caroline turned to Anna and Second. "Is that how we do it?"

They shook their heads, with Anna replying. "No, but we are also larger than Fittrel and have been developing our envoy program for longer than them. It sounds like they only just started to concentrate on their program. Given time, I imagine that they will move beyond their current methods."

Second agreed, leaning heavily on his cane with every step. "I agree. They have taken some good first steps. They realized there was an issue and found an immediate workaround. Hopefully, they are still working on a true fix for the issue as well."

Orlo led them to a room filled with food and a waiting butler. "Zack, Princess Zara, you may give him anything you wish brought back to your dorm. Your dorm matron Edith will make sure that it is delivered safely." He told them once they had all stepped inside.

Nivean's eyes widened. She hadn't realized the young girl was a princess. No one in Fittrel had.

Zack felt the pocket of his uniform for the scrap of suit Zara had cut off before handing the pack over to the man.

Zara took a moment longer before handing him George. "Can you take Aisha back as well?"

"We will, dear," Edith answered her without hesitation. She knew when she was being excused. The conversations they were about to have were far above her paygrade.

Zara gathered a plate of food and sat next to Zack, away from everyone else.

"Now, who wants to start?" Second wondered, his hand tapping on the top of his cane.

Zack smiled as an idea came to him. "Is our old deal still in place?"

The old man blinked and began to laugh. "Sure, I haven't even paid you for the last time, but absolutely. What have you got for us?"

"We know why the portals are growing more powerful and and will eventually lock everyone out." Zack led with one of the more important secrets.

The cane fell to the floor as the room grew silent.

"Is that true?" Anna dared to ask.

"We learned it from the people who rescued us while we were inside the portal." There was another round of shocked inhalations.

"They actually helped you?" Orlo was shocked.

Zack glared at him. "I knew it! You all did know there were intelligent beings inside the portals."

Second and Anna had the decency to look away while Nivean simply looked confused. The Major seemed determined to say as little as possible and sat to the side nursing a cup of tea.

Queen Caroline handed a plate of small sandwiches to Zack before sitting next to her husband. "You should really eat something. This conversation is not going to be a short one."

Orlo glanced at his wife gratefully, taking her hands lovingly as she sat down. "In response to your somewhat inappropriate accusation, do try to remember to that we are the rulers of a country. The answer is yes, we've always known about them. All the leaders with a portal in their domain learned of them when the portals first appeared."

Second picked up his cane and took over the narrative. "The first travelers through every portal met them. They hadn't realized or known that a new portal had been formed in the area. They weren't expecting us to appear, and we, by which I mean Aperran's, weren't expecting them. Most of the encounters ended with them subduing the new travelers and then leaving the area. A couple were more ferocious and killed nearly the entire team involved."

"Needless to say, we, or rather our predecessors, all decided it was better to hide their existence from everyone after that. A task that was made easier as they disappeared and avoided us, and the areas we could easily reach." King Orlo finished for him when Second paused to take a drink. "Since then, different countries have had one or two meetings with various races. Usually, they are a ruler class being or accompanied by one. Each time, they have given us some ominous hints about what is to come, something they call the Change or the Great Change. It's honestly rather confusing."

"We can make it less confusing for you. It was, in fact, fully explained to us." Zack took a bite of his sandwich, enjoying the rare chance of having a king and queen hanging on his every word.

Zara elbowed him lightly as she continued to eat and ignore everyone.

He swallowed and took a quick sip of tea before continuing. "The Change and the Great Change are two separate events that we need to worry about. The more immediate one is the Change. It's where Aperra will begin generating magical energy of its own, meaning that we'll be able to use magic here. I'm not sure if mana crystals will form here naturally, but even if they do, the other races still mine them from the portals. So, there must be a reason. Either they are of a higher purity, or it's just better to leave the ones from their homes alone."

Zack stopped speaking to eat some more and let them talk amongst themselves.

"What does that have to do with the portals?" Nivean questioned after a few minutes of back and forth.

"Who said it had anything to do with them?" Zara elbowed him again, harder this time. He grunted and tried again. "The portals all go through their own Change as well. Each world, fragment, and portal have to go through them at some point. From what we gathered; it seems like the portals go through a change every time a world they are connected to does. It makes them bigger, closer to a real-world, or a fragment of a world at least. When that happens, they'll stop being a portal and become a home for someone. It's been so long since it last happened, even the snow elves weren't entirely sure about the details."

"Does that mean the portals are going to remain locked until they complete their change, or until we complete ours?" The Major questioned, speaking up for the first time.

Zack held back a shrug. "That's likely to be the case. We didn't think to ask how long the change for a portal normally takes. We had other concerns on our mind at the time."

"Did they say when Aperra's Change would happen?" Second's hand had a death-grip on his cane, despite his calm tone.

"No, but I would guess after all or nearly all the portals have begun their Change."

The adults in the room each stilled.

"That will throw our entire economy into disarray. Prices for everything will skyrocket, and that's assuming that we'll even have enough mana crystals to supply energy everywhere." Orlo slumped against his wife and began massaging his eyes. "How many portals do we even have left open now?"

The Major coughed. "Strictly speaking, all but two are still open, your majesty. They aren't actually locked. It's just the term we've been using since no one is willing to enter them after their power bands become fully black. The beasts and monsters inside are too strong. The travelers and miners aren't willing to risk it."

"Each of those is on the cusp of beginning their Change. It sounds like," Zara spoke up, having finished her plate of food. "In time, each portal may start it on their own, but it would be faster to continue sending in travelers to push it over the edge. The problem with that is, they might also get trapped inside like we did. However, I'm inclined to believe that happened due to special circumstances. From what we learned, normally travelers have a rather large window of time to make it back to the portal and their world before the portal actually begins its Change."

"What makes the portal at the research institute so different in the way it acted, then? It didn't follow any of the normal patterns." The Major stared at the siblings, sure that they knew more than they were saying. "It ejected the travelers that were inside it at the time and somehow wiped their memory. Then its surface darkened and stopped moving, becoming hard to the touch. Only after all that did the power rings around the edge suddenly thicken, multiply, and become solid black."

"How would we know? We haven't been back to that accursed place since you rescued us." Zack answered him blandly. "Look, we're offering to help explain the situation to you all."

Zara jabbed him in the side repeatedly.

He breathed in deeply, regaining a smidgen of control. "There is a lot more that we know, and you don't but should. We don't have answers to everything. There simply wasn't time for that number of in-depth conversations to occur."

"The Great Change is one that affects everyone. It's not localized to just Aperra. Whenever it happens, it will change everything, and that's really all they could tell us." Zara pushed the conversation forward. "What everyone needs to worry about is something called the equalizing that will happen during our Change."

She spent a few minutes describing how it worked to them.

Anna cursed and angrily shoved a cupcake into her mouth.

Second reached inside his vest and pulled out a plain metal flask. "I think news like that requires something a little stronger than tea."

Caroline sadly shook her head. "There's no way. It takes too much time to train stats normally. We could maybe ask the students from the various academies to hold off on placing their accumulated status points. However, I doubt any would do as we asked. They see those points as the way forward. Their path to strength, because that is the way it has been for the last hundred years. No one would believe us if we were to suddenly say differently."

"I'll force Tessa to stop using them if I have to!" Anna growled, spewing cupcake crumbs everywhere.

Orlo's hand reached up towards his face and Caroline quickly smacked it down. A second later, it started to drift up again. This time, she took a firm hold of it and held it with her own.

"Don't start rubbing that spot again. It'll turn into a sore like last time."

The king smiled gratefully at his wife and promptly sat on his other hand, not caring about the other people present.

"Nivean dear," Caroline smiled at her, like a wolf about to devour its next meal. "I think it's time we renegotiated the terms of our agreement. Clearly, the information they have provided has gone far beyond what we expected. How about the two of us get in touch with your superiors and see if we can make another deal? Something slightly more favorable for us this time."

"Nivea, we'll talk later. Don't go leaving before then." Second told her softly as she passed.

Her foot paused in the air before she nodded and followed the queen from the room.

"I think we've covered the basics of what we needed to tell you. Jean can probably provide you with the details about our adventure better than we can." Zack was eager to get back to something more normal. "Wait, what's today?"

"Today's Holztag, you managed to miss an entire week of school," Anna answered.

"Speaking of which," Orlo put on a stern face. "Young lady, you may be a temporary princess of this country, but that doesn't mean you are allowed to skip an entire week of school. I expect better from you in the future." He laughed and looked around the room. "What?"

"Orlo, you can't act like that around people who don't know you. They might think you were serious." Second took a long swig from his flask, screwed the cap on, and stored it back in his vest. "I must apologize for him. The king and queen don't get to see their children very often at the moment. There are a few rather stupid royal traditions that have yet to be abolished for some reason."

"Trust me, I wish I had abolished them years ago as well. It would have saved Caroline and me a lot of heartache. Not to mention the kids, they hate it. Maybe I should just get rid of the tradition next time they're home? It sounds like everything is going to get tumultuous soon in any case. I would rather enjoy some peaceful times with them both while we can."

Zack reached into his pocket and withdrew the suit scrap. "And with that, I think it's time for us to go back to our dorm. Here, Jean knows what to do with this and what it's worth." He handed it to the woman, who had barely said a thing since they entered the room. "Get us a good price for it," He whispered to her.

"Oh, Zack." Second called. "Our meeting last week never happened. How about we reschedule for tomorrow? I'll pick you in the morning, with all the money you've earned from our deals in tow. I believe there is one more deal we have yet to discuss as well. If you are still interested, that is? Regardless, there are some people I want you to meet. I believe it may prove enlightening."

Zack thought back to the deal he was originally going to make with Second and the information he promised to find. "If you have the information, then I'll still make that deal."

"I do."

"Then I'll see you in the morning," He bowed to the King, while Zara curtsied clumsily. "Your majesty, it was an honor meeting you and the queen. Major, I'm sure we'll be talking again soon. Anna, say hello to Tessa for us." Then they left before anyone could say otherwise.

"Do they even know where they are going?" Anna wondered a moment after the door closed behind them.

"I didn't even say they could leave," Orlo chuckled. "Cheeky little brat. I miss my kids."

Chapter 16

Zara began filling the tub with hot water as soon as they were home. They had washed the bears at the base when they first arrived, but they had better cleaning supplies here. There they had been limited to shampoo and bar-soap, neither worked for the sort of deep cleaning the three bears desperately needed.

Zack went into his room and stripped down, removing the suit for the first time in days and changing into some comfortable clothes. "It almost feels weird to not be wearing that suit now."

Zara dropped the bears into the steaming water to let them begin soaking before answering him. "It really does." She had changed while in the bathroom and was cradling her suit. "Look at this." It was turned inside out and had already been wiped down. Faint purple lines extended outward from where the crystal was in a complicated fractal pattern.

"It's already started to change the suit then."

"Yup, and check this out as well." She flicked him the small mana crystal he had given her on the airship that first day.

"It looks a little dimmer," He guessed, not really remembering what it had looked like originally.

"Exactly! You were right, well I guess so was I, but as long as I keep that touching my skin the entire time, then I can absorb some of the mana it gives off naturally."

"We'll need to buy a supply of smaller mana crystals then. Some for you, and some for me." He handed it back to her. "How many puppets do you think you can support over here with one of these, then?"

"Doing both our suits shouldn't be a problem, especially with the new spell level. I can maybe squeeze Zelda in as well, but that will be pushing it to the limit. That small mana crystal might not put out enough ambient energy to keep up with the expenditure."

Zack pointed to the pack. "Then carry two of them. Your natural mana regeneration in the portal is high. You could probably carry as many as you wanted."

"That sounds expensive."

Zack laughed and hugged her. "At least we don't need to worry about buying food now. The academy provides that. Not to mention tomorrow we'll see how much all that information was worth to Second."

"Probably not much. You kept giving it to him while other people were there. He'll only give you a tiny portion of its true worth in all likelihood."

"That's true for when we came out of the portal, but today was with the king and queen. I think that'll even out the odds a fair bit. All, or at least most of the information he buys, goes to them, anyway."

"That might be true." She agreed slowly. "In any case, I'm going to go let Edith know that we're back from the castle. Can you please get started on

Zelda and the others while I'm doing that?" Zara grabbed her suit and went back into her room to change into it before leaving.

Even just walking down the hall to Edith's door was scary without her puppet-enhanced suit on. Knowing that she had magic when others didn't helped to embolden her. It was a crutch of sorts, but everyone used them when they were recovering. It was important to remember that each person recovered at their own pace. That was especially true when you were as damaged as Zara and he had been.

Zack was simply glad that she had found a path forward.

He grabbed the scrub brushes and the specialized cleaning soap. He had managed to recover them from the trash of an early construction job. They tried to use the soap sparingly, as they couldn't afford more and had filled the bottles with some water when they first found them, diluting the mixture.

"At least you don't smell anymore," Zack muttered as he pulled George from the hot water. He brought him over to the sink and began scrubbing him down. The washing they had given him at the base had gotten rid of the bear's initial funk and dried blood. This was when, hopefully, he would be able to remove the stains and anything that had seeped inside the bears.

Behind him, the bathtub water had turned a weird, mottled shade of nasty as a varied array of colored blood began to seep out and mix together.

In the sink, soapy, discolored suds began to form as he gently scrubbed the treasured bear.

"We're going to have to do something about you soon, little guy. You have more bald patches than last time, and even your cloth lining underneath is getting kind of ragged." Zack paid special care to those areas, unwilling to damage them. "It's too bad Zara can't fix damage from something before it became a puppet."

He scrubbed and washed down each bear twice before leaving them to hang dry over the tub.

"Is Edith alright?" He asked as Zara walked back in when he was drying his wrinkled hands.

"She was fine. The royal butler fellow was apparently rather snooty to her. Other than that, she's just making sure everything is where she left it. I think she was just looking to regain some control and a sense of safety."

He could understand that. She had been attacked in her own home. A place that was meant to be safe, where she could be in control and herself. It would be a while before she found that again. If she did, not everyone could. Some had to move somewhere else without those haunting memories and start over.

The fact that it was simply a punch to the face mattered little. It was what it represented. What could have been if it had been anyone else other than Dorn, someone with other intentions.

"Is that what took so long? You were keeping her mind off of what happened."

"It's not good to obsess over those memories. She'll do enough of that tonight when she's trying to sleep. I figured it was the least I could do for her, even if she doesn't know what it means."

Zack pulled her close and put his chin on her head. "Good girl. Even if she never figures it out, you did the right thing." He held that position a moment longer, enjoying the quiet moment with his little sister. "Now, let me show you the sopping wet puddle bears you get to cuddle with tonight."

"Nooooo," She whined. "That's right, there's no way they'll be dry in time for dinner, let alone bed!"

"Hold on," He stopped her before she could have a breakdown. "I had a thought earlier when I was washing George. He needs a lot of work! You've rubbed the poor guy bald in several places, and the cloth beneath those places is fraying."

Zara agreed, suitably distracted for the moment.

"I was thinking, can you use *'modify'* on him to fix him? Maybe fix the cloth so it's no longer fraying, and then cover him up with some clothes. I don't think you can just grow him some new fur when you modify him. Can you?"

"I can do all that, except maybe growing him some new fur. Modify uses existing material as the base, so it might be possible if we added some things to him. The new fur wouldn't match, but I can probably spread it around the old and simply redistribute everything. That might work." She was silent for a few minutes, thinking over the limits of her spell. "What does any of this have to do with them being wet?"

"Now, admittedly, you've never exactly told me the limits of your spells, so I have no idea if this is even possible. I thought you might be able to just turn them into puppets for a minute and then force the water out of them. Barring that, maybe use modify to wring it out of them?"

It sounded stupid when he said it out loud, but it really did depend on the limits of her spell. If she could force her puppets into impossible contortions, then it would be easy to wring every last drop of water out of them. Plus, if they were puppets, then she didn't need to worry about them getting damaged.

"I... have no idea myself. I've never tried those kinds of things with them. We never really had the time or freedom to experiment after that first time through the portals."

It was true; they had been left alone for nearly thirty gloriously unsupervised minutes that first time. It had been heaven, and it had never happened again.

"Right," He smiled at her, forcing away the memories. "Well, there's no better time than the present to learn what your class and spells are truly capable of. You didn't know that you could turn clothes into puppets before, so let's start experimenting. Then tonight, you can tell me more about how to control my magical energy."

They had begun the discussions during their time on the airship. At night, and then at other times when they could guarantee they were alone. Unfortunately, it was slow going without him being able to actively feel the magic coursing through him. Regardless, it was good knowledge and practice for the next time he went through the portals.

Zack and Zara went around the dorm apartment, gathering everything they could think of for her to experiment on. Soon, a pile of old clothes, shoes, and a backpack had formed. It was joined moments later by a plate, a chair, and then the kitchen table.

Zara frowned. "Is that really all we have? It's mostly our old worn-out clothes and junk from the apartment. We should go on a shopping trip tomorrow when you get back."

"I'm fine with that. We've been in need of a few new things for a while now. We just didn't have the money. As long as we don't go overboard with the money you brought back from the Albright's, it could last us a long time."

"Why do you keep saying it like that?" She demanded, glaring at him.

"What?"

"You keep saying, 'the money that you brought back.' It was both of us that brought it back! It's our money, not just mine!" Zara stamped her foot angrily.

Zack scratched his chin, unsure of how to properly put his thoughts into words. "If it had been just me, I probably would have just left the pack there. I don't have a puppet spell like you do, and we were only able to bring it back because you do. Sure, I may have helped when I could, but this was mostly you, Zara. I don't want you to feel like I'm ungrateful or trying to take it away from you."

He scratched harder. "I'm not phrasing this very well, and I know that. What I'm trying to say is that I truly do think it was mostly you who deserves all the credit. Either way, I'm grateful and thank you."

Zara sniffled and glanced away. "I know we don't really need it now, but it'll keep us fed if we ever end up on the streets again. Not that it seems likely anymore. Besides, you've done so much for us, I had to do something when I saw the chance."

Zack swallowed back a sudden rush of emotions and wrapped her in a hug. "You never have to do anything for me, but stay safe. You're my little sister and I love you more than anything. Although I'll admit having the option to wear another pair of nice clothes outside of the academy uniform will be nice."

Zara hiccupped and sniffed, nodding her head against his chest. "Now let's see what kind of weird things I can turn into puppets." She wiped her eyes and grabbed a dinner plate from the pile.

The glow from the puppet spell faded as it took control of the plate and then did nothing.

"Can you modify it? Give it some legs or something."

Zara concentrated on the plate, and the surface began to deform into an upside-down bowl. Her hand began to shake, and with a gasping scowl, she abruptly canceled both spells. "Whatever that plate is made of does not want to be changed easily."

Zack flicked the edge with his fingernail. "It sounds like some kind of thick glass."

"Humph, well, either way, the plate took both spells, even if it would be useless as a puppet"

"At least you can fix it if it ever breaks." He joked, scooting the chair towards her.

"Yea, just what I always wanted to do, fix household supplies and furniture." She rolled her eyes good-naturedly and began laying her puppet spell down on the chair.

Unlike the plate, it was able to scuttle slowly around the room. However, her modifying spell was as ineffective as it had been on the now ruined plate. She did remember to fix the chair before ending the spells this time, though.

"Do we have anything metal besides the pots?" She asked, pushing away the kitchen table. It was another hunk of wood and she doubted it would react any differently than the chair had.

"We have my sewing scissors, and then both your and Zelda's daggers, but that's it."

Zara brought her daggers out of her room while she decided what to do. Turning them into puppets brought certain positives along with it. She would be able to fix them if they ever broke and make them stronger and sharper. Assuming they took to modifying easier than glass and wood did. Really, it was all pluses as far as she was concerned.

"How are you doing on energy?"

"I'm starting to run a little low. The modifying spell took a lot more than I thought it would. I'll just sleep with a couple of the mana crystals tonight, and hopefully, I'll be fine in the morning." She smiled at him, her eyes dancing. She was having fun playing around and experimenting with her magic like this.

Once again, she began laying the complex layers of her puppet spell, taking the time to include both daggers. When she finished, the purple magical glow sank into the metal weapons, signifying it had been successful. She moved on to modifying them without delay, sharpening the edges and removing the chips from the blades.

She ended the puppet spell on them both and picked up the two daggers.

"Well?" Zack wondered.

"Everything we tried took the puppet spell without a problem, but only things with legs can move. Cloth is by far the easiest and cheapest to modify. Even the suits which are made from some weird mix of other materials are easier than these. Metal is doable, though still difficult and slightly expensive energy-wise. Wood and glass, however, are going to be impossible." She stopped and picked up the ruined plate. "Well, I should say, impossible here. Inside a portal, I might be able to manage it. It would still be hard, but it might be doable. Just not really worth it."

"What about the puppet spell? Did it require more energy to make that chair walk than it did the suit?" Depending on her answer, then Zara would have a lot of options open to her in the future.

Zara took a moment to think and then nodded. "I think so. I only had it walking around for a minute, but I think it took more than the suit would have."

"I wonder if that correlates at all with the increase in cost for your modification spell. Like maybe a metal puppet that could walk would be cheaper than a similar glass puppet?"

"That's a fair leap to take from just one experiment," Zara nibbled on her lower lip and glanced at the pack of money in the corner. "Ugh, fine. Tomorrow, after you get back when we go shopping, we'll get a few figurines to experiment with. You might be onto something, and it would be nice to know for in the future."

"Alright, now that we have that decided, what are going to do with this plate?"

"Um, conversation piece?" Zara really didn't want to try and change it back to normal.

He rolled his eyes. "Whatever, grab whichever clothes you don't want anymore and put them on the table. I'll grab George, let's get him patched up and get this done with."

The three bears were still dripping slowly into the tub when he walked into the bathroom. Zack gave George an experimental squeeze, and a small dribble of water cascaded down. Deciding that was close enough, he grabbed a towel and the bear.

"He's still wet, just not waterlogged." He announced, placing the folded towel on the table and then George on top.

Zara had cut apart an old pair of wool socks that wouldn't clash too terribly with the bear's current coloring. She had even brought the needle and thread Zack had taken from the tailor's box in Fittrel.

"How much of it needs to be attached, do you know?"

Zara shrugged. "No idea. I think it just needs to be enough that it's recognized as a part of him. What you did to the suit before was fine."

He laid the sock over George and sewed it into him using wide, gaping stitches, which weren't good for anything but what they were about to do.

With that done, they carried George back into the bathroom and Zara turned him into a puppet. The water was then wrung out a second time by Zack. Now that Zara was able to reinforce the bear's body, he didn't need to worry about damaging the bear. It would take a while longer for it to dry the rest of the way, but she would be able to sleep with him that night.

The modification spell was interesting to watch in action as it sucked the sock into the fur and began to redistribute it. Soon enough, George no longer had any bald spots, and his fur pattern had become more interesting.

Zara canceled the spell and sagged against the sink. "I think I'm done for the night. I don't even have enough energy to maintain the spell on my suit for much longer." She canceled that one as well. It was a good thing they hadn't had her try to dry George with the modification spell after all. She wouldn't have had enough energy to finish doing everything else otherwise.

"That's fine. Why don't you grab the other mana crystals from the pack? I'll go and see if they'll still let me bring the food back." Zack followed her out of the bathroom and took a step towards the front door before stopping. "Maybe I should put on the suit before I go out as well. The Oracle did say they were good at absorbing blunt attacks."

Dorn may be gone, but he wasn't the only one who had attacked him that night. Zack would like to think that it wouldn't happen again, and maybe it wouldn't. Zara was now a princess, and his status should be raised by association.

However, people were stupid, and they did stupid things all the time. He couldn't rule out the possibility that it might happen again.

Even if it wasn't that night.

He changed and went to get their dinner. It was still a little early for most people, and luckily, he was able to avoid the dinnertime rush while securing them both some extra food.

Chapter 17

"What are you doing here so early?" Zack groused, leaning against the doorframe while he rubbed his eyes and yawned. He and Zara had been up late talking about the specifics of magical energy control. She was beginning to make some progress in it, since she was actually able to practice. Unlike him, who was confined to just talking about it and memorizing everything she said and learned along the way.

Second quirked a brow. "It'll take us an hour to get where we need to go. I decided it was better to show up early and get this done with, so you would have the rest of the day to spend the money I brought."

"Right, the money!" Zack straightened, suddenly wide-awake. "How much did you bring? Is it enough to fill a couple of packs? Should I get changed and help you bring it in?"

Second chuckled. "You should get changed, but only so we can go. It's all in this one bag right here."

Zack's face fell at the sight of a single bag. It was maybe a quarter of the size of the one Dorn had been carrying. He didn't really know what he had been expecting, but a part of him had been hoping for more than that.

"Oh, don't make that face. It's full of nothing but large bills. Trust me, that information you gave us yesterday was incredibly valuable."

"Okay, let me put this away and get changed. I'll be back out in a minute and then we can talk about the other deal on the way."

Second agreed, and Zack closed the dorm door. He briefly opened the bag, checking to see how much money was inside. The old man hadn't been exaggerating. There really was nothing but large denomination bills inside. He had no idea what the final amount was, except that it was a lot. Zara would take care of counting it while he was gone, but it was clear it had been worth giving them the information.

Zack quickly dressed in the Shouvain suit, with the school uniform on top. He wrote out a note to Zara and then left with Second, making sure the door was locked behind him.

"Do you have an actual name?" He asked as a chauffeur opened the door of a luxurious-looking Alberitas vehicle. Envoy Nivean was waiting inside, looking over some documents while she waited for them.

"What do you mean?"

"Well, the name Second came from you being second-in-command of Faluers' Fist, didn't it? Last I heard, you were due to take over the entire operation. As such, the name no longer fits." Zack slid across the comfortable seats, coming to a stop facing the Fittrel envoy.

"You're right, it no longer does. Should I just have you start calling me 'First' instead?" The older man asked, the door closing behind him.

"No."

He laughed. "Very well. I'm sure you would have learned my name at some point, anyway. It's Amar Holt."

"It's nice to properly meet you." Zack glanced at the man's daughter, who was ignoring them, unsure of why she was there. Movement from the side of his eye startled him and he realized they had already left the academy behind. "Hmm... your driver is very good; I hadn't even realized we'd started moving yet."

Amar nodded in agreement and relaxed into his seat. "It's a bit of a drive, so you may as well get comfortable."

Zack endured a few minutes of what he considered stressful silence before he couldn't bear it anymore. "Did Mrs. Ricerca really retire from being a hidden advisor to the king? She was there yesterday. Did they give her a new position?" It was the first subject that came to his stressed mind.

Amar's hand tapped thoughtfully on the ever-present cane before answering. "She did retire. Her last announcement, in fact, was announcing your sister as the special scholarship holder before the citizens. It caused quite a stir. Both announcements did, in fact. It's not every day someone returns from the dead, a hidden advisor to the king is revealed and then willingly retired, not to mention an unknown girl is raised to temporary royalty status. It was great. You should have seen how the nobles were panicking." He finished with a chuckle.

"And? Did they give her a new position?" Zack asked again, wondering why she would have been there yesterday otherwise.

"You're curious why she was there yesterday. Aren't you?"

Zack nodded.

"You have much to learn about the world of nobles, my boy. It isn't like what you are used to. When a commoner retires, if they have the opportunity and the resources to, that's it, they are done. That isn't the case for nobles. We owe favors, run estates, businesses, countless other things of similar natures. As long as they are of a responsible sort, then they'll keep going long past when they would have otherwise retired. For us, there is no such thing as retirement, not one based on age at least, and certainly not one for such unique a position as what she held."

"So, what you're saying is that even though Anna is officially retired, that isn't actually the case?" He clarified, looking to understand.

"Indeed. Retiring was merely the method for her to step out of the shadows and back into her family's life properly. She still has valuable knowledge and skills the crown has need of."

Zack had calmed himself somewhat by that point and was ready to talk about their other deal. "Do you have the information about my parents?"

Amar lifted up the middle seat and opened a small hidden safe. Inside were three folders and a couple of mana crystals. He selected one of the folders, a thin one, and began to close the safe before Zack stopped him.

"We'll need one of the mana crystals for my information to be verified."

He looked curiously at him but withdrew one along with the folder regardless. "You have no idea how hard it was to find out the small amount of information that I have here." He held up the folder, not yet offering it. "Years have passed since you and your sister became orphans. That's a lot of information to become lost, buried, or even changed. I just want you to understand that and temper your expectations before opening this folder."

"Anything is better than what we have now. Besides, considering the time-frame you've had to work with, just having something already is impressive."

Amar shook his head and handed the folder over. "No, it's not. Trust me on that. With my resources and network, I should have been able to get enough information to write their life story."

Zack opened the folder and a single, lonely sheet of paper fell out and onto his lap. His parents' first names were listed at the top of the page. *'Zane'* and *'Miranda'*. Like always, no last name was listed.

"They were officially registered travelers. How can there be no last name listed?"

Amar sighed in disappointment. "I don't know what to tell you. That single sheet is all I was able to uncover on them. Despite a few records stating they were at least specialist classes; I had never even heard of them before this. No one seems to ever remember working with them, either. To say it is odd would be a gross understatement."

Zack scanned the rest of the document and closed his eyes. "So, when they disappeared, no one made a fuss because they didn't know anything about them? How does that make sense? What about whoever they were working for to get access to the portals?"

"That's what it seems like, and as for the corporation they were working for... There was none listed. I had to go through the records of every entity working the portals anywhere close to where you were living back then." He laughed hollowly. "My people came up empty. The lack of a last name presents some rather unique problems in finding information related to your family. Your parents were ghosts."

Zack snorted. "That sounds familiar, having all records related to us getting lost and then magically disappearing."

Amar's gaze sharpened and came into focus. "Indeed, it does sound familiar. You may be onto something. I'll have my people look closer, see if there is any record of someone else scrubbing the records before they got there."

They went over the few remaining details, and then Zack returned the page and folder to Amar.

"Do you have a knife?" Zack asked, ready to pay the fee for the information he had gathered. It wasn't much, but they had a deal, and he was going to abide by it.

The older man stared at him, his fingers tapping slowly on the top of his cane. "I do," He said at last. "Our deal is not complete. I have not yet sufficiently delivered on my end of the bargain. Whereas you have repeatedly demonstrated your ability to fulfill your side."

Zack shook his head. "This was our only official deal; the others were simply you humoring me. I appreciate the fact that you are going to keep looking. However, once you see what I have to offer, it may make you look harder and longer."

The fingers tapped for a second longer before reaching into his suit pocket and retrieving a pen. "I wouldn't say I was simply humoring you. The information you provided truly was valuable, and after their majesties have made their plans, I'll make mine. Faluers' Fist has many sides to it, and now that I'm its head, the business will grow. I have the perfect way to sell information without implicating my private information network."

Zack accepted the pen, unsure of what he was supposed to do with it.

"It's a penknife. You pull it apart, and a knife is nestled inside."

He pulled it apart and sure enough, there was a sharp but thin blade inside the top portion. Carefully, he rolled up the sleeve of his suit first, and then the sleeve of his uniform. Gripping the knife, he was about to cut his arm when he stopped.

"Uh, this might get messy. I'm not actually sure if you want me to do it inside here or wait for someplace easier to clean."

"I have to admit you have me becoming more and more curious." He retrieved his crystal pocket watch and thumbed the catch, springing open the protective lid. "We still have a few minutes before we should be arriving. Nivea, do you perhaps have anything for a bloody mess?"

The envoy put away her papers and rubbed her eyes. "Think about what you just asked me, father. That phrasing! It's a miracle Beth still puts up with you."

"I'll have you know Beth-"

"Nope, none of that. I do not want to hear about the woman you found to replace mother."

Amar's cane creaked, as his grip on it hardened. "That is hardly fair, and you know it. Your mother not only injured me but also betrayed me and this country. Then you went along with her." Any progress they had made in repairing their relationship was undone in an instant. "Now, do you have something or not?" He asked in a coldly neutral voice.

She reached into a bag at her side and withdrew a package of cleaning wipes and a sanitary pad. "I'm a lady, of course, I have some things on me."

"Crap, we need to get these for Zara soon," Zack muttered to himself. Now that they were getting healthy, their body's hormones would eventually fall back into their natural rhythm. He would need to be prepared for when that happened to her. Unhealthy eating, combined with everything else that had been done to them had delayed certain bodily functions for both of them.

The blade of the knife cut into his arm, deep enough to prove his point while avoiding damage if something went wrong. He wiped the blade clean and stored it inside the pen before handing it back to Amar. His arm dripped onto the pad for a few seconds while he grabbed another cleaning wipe.

Zack hissed as the alcohol in the wipe hit his self-inflicted wound. "Alright, as you can see, I am clearly injured here. Nothing special about that."

Amar and Nivea nodded.

"Now hand me the mana crystal and keep watching," Zack told them, continuing to wipe away the blood. He held the crystal with his injured arm and felt the healing begin. Almost immediately, his blood began to clot, and one last wipe was enough to leave his arm clean.

The father and daughter leaned closer, their interest peaked at the sudden and for them unexpected change.

Over the next few minutes, his skin scabbed over and healed before their eyes.

Zack was glad he hadn't made the cut any worse, otherwise it might not have healed so quickly.

"How is that possible?" Amar wondered at last, as Zack began rolling down his sleeves.

"It's an ability of mine. It gives me a certain amount of passive healing whenever I am near a magic source." He held up the mana crystal. "This little demonstration, as I'm sure you are already imagining, could have implications on a wide scale." He shrugged. "At least until Aperra's Change happens."

"That is not what I was expecting." The older gentleman looked positively shaken by what he had seen and heard.

Nivean was reacting little better and was as pale as she could be with her coloring.

"Researchers have always believed that magic in some form had the potential to work here. They've just still been working on adapting the spells and rune frameworks to work with mana crystals. A lot of people think it's a lost cause, and they might be right." Amar flexed his hand and stared at Zack. "Thanks to you, we now know why traditional magic doesn't work here. Something was missing all along, and the coming Change will fix that."

"How many others possess abilities like yours?" Nivea asked haltingly.

Zack rolled his eyes and bundled all the used wipes into the sanitation pad. "How am I supposed to know that? It's not like everyone tells me what their abilities are." He handed her the package of cleaning wipes with a quick thanks. He didn't want to tell them it was unlikely that any but him and Zara had the ability. That would devalue the information he had given them.

The information had value in and of itself to people like Amar and the king and queen. Just because he didn't know what it fully meant, didn't mean everyone else was as ignorant as him.

Everyone was lost in their thoughts as the rest of the ride passed in silence.

"Come," Amar winced, his bad leg twisting as the chauffeur helped him from the vehicle. "Let me show you your surprise."

Envoy Nivean followed them out

"Wow, it's a large imposing military building, just what I've always wanted." Zack quipped, suddenly uncomfortable and wishing he had waited to show his healing ability until later.

"It's what's inside the large, imposing military building." Amar leaned on his cane with every step. "Let's hurry. I imagine Anna is already impatiently waiting for us inside."

Zack followed along, keeping his questions to himself, and maintaining his grip on the mana crystal. His arm had already visibly healed, but he was hoping to ensure that no scar tissue remained from his little demonstration.

Anna was indeed waiting for them. Her stylish clothes had been exchanged for an undecorated military traveler's uniform. Her arms were crossed and the scar on her cheek stood out in sharp relief against her unnaturally pale skin. A small tool chest sat on the ground by her feet.

"Good, you're finally here. You've made me wait long enough to finish this." She glanced at Zack. "If anyone ever tells you that getting revenge isn't worth it, that you won't feel at peace afterward... just spit in their eye.

"It's not about feeling peace. It's about being able to move on. I'm not a saint. I can't forgive people who have wronged me like the Albright's did. But after I kill them, and take everything from them, I can move on. Finally. I can be the mother Tessa deserves, and the wife Mathew thought he married."

It all clicked together in his head. "Is that who we are here to see? The Albright's."

Amar nodded, beads of cold sweat dotting his brow. His leg was bothering him with every increasingly painful step. "I thought it might be informative for you to see the people that had raised someone like Dorn." He sighed and looked away. "Though I admit, I have badly misjudged them. I had thought his grandfather better than this. His grandmother certainly was, bless her soul."

Nivea snorted and looked away. "I never liked them. The entire family always gave me the creeps." She saw her father's glare and quickly continued. "I never met the grandmother, so I can't speak for her."

"Are we done?" Anna interrupted coldly. "I would like to get this over with today, so I can finally move on with my life!"

Zack really wanted to know what they had done to her, to foster such intense hatred. Not that he would ever ask the extremely intimidating and rather terrifying woman. She was beautiful, and a more mature version of Tessa, but she was crazy.

Not to mention she had used him in her plans. Which then led to him, and Zara being kidnapped multiple times. He would rather avoid her entirely for the time being if he had a choice in the matter.

Amar withdrew a key from his suit pocket and handed it to her. "Contain yourself for a little longer, Anna. No matter what, I promise you they won't live to see the end of the day. I am merely here to ask them a few questions, and then they are yours to do with as you please."

Her jaw clicked, and the sound of teeth grinding together was audible. "Fine. I'll remain out here then. I doubt I'd be able to contain myself otherwise." She kicked the tool chest, popping open the top section. "I'll just start sharpening some instruments for when I get to play later."

A row of scalpels and skinning knives rested alongside a sharpening stone.

Zack shivered at the sight of the familiar instruments. His scars were gone, healed by the snow elves, but his mind imagined that they still itched at that moment.

Looking away, Zack grabbed the key from her and jammed it into the locked door.

The talks with Edith had been helping him to better explore the damage to his psyche and emotions. It would be a while yet before he had enough control to act normal in the face of a reminder. It would be even longer still until it was no longer just an act.

He pushed open the door and saw three people in chains, underneath dim yellow lights. They looked ordinary, like any other person he might see on the street. They had been dressed in matching grey jumpsuits that highlighted every bruise on their pale skin.

All three had defiant expressions on their faces, as though they were expecting to be rescued.

Zack turned to Amar. "You haven't told them yet. Have you?"

He smiled somewhat sadly and limped slowly into the room. "No, we get to do that today."

Chapter 18

Nivea finally gave in and helped her father to the seat across from the three chained Albright's. He sat down with a heavy grunt and extended his bad leg in front of him.

"Damien, Paula, Dean, you all look less black and blue since the last time I saw you."

Each of the three flinched when he addressed them, ending with the grand-father.

"Why did you do any of this?" Amar asked the question with the air of one he had asked many times before.

"Holt!" Paula spat. "Do you really think you can get away with doing this?"

Zack held back and watched. First in shock and then in understanding, as the woman continued her vitriol-fueled tirade. She at least had begun to realize that no help was coming for them.

Amar shifted in the uncomfortable chair when she finally stopped and looked at her pityingly. "What happened to you, Paula? You didn't use to be like this. What changed? For that matter, what about you, Dean? What would your wife have said if she knew about any of this?"

"You don't understand," Paula muttered sadly.

"I know. That's why I'm here asking questions."

Zack shifted uncomfortably as the silence stretched. Beside him, Nivea maintained a bland, dissociated expression.

Overhead, the dim lights flickered as the old control conduits that led to a distant magi-crystal fought to keep going.

Amar sighed and shook his head. "Very well. If you don't wish to talk, then I have no other choice but to do my duty." He reached around his neck and retrieved a medallion similar to the one Anna had carried. His was attached to a magnetic coin insert that held the medallion in place. "Do you have any last words?"

"What happened to my son?" Damien asked. The defiant look from before had been stripped away. Each of them recognized the medallion in Amar's hand, and what it represented. When he flipped it into the air, he would be speaking with all the authority of the king and queen themselves.

"He's dead. He has been for a week now. Your poor misguided attempts to take over the Ricerca's, and then get revenge on a pair of orphans, led to your entire family's downfall. Although, I guess I should say, someone has been manipulating you towards that end for the last twenty years, at least."

"Why?"

Amar laughed hollowly and balanced the engraved and decorated coin on his fingers. "If you are going to massacre an entire family, make sure you get the entire family. Don't leave one of them alive to tell the tale of your atrocities. We couldn't do anything then because her family weren't nobles of our country, and for whatever reason, her country wanted them gone. You all went too far. The stories she tells…"

He abruptly flicked the medallion into the air, where it hung seeming to defy gravity as it spun, giving off a hum.

"As is my right as the queen's hidden advisor, I hereby renounce all claims the Albright family has upon any form of nobility and the protections that were once granted upon them."

This continued for several minutes as the man listed out one crime after another. His steely eyes never wavering an inch. Finally, he came upon the last two accusations.

"Furthermore, for their crimes against Albion's royal princess Zara and her brother Zack, they are given the death sentence."

All three snapped their heads up at that. It was a given they were going to die by that point, but when had they messed with the royal family?

"And lastly, for the eradication and frankly borderline unspeakable crimes against the noble family 'Testa', your punishment is to be executed by the last surviving member. Take your despicable secrets to the grave. I hope it was worth it." Amar snapped his fingers, and the medallion abruptly stopped spinning. A deep bass note burst forth from it before falling down into his hand.

Zack barely held back a snort; Anna had named her daughter after her family name. He wondered if Tessa knew.

Amar slipped the medallion back into its magnetic holder and hid it beneath his shirt once more. He slowly got to his feet with the help of his cane and turned away from them in disgust.

The three Albright's had lost their haughty and defiant expressions. Tears streamed down their pale, bloodless faces.

The grandfather spoke as they reached the closed door. "Those orphan kids that were with the Ricerca girl? They belong to someone who wants it to be known, that if they can't have them back, then no one can have them at any cost. We learned that just a few minutes before you raided our estate. I hope that helps in some way."

"Those two 'orphans', as you call them, are the royal princess and her brother," Amar replied without turning around. He opened the door and walked out.

The door shut behind them, and Zack let out a relieved sigh. "That was a long list of crimes! How could the king and queen let people like that live, let alone remain as nobles?"

"Most of the crimes I mentioned were discovered from records we recovered from their estate. Others, like the matter concerning Anna's family," He glanced at the red-headed woman who was packing up her knives. "Albion has no jurisdiction in that country, and the royalty there appear to have sanctioned the attack. We had to wait until something like this came up where we could bundle the accusations together."

"That makes no sense."

The older man shrugged. "That's politics, combined with noble law. It doesn't need to make sense. It just needs to protect the nobles from getting in trouble for the crimes they've committed. Orlo and Caroline have made some progress in overturning several of those laws. It might not surprise you, however, that few of the nobles want them gone."

"Can I go in now?" Anna asked, interrupting them.

"Yes, they're all yours. One thing though. As we were leaving, Dean mentioned Zack and Zara belonging to someone. It sounded like the organization behind the research institute, find out what they know. If you can, please."

Zack noticed that the crazed look in her eyes from before had vanished. Something more akin to sad resignation had taken its place. She was approaching the end of a journey that had consumed her for years. He had no idea how she had done it or gotten away with it. Somehow, she had, and now the end of it all had appeared.

She picked up her tool chest. "I will. By the way, Zack. Tessa will meet you at your dorm just before lunch. She wanted to take you and Zara out to see the city."

"That'll work out great. We had planned to do some shopping later anyway." He pulled at the academy uniform, noticing that it no longer fit as well as it did before. Even getting them slightly loose, he had filled out, straining the material around his muscles and increased healthy body mass. "We can't wear these all the time."

"It looks like you need new ones of those as well."

"Yeah, the uh, snow elves did a great job healing us." He scratched at his head nervously. Anna had always unnerved and scared him. Her manipulative ways, combined with her overall ruthless aura, kept him from completely trusting her. Now he was seeing another side to her, and he wasn't sure how to handle the sudden contrast.

"I'll let her know," She breathed in deep and opened the door, retrieving the key as she went in. No one would be coming in after her. This was her personal business to finish.

"How many other nobles are like the Albright's?" Zack asked as they walked back to the waiting vehicle.

"You mean that bad, or that bad, while being powerful enough that the crown couldn't touch them without a good reason?" Amar panted out, his bad leg beginning to drag behind him.

"Yes, either, both."

Amar stopped walking and dabbed at his sweaty brow with a handkerchief. "Noble law protects them from the crown interfering without good reason. It was never about the Albright's being too powerful, despite what you may have thought."

He stopped talking to think. "No, I take that back. It is a little about that. The crown makes the laws, but they like to play within them as well. If the nobles and everyone else sees them working around them, then it would be pandemonium. The crown wants to avoid a revolt and the nobles banding together. That is why each situation has to be handled so delicately. It can snowball into a huge affair otherwise."

Nivea sighed and took her father's arm. "Why haven't you gotten your leg looked at after all this time?"

He shook her off, stumbling into Zack as his leg crumpled. "It's a reminder of you and your mother. It helps me to remember the price of betrayal."

Nivea reacted as though she had been slapped. "I didn't have a good choice back then! No matter what I was betraying one of my parents, at least with mom I thought she would be around."

"I hope you were happy with your choice," Amar murmured lifelessly.

"No, I wasn't. Mom was never around, either. She had to work all the time." She told them in a defeated tone.

"Funny how that works, isn't it? People actually having to work for a living to survive, I mean. She must not have gotten as much money for the information she stole as she thought she would."

Nivea burst into deranged laughter. "Money? They never even paid her. She ruined our lives and then didn't even have anything to show for it. How do you think we ended up in Fittrel?"

The father gazed at his daughter for a long moment before turning away with pained eyes. "Come along. I'm sure Zack doesn't want to be hearing about all of this."

Zack steadied the older man and helped him walk the rest of the way to the vehicle. "I don't mind. My own parents aren't exactly glowing examples of awesomeness. It's rather nice knowing everyone's parents suck, actually."

Amar lightly jabbed him in the side with the head of his cane. "Watch it, I'll have you know I was the perfect father until my wife ruined it all."

"Alright," Zack waved to the waiting chauffeur. "I'm sure you were the greatest father to ever walk the land. All others bowed down to your excellence and worshipped at the altar of your polished shoe."

Amar coughed. "I wouldn't go quite that far. I certainly made sure my family never went hungry, and I made sure my daughter knew I loved her. It's too bad she's dead to me now."

Zack rolled his eyes as the man pushed the metaphorical blade just a little deeper inside the woman behind them. She was most definitely his daughter. Both sides appeared to know how to carry a grudge like nobody's business.

***

Zara was waiting for him when he got back to the dorm. Piles of money had been spread around the dining room table and placed into neat little stacks.

"So, how's it looking?" He asked after hugging her.

"I've already separated it into a few different piles. The money that we'll put into the bank. The bills that we'll carry for everyday things. Not every place will accept the cards the academy gave. Then the pile we'll hide in the apartment in case we ever need to run."

"Good. Did you include the new bag of money? That was from Second for all the information we gave him. His real name is Amar Holt, by the way."

She wrinkled her nose. "Amar Holt? Weird, Second just seems to fit him better. I counted it, and there is more than I was expecting in it. I was thinking that would be the bag of money that we hide here. It has enough to keep us going for a while. I did exchange a few of the bills for lower denominations. There was nothing but large bills in there."

"That's what Amar told me." He glanced around the apartment. "We need to get this all cleaned up though. Tessa is going to be here in a bit to take us shopping and see the city."

"How did you find that out?" She handed him some money and started packing the rest up.

"Anna was there." Zack gave her the whole story while they cleaned up the apartment.

"So, that's why she faked her death and became a hidden advisor to the king? All so she could get her revenge on the Albright's." Zara was more than a little impressed with the woman's drive and cunning. "What do you think she is going to do about the people from her country that let it happen?"

Zack tossed her a shirt. "If it was me, I'd wait until the Change happens and then go after them. With the information we told them last night, as long as they keep it from those people, she could have the advantage. Past that, I'm sure she has some plan to deal with them. She must. Anna doesn't strike me as the kind of person to let something like that go." He snorted. "Actually, she said as much to me earlier today."

They finished cleaning and prepared to head out.

Their stomachs were rumbling, and they were anxious for Tessa to arrive. Neither had eaten breakfast yet. Zack hadn't had the opportunity before Amar arrived, and Zara hadn't wanted to go to the cafeteria alone.

She was hesitant to bother Edith over something as simple as breakfast at the moment. The older woman was dealing with her own issues and didn't need the young girl distracting her. Or maybe she did. Zara didn't know. People were confusing, teddy bears were better.

Zack was inspecting Aisha when there was a knock at the door. "If that's Tessa, can you have her come in? Maybe she can help."

Zara tentatively opened the door and then invited Tessa and her chauffer Ben inside their apartment. They had been warned about letting people inside, but saw no harm with letting her in. She lived off-campus and was the closest thing to a friend they had outside of Edith at this point. If she couldn't be allowed inside, then truly no one ever would.

"What's the problem?" Tessa wondered.

Zack glanced up. "We weren't able to wash Aisha and the other bears in time. They've gotten stained. I was wondering if you knew of something effective in getting blood and other nasty stains out?"

Tessa looked lost and turned to Ben.

"What have you been using?" He asked in his deep voice.

Zara ran into the bathroom and retrieved the cleaning supplies. She presented them to the tall man.

"These are for carpets. The cleaning solutions would be rather rough on a plushie." He thought for a moment before handing them back. "I know of a specialty cleaning service in the city. I can inquire as to whether they have anything that would work on them."

"Thank you," Zara smiled shyly and retrieved the cleaning bottles.

"We need to make a stop at the bank, and then we are yours," Zack announced, picking up the pack of money.

"That's fine-" Zara's stomach rumbled, interrupting her.

"Sorry, we, uh, haven't yet had the chance to eat breakfast... or lunch. We weren't sure when you were coming." Zack scratched at his nose while his sister ducked behind Zelda.

"It never used to do that." She complained softly. "Those stupid snow elves must have broken something when they were fixing us."

Tessa eyed her, but let the odd and slightly disconcerting comment pass. She had heard stories of how the functions of people's bodies changed when they starved or were malnourished for long enough. "Shall we?" Her voice came out strangled and laden with a sudden burst of emotion. She swallowed and tried again. "Shall we? I know of a restaurant near the bank the academy does business with. We can eat there after you finish your business."

They nodded in agreement, and a few minutes later were on their way.

"How was your first trip inside the portal? Did you get a good class?" Zack remembered how excited she had been to go through.

"It was good. I did get something of an odd class though. Not aberration odd, but not one I or the others had ever heard of before." She fingered her red hair. "I had always figured that my elemental affinity would be fire, my mother's is, and that seems to be the case for her entire family. We're not sure if it's a bloodline class, but it's called 'Tiny Drak Mage'."

Zack nodded along. "Okay, so you're some kind of special fire mage class?"

She shook her head. "Not exactly. We had to look it up, but apparently, a 'Drak' is a fire spirit of sorts. My first spell is a variation on the typical fireball all fire affinity mages get. What my mother and I are guessing is that later on, the class will interact with the spirit of fire in some way."

"That sounds like a cool class to have," Zara piped in, continuing to hug Zelda.

Tessa tilted her head at the girl. "I'm not sure I should ask this, but what about you? What is your class? Is it perhaps related to your bears in some way?"

She and Zack had already had that conversation and were fine with answering her.

"Why wouldn't it be alright? I'm a member of the class now as well. That means I'll be going through the portal with everyone at some point. It would be rather silly to try and hide my class from everyone..." She trailed off.

"There are two answers she can give you," Zack picked up where she left off, just as they had agreed. "Which do you want? The truth, or the one we'll tell everyone else in the class."

"Just give me the same answer, you'll tell everyone else in the class. It'll make it less confusing."

"Good answer. My real class is a variation on puppets. As for what we'll tell everyone else, the name will probably be 'Bearmancer' or maybe 'Tiny Bearmancer' like yours. My bears can come alive while inside the portal."

Tessa blinked and sighed. "That is not what I said, but thank you." She turned to Zack. "Is your class as... special?"

He bit the inside of his cheek before answering. "In a way, but it'll be easier for me to pass off as a simple mage. Well. One with a very strong affinity."

"This is going to be an interesting school year," She muttered.

The siblings laughed at the understatement.

Chapter 19

Depositing their money at the bank started them off on an odd foot. The initial steps were easy with the use of their cards. The problem began when Zara asked the teller what last name the academy had listed on the account. Despite the odd question setting off some obvious red flags, and a rather curious stare, the teller answered, regardless.

"It says '*Nameless*'."

Unfortunately, that just left them unsure as to whether the school had listed that as their name, or left it blank and the bank put it there instead.

Shopping after that started out better than Zack had been expecting. It was easy to find clothes for Zara and himself. Plus, they were even able to find some small doll clothes for the bears. All of that came crashing to a halt, however, when he recognized someone well away from his established stomping grounds.

Zack grabbed Zara's arm and pulled her to the side of the closest building. His eye's never left the man-eating at the outside seating area of a restaurant in front of them. The man was sitting with a group of others, all enjoying their meal and talking loudly.

"Do you know those people?" Tessa inquired. She and Ben had followed them to the side of the building.

"Do you remember the story of how we got the headmaster's brother-in-law fired?"

Tessa nodded slowly. They had told her the story themselves before, and she had found the tale rather memorable.

"One of the men sitting at that table is Cooper. The leader of the gang that was trying to capture me." Zack held his sister close, not letting her move. "I just don't understand why he would be here. The town we came from is hours away from the capital. This shouldn't be his territory, and he was a small-time thug when I knew him."

"Do you wish to confront him, or simply have someone tail him and his associates?" Ben laid out some options.

"Do you have people nearby who can do that?"

Tessa blushed and looked at the ground. "After what happened with Faluers' Fist, mother has become rather overprotective. There are always people following around me now. She couldn't do that before because she was supposed to be dead."

Ben made a signal with his hands and a moment later, they were approached by two shoppers. The two were dressed like everyone else around them and blended in perfectly with the crowd. They never would have known the two were anything other than normal people if they hadn't approached them at that moment.

"Dispatch some people to follow each person at that table. Assume they are dangerous and do not approach at this time. Normal reconnaissance and intelligence gathering tactics only. We'll want to know why they are in the capital and meeting together." He gave them their orders, and they retreated back into the crowd without a word.

"Where to next?" Tessa wondered.

She had been enjoying the day with them so far. It wasn't often that she got to go out and just mingle with someone like this. Before, everyone had been trying to get close to her because of her father's research. Now it was because of her mother *and* her father.

Spending time with two people who so clearly didn't care about her parent's was rather refreshing.

"Well, I think we now have more clothes than we ever had in the past, and certainly far nicer ones, for sure. I think the next items we were looking to get were some large packs, as well as a few smaller mana crystals?"

The packs they had left at the school portal when they were abducted had been returned to their apartment. However, they were too small to carry enough supplies the next time they got stuck inside a portal. It was time to upgrade to something new that could carry everything they would need and more.

Zara nodded. "Maybe a few figurines as well, if we can find them for the apartment. Just some things to make it a little more ours." At least that was the excuse they were going with. She was hoping to use them for more experiments. Figurines tended to be easy to find, were fairly cheap, and came in a variety of materials.

They would be the perfect experimental material if it wasn't for their small size. She had never tried her puppet spell on anything so small before.

Tracing down the layers correctly would be a struggle for her. Luckily, these were for practice and not for the battlefield. In the safety of the apartment, she might be able to manage it with time and concentration.

Tessa pulled them from one shop to the next over the next few hours. They didn't always buy anything; in fact, they rarely did. It was more about spending time together and seeing the area. Despite that, they found enough figurines of differing sizes and materials that Zara would be able to experiment for several weeks.

They also found a plushie shop that they had to pull her out of. Maybe someday she could have an army of teddy bears and other stuffed animals following her around. Unfortunately, that was not today. It would draw too much attention, and frankly, there was only so much attention she could pour out on the three she already had.

Zack poked his pouting sister's puffed up cheeks. "Come on, you know you would have been spread too thin with any more bears. Aisha already feels like she doesn't get enough attention because she's the biggest bear. If you added another one into the mix, it would be bad."

"I know," She whispered, losing the pout. "But they're all so cute and cuddly. I can't help but want them all."

The crowning event of the day happened when they stumbled upon a shop that sold prank items. Leaving Tessa outside, they went inside and bought all of the itching powder they could carry. The store had other items as well. However, the odorless, and mostly harmless, itching powder was best for what they had planned. Which was getting petty revenge on some of the teachers.

Although, for the math teacher, they planned to use more than anyone else.

"Where to now?" They asked in grinning unison as they exited the store.

"That's up to you. We can get dinner, and then go back to your dorm apartment, or we can do something else?"

Zack stared at her. He thought he had heard something odd in the way she said that sentence. "What would you be doing if we went back to the apartment?"

"Reading," She answered readily.

"And what would you have been doing all day if we weren't around?"

Her response came a little slower and softer this time. "Reading, training, maybe spending some time with my mother if she had time."

There was no mention of spending time with friends.

"That's what I thought." He glanced at Zara, who nodded. "How about we get some food and then find a game shop? Then we can head back to our place to have some fun."

The other girl hesitated.

"Please," Zara went in for the kill. "We've never played any board games before. The other kids at the orphanage were always using them and we couldn't afford them afterward. We'll need someone to show us how they are meant to be played."

Ben smirked from behind Tessa. He understood what the two were doing, and he approved. "Young miss, I haven't heard back from the teams we sent to follow those men earlier. The earliest reports should be coming anytime now. I'm sure the princess and her brother will be most interested in hearing them as soon as possible."

"We would actually." Zack lost his grin. "Anything Cooper is involved in can't be good. The guy is worse than scum. If it's something that involves him and is big enough to pull him away from his territory..." He shrugged, letting the thought dangle.

She rolled her eyes and flicked her bright red hair over a shoulder. "Very well. I shall assist you in learning how to play some games. I must admit, it has been some time for me as well. I haven't even played any of the newer games. This will be... fun." She finished tentatively, feeling out the word.

"Of course, it'll be fun. That's the entire point of playing games with people." Zara held tight to her brother with one arm and Zelda with the other. "Show us where to go next. You're the ones who know the area."

Tessa turned to Ben. "Do you know where a game shop is around here?"

"Not around here, no. However, if you are willing to let me take care of the food and the games, I can have them waiting for you at their dorm."

"What do you two think?" She presented the option to Zack and Zara, since they had been the ones to offer in the first place.

"It sounds great to me!" Zack agreed. "I wouldn't have known what to choose game-wise in any case."

"As long as there's lots of food, then I'm happy as well." Zara smiled from behind her bear.

"Let's head back to the vehicle, then." Ben made some more of his cryptic hand signals, and a person eating a sandwich pulled away from a nearby window.

He spent a few seconds giving the man some whispered instructions, and then they were off.

"How do we even get back to wherever we started from here?" Zack wondered, looking around. He had gotten hopelessly turned around throughout the day.

"It's actually not that far. We just need to cut through that area over there and we'll be more or less back where we started," Tessa explained as they began walking.

"We went in a circle?"

"Well, only if you're really bad at geometry. We zigzagged around a lot, but sure, if that's how you want to think of it, then yeah, we went in a circle." The red-haired girl chuckled and then began to laugh as something inside her finally relaxed.

"Are you feeling better now?" Zack asked her once they were safely inside the privacy of the vehicle.

Tessa giggled, and then sighed a couple of times, slowly regaining control of herself. "I must apologize for that uncouth display. It has been a while since I last embarrassed myself in such a fashion."

Zara groaned. "She's doing it again. Make her stop!"

"Why are you apologizing for laughing in front of us? And she's right, quit talking in your overly proper and polite voice. It's annoying."

She coughed and looked away, her cheeks blazing red. "It wasn't the laughing I was apologizing for. I inadvertently mocked you and your lack of knowledge. That is something only friends should be doing with each other. I..." She played with her fingers and continued staring out the window. "I didn't think we were there yet."

Zack remembered their conversation from before, about what she would have been doing if they hadn't been there. Then he remembered how everyone had always been hanging onto her during class. She had never been the one talking to them. They were always talking at her and each other.

"You don't have any friends, do you?" The blunt question hung like a pall in the air between them.

"Well, you didn't have to say it so frankly," Tessa complained, sinking into her seat. "No, I don't. I never have, or at least, not since I was a child, and began to understand what they all wanted me for. They wanted to be my friend so they would potentially have access to my father and his research. Now they all want to be my friend so they can gain the ear of the king's old advisor, and because of my father."

"That explains why I always see people around you at school, but rarely see you talking to them."

She nodded. "It's exhausting, and I had given up on them until you arrived. Mother's plan forced us to interact, and I quickly realized that you were different from the others. Part of it was from ignorance, but a larger part of it was because you simply didn't care. You had access to people of your own and didn't need my mother. Your compatibility results already prove you don't need my father."

"And now Zara's a princess."

She laughed at that. "I must admit, that is rather amusing for me. Yes, I'm the one chasing a friendship above my station this time. If it makes a difference, I had already planned on getting closer to you both after our little adventure together. Zara, becoming a princess, had little to do with my decision."

"I don't know that I'm really a-"

Something crashed into the front of the vehicle and sent them careening off the side of the road. The windows cracked but refused to shatter as the armored vehicle rolled twice and came to a rest on its roof.

Zack groaned and cursed. His head had taken a beating, however, the rest of his body was in decent condition. Thankfully, he and Zara had taken to wearing the suits all the time. It had helped to blunt the worst of the damage.

"Zara, Tessa, you both alright?" The words came out jumbled and felt wrong. He blinked and wiped some blood from his eyes. Hanging upside down with a bloody nose was disgusting. He braced a hand on the ceiling and undid his seatbelt, falling with all the grace he could muster.

Picking himself up, he saw that Tessa was out cold. Her face had been right next to the window when they'd been hit. Undoubtedly, she had taken a good hit to the head. Behind him, there was a soft thump as something fell to the ground.

Spinning around, he ignored the rush of vertigo and saw that it was Zelda who had hit the ground. In seconds, he had the belt restraining his sister undone and had her cradled in his arms. Like him, her suit had protected her from the worst of the damage. Hers had actually probably done a better job even since it was a proper puppet.

Zack kept a sharp eye on the windows while holding his sister. He had no idea what he was supposed to do in the situation. Should he put her down and help Tessa? Or should he try to open the door? Was this an accident or a deliberate attack on them?

His thoughts were fuzzy, and not everything was making sense. Thoughts kept falling away, refusing to cooperate.

He shook his head, but that just made it worse.

"Zara," He mumbled, she would know what needed to be done. She was the smart one, while he was meant to be her shield. That was his role as the older brother. He was meant to be her protector.

He tapped her on the cheek, ignoring the blood that dripped from his nose onto her clothes. "Please Zara, I need you."

She stirred as he continued to tap weakly at her cheek.

His mumbled words grew stronger with each iteration.

Zara opened her eyes at last and hissed in pain. "What happened? It feels like my neck has been snapped off!"

Zack blinked slowly. "I... think... something's... wrong... with... me..." It took him several seconds to form and say the simple sentence.

Zara rolled up her sleeve and retrieved her small mana crystal from the small divot she had formed in the suit for it. She pressed it into his hand and forced him to hold on to it.

"We should have started making you carry one of these as well," Zara muttered, noticing the glassy look in his eyes. "What is with you and taking hits to your head?" She pushed Zelda into his lap and then carefully went over to help Tessa.

It had only been a couple of minutes since the accident, and yet it was too quiet outside. There was no one out there offering to help them. Nor was there anyone trying to break down the doors to capture them. It made no sense; the road shouldn't have been that empty at this time of day.

Zara felt her mind racing as she struggled to support the older and taller girl's weight. She wouldn't be able to undo the seatbelt otherwise. Finally, she used her suit as the puppet it was to help support the weight and then lower her to the ground.

She peeked out the cracked window, only to pull back in a rush. The entire vehicle was surrounded by people, and it wasn't Faluers' Fist this time.

What were they going to do? What made more sense, delaying them or going with them? She could potentially turn the vehicle into a puppet, using her magical energy to keep it intact a little longer. It might buy them some time. She had never tried her puppet spell on anything so large or complicated before, so it might fail.

There was also the problem that with so many people out there, they would likely burn through her meager amount of energy in seconds. That option was out.

So, then, it made more sense to use her puppet spell on Zack's suit, ensuring they couldn't take it off him.

With that decided, she got to work, inlaying the first of many spell layers onto his suit. She could only hope that the people outside didn't notice the slight purple glow her magic was producing. Well, that and that they'd give her enough time to finish.

Whoever they were had already waited this long. Surely, they would wait another minute and a half.

Right?

They didn't. It turned out they hadn't been waiting at all. They had been repositioning their own vehicle. The first one that had been used to crash into them had simply taken longer to clear from the road than they had anticipated.

The Ricerca's vehicle was armored, and the people outside had no chance of getting inside on their own. They would need the help of something with more power behind it to rip the doors open to get at the kids inside.

Furiously, Zara kept working, desperately tuning everything out, going on outside. She couldn't afford the distractions. She couldn't even spare the time to think about where Tessa's guards were, and who knew if she even had any assigned to her yet. They had only just returned from the portals and Fittrel, after all.

Metal groaned and screamed as the roof slid across the ground. They were being shoved towards something. The noise grew louder as they picked up speed.

Zara finished her spell and rushed to latch onto Tessa with one puppet-enhanced arm and onto her brother with the other. Zelda was squished in-between the three of them.

Zack licked his chapped, bloody lips and turned them so his back was to the door. "Hold on," He mumbled.

The stop came abruptly, launching them across the intervening foot long divide to the door frame. The air rushed from Zack's lungs as the reinforced puppet suit kept his ribs from breaking. He would have some bruises, but no broken bones at least.

The vehicle bent as the reinforced, armor-plated metal reached its stress point and began to flex.

Chapter 20

T he windows buckled and shattered first. The thick, laminated panes of heavy glass cut Zack's uniform to ribbons as he protected the girls. His mind was still foggy and disconnected, but the small mana crystal and the healing it gave him was helping to bring everything into focus.

Across from them, the doors popped open as the frame finished giving way.

He shook Zara. "Quick, release us." Her suit puppet was still holding them together. It would cause problems if whoever came in to get them couldn't pull them apart. Then again, maybe it would actually help.

Before he could say anything else, he felt her grip on him relax. Looking down, he saw her weakly holding onto him and Zelda. A trusting but scared look in her eyes.

"It'll be alright. Whoever these people are, they'll have to contend with the Major, Anna, and the Crown. They are either stupid, reckless or after something else." There were a few other options he didn't mention. Without knowing anything more, it was pointless to speculate.

Personally, his money was on these people being amateurs, but that also felt wrong. In his mind, professionals operated faster, smoother, with less lag and room for error. Why try cracking open the vehicle here when they could just load it up and take it somewhere else?

Amateurs, on the other hand, wasted time like these people had. Except they had known and been prepared for the armored nature of the vehicle. Which meant this wasn't a random hit on any passing person. They had been targeted.

It was an odd mix of professional and amateur grade work.

Zack gripped the mana crystal tighter. He was sure he was missing something. It was obvious, whatever it was. The fog in his mind was clearing, but not quickly enough. He shoved the crystal under the sleeve of his suit where it would be hidden and kept thinking.

A gloved hand reached in and opened the door.

Could they have been hired by someone else? Did that even make sense? Disposable goons, perhaps. Wasn't it better to get the job done the first time, instead of risking failure and alerting everyone?

He blinked, then again. Who said they had failed?

The door opened, and a masked man holding a knock-off Majair appeared. "Good, one of you brats is still awake. That will make this easier. Come towards me and no one will get hurt."

"I'm already hurt," Zack coughed and played up his injuries. "We weren't wearing our seatbelts when you hit us." He coughed again and let his head fall back. "I think," He coughed again, feeling his headache coming back. "I think they're dead." His voice fell to a whisper as he finished.

The man cursed and pulled back, looking for a light.

The scene that he saw when he came back easily exceeded whatever he had been expecting to see. Zack's nose had bled everywhere, and the harsh light painted a rather gristly scene to someone not looking closely.

All the while, Zack remained still and tried to breathe as shallowly as possible. No professional would have bought his act, further proving his theory that these people were anything but.

The light vanished as the masked man pulled back with another curse.

"Your acting sucks," Zara whispered, from her place in-between him and the unconscious Tessa.

"It wasn't acting," He protested with a grimace. "My head is killing me. Those fake coughs made it worse. Now hush, we're supposed to be dead in here."

The light returned a minute later, with more people in tow.

"What are we supposed to do with them now?"

"We can't do anything with them if they're dead."

"Are you sure that they're dead? Did you crawl inside and check? Maybe they are simply injured and unconscious."

Zack felt his back go cold as a new voice joined the others outside the wrecked opening of the vehicle. Something fleshy smacked into the door, making it groan in protest.

"Get in the car and check on them. If they're alive, then pull them out."

Zack had forgotten that vehicles had other names as well. Tessa had mentioned them to him once before. They were based on old names from before the portals had appeared. When other forms of energy were still used to power everything were still in development.

"What if they're not?"

"Then it doesn't matter. We'll still have accomplished what we agreed to do. It'll be sad for us since we won't get our second payday, and it sucks for the kids, but nothing more."

Zack shivered as a feeling of dread washed over him. Were they really going to be captured again, just like this? Without him being able to do anything to stop them.

He refused to accept that, but at the same time, was there anything he could even do? He felt his sister shift and knew that no matter what; he needed to at least try. Besides, the person in the most danger was Tessa, not him or Zara.

They had the suits on and were at least semi-protected. Not that he was interested in learning if they were capable of stopping a Majair's bullet. The suits were good for stopping blunt attacks, not so much for piercing damage, and he had a feeling which the bullet would fall under.

Having them reinforced by Zara's magic might save them from one attack, possibly two. Her energy reserves were finite, and there was no telling how much each attack would take from her until it happened. It was better to avoid the situation if at all possible. He just didn't see how that was going to be a choice if they wanted to avoid being captured.

Which, obviously, they did. That went without saying.

He cracked his eyes open a hair and quickly looked around the back of the car. Shadows pervaded the space, preventing him from spotting anything useful. Not that he would have been able to move and fetch it if he had seen something.

The act of looking at least let him feel like he was trying, that he hadn't given up without a fight.

Light flashed erratically over everything as someone crawled inside. Mumbled grumblings filled the space. "Why did I have to be the one who crawled inside? I have bad knees, everyone knows that. Ugh, that's disgusting. I can't believe I just touched that. Where did all this blood come from if they're not dead?" The mutterings continued as the whiny person drew closer to them.

Zack breathed as shallowly as he could, not daring to take anything deeper.

"Whose plan was it to hit them like this anyway?" He reached out and touched Tessa's shoulder, shaking her.

Zack felt his suit stiffen, a sign that Zara was taking over the puppet. He made a firm fist and waited for her to act. She would be able to exert more force using the puppet than he could with a punch in the limited space. Puppets had no need to build up speed or for large areas to fully utilize their muscles.

That wasn't how they worked. They were magic and absolutely the best choice in this instance.

The man shook Tessa harder, shifting her away from Zara and allowing her to see him. It was the opening she needed.

Zack's arm snapped across the distance and smacked into his open jaw, dislocating it. The hit instantly knocked the man out and strained Zack's shoulder muscles. The abrupt, powerful movement was too much for them. His hand, at least, had been prepared. The knuckles would still be sore later, but nothing was broken.

"What was that? Derrek, are you alright in there?" A female voice called from outside the car.

Zack grabbed the light and shined it back towards the door. "I'm fine, just slipped is all." He grumbled loudly, in what he thought was a decent imitation of the man.

It didn't need to be perfect, it just needed to buy them some time.

Zara and he began stripping the man of everything useful. Which amounted to a dagger, the knock-off Majair he had seen earlier, and the flashlight.

It was not enough to ensure they could escape, but it might be enough to keep the people from coming closer. It just depended on what their goals were, and Zack had a feeling that abducting the three teens wasn't it. The plan they had used could have easily left all three of them dead or severely injured. Dead people didn't exactly make the best hostages.

"What should we do?" He whispered to Zara, as the small weapon began to charge with a soft whine.

She pulled Tessa to the side with a worried look. "I thought she had guards following her constantly! Supposedly I do, or am supposed to as well, for that matter, though I don't know if that has even started yet. Regardless, it shouldn't be long until others are here. We just need to hold them off until they arrive. I'm worried that she hasn't woken yet though. I didn't think the suits would make such a difference for something like this."

"I'm glad they did." He muttered.

"Derrek?" The female called out hesitantly. "Are the kids alive?"

"Stay to the side," Zack told his sister, handing her the dagger. With his strained shoulder, he could only use one arm at the moment. He nudged the unconscious Derrek towards the door, staying behind him.

"What do you all want with us?" He asked, dropping the act without any preamble. He was hidden behind the larger man, with only the muzzle of the pneumatic powered pistol showing.

"So, you did manage to survive. Good, that will make things much easier on us when this is all over. Is Derrek alive at least?"

"He is. I just knocked him out." His shoulder ached as he shifted position. "Now answer my question. What do you want with us?"

More people arrived just outside the beam of his light, their dark forms melding together.

"Nothing. Your capture was merely a bonus for us. We were paid to do exactly what we have already done, then leave a card here and nothing more."

"I was right then. We're just a distraction. A group of people of suitable importance to invoke the desired response." Zack wasn't sure if that made him feel better or worse. "Where do we go from here?"

"What do you mean?" The woman who had been speaking to him stepped closer and crouched in front of the door, blocking him from shooting anyone else. She wore a cheap mask and outfit that was vaguely meant to resemble Faluers' Fist.

"I mean, I'm rather against us being captured. It has happened a few too many times recently and I don't care to experience it again. Which means no bonus for any of you. However, I'm also fairly certain that you all don't want to be shot. Even if I only get one shot, I can make it count at this range. I've seen what these things can do from such a short distance, you won't be the only one it hits."

The shadows behind her shifted and moved back.

"You're a cheeky little brat, aren't you?" She sighed and turned to look at those behind her. "How much time do we have?"

"Repositioning took longer than we thought. If we leave now, we might get away clean."

She glanced back at Zack. "I'm pretty sure the driver is fine. He was still breathing when we checked on him, it looked like he had just been knocked out by the impact. Assuming the other two with you are fine, how about you give me Derrek and we just go our separate ways? No extraneous harm, and no more actions on either of our sides. We don't know any of you. This was simply a paid gig, nothing more. We have families to feed, and prices are going through the roof on everything."

It was the second time they had heard that excuse recently. The first time it had been from a soldier. Now it was coming from someone he was guessing was a normal, struggling person.

"How is she, Zara?"

"No change. She is still unconscious."

He had to make a choice.

"Tell us who hired you, along with what the card says, and then you can leave with him." He hoped it was the right one, and that nothing was seriously wrong with Tessa. Anna would murder him otherwise; she might do it anyway, regardless of the information.

"There isn't much to tell. They had accents and lots of money. They provided the plans and the vehicles, everything we needed to do the job. They never told us their names, or what they were really after. As for the card, here you can have it." She passed him a metal card that he shoved in his pocket without looking at.

He cursed and shoved Derrek at her. "Fine, leave the vehicles and I'll do what I can to make sure no one goes after your group. Assuming, of course, that you're telling the truth."

She pulled Derrek away with a muttered, "I am."

Zack kept his light on them as the shadows peeled away in clumps. "Why did you have such a big group for such a simple job?"

"We weren't sure how easy it was actually going to be, and besides, there are more than a few of us in need of money."

He snorted. "Trust me, I know. My sister and I used to live near the slums in a town a few hours from here. Rotten food and spoiled meat were all we could afford on the good days. I would have done worse than this if it meant I could feed her some decent food."

"What changed?" She asked softly.

"I awakened as a traveler, and the academy let her come with me. We have to put up with some real stuck-up nobles, but we get to eat consistently now. Plus, we've made a friend."

The last of the shadows left, carrying Derrek with them.

"The people that gave us this job, and all the money," She began, peering around quickly to make sure no one was in earshot. "They wore odd outfits similar to yours, under their clothes. I hope that helps."

Zack stared down at his destroyed school uniform and saw his Shouvain suit peeking through. When he looked up again, she was gone.

"Come on, let's get her outside and onto the ground. Then we can get Ben."

Tessa groaned as Zack was helping the unconscious man out of the driver's seat. The older man had a nasty bump on his head, but otherwise seemed unhurt. Her eyes fluttered open as Zara helped him drag Ben to her side. His strained shoulder wasn't up to the task of doing it alone.

She gazed unseeing up at the star-filled sky for several seconds before saying anything. "I remember us shopping, and then coming back to play games and eat dinner at your dorm." She winced and raised a shaky hand to the side of her head. "Then something happened to the car..." She fell silent for a moment. "Now I have a massive headache and my chest hurts."

"Yeah, you could say something happened. We were in a planned accident, of sorts." Zara told the other girl everything.

During which Zack used the flashlight to give the chauffeur an amateurish once over.

"I thought you had people following you everywhere?" Zack asked her once his sister was finished. "We thought rescue was already on its way as soon as the accident happened."

"It was smart of them to push us away from the road like that. At night, no one will see the marks unless they are looking for them. As for my mother's people and Zara's guards, I have no idea what's going on. It hurts to think."

"What do you think the people who hired them are really after?" Zara whispered to him.

Tessa's eyes had drifted shut.

"I think Shouvain hired them. The lady I was talking to said she saw them wearing similar outfits under their clothes. They don't know we have the suits, otherwise, they would have come for us, not used us as a distraction."

Zara frowned and poked at the ground. "That means they're either looking for their lost spies or are truly after something. We talked about their mana-tech research being top-notch before. Maybe they feel threatened."

"What? Ohhh," He nodded in understanding. "How did they get enough people here in time to make a play for it?"

"Who knows, they probably began planning when we first left Fittrel or something."

"Ugh, spies, they're everywhere," Zack muttered. "Come on, we might as well make our way back to the road. They won't find us till morning if we don't."

Carefully they got Tessa onto Zara's back, and then with Zelda in her arms she took one slow trembling step forward after another. She had to keep dipping into her magical energy reserves, using the puppet to support her weak legs.

Behind them, Zack dragged Ben, mentally apologizing to the unconscious man for the indignity of the action. The trip back to the road was cut short when they were finally rescued. They had spotted the light Zack was holding and converged on them.

They found out later that the guards assigned to Tessa and Zara had been ambushed and were dealing with some armed elements farther down the road. Apparently, the people who had hired the Albion citizens hadn't been keen on leaving loose ends. After the job was completed, everyone involved would have been silenced permanently.

It turned out to be lucky for them that they had stuck around and tried to get something extra. If they had left right away, like the plan dictated, they would have been murdered. The guards would have broken away from the fighting and gone to rescue their charges.

Zack gratefully relinquished Ben to their rescuers while Zara did the same with Tessa. They were all then bundled up and taken to the Ricerca estate. A team of nurses and doctors were to meet them there to check them each for any unseen injuries.

The siblings fell into a light slumber, exhausted from the events. Their bodies ached, and in the case of Zack, his shoulder and head needed some time to heal from the damage he had suffered. The small mana crystal he had stuffed up his sleeve would only heal so much. It just didn't have enough output to keep up with what he needed.

They woke when the transport stopped in front of the mansion.

Chapter 21

"What were they after?" Zack asked as Anna walked into her fake office. He had begged away from the nurses and doctors and found his way up there alone. He didn't feel bad about avoiding them. He could heal. Zara, on the other hand, he had made sure got the full inspection.

The older woman seemed calmer than when he had seen her that morning. It was clear that she was worried about her daughter and angry, but that was all. The edge that had made everyone walk on a knife's blade around her was gone, for the moment.

"The airship. We'll talk about that in a minute. I need a drink first." She collapsed into a chair opposite him and poured herself a stiff drink.

"Was this morning worth it?" He wondered softly, feeling the edge of the card in his pocket.

She swirled the liquid before downing it all in a single go. "Yes. Will I have nightmares about it? Probably. Am I disgusted by some of the things I did to them? Yes. Can my family finally rest in peace knowing I got revenge for them? Again, yes, so it was most definitely worth it. Who cares if I am a monster? I will still never be like the Albright's. With them gone, I can finally let this chapter of my life go."

He watched as she poured herself another drink.

"What about the royal family that let it happen?"

She laughed dryly. "A person has to know their limits. Besides, I'll be getting some revenge on them as well. The king and queen have agreed on a total information blackout regarding everything you told them. That country will know nothing about the coming Change, or the equalizing. All of it will blindside them. They might not collapse, but their power will be diminished." She smiled hatefully. "Who knows, maybe after that I can do something to them."

"Is that where it ends, with them?"

Anna set the glass to the side and stared at him. "Why do you want to know?"

Zack reached into his pocket and withdrew the metal card the woman had given him. "The accident, attack, diversion on us. Whatever you want to call it. This card was supposed to be left at the scene."

He leaned over and handed it to her.

Anna took a moment to inspect it before looking up at him. "I don't understand the connection."

The card had a simple message printed on it that said, 'Thanks for the opportunity. It would have been more complicated without you. It's why we let you live this time.'

"Hold it up to the light and look at the upper left-hand corner. That indentation before the first word. If you look at it just right, you'll notice an image."

It took her a moment to tilt the card the right way. "I see it. How did you know it was there?"

He snorted. "I didn't. I tossed the stupid thing at the wall and thought I noticed something glinting in the corner when it bounced off."

"What does the symbol mean?"

The symbol on the card was of an ouroboros dragon. The tail curled around behind it to form the symbol for infinity and then ended inside its mouth. Wings had been drawn at the intersection of the symbol, with the one on the bottom reversed and facing a different direction.

"I can't be sure, and Zara would remember it better, but I'm certain that the researchers who held us back then..." He swallowed and clenched his fist tight. "Their equipment, all of their specialty items. They all had that symbol, or something like it, printed on them."

"I'll have to check if it matches what was recovered from that place." She flicked the card back at him and took a sip of her drink. "It might get you one step closer to finding out who they are, but that's all."

"Did they get the airship?" He changed the direction of the conversation, wanting to know that before revealing anything else that he knew.

"No," She took another swallow and sighed, reaching for the ever-present water instead. "Our people and the guards Fittrel had stationed aboard it fought them off. They weren't expecting there to be guards on board the ship. Besides, Orlo isn't an idiot, and neither is Caroline. As soon as they heard our armored vehicle had been attacked, they knew something was wrong.

"They made a show of ordering their personal soldiers to go rescue the princess, her brother, and, of course, Tessa. Meanwhile, they had me moving the Major and his people as close to the castle as they dared without being seen. From there, it was just a matter of waiting to see if anything actually happened."

"We never saw the soldiers," Zack protested, flipping the card from finger to finger.

"They're outside don't forget the castle is still around an hour from the academy. By the time they arrived, the security I had watching Tessa, along with the two royal guards assigned to Zara had already finished taking care of their own ambush and gotten to you. I came from the castle as soon as I heard the four of you had been brought here."

That explained what had taken the guards so long, they had been ambushed as well. "How are they?"

"Your sister is fine, just some minor whiplash. Her neck will be sore, and I imagine she'll have some nice headaches for a few days, but that's it. My daughter has a mild concussion from hitting her head on the window. She's fine otherwise. As for Ben, however, the hit he took to the head from the steering wheel is a bit more severe. It's too early to say."

"Can he go through the portal and be healed?"

She shook her head. "No, Ben isn't a traveler."

He caught his nail on the edge of the card, making a soft ping sound. "I made a deal with the people who did this to us. In return for some information, and them leaving all the equipment, you wouldn't go after them."

She shook her head in disbelief. "That had better be some unbelievably good information for me to go along with that deal."

"It wasn't originally. The people who hired them paid for everything and made the plan. It's why I had them leave everything. I thought it might be useful for you. It was a comment she made at the end that made it all worth it. She said that people who hired them were wearing similar outfits as mine under their clothes."

Zack had denied a change of clothes earlier for this exact reason. He was letting her see the shredded state of his uniform and what he had on underneath it.

"Is that?"

"It's a Shouvain suit. One entirely made of the material Jean was supposed to sell to the king and queen yesterday."

"She did don't worry, they already passed it off to George Trask and his company," Anna mumbled, her mind scrambling to keep up. "So, you're saying that Shouvain is the one who attacked us for the airship and that they're related to the research institute?"

He nodded. "That's what it looks like. It's by no means definitive, but it does give you someplace to start looking. Now if you'll excuse me. I need to go find my sister and have her look at this symbol."

"Of course," She agreed distractedly. He had given her much to think about.

Zack found his sister resting a while later. She was in the same room they had been in as before. Zara had a brace on her neck and was looking bored while she idly played with Zelda.

"There you are! I was wondering where you had run off to."

"Sorry, your royal highness, I was speaking with Anna. I thought you might want to avoid that particular meeting." He teased her while easing onto the bed beside her.

"I don't know," She responded seriously, instead of joking as he had expected. "I think I'm getting used to her. She's still scary, but I think that actually helps. Knowing that she's a dangerous person, but also a loving and caring mother to Tessa, seems to be setting her apart from everyone else. I saw her earlier, briefly before she left. I'm guessing to meet you, that's when I noticed it."

He gently wiped the wet glimmer from her eyes and held her close. It was easy to ignore the pain in his shoulder when he saw how relieved the simple gesture made her. "How are you feeling?"

She inhaled sharply. "Do you mean physically or emotionally? Because those are two entirely different questions and answers."

"Both."

"Physically, my neck hurts, and I'm sure the rest of me will be sore tomorrow. Other than that, I'm fine. The suit spread out the impact. Emotionally..." She sighed and glared up at the ceiling. "I'm not sure myself right now. I'm angry that these things keep happening, glad that it wasn't worse, and sad that I was mostly useless. I was hoping that the suits and being able to use my magic here would change that."

Zack was quick to cut off that line of thought. "The suits are the reason we were able to escape as easily as we did. Not to mention you using your puppet magic on them. Don't think for a second you didn't help. Without you making the suits into your puppets, we wouldn't have been able to knock that man out."

He let that sink in for a moment before taking Zelda from her and tossing the bear into the air.

"Don't forget, your magic is limited here. There is only so much you can use, the fact you can use any at all is already amazing. We're relatively low level as well, and without access to our portal stats. Any magic you use here is getting done off of your normal Aperran based stats."

"You're right. I had forgotten that." She caught Zelda as he tossed her into the air a second time. "I was just hoping we would be at home playing a game with Tessa and eating some good food. Not dealing with something like this."

"Maybe we can still do that tomorrow, and just do it here instead of there."

"Yeah, tomorrow." She agreed. "What were they after?" Zara asked softly, after they had been resting in silence for a minute.

"The airship." Zack pulled out the metal card and went through the entire conversation he'd had with Anna.

"You're right, it's the same logo." She examined each edge of the card closely, looking for anything else that might be hidden. "I guess the next question is, how is the research institute related to Shouvain? Does the country own them? Is it a division of one of their magi-tech research corporations, or are they partners?"

"I think partners would be worse," Zack muttered, getting up. "At least if Shouvain owns them, they're somewhat limited in scope. If they are merely partners, then they could be working towards having people everywhere."

"They're not there yet if it's the latter. Otherwise, they wouldn't have needed to wait for the airship to leave Fittrel."

"True. In any case, those things have nothing to do with us. Anna knows about the connection now. I'm more worried about the message. Do you think it was meant for us, or just a general one meant for whoever was in the car?"

Zara flipped the card over to read the message and sucked on her lips, thinking. "It's vague enough that it could be both."

"So, in other words, they may know where we are."

"We always knew that was a possibility."

He nodded. "But it doesn't seem like they want us back, at least. They got their use out of us and then cast us aside. Good riddance."

"That just means we have a little more room before we get our revenge on them. Whoever they are," She flicked the card into the air at him. "And whoever supports them."

He caught it and stored it in his pocket. "Now I'm going to get washed up and then let's get some sleep. I'm tired."

***

Zack passed the dimming but still good mana crystal back to his sister the next morning.

She hid it back in her sleeve and gingerly felt at her neck.

"How is it? Are you going to live?"

She chucked Zelda at him and continued to feel her neck. "It's stiff, and sore is all. I'll probably keep the brace to sleep in and raise the collar of the suit to get me through the day. It's a good thing some of the clothes we bought yesterday came with high necks." She sat up with his help. "I just hope that everything made it through alright. We spent a lot of money on those clothes and items."

"I'll go ask. Meanwhile, if you want to go take a shower. Neither of our uniforms are in the best of shapes at this point." That was the understatement of the year when it came to his. Hers, at least, was still in one piece.

He found a pack full of their new clothes waiting just outside the door for them.

Zara came out to find him changed and waiting for her. There were even some clothes spread across the bed for her to choose from. He had even dressed Zelda in a little dress that had somehow made the trip.

"That cold water helped my head, but tightened my neck," She complained lightly, grabbing an outfit that looked cute.

They found Tessa waiting for them downstairs. A bandage was keeping a cold compress pressed against a bump on her head.

"Did you sleep alright?" Zack inquired, keeping his voice low in case she had a headache.

"Like the dead." Her face looked unnaturally pale against the backdrop of her fiery red hair. "Ben's still out of it, but he's breathing without an issue. It's just a waiting game at this point."

They walked alongside her to the dining room, where breakfast was waiting for them.

"What are the two of you going to do today?"

"Well, that depends on you," Zack peeked at his sister to make sure she hadn't changed her mind. She hadn't. "We were thinking that since we didn't get to play any games yesterday with you. We could just play them here. If you still want to, and feel up to it, I mean."

He carefully dug into breakfast, minding his manners, while she thought the offer over.

"That sounds like fun and is probably for the best anyway. I think mother, along with the king and queen, would prefer it if you stayed out of trouble."

Zara snorted and then moaned, grabbing her head. "We had nothing to do with this one. Blame Fittrel and the people who wanted the airship, not us."

"Somehow, I don't think that's going to work," Tessa remarked impassively, popping a piece of fruit into her mouth.

"I'm a good little princess, I tell you!" She protested in faux outrage while picking up a large, sweet berry. "I couldn't be more innocent if I was asleep and trapped in a tower."

Tessa stopped chewing and swallowed, covering her mouth with her hand. "That makes no sense."

Zara shrugged. "It makes sense to me. That's all that matters."

"Not to change subjects here... but to change the subject, do you have any board games here?"

The girls both rolled their eyes.

"The people Ben sent off yesterday to get the games ended up bringing them here after everything that happened."

"Oh, good!" Zara bounced happily in her chair, groaning in pain as one hand went to her head and the other to her neck.

"Would you be careful," Zack admonished her, moving her hand away from her neck and lightly massaging it. "When do you feel like beginning? We don't know what else you have to do this morning or today."

"I..." She bit into a berry with a complicated expression. "I'm not sure. Father is busy with his experiments. Meanwhile, mother is dealing with the aftermath and fallout from everything that happened yesterday. I suppose that means that as soon as we are done eating, we can start."

"Is this the best room or should we play somewhere else?" Zack wondered.

"There's a sitting room, with a smaller table and more comfortable chairs that we can use."

He nodded and picked up his fork. "You wouldn't happen to have any mana crystals lying around, would you?"

"Why?" Tessa asked in confusion.

Zack pointed his fork at his sister. "If it's a big enough one, she might be able to show you something interesting." He was thinking that Zara might want Zelda to come out and play with them. She could use the extra support, and now that Second, or rather Amar, already knew he could use magic in Aperra, hiding it from Tessa and Anna wasn't worth the extra effort.

"Are you saying?" Zara's eyes flicked down to Zelda, who was sitting motionless in her lap.

He nodded. "Amar already knows about me. So, it's up to you, but I figured it would be fun for both of you. Besides, I know it would help you to feel even more secure with her in that state."

Tessa looked from one sibling to the other, unable to follow their conversation. "I have no idea what the two of you are talking about. However, we do keep a supply of mana crystals here for emergencies and for when my father needs them for his experiments. Taking one or two won't be an issue, as long as I remember to tell mother afterward."

Zack felt gloomy at the nonchalant way she said that. One of the main reasons they had gone through the school portal the week before was to get mana crystals. They had walked away with that weird purple one the ruler had given them, and a small one. That was all they had to show for their efforts after risking their lives.

Then there was Tessa talking about them like they grew on trees or could be picked from the ground like a common cabbage. The nobles and rich truly were a different breed.

"Let's just finish breakfast," He grumbled after a moment, suddenly feeling the gap between them.

Zara was smiling happily and didn't seem to care either way.

Chapter 22

A pile of games had been brought into the bright sitting room by the time Tessa returned with two mana crystals. Both were high quality and dense with mana inside. Just one of those would let off enough ambient mana to keep Zara going strong. Two of them were overkill.

Zara politely, but greedily, accepted one from her, while the second was put to the side for the moment.

"Tessa, just uh, don't go telling everyone about this, please? Amar already kind of knows, so I'm sure your mother and the crown know as well."

Her brows furrowed in confusion, regardless she agreed without needing to think about it. Even if she forgot her personal feelings about the siblings, strictly speaking, Zara was a princess. Anything she said could almost be considered an order, not that she was all that hard to convince. Tessa was curious by nature and already considered them both friends. If they wanted her to keep something a secret, then she would.

Zara held the crystal in one hand and placed Zelda on the polished wood floor. Without wasting a second more, she began the animation process on her beloved bear.

Tessa gasped, her eyes widening as a purple glow began to exude from the stuffed animal. "Is she performing magic here? But that's impossible! Isn't it?"

"She is, and yes, it is, for most people. At least for a while longer. The world will be changing soon enough."

A minute later Zara finished awakening Zelda and crouched back as she sprang up and hugged her. "Yes, I love you too." She whispered, hinting at the one-sided conversation going on between them.

"That really just happened," Tessa mumbled in shock.

"Yup, and now we have a fourth player for our games." Zack had already begun looking through the pile.

"Wait, you mean that bear isn't just a puppet? It's a thinking and living... toy?" She didn't know what to classify Zelda as.

"Thinking yes, living, that's harder to define, but she does feel pain, so sure. Zelda is a living, thinking, stuffed animal." Zack turned away from the games. "By the way Zara, you should raise up your collar now, so you don't keep hurting yourself."

She looked up from hugging Zelda. "Hmm, probably a good idea."

Her hand started to glow as she used her modification spell. The material around the collar of her suit began to creep up, supporting her injured neck. It took the excess thickness from the places she had left padded for future growth.

"That's better," She moaned in relief when she finished. "Even better than that stupid brace I had to sleep in."

Tessa blinked again and shook her head. "I just... You know what, whatever. Your name is Zelda, right?"

The bear nodded from her place on Zara's lap.

"Do you want to play some games with us?"

She nodded and then shook her head.

"She says she doesn't know how to play." Zara translated for them. "None of us do, though, so we can all learn together."

Anna found them several hours later, laughing and having fun. When she opened the door, Zelda was standing on the table moving her character piece several places across the board.

"Well, you don't see that every day. I guess you didn't tell Amar everything then?"

Zack pushed a card to Zelda and then looked up at their host. "I rarely do."

"Smart." She wandered over to Zelda and tried to poke her with a finger.

"Mother, don't do that! She doesn't like it, and we're in the middle of a game." Tessa scolded her curious mother.

"Oh, how do you know that she doesn't like it?"

Tessa flushed and turned away. "I may have gotten carried away myself, okay? It's not my fault she's so soft and cuddly. I couldn't help it."

Zelda waved a toothpick at them both imperiously, and then flipped over the card Zack had given her. She did a little dance and moved her piece forward to the square the card dictated. She was now firmly in the lead.

"What did you come in here for, mom?" Tessa wondered, grabbing the dice and blowing on them in the hope that it would grant her better numbers.

"Oh, I was just going to let you all know that everything had been retrieved from the accident site. Everything in the back seems relatively undamaged. The boxes were slightly squished, is all. The clothes all came through without a problem, though they will need to be washed. It seems as though a powder of some kind exploded all over everything."

Zack cursed softly at the mention of the wasted itching powder.

"What kind of powder was it exactly?" Anna's smile remained the same. However, her eyes had gone cold.

"Nothing illegal, if that's what you're worried about, or at least I don't think it was. It was just some itching powder we bought. We were going to douse a couple of the teacher's apartments who annoyed us with the stuff." He saw no harm in explaining their plans to her. They had lost the powder already; in any case, she was a proponent for revenge. Even if it was slightly petty.

Her cold gaze went back to normal. "Oh, is that all? Well, why didn't you say something? I can have Matthew mix you up something that will have them trying to tear their skin off?"

Tessa dropped the dice in surprise. "Mother! I don't think it needs to be that powerful. How about just strong enough that it will leave bloody tracks while they desperately scratch at themselves?"

Anna appraised her daughter. "I didn't expect that. Do you have something against one of these teachers as well?"

She sniffed and carefully picked up the dice. "Mainly just the math teacher. He kept disrupting the class to pick on Zack. I'm there to learn, and he was getting in the way of that. He needs to be taught a lesson." She began to move her character piece, only to stop a moment later. "Actually, come to think of it. He's the only teacher I've seen truly annoy you. You missed history and mana tech applications. And I know you don't have anything against our homeroom teacher. He's great!" She finished with a laugh.

Zack slipped her a card from a different pile this time. "He is indeed. However, don't forget we live on campus. There are plenty of opportunities for all of the other teachers there to do something if they want to. Hopefully, it will stop now, but who can say? Either way, a little petty revenge never hurt anyone."

Anna nodded, tapping her cheek thoughtfully. "A compressed, aerosolized form injected through a small hole in, say, the window or under the door should easily cover a teacher's room. Depending on where their clothes are, they might get a stronger hit or a weaker one. It would be a faster and safer option for the two of you as well."

Zack and Zara shared a look. "Sure," They both agreed. "As long as it's not any trouble."

"Don't worry, he loves to do random little things like this every once in a while. It helps to exercise his mind."

"Crap." Tessa had flipped over her card. "My piece gets sent to the nearest portal for one turn, without having fully awakened as a traveler yet." She retrieved one of the cards she had gotten from a previous turn. "Can I use this one now?"

They each shrugged. None of them had any more idea than her when she could and couldn't do something in the game.

"I'm going to use it then." She threw the card into the middle of the table. "Something goes wrong with my awakening, and all the monsters that were attracted by the light show die. I gain..." She quickly rolled a single dice. "Four levels. Wouldn't that be nice?"

Zack shot Zara a knowing look.

"That ends my turn. Zara, you're up."

"What is this game?" Anna was glad that her daughter was having fun with them. "We should buy it."

Zelda pointed her toothpick to the box on the ground by the table.

"Um, I think it is yours," Zack informed her, passing the dice to his sister. "Speaking of which, did Ben's people find out what Cooper and those other people are up to?"

"Portals of Agreishia, we'll have to play it together later with your father." She placed the lid back on the floor. "They did actually, and it's tangentially related to you... in a way."

"Really?" He hadn't been expecting that.

"Remember how you said that Cooper wanted you because he was trying to expand his operation? To develop his own force of travelers?"

Zack nodded.

"Well, he has done exactly that. All of them have. The other people with him were all small-time gang operators as well. It seems that they have been kidnapping every potential traveler they can get their hands on. We have no idea who they are working for just yet, but it appears they do have access to a portal somewhere."

Zara rolled her dice and directly moved her piece into the nearest portal. "What are you going to do about them, then?"

"That's the question, isn't it? We can rescue everyone now and save them, but miss out on whoever put this all together. Or we can let them suffer for a little longer while digging deeper into everyone involved."

"Which one are you likely to do? I need an action card, please." She informed her brother at the end.

He had gotten distracted by the conversation and quickly passed one to her.

"I haven't decided yet. I need to discuss things with Amar first, preferably without his daughter around. The information only reached my desk this morning, and I have been somewhat distracted." She grinned sardonically.

Zara picked up the card and glared at her brother. "My brand-new bow breaks as it goes through the portal. I roll one die to decide if any monsters heard the possibly loud noise, and one additional die to decide if there are any helpful travelers nearby."

"Does that even count as an action card?" Zack muttered. "Well, I'd love to watch whenever you all decide to take down Cooper."

"Just watch, not help?" Anna teased.

He rolled his eyes. "I'm not trained for those sorts of things, nor am I an idiot who thinks he's some sort of hero." The look in his eyes changed, losing some of their cheer. "I know what I am, and I know what I'm capable of, especially in this world."

"That's good, too many young kids or impetuous adults have died before their time because they rushed into something. Always take the time to learn and plan when you can. Delegate to those who specialize in a field, there is no shame in doing that. The myth that a hero must do everything themselves is exactly that a *myth*. No one is all-powerful, not even aberrations.

"That's why people work in teams. Each person makes up for something that another lacks. You must have the knowledge and the ability to use it." Anna sighed. "I apologize. That was a lesson I had to learn myself early on. Don't make the same mistakes I did. It nearly cost me everything. You might be more successful or less. Either way, it isn't worth the risk."

Zack waited as Zara rolled each die in turn, before replying in a quiet tone. "We know. It's a topic we've discussed at length over the years. There was a time we believed in those stories about heroes, then we were taken. Trust me, that experience opened both our eyes to the truth of the world. One person's strength is limited in this world, and we know that."

"Three monsters somehow heard the bow break, and there was one traveler nearby." Zara interrupted. "We'll have our revenge, but we'll do it right, and together. Now, someone, please get the instructions out and tell me what to do next."

Anna stayed a while longer, watching them play the game. She enjoyed the sight of her daughter having fun with the two of them. Eventually, however, she left to go speak with her husband and then she would meet with Amar later.

Zelda ended up winning the game, without ever having her character go through the portals. Instead, she had become the head of a corporation that then wound up employing the other character's pieces. The little bear had the time of her life, dancing around the table and gloating about it.

"What now?" Tessa asked when Zelda was finished.

"We probably need to be getting back," Zack sprawled back onto the carpeted floor. "Edith is probably worried, and we need to get new uniforms made as well. I've grown some already, so they don't fit right, and Zara's have all been destroyed now."

She tried to hide her disappointment when she nodded. "I understand."

Zara flicked Zelda's toothpick at her. "I don't think you do. Despite our somewhat rocky beginning, we've decided we like you. Unfortunately, we still have things we need to do as he mentioned. Tomorrow, after classes, you can certainly come over if you want."

Zack stretched, popping his back. "I hope Ben gets better; I know your family cares for him. How are we supposed to get back, though?"

"I'll ask mother, she'll know what to do."

They packed up the game and got their pack from the room they had slept in while Tessa went to find her mother. Anna found them waiting by the stairs. She had four aerosol cans with metal-tipped extensions on them in her arms.

"I didn't know how many you needed, so I had him make four of them. And before you ask, yes, he enjoyed the distraction, so thank you for that."

"We only needed three, well, kind of four, but we don't know where the headmaster sleeps," Zack told her while carefully taking them and putting them in the bag with their clothes.

Zara tried to hand over the two mana crystals to Tessa, who shook her head.

"Keep them. Mom said it was alright." Anna nodded from beside her daughter. "Just keep Zelda awake. I want to play with her again tomorrow after classes are done."

"Of course, she won't be moving during our regular classes, but she'll be awake." Zara couldn't bear to part with Zelda now that she had awoken her in Aperra.

She just wondered how it would affect her when they went through the portal the next day. Crossing over from the portal to the snow elf world, the bears and her puppets had been fine. Normally, she had to redo the spell every time she crossed over. Now she was depending on the bracelet to let her do magic on Aperra. She couldn't help but wonder if it would work the same way?

The trip back to the dorm was a fast-nail-biting affair. Anna was a great, if incredibly reckless driver who loved to go fast. She just drove as fast as her vehicle would let her, paying no mind to anyone else around her. Tessa was used to it, Zelda absolutely loved it, and Zack and Zara just wanted Ben to get better as quickly as possible.

"We'll see you tomorrow. Stay safe on the way back." They called out as the car sped away again. Both of their faces were slightly green, and they were taking constant deep breaths to offset the nausea.

"Why don't you get Edith all caught up? Meanwhile, I'll start putting everything away that we bought yesterday?" Anna had made sure their belongings were dropped off at the dorm safe and sound earlier.

His sister broke off at the Dorm Matron's door while he continued on.

He separated their new, and freshly laundered clothes first, and then began working on unpacking the many other items. The packs they would be bringing into the portals with them, along with their new camping supplies, were placed to one side. They would need to go through them later.

The numerous little figurines he began placing carefully on the table. The tallest went at the back, with the smallest in the front.

He had just finished placing them when Zara returned.

"Edith wants to have a session with you after we get fitted for new uniforms." Zelda jumped from her arms and began exploring the dorm apartment.

"You're supposed to say, *'I'm back'*, or *'hello brother'*." He playfully tossed a ball of wrapping tissue at her. "And why? I just had one with her..." He stopped to think. "Okay, so maybe it was a couple of days ago now."

She nodded and picked up a small clay wolf. "She wants to do them every other day if we can, or every three days. Whichever we think works best."

"I'm fine with either option. I won't say talking to her is magically making everything better. That was never the goal." His finger ran along the fine lines of a tail feather on a shiny bird he didn't recognize. "This is a long-term process. I'll go along with whatever you decide is best. You probably know better than I do on this one."

It was true. She had spoken in-depth about the subject with both Edith and Jean. While neither of the women was an expert by any stretch of the imagination, they both knew more than the siblings had.

"Let's go with every three days," Zara decided, setting down the wolf. "She's already helping us with our tutoring as well, and we need time to sort ourselves out after each session. We can change it later if we need to. For now, though, I think this will work best."

"Now that, that has been decided, let's go get our uniforms done before they leave for the day."

"After we get back from Edith's tonight, I think we can move the crystal from my suit to yours as well. It's been in it longer now than it was in Zelda originally by a couple of days."

"How does it look?"

"There are thick purple veins running everywhere inside the suit, and it's no longer silver-gray on the inside. Everything has taken on a purplish tinge. It might be less pronounced because the suit is just so much larger than Zelda." She had checked it that morning after her shower. "I figured after we used the crystal on George and Aisha, if there is anything left, we'd use it in the suits again."

"That works. I'll need your help in making it comfortable later, please?" Zelda popped out of Zara's room with her dagger belt in hand. "I'm not sure you're allowed to wear that on campus."

Zara looked away, holding back a laugh at whatever the bear was saying to her. "She says that if we let her wear it, she'll use one of the aerosol canisters on the headmaster's office for us."

"Deal, come here so I can help you put it on." Zack didn't even need to think twice about that particular offer. He'd even give her two of the cans to use. It didn't matter that Zelda would have helped them either way. What mattered was that she had offered.

Chapter 23

Zack yawned as Quinn talked about the monsters inside the school portal. Beside him, Zara did the same. It had taken them more time than they had thought it would to deploy the itching powder on the teachers. Mainly because they had to wait for them to fall asleep first.

The other students in their class kept glancing back at Zara and the dress-wearing bear sitting on her desk. They had all heard stories about the special scholarship holder. The overnight princess, supposedly one of the youngest people to ever go through a portal. Outside of the odd glance in the cafeteria, for nearly all of them, this was their first time seeing her.

Quinn clapped his hands, catching everyone's wandering attention. "Our time is up. You know the drill from last week, I'm sure. Just in case you managed to forget, head over to the cafeteria, pick up your prepared lunch, and then go down to the training field. From there, you will be taken to the portal for your training period." He winked at Zack and Zara and then shooed everyone from the room.

Tessa sidled up beside them as they walked to the training field. "Mother says the king warned Fittrel to prepare for war. As soon as they firmly identify the attackers, they'll retaliate. For now, that is really all they can do, unless you know who trips up."

"They seem to want that airship, so it might just happen," Zara whispered to her, before skipping ahead to present herself to Jean. She needed to get her training uniform still.

"She's so different from the girl I met during that first week of school," Tessa commented uncertainly. "She was so timid and afraid of everything. It was heartbreaking."

"She still is. Just now, she has the power to fight back. Not a lot, as we saw on Erdetag. It's enough to let her be more confident in front of most people. Besides, she likes you, and she's gotten used to Jean."

"Still, it's a remarkable change."

"Yeah, it really is." He agreed. "How come I don't see you being swarmed by your groupies today? What happened? I figured your mother's announcement would have made them even worse."

She shivered. "They were practically feral that first day back. They created a huge problem for everyone inside the portal. Rose, and of course Quinn, came down hard on them all. When mother found out, she apparently went to visit their families in person."

Zack felt his brows rise in surprise. "I bet that went over well."

"Well, I haven't been bothered since, at least. I'm not sure what she said to them, but the reprieve has been pleasant."

"I'm beginning to understand more and more why you were so excited at the prospect of playing games with us." Before, he had thought she was just lonely, someone who wanted friends. Now he was thinking there might be a desire for normality in there as well.

"Speaking of, are we still on for after classes?"

"We can't do it all night, but yeah, Zara and Zelda are both excited." He glanced at the other approaching students and stepped closer to her. "We have tutoring we need to do after that, which is why we can only play for a couple of hours."

"How many subjects are you behind on?"

Zara came back to them with a specially made small training uniform in hand. There were few girls and boys in the academy as slim and diminutive as her.

"Math is the big one, history most likely as well. I just didn't have a lot of time growing up to attend classes, not if we wanted to eat regularly."

She didn't know how to respond to that casual remark.

"Did you ask her?" Zack asked his sister as she returned.

She nodded and crowded close to them. "The rings still have plenty of room for growth she said. Nothing should happen with the portal anytime soon."

They had been worried about going through the school's portal and creating another Change event. Except for this time with all of their classmates in tow. It would have been a disaster. Now they could just enjoy their training inside the portal like everyone else, without worrying needlessly.

Tessa looked on in confusion, missing her chance to ask for clarification as the rest of the class arrived.

Rose was sucking on a lozenge for her throat and pushed Jean forward.

"Due to my unexpected absence last week, instructor Rose's voice has taken a beating. So once again, I am the one who will be doing all the talking. Go change into your training uniforms and grab your weapons if needed. Remember, this is a training class. The idea is to get you used to handling your weapons of choice, abilities, and standing up to monsters. Not to fight each other."

A few of the students shifted uncomfortably at that announcement.

"Anyone caught starting a fight with another student will be expelled from all future portal training classes for the year. I would suggest you not even think about it, as it's not worth the risk. Now hurry up, our ride will be here in a moment. Any student that misses it will be running to the portal."

Everyone broke for the changing rooms, rushing to ensure they didn't get left behind.

Tessa and Zara were the first of the girls out. Still, Zack had beaten them by a minute and was inspecting a small staff while holding the pack with Zelda and her belt of daggers inside. They had decided to leave George and Aisha inside the dorm for their first run with the other students.

"Tessa, I meant to ask you earlier, but how's your head feeling today?" Zack opened the pack so his sister could retrieve her bear.

"Thankfully, the swelling went down enough for people to barely notice it. My thoughts can sometimes be hard to keep track of every once in a while still." She shrugged, dismissing the lingering effects of her concussion. "I have medication for the headaches at least. It keeps them bearable."

They had gotten something similar for Zara's neck pain from the academy nurse the night before. The doctors that Anna had brought in that night had not been carrying enough medication. Most of what they had thought to bring went to Ben.

"How about the two of you?"

"I'm perfectly fine." His shoulder had long since been healed.

"My neck is still sore, but as long as I keep it supported, it's mostly fine. I'm the same as you when it comes to my headaches. I just take some meds." Zara shrugged and closed the flap on the pack. "We survived; we can't ask for much more than that."

A modified troop carrier trundled up to a stop nearby. It had long benches inside with an extended rear seating area. Anyone who was unlucky enough to not get a seat would have to stand. That said, there were plenty of seats for their class. Each class had a minimum of twenty students, and there were six classes per year. With the addition of Zara, their class now had twenty-one students in it.

Quinn was the driver and glared at each student as they got on board. He was determined to make sure that nothing happened to his wife again.

Jean tapped his shoulder just as the last student rushed through the door. "And time! They just barely all made it on time. Let's go."

A few students glared at Zack for sitting next to Tessa, only to look away when they remembered who his sister now was. She was a princess. He was out of their reach and could sit with whoever he wanted.

Spencer could only grind his teeth and duck down in his seat. He knew what was coming his way eventually, and there was no way to avoid it.

Zack had every right to issue a duel against him and the others that had worked with Dorn that day. With the crown as his backer, there was no way they could avoid them either. They had well and truly backed the wrong person this time.

The siblings paid close attention to the power marking rings around the portal. Jean hadn't been lying to them. There was indeed plenty of room left before they went all black. Neither knew how fast that process would take, but they were confident it wouldn't happen while they were inside this time.

"Line up! Rose will go through first, along with Quinn. Only then can all of you start going through. I'll come last, to make sure we haven't left anyone behind."

"Let's go through first," Zack whispered to his companions. "It'll make it easier to hide Zelda that way. We can just pretend everyone else just missed Zara doing the spell or something."

"What about the teachers?" Tessa questioned.

"They should be paying more attention to danger than us at the time, or at least I hope."

"No one knows what my magic looks like, so it shouldn't be a problem to hide it. Just stand over me when we get inside." Zara held Zelda at the ready, in case she did need to actually cast her spell when she went through.

The teachers went through, and at Jean's nod, Zack led the way for his group next.

The portal's energy welcomed him and then spat him out on the other side. The other two were right behind him.

"Well, how are the spells?" He asked his sister, keeping one eye on the teachers who had both spread out ahead of them.

"They're still good and active." They stepped to the side while she began acting as though she was awakening Zelda.

What she didn't tell him, mainly because Tessa was there, was that the spells would likely fail on their way back through the portal. They had the last time at least, and there was no reason to think that would be a onetime occurrence. Knowing him, he remembered, or had at least thought it was a possibility.

She didn't mind Tessa anymore, but this was information that concerned their safety. It was best left to just the two of them. The fewer people that knew it, the fewer that could let it slip by accident. You never revealed a possible weakness to people. That was basic. It didn't matter if they were friends, you just didn't do something like that.

More students joined them in the clearing. With most taking a moment to look for the floating island. It had drifted over to the distant mountains, and was little more than a speck in the sky right then.

They kept up the charade for a few more seconds and then let Zelda climb up onto Zara's shoulder.

The sight of a moving bear shocked all of the classmates that saw it. Few of them had actually believed that she would be able to go through the portal. Now they had just seen something even more incredible. Her bear had come to life.

One of them dared to step forward, carefully approaching the three. "Um, if I might ask, what is your class?"

"Tiny Bearmancer," Zara answered succinctly. If they were to believe it, then the 'Tiny' in the name would likely imply she could only animate one bear at a time. Which was why they had decided against bringing George or Aisha along that day.

Jean clapped her hands as she came through the portal. "Rose and Quinn will be sticking together. Since they have an additional adult, they will be getting more students. Twelve of you will go with them, and the remaining nine will be with me."

She glared at Zack and Zara as though daring them to choose the other teachers.

Obediently, they went over to her.

"Now, who wants to team up and go first? I would suggest teams of two or three, otherwise, the experience gets spread out too thinly. That said, we are here to train, so the decision is up to you."

"I'll go," Zack volunteered. He didn't need a team, and neither did Zara. However, if Tessa asked later, he wouldn't mind helping her.

Jean rolled her eyes. "Fine, we're heading to that section of the woods. Let's see what you got for us."

Zack grinned. He had been waiting for this. When they were on the snow elf world, the Oracle had given him the '*Blink*' spell to learn. Shortly after learning it, they had left without him ever having had a chance to use it. With Skye's help, they had sped through the world inside the portal. Then, with the end in sight, they had been forced to run because of the time limit on Edith and Jean.

He could finally use the spell. He just needed to get inside those woods first, where fewer people would see him use it. His normal attack spell could be passed off as an odd mage spell. That wasn't the case for blink, not that he was going to let that stop him.

Jogging ahead of the others, Zack barely slowed before entering the trees. It was a risk that Jean was only willing to let him take because she had seen his power before. Behind him, he could hear her lecturing the students against doing exactly what he was doing. He tuned her out and focused.

The last time they had been inside this portal, they had encountered a lot of different beast-type monsters. This time, they were entering the woods, and he was expecting some plant-based monsters as well.

A living vine crept along the loamy, leaf-riddled floor, stirring them up as it tried to catch its prey unawares. Zack stepped on the vine, feeling it squirm underfoot as he searched for the host body. Plant monsters were more of a pain to deal with than most thought. They could hide, use poisons, attack from every direction and with a variety of weapons.

They were annoying if you underestimated them.

That was a mistake that Zack was unlikely to make now. Not after he had learned those lessons the hard way several times when he was a kid.

The leaves shifted and flew into the air as the vine wriggled. The length of creeping plant gave him the general direction of the main body. He took a few steps farther into the forest before stopping. This was a class training exercise. There was no reason for him to go after a monster hidden so far inside.

Looking behind him, he made sure he was hidden from view before peering up at the branches above. They were all well out of reach even if he was to jump, not if he was to use blink, however.

He focused on the branch he wanted and then looked past it to the tree trunk. The spell worked with line of sight only, which meant he had to appear slightly above it. He also didn't want to go too far, not on this first attempt. The spell description said it was mana intensive. He wasn't interested in going too far and ending up with his astral form trying to eat his body again.

Experiencing that once was more than enough for him.

The instant he cast the spell, everything shifted. He was up in the air staring at bark, falling awkwardly onto a large branch. All the while, a large portion of his magical energy was torn from his body to fuel it.

A distance no more than thirty meters had taken around half of his natural available energy.

It was indeed mana intensive, but not nearly as bad as he was fearing. For long distances, sure, the spell was unusable. For anything relatively close, it would come as a nice surprise. There were a few more experiments he wanted to try, but now wasn't the time.

He had just spotted a couple of beasts walking into view.

Zack calculated the distance and took a running leap off of the branch. Well, maybe he had enough time for one more experiment.

The jump carried him farther than expected before he began to fall to the ground. It wasn't close enough to the beasts, though it had alerted them to his presence. A few meters above the ground, he blinked away, appearing above the first of the boar-like beasts he had seen. Just as he had hoped, the spell did nothing to negate his speed.

He shot down, almost forgetting to activate his *'Arcane Armor'* at the last second. His protected fist pummeled the beast into the forest floor. He could hear its legs snapping like twigs under the might of his speeding fall.

Zack fell to the ground beside it while the other boar took off at a run. Using blink and arcane armor in rapid succession had nearly drained him dry. He raised his hand and sent an arcane bolt through the boar's skull beneath him, before it could move. The spell drilled deep into the ground before fading away, he still needed to practice his magical energy control.

He didn't bother to look for a mana crystal inside such a weak beast. If he managed to find anything, its small size would make it more trouble than it was worth. A few weeks ago he would have been salivating at the thought of any mana crystal no matter the size, now he was possibly passing one up because it was too small. How quickly things changed.

With a groan, he got to his feet and took off after the other boar. If he could herd it towards the clearing, then Zelda would be able to take care of it easily.

Honestly, there were plenty of easier ways to go about this exercise. Except, he hadn't been able to resist finally having the opportunity to try out that spell, and he hadn't been disappointed. It was everything he had been hoping it would be, and more. Or at least that was true as far as he could tell from the limited information, he had gotten both times using the spell.

A bolt shot out, skimming the backside of the running boar and destroying the side of a tree. The boar squealed and changed direction, heading back towards the clearing it had been trying to avoid.

One more bolt was enough to convince it to run into the open space.

"Hey Zara, I brought you a present!" He called out, unable to find the group for a brief moment.

A sharp whistle to the side gave him a direction, and he began the process of herding the boar all over again. Coming over a small rise, he saw Zelda jump onto the boar's back and began riding it like a mount. It was only when it got close to the students that she pulled out her daggers and began to bloodily carve the beast apart.

It slid to a stop at Jean's feet, dead. Zelda wiped her blades off on its hide, took a couple of bows, and then hopped off and back into Zara's arms.

"How many did you see inside?" Jean asked him, seeing spots of blood on his own uniform.

"Three, two of these boar beasts, and then one plant-type monster. It's actually rather quiet inside. We'll need to make some noise to bring them to us."

"Stupid overzealous company travelers," Jean snorted. "They've been messing with all of our training days lately. By cleaning out as many monsters as they can before any of our classes can enter for the day."

Chapter 24

"What now?" Tessa wondered. "Is this the end of our training exercise already?"

Jean glanced at her and grinned. "No, we're just going to do like Zack suggested in a way and make some noise."

The other students in their group backed away from them, not liking the look in her eyes.

"How much energy do you have left, Zack?"

He breathed in deep, smelling the scent of blood, freshly over-turned grass and the forest nearby. "Enough for a couple more spells, is all. I used a lot herding that boar-monster over here."

Jean nodded and turned to Tessa. "Here's what I'm thinking. Why don't you and Zack use a couple of your spells to scare the monsters in the forest into coming out? You light some trees on fire, and he'll make some noise."

"Will that even work?" A student with a sword asked doubtfully.

"Of course, it's a tactic a lot of the traveler groups use when no one has been inside the portal for a while. It grabs the monster's attention easily and brings them to you. Which means you have the freedom to choose the battlefield and how you want to set it up. Including what traps you want to use, if any, or just simple hit-and-run tactics using the portal.

"Though, to be honest, those aren't the best. Most people tend to be disoriented for a moment or two after they come through. That is plenty of time for a monster to kill you. If your team leader ever suggests that plan, refuse to go along with it.

"The only questions this time is if the two of them will be enough and if the corporations even left us enough monsters? It doesn't matter how big of an attention-grabbing mess they make if there are no monsters around to notice it."

"Shall we?" Tessa wondered.

Zack shrugged. "Sure, maybe we'll get lucky."

They jogged towards the tree line while the rest of the group began preparing to receive any beasts and monsters that might appear.

"How far in do you think we should go?"

"Can you toss you fire at all?"

She nodded.

"Then not far. In my mind, at least, we want the fire behind the monsters. So. I'll use my magic first and then you can use yours. It's up to you whether you use yours in here or outside the trees."

"Definitely outside the trees where I can arc it up and over."

Zack raised his hand and pointed straight ahead. He had already decided to only release three bolts. One ahead, and then one slightly to the left and then one to right. With how much damage his spells were doing now, there was no telling how far into the forest they would go before stopping. It was better to not go overboard at this stage.

The first arcane bolt fired, taking the last of his normal magical energy with it. The next two bolts would come from his astral form. At least he could cast the spell quicker that way. He shifted his hand and fired again, followed by the third time a beat later.

Trees thundered down as the forest erupted into noise. The three bolts ate their way deep into the forest before finally disappearing.

Tessa stood behind him with her mouth hanging open. "I don't think we need my fire spells; they can't compare to that display in the slightest."

"It's better to be thorough, and it isn't a matter of comparing spells. Besides, remember that Zara and I were just stuck inside the portals. Our levels are naturally higher than yours."

She thought that over while they walked out of the forest. "That's not all of it, though, is it? You are an aberration, just like your little sister, aren't you?" She didn't wait for him to answer before continuing. "Aberration classes don't run in families, to my knowledge. They aren't like bloodline classes, they're the rare outlying oddities. It makes no sense for you both to have aberration classes."

The rhetorical questions went unanswered as she began to gather her energy into a little ball of fire on the tip of her finger.

"It's called *Flame Shot*, the description says that after I level it up, its form will change. It supposedly has a lot of versatility, especially being the first spell I got."

Zack wondered if that was true of his own *'Arcane Bolt'*? The spell was still level one, despite how much he had used it. Hopefully, it was getting close to leveling up soon. Zara's puppet spell had just leveled up. Surely that meant his first spell was getting close as well. Right?

Tessa aimed her finger into the air and above the trees. The fire streaked from her finger and shot straight for over forty meters before beginning to fall back down. She adjusted her aim and let loose with another flame shot. Soon she had released ten of them before deciding to take a break. She would need some magical energy left over to fight any monsters that appeared from their efforts.

Curls of smoke drifted up from the forest in a few places. There was no blazing inferno that promised death to every being that came upon it. Not yet at least. What could you expect from someone who had only been inside the portal once before? Frankly, they were lucky to get what they had.

Zack didn't even know if she had reached level two yet. He pulled her along behind him, hurrying back to the relative safety of the group.

Trenches designed to trip anything running towards them had been dug in the short time they had been away. Small holes which the melee students could hide in had been dug next to each of the trenches.

At the back stood Jean, a female student he didn't know who used a bow, and Zara, with places for him and Tessa as well. They were the only ones who could fight at a distance. Their place was obviously at the back.

They took up their positions just as the ground began to rumble. The smoke had begun to thicken above the trees. The magical fire gradually consumed the trees it had hit and began to spread. The hot flames paid no mind to whether the wood was wet or dry, it just wanted to burn it all.

Against their expectations, the flames began to spread, jumping from one tree to the next.

"Does anything that dies from that count as a kill for me?" Tessa asked their teacher hopefully.

Jean snorted. "You wish, maybe if you were close enough, it's possible. Of course, then you would get burnt as well. Unless your elemental affinity is truly off the charts, I wouldn't suggest trying it. Still, most everything that would die in that fire wouldn't go to you even if you did manage it. Once the fire changes from your elemental attack to normal flames it would no longer count towards you in any case. Ask Quinn about *'Area of Effect'* spells later and their maximum range for experience gain. You go beyond that range or initial time limit in the case of your flames and that experience is lost."

Tessa put the information away for later, content with the knowledge that others had tried it before her.

Quinn and Rose hurried over with their group of students as the first of the monsters burst out of the trees. Soon, five beasts had cleared the trees and were eyeing the students wearily. At their front was a small fox monster with two tails and an intelligent, calculating air. It spotted the second group of student travelers, and the five monsters took off at a run, away from them.

A moment later a snake appeared, and this time Jean wasted no time in ordering the archery student to aggro the beast. They couldn't afford to waste this opportunity by letting all the monsters run away.

The arrow arced through the air and skittered uselessly off the scales. The archer had been in training since she was young and had phenomenal aim. Regardless of its inability to damage the beast, the impact drew its attention. The snake came at them with a vengeance.

"You weren't having any luck finding any monsters, either?" Quinn asked as they drew close.

"Nope, the corporate travelers must have been ordered to clear all the close ones out before our training sessions."

The new group of students didn't have the advantage of the holes that Jean had forced her group to dig. However, they were plenty able to stand inside the trenches and use them to their advantage. Something that they did as soon as the snake drew near. None of them wanted to miss out on any experience points.

Only Zack and Zara could afford to be more lackadaisical, since they had already gotten a monster each.

Under the concentrated efforts of the students and with the help of the teachers, the snake's scales were soon broken. It perished soon after that. The arrows in its mouth and Quinn holding its tail had kept it from hurting anyone.

At the back, Zack was taking the chance to train his magical energy control. After talking over the theory with Zara, and her telling him how she did it, it was finally time for him to practice. He needed to get the cost of his arcane bolt spell under control.

Zack doubted there was anything he could do for blink or arcane armor. The way they worked seemed to prohibit someone from actively controlling energy with them. His greatest hope was being able to make his arcane manipulation ability more effective. If he cut the cost of using that down even a little, then it would open up a lot of avenues for them.

He had a feeling that was another pipe dream. Either way, it was a great skill to have, and one that would prove useful in the future no matter what.

One monster after another appeared from within the forest, and under the teacher's guidance, the archer would target one of them at a time. Sometimes the beasts would come at them willingly. Usually, they simply ran in a different direction without ever looking at them.

The experience points were spread liberally between all of the students, as well as the teachers. Still, due to the large number of monsters, they ended up getting more experience than normal. Nearly every member of the class had approached the border to level two, and some had even crossed over it completely.

It was only later, as they discussed these differences, that they would remember Quinn's words about Zack. They were already starting to see differences among themselves, granted it was likely because those people had done more damage to the monsters than anything else. Still, it served to drive home his message from before.

Zack would someday stand above them in levels, and for travelers, levels equaled power. Not to mention with his sister as the princess now, it was apparent all of them had badly screwed up.

Only Tessa was close to the two of them, and it was doubtful if they would let any of them into their little group of friends.

"Everyone, our time should be nearly up for training. I want everyone to start heading towards the portal." Jean called out, as the latest beast fell to their combined might. "Zack, Tessa, Zara, can you handle covering our backs along with Quinn?"

The three shared a quick look and then nodded.

Tessa still needed to get some more experience. She hadn't been able to freely use her flames before with how bunched up everyone was. Now was the perfect time for them to bag her a monster or two. Splitting the experience between just two or three people would keep it reasonable.

"Send Zelda out. She can hop onto one of them and steer it to us for Tessa," Zack whispered, as the students began to carefully walk past them.

Zara walked over to Quinn, handed him Zelda, and then pointed to the trees. "Can you toss her, please?"

"You sure?" She nodded, and with a shrug, he hauled back his arm and threw the bear into the air.

Zelda spread her arms and spun, enjoying the short flight, before crashing face-first into a tree. She dropped to the ground and sprang back up, straightening her dagger belt.

Zara grinned as she watched the bear run to the side while drawing her daggers. Zelda was keeping a running commentary going in her head about the joys of flying, and how Tessa was doing the right thing by burning all the nasty, hateful trees down. There were still the occasional times Zelda would fall silent and forget to speak, falling back on miming things.

She hoped that awakening her in Aperra, the place that had originally caused her to be so reclusive, would help. Before, when they were younger,

Zelda was a lot chattier. Her time in Aperra, where she could only watch as Zara suffered but could not help, had changed that. It had nearly taken her voice, her words, from her.

That wasn't something Zara would allow to happen if she could help it. Zelda was too precious to her for that.

Zelda began to run and then jumped as a sleek bear beast appeared. Her daggers bit into the top layer of its fatty layer and stopped. It was enough to grab its attention, but not much else. She would need to go for the eyes, ears, or mouth if she wanted to hurt it.

"Here it comes," Zack informed Tessa, shaking her from her stupor, as the large beast turned towards them.

A bright ball of fire appeared on the tip of her finger; she was just waiting for it to get closer.

The last of the students hurried past them, just as the bear stepped into the filled trench.

With a grunt, she released the flame shot, and Zelda jumped from the unsuspecting bear's head. Bears were naturally greasy animals, and while there was no guarantee that under normal circumstances they would go up in flames. This time they were dealing with some of the magical variety, and they had already seen what it did to the trees.

The shot hit the bear in the chest, doing little initial damage. It was only when the beast arrogantly tried to brush the fire off it that her magic began to shine. It immediately began to regret the action as the small flame spread across its chest in an arc, and onto its paw.

The distracted beast tripped and fell onto the pile of corpses. The magical fire ate at its greasy hair and fatty layer, spreading all over its body. From there it spread to the dead monster bodies in the trench, sending up plumes of noxious smoke.

Despite the hot flames eating at it, the bear gradually stood and roared at Tessa, venting its fury at her. The fire hurt, damaging it slowly over time, instead of dealing large amounts of immediate damage.

Zack took careful aim, glad that there were no longer any random students around to see what he was about to do. A hand dropped onto his shoulder, stopping him.

"Hold on, she has this." Quinn rumbled to him.

Nearby, Tessa was taking aim for the bear's head and firing one flame shot after another. The flames grew stronger, eating away at the beast's eyes and climbing their way inside its skull. It began to scream and tear at its face with its claws, tearing long strips of cooked flesh away with each pass.

In seconds, it had done more damage to itself than Tessa had managed with her attacks.

A painful, keening wail that resonated with Zack's soul burst from its mouth. It was a sound he had made before and knew too well. Without a second's hesitation, he took aim and fired. The bolt erased the bear's head and burrowed deep into the ground behind it.

He still had a long way to go with his control.

"No one and nothing should make a sound like that when suffering. It's better to just put them out of their misery." He told them.

A pale-faced Zara was holding tightly to Zelda, nodded.

"Come on, we won't be collecting any mana crystals from the bodies this time around." Quinn pushed them towards the portal.

"Are we all here?" Jean asked once they had arrived. She did a quick headcount and then nodded to Rose, who walked through the portal first.

One by one, the rest of the class filed their way out, content with their gains. It had been a productive training session for all of them.

"Sorry, I didn't mean for it to take that turn," Tessa apologized while they waited.

Zack shook his head. "No, that sound it made just brought back memories for me. You need to fight with what you have and did nothing wrong. Did you at least get a level from this, or did I steal too much of the experience by killing it at the end?"

She was silent for a moment as she pulled up her status page. "I did actually! I'm only at the beginning still, but I got the level. That bear must have been rather high-leveled." She looked at Zack with narrowed eyes. "And yet you were able to do that to it..." The side of her lips quirked into a half-smile. "I don't care. I'm just glad no one else saw but Quinn, and he doesn't seem interested in saying anything."

Jean shook her head as they approached the portal. "Really Zara? Look at Zelda! You got her such a cute dress, and then go and ruin it by getting it all bloody the first time you go through a portal."

"It's easily washable material that's supposedly resistant to staining." She protested, hugging the bear closer.

She shook her head. "Zara, sweety, nothing is that resistant to bloodstains. Either way, thank you Zack and Tessa for setting up such an effective monster driving field. We'll probably have to use it again next time as well. Thanks to your efforts, this training session wasn't a complete waste."

When they got back to the academy, they discovered that two of the nurses had been called away unexpectedly. Leaving the medical facilities short-staffed and the injured students waiting in a line. Thankfully, none of them were severely injured this time around.

One of the overworked staff let slip that they had been called away by the headmaster and a certain annoying math teacher.

Zack and Zara shrugged and let their classmates suffer their minor injuries. It was a petty form of revenge, yet it still brought grins to their faces.

Now Zack only had to deal with Spencer and the others that had attacked him with Dorn, and they could fully move past that event. It felt good to be able to check things off so rapidly on a list like this at times.

Chapter 25

Zara finished redoing the spells on both of their suits before Tessa arrived at their apartment after class. She had needed to retrieve the game they were going to play. Zara had previously reawakened Zelda during a bathroom break shortly after they got back from the portal.

The four played for a couple of hours and then Tessa left so they could go get some tutoring done with Edith.

The next day was much the same, except without the training session. Math class was also taught by a substitute teacher, someone who treated them all the same, this time. Unfortunately, the information was still beyond Zack, though somehow Zara seemed to be able to understand some of the theories.

Mittwoch was the day the siblings had been looking forward to the most. Their mana tech applications class was that day, and it was a subject that neither knew anything about.

The three walked over to the mana tech building after lunch, with Zack paying special attention to glare at Spencer as he walked past. He was just waiting for his handling of the staff to get better before challenging the boy to a duel.

"What are you waiting for? You should just do the same thing to him that he did to you. I'll even help!" Zara saw even less point in sticking to the rules than he did on this one, especially when others had already flaunted them.

"I don't know, I just thought that it would have more effect on them mentally if I beat them at their own game." He hadn't actually given the matter a lot of thought if he was being honest. For whatever reason, he had just gotten it stuck in his head that he needed to go about the matter properly. Probably because Zara was a princess now, everything he did could have an effect on how people would view her.

He knew she would never blame him for this one, and she wouldn't likely even care. Still, now that he was giving it some proper thought, it was better to start changing their behaviors now rather than later. They might not be from Aperra, but there was no telling if they would ever find a way home.

Everything that had seemed within reach while on the snow elf world had started to appear less realistic now that they were back in familiar territory.

Unfortunately, their mana tech applications class was a disappointment. Quinn hadn't been joking before when he said that all they were going to be taught was how to process the mana crystals that they brought back. It was a topic that the academy apparently believed needed to be covered in great, exhaustive detail. Only after every detail was ingrained in their very being would they be allowed to move onto anything else. However, even that depended on the entire class for the first year, and not on a person's individual aptitude.

For people like Zack and Zara, who already knew most of what was being taught, it was the worst. There were details, every now and again, that they didn't know. Little nuggets of information that were somewhat interesting to know, while also being absolutely useless.

If it hadn't been for Tessa's presence, they would have walked out of the class early. As it was, they barely managed to last the entire period.

"That was a waste of time," Zack ground out angrily once they were free.

Zara nodded. "I'm sorry, Tessa, but I doubt that either of us will be attending that particular class again until they switch subjects."

"That's fine, I understand. From what I've been told, a lot of people actually treat this as a free period in the beginning. Many nobles and children of travelers already know all of this information. There is no reason for them to learn it all again."

"What about you? Are you going to keep going to it?"

She hesitated, debating her answer before replying. "It depends on what the two of you are going to do instead. Most students who skip it hang out with their friends or go to the library for some extra studying. I don't need to read up on anything I can't find at home, and as for friends, well, we've already talked about that before."

"Well, I mean, we just barely made the decision. I don't see why we can't all decide together." Zack nudged his sister, looking for confirmation.

"Is there something that you want to do in particular?" Zara brushed some dirt from Zelda's top.

"No," Tessa shook her head. "I just don't want to spend the time alone."

It was a sentiment that the siblings could understand. They had always had each other, yet there were also still plenty of times when they had been forced to be alone. It was a feeling that was always uncomfortable, despite knowing the other person would return. Tessa had her parents, but that was a different relationship than one would have with a close sibling or friends.

"Well, in that case, how about after class today instead of resuming our game from yesterday right away, we discuss some options? Whether those are just going back to the dorm to hang out and play or doing something else."

The girls both nodded.

"Good, now how is Ben doing?" The trio stepped off the path and out of the way of some jogging seniors.

"He's still drifting in and out of consciousness. Mom and dad have both tried talking to him the last couple of times he's been awake. I believe their descriptions of him were along the lines of loopier than a three-legged animal with no sense of direction."

"Your parents are strange." Zara curled up her nose, refusing to laugh at the weird phrase.

"They have their moments for sure," The other girl agreed.

"Has your mom said anything more about Shouvain or the attack on the airship?" Zack wanted to ask before he forgot later. It was a topic they had been avoiding during their games, really anything serious during those times was taboo to talk about.

"Not yet. I do know that the ship left last night for Fittrel, while Nivea is still here. Amar is struggling to get to know her again, mom says."

They walked inside the building, only to be stopped by a glaring Spencer. "I challenge you to a noble's duel."

"On what grounds, and why should I accept?" Zack shot back. He wasn't a noble and cared little for what others thought of him.

The question stumped the poor VanCamp boy.

"In that case, I refuse." He was tempted to just kick the boy right then and there and be done with the whole situation. He couldn't, though, not with everyone watching. It would cause too many other issues for the momentary pleasure to be worth it in the long run.

Brushing past him, they made their way up to Quinn's classroom for the last class of the day.

"I don't think that is going to work a second time. He'll be prepared to answer next time." Tessa whispered outside the room.

"Then I'll just prepare a different question. Is there a rule that says I have to accept the duel?"

"I don't believe so. As far as I know, it is only related to how the other nobles and students perceive you. Of course, in your case, there might be a bit more latitude. Everyone knows you were attacked, unofficially, by Dorn, Spencer, and a few other students. Then there was your general lack of physical ability when you arrived. Even if Spencer did win, he would lose a lot of respect."

Zack pushed open the door while considering what she had said. "So, I could probably get away with saying no once or twice more, but that's all?"

"It depends on how long he takes between each challenge, but that's the gist of it, yeah."

Quinn, who was sitting behind his desk for once, instead of on top of it, looked up when they entered. "Zack, princess, you two are excused from attending my class this period. The headmaster wants to see you right away."

Tessa waved as they backed out the door.

"We'll meet you back at our dorm after class."

"What do you think he wants?" Zara asked once they were back outside.

"It could be anything. Maybe he wants to apologize for being a jerk to us or thank us for helping with the training session. He could also have figured out that we were the ones who doused his office with the itching powder." Zack shrugged. "Anything really. There are lots of options."

The lift ride up was a short silent affair, and the nice secretary lady from before waved them right in when they arrived.

The headmaster was standing in front of the large windows that overlooked the campus. His skin was bright red, and the office smelled of disinfectant and cleaning agents.

"I don't know how you got in or did it, and I don't care. I know it was you and that is enough. Our little squabble ends here with this. Is that understood?" His voice was tired and lacked all the bluster from before.

"Putting aside the rather egregious assumption that it was us who did whatever you think we did. Will the as you call it *'squabble'* end here? You sicced your teachers on my brother and me when all we wanted to do was nothing but learn in peace!" Zack put his arm around his sister as she began riling herself up.

"She's right, you and your brother-in-law started this mess headmaster. We would have been perfectly content staying beneath everyone's notice. You all just couldn't let us have that. So, tell us, how can we trust anything you say?"

He turned to face them, revealing the bloody scratches he had dug into his face, several of them coming close to his eyes. "You think I would dare to go against the crown and a royal princess?"

They shrugged.

"Why not? You knew who brought me into the academy and went against the military readily enough."

He had no reply to that. It was a fact he had known, and had still turned the teachers against them.

"I have an idea," Zara spoke up with an odd gleam in her eye. "No one ever did anything when Zack was attacked that first week by Spencer and the others. Now, Dorn and his family have already been taken care of. The others, however, well, they were never punished. Do something with them and then we'll believe you. Our differences can end with that."

He nodded sharply, seemingly relieved that was all they wanted to end their conflict. "I'll call for the boy after this immediately. Do you know who the others were?"

Zack shook his head; Spencer was the only one he had known. All he could give the headmaster was the number of attackers that had been there, and after also discussing their work situation, they left.

Both sides felt lighter after the meeting, as though an invisible weight had vanished from their chests. For the siblings, it was nice to not have to worry about their teachers having it out for them. The headmaster felt as though he had come within an inch of losing his life and had gotten a second chance. He was determined to beat some sense and discipline into his brother-in-law when he went home that night.

Zelda wiggled out of Zara's arms and onto her head when they were inside the lift.

"Yes, you did a good job finding that vent to spray the canisters from. Even if it did take you hours to carry them into position." Zara rolled her eyes and blindly patted the bear on top of her head.

"Yup, him approaching us like this was definitely because of what you did for sure, Zelda. Without this tipping him over, it would have taken him forever to admit he was in the wrong. During which time we would have had to keep putting up with crap from all the teachers... Maybe... Some of them, I'm sure, would have been scared off by Zara's new title. Either way, this for sure helped. So, thanks." He smiled gratefully at her.

The silly bear preened, running her paws down her dress. She tumbled unexpectedly off Zara's head when the lift shuddered to a stop at the bottom.

Zara caught her at the last moment and stuffed her close to her chest as the doors opened.

They walked back to their dorm while dissecting the short but interesting meeting. A lot had happened in a short amount of time.

"Are you going to let them all off if he actually punishes them?"

"You mean instead of challenging them all to duels?"

Zara nodded.

"I don't know, probably. I'm hoping it will give me time to train more than anything else. At the same time, while I dislike them and what they did, it's not to the same level as with Dorn."

She snorted and gripped Zelda tighter. "Speak for yourself. I'm the one who had to watch you collapse, not knowing how badly you were hurt!" Tears filled her eyes as she shouted at him, disturbing some birds that were resting in a nearby tree. "If anything had happened differently, I could have lost you. What would have happened then?

"Would anyone have even helped me get revenge for your death? Would I have died trying or do you think something worse could have happened to me? Make no mistake, I hate Spencer and whoever else was involved. Yes, we are doing better now, but we weren't then. Everything could have ended so easily because of their actions."

It was a scenario he had avoided thinking about, just as it was abundantly clear that she had not.

"You forget, Ben was watching in the shadows the entire time. Yes, I was hurt, but Tessa did say he would have stepped in if they had gone too far." He was making excuses, and they both knew it. "I don't know what to tell you, Zara." He finished softly, after struggling to find the right words and realizing they didn't exist.

"Tell me that we'll be alright. Tell me…" She began to sniffle and cry.

He held her close as they walked inside the dormitory building and to their apartment.

"We've already lost mom and dad. I can't lose you too." She whispered as the door closed behind them.

"You won't. Not now. We have the suits that you have strengthened with the crystal and your puppet magic. Plus, I can heal as long as I have a mana crystal on me, and I always have one on me now. We're stronger than we were a couple of weeks ago. I won't say we're indestructible, but we're tougher."

Zara rolled her eyes and hiccupped. "You're terrible at motivational speeches. You know that, right?" She reached for a tissue and blew her nose.

"Yeah, well, you mentioned mom and dad. It made my mind go blank. You haven't willingly mentioned them in years."

Zelda jumped down and went to go play while they talked.

Zara collapsed onto the couch with a nod. "I know, and I still don't want to quite yet. Consider it a momentary lapse in judgment. I've just been thinking about what the Oracle told us about where we are really from. The idea that we might have more family out there keeps popping up."

Zack laid down on the floor next to the couch, snagging a pillow on his way down. "I know. I've thought about it as well. All of that is in the future, far in the future, unless we get lucky."

From his place on the floor he could barely see the small sprouting seed they had planted in a pot on the table. It was the seed they had recovered from inside Zelda back in Fittrel. Not much had changed with whatever it was. The sole leaf on its tiny stem was still green, and it was still small. For all intents and purposes, it was growing like a normal plant. Which they had to admit, kind of annoyed them both.

Zelda toddled over a minute later with a figurine held in her paws, offering it to the girl on the couch.

"Is that the last of the small ones?"

The bear nodded.

"I think we still have awhile before class lets out if you want to give it a try."

Zara sat up and grabbed Zelda, looking at the object in her hands. "What is this one even made of?"

"Some springy substance, I think the seller mentioned it came from a tree of rubber, whatever that is."

So far, Zara had been unable to find any that she was able to modify with relative ease. Either she had gotten lucky with the suits and fabrics. Or, as was more likely the case, it was because that was the first item she had tried the spell on. She could still use her modification spell on them. The energy expenditure to do so and the difficulty, however, went up significantly.

It was no different this time, either. The small, slightly bouncy object fought against her attempts to modify it. Making it the hardest one to work with yet. At the end of the experiment, she had only managed to make its ears longer by a hair.

Zara was panting and sweating when she ended both spells to it. A frown marred her face as she picked up the small sculpture and looked at it closely.

"Nope, I am not working with this material again." She tossed it to Zelda and stood up. "I'm going to shower and change. "Why don't you get changed as well? I'm sure Tessa will be here soon."

The shower was still running when there was a knock on their door a few minutes later.

Zack opened it and sighed. "What's wrong?"

Tessa pushed him aside and closed the door behind her. "I swear I wasn't that easy to read when we first met."

"You still aren't, but after spending some time together, you have relaxed your mask around us some. That combined with a small amount of familiarity certainly helps at times."

"Oh, well, that's fine then." She spun around. "Mom's outside waiting. She stopped me on the way in."

"And?" He prompted. "Is she taking you home early, or did she want to join in the game?"

She chuckled at the thought. "Unfortunately, no. She's here to see if you wanted to watch the Major and his group take down those kidnappers you alerted her to."

It took him a moment to understand who she was referring to. "You mean Cooper and the other gang leaders? They are going to go rescue the travelers they kidnapped?"

She nodded. "That's what mom said."

"She got permission to take Zara along for something like that?" He asked in disbelief.

Tessa nodded with a half smile. "We'll be watching, not doing anything, and besides there will be loads of soldiers there. I can't imagine it was hard."

"Zara," He called out. "Hurry up!"

The shower shut off a moment later, and the door cracked open enough to let out a wave of steam.

"What's the rush?" Zara called back.

"Anna's here. They're going to take down Cooper and the others. She wanted to know if we wanted to go and watch it all go down."

"Yes, we want to watch!" Came the emphatic cry.

"Apparently we want to watch." He reported dryly.

"Are you sure? She didn't sound all that enthusiastic. Maybe I should just tell mom neither of you was interested?"

"Don't you dare!" Zara cried out slamming the door shut.

Chapter 26

A nna drove them all to a small military waystation outside the city. The trip had taken around a half an hour at her normal top driving speeds. Meaning they were already well away from the capital by that point.

Sergeant Grieves and the rest of his squad were waiting for them at the waystation when they arrived. He had just finished going over the plan when they stepped out of the vehicle.

"Each of you put on these uniforms and helmets. You are here to observe and learn, not to act. If you see something, let one of us know. If one of us is not nearby, then you do not go after it yourselves. Is that clear?"

"Yes, sir!" The three kids shouted. Off to the side, Anna had grabbed her own uniform from the vehicle and was waiting for them.

Zack slipped into a small locker room and quickly changed into the uniform, pulling it on over the Shouvain suit. Thankfully, they not only didn't know his size, but they also weren't designed to be worn tight, so the extra layer didn't cause any issues for him. He retrieved his clothes and stored them in the back of the Ricerca car, along with everyone else's.

Grieves piled them inside the troop transport as soon as they had all finished changing. Several lights turned on in the back as they trundled down the road a minute later. The thick canvas flaps had been secured beforehand, cutting the wind noise down to a dull roar.

"The Major and the rest of a platoon are waiting near the operation site. After monitoring them over the last few days, we have been able to establish a basic schedule. Their command structure is fractured and activities during the day happen at erratic times as a result. However, at this time, they are not making full use of the portal and working through the night.

"Each night that we surveilled them, they were all asleep before full dark. The reason being the portal they are using is deep in the mountains and the location is without any form of modern lighting or other such conveniences. Any mana crystal they used to power their lights, or heat their water, they have to provide themselves.

"Our goal is to rescue the kidnapped travelers while taking as many of the adults as possible alive. Do not put your lives at risk to do this! We want answers from them, but not at the cost of your lives. Is that understood?"

"Sir, yes, sir!" They all shouted exuberantly. The Major and Sergeant Grieves never put their soldier's lives at risk without a very good reason. It was why they were all so loyal to them. It was rare for commanders to care so much for their troops.

"You all already know the plan. Spend the rest of the trip getting into the right headspace. I want everyone ready to hike the remaining distance and be prepped for action once we arrive."

Anna and Grieves put their heads together and spent the trip poring over the plan and maps of the area. Tessa and the siblings did their best to talk for a little while, but their position by the back gate made it nearly impossible.

The wind and road noise that crept in around the edges of the flaps was terrible.

Eventually, the three simply closed their eyes and did their best to sleep while they could.

Zelda discreetly woke Zara a while later, as the transport began to carry them up an unmarked mountain road. The bear had been stuffed inside her uniform top, with only her head showing. She, in turn, nudged her brother awake, who then woke Tessa.

Grieves noticed they were awake and nodded in approval. "We have a short hike of two kilometers to the waiting area where we will meet up with the Major and the rest of the platoon. After that, we'll have another one-kilometer hike to the operation site. Let's do this as quickly as we can. It's currently almost dusk, and I don't want to alert anyone that we are on the mountain with lights."

There was a round of affirmative noises from the soldiers as they each began checking their equipment.

Zack and Zara, for their part, made sure their mana crystals were secured and hidden under their suits. Neither removed them outside of checking them each day, but it never hurt to be careful. Those were their lifelines if they got in trouble.

The brakes squealed and shuddered as they locked up, throwing everyone in the back forward.

Sergeant Grieves banged on the back of the cab and cursed at the driver. "What was that?"

"Sorry, sir, there's a tree in our way. We couldn't see it until after we came around the corner."

"How far are we from the drop-off point?"

"A little over a kilometer, sir."

Grieves pulled back. "I don't like this. The Major and everyone else should have made it through earlier without any issue. Everyone out, we're walking the rest of the way from here. Grab all of your equipment and keep your eyes open for any signs of an ambush."

He locked eyes with Anna. "Ma'am, what would you like to do with the kids?"

"Give Tessa and Zack each a Majair pistol, if you have any to spare. I know they both can handle them. As for Zara, give her some daggers, a belt of them if you have one." She finished with a smile. The woman knew Zelda would be fighting for her, and that the bear had a particular penchant for sharp pointy objects.

"Yes, ma'am." He found them the requested weapons and had each strap them on while he watched.

"Sir!" A soldier from outside called. The back flap was thrown open. "The tree was definitely cut down within the last couple of hours. There are wood shavings at its base, and they smell fresh."

A murderous look crossed over Anna's face as she strapped on her own weapons of choice. Two customized Majair pistols, one on each hip, and a pair of long curved blades that crossed behind her butt.

"Tessa dear, stay close to Zack and Zara. You two, keep her safe or else!" The unspoken threat was unneeded as they strapped on their helmets. She was their friend. Of course, they were going to keep her safe. "Sergeant, when we get back, I want to know how word of this operation got out. And I want to know if they are targeting us, or the Major."

"That's easy. They're targeting the Major," Zack spoke without thinking. He bit his tongue and turned away from them.

"Why do you say that?" She asked, curious as to his thought process.

He sighed and turned back to them. "It's simple. They let us get out of the carrier already. If they were targeting us, then they would have ambushed us before anyone ever got out and was ready for them. Heck, I would have thrown a bomb in the back when the back flap was first opened and gotten rid of ninety percent of us. I'm just a kid and I can think of that. Surely Sergeant Grieves and the others can as well."

"He's right. I wasn't going to say anything until I was sure, but it is likely that the Major is the target. Any resistance we meet on the way to him, and the rest of the platoon, will be a fragment of their main force."

Her finger tapped thoughtfully on the edge of the helmet she had yet to put on. "We had better hurry then. Sergeant, you know what to do, don't let me get in your way."

His face hardened. "We'll be setting a hard pace. Don't fall behind."

"Even if we do, keep going. I'll stay with them. We'll be able to take care of ourselves." She sighed and cracked her neck before strapping the helmet on. Her long red hair was already curled and tied together in a loop where it wouldn't get in the way. "I have no idea why I agreed to this. The Major must have been out of his mind! We both must have! This was supposed to have been a simple watch and babysit job. I should have known better. Nothing has been simple lately!" She muttered to herself while tightening the straps. "I even brought Tessa along, Mathew is not going to be happy about that when he finds out."

They climbed out, and after skirting around the fallen tree, immediately began hiking up the dirt road. The main group of soldiers kept their eyes on their surroundings, while two others would scour the trees on each side. The groups would exchange soldiers every couple of minutes in an effort to keep everyone's eyes as fresh as possible.

Despite their caution, the pace they set was fast, and it only took them a few minutes to cover the intervening kilometer and reach the formal drop-off point.

Everyone spread out and inspected the vehicles for traps before coming back together. Nothing appeared to be out of place. With one last look around the clearing, the group headed for the unofficial trailhead.

The trail was one created by the military platoon while they were surveilling the site.

No one but them knew it was there, just like no one should have known the dirt road was there either.

Grieves spread everyone out the same as before and started them up the trail with himself at the head.

"Wait!" Zack called out after they had been hiking for a bit. His sixth sense had just filled him with a sense of dread. The call went unheeded.

Anna and the kids were still in the rear position when the bomb went off.

It had been buried to the side of the path and then covered with the rocks and brush that littered the area. All it took was one soldier stepping on the wrong branch and it went off. The nearby explosion threw them into the air and against some nearby saplings. The short distance they had at the back, and the small nature of the bomb, were enough to save their lives.

Unfortunately, the same couldn't be said for the soldiers who had been closer.

A few had gotten lucky in that their armor had protected their vitals. The two closest to the explosion, however, looked more like shredded and charred hamburger than anything that had once been living.

Secondary fires from the explosion burned through the underbrush, creating a constant wave of heavy, dark smoke.

They were over a kilometer in by that point, past the halfway mark. There was no turning back for them. They would find help closer with the rest of the platoon and the Major, than they would by going back to the vehicles. Assuming they were alright.

The problem was, several of them could no longer walk, including Grieves, who had taken some shrapnel to the thigh. His plan of spreading everyone out had saved the bulk of the squad from any serious injuries. That didn't mean they weren't injured, simply that they weren't at risk of bleeding out soon.

Anna had truly begun to regret bringing her daughter with them. This was supposed to have been a simple operation, something without risk for the kids. A reward of sorts, where they would be able to see the good they had done by reporting Cooper and what they knew.

Now, she swore she would find out who was responsible for leaking their plans and make them pay. They had made this personal, and she always repaid personal favors of this nature in kind.

The few uninjured soldiers stood guard, while Zack, Tessa, and Zara began administering emergency first-aid. It was a basic skill that all travelers were taught. Zack and Zara had picked it up years ago, while Tessa depended more on the advice of the soldiers she helped.

It was something Quinn was teaching them during the last class of the day. Unfortunately, the academy's school year had only been in session for a couple of weeks. It took far longer than that to become proficient in the skill, and that was assuming it was the only thing he taught them during that time.

Anna scouted ahead while they helped to stabilize everyone. She carefully brushed the debris away from every spot she found. It made for slow progress, but she was able to uncover another two such bombs without setting them off. Both had been placed just off to the side of the trail, where any careless boot could step on them.

It made her wonder how many they might have unintentionally missed on the way up. Going back might prove just as dangerous as moving forward.

Turning around, she retreated, and let the injured sergeant make the call after informing him of what she had found.

Grieves looked over his squad, and the three kids helping the more experienced members. Then he stared at the two ruined corpses of men closest to the blast. Of the original fourteen members of his squad, just over half were still sufficiently mobile to continue onward. The rest would only slow them down.

He ignored the rage burning inside and forced himself to make the hard decision. "Anna, take seven of the squad and continue on toward the Major. Leave one to help us move off the trail and into the trees. Avoid the path going forward."

She nodded. "Don't worry, we'll be sticking to the trees ourselves. It'll be slower going, but it should be safer. They can't have placed bombs everywhere."

"What about the kids?"

She glanced back at them just as Zack dug a small branch from the meat of someone's leg. Another soldier was by his side with a pair of tweezers and some tape to close it up after they had finished.

Anna sighed and shook her head. "I know it's irresponsible, but I'll bring them with me. I need to be able to keep an eye on them, on my daughter. I won't feel at ease otherwise, even if it means bringing her to someplace potentially more dangerous. It's not as scary as the unknown."

"Have them take the two rifles, at least if they're still working. You might need them. Now, get going before the smoke gets worse." He ordered.

Anna inspected both of the Majair rifles on the bodies and found that only one of them was in working condition. She handed it to Zack and then gathered everyone together.

"I need one of you to stay behind and help take care of the wounded here. Which of you eight is the best at first-aid?" A mental debate occurred between the soldiers in that instant. They all wanted revenge, but taking care of their teammates was important as well.

A large, brawny man in the middle of the group raised his hand. "I probably am, ma'am. Our squad doesn't have a designated medic. We all just take care of ourselves. I tend to help out the most, though."

Anna took in his size and nodded. "Good, you'll stay and take care of them. Move everyone away from the path and into the trees as soon as they are stable. The rest of us, let's go. The Major could be in trouble." No one heard her muttered, "Let's hope not. What can eleven of us do that a platoon of soldiers can't?"

Zack quickly familiarized himself with the rifle, finding that it was mostly a larger version of the pistol in operation. The places where it differed were items that he didn't need to worry about at the moment. As long as he could fire the weapon, then he was fine.

In front of Zara, Tessa stretched her back with a slight grimace. Where he and his sister had been wearing their protective Shouvain suits, she had nothing but a uniform to protect her when they crashed into those saplings earlier. They hadn't been given armor of any kind since they weren't supposed to see any action.

Her bruised back and side were complaining about that decision now.

They ran and limped through the trees, barely keeping the path in view most of the time. Anna was taking no chances now. Despite that, the group's pace was faster than before. It needed to be if they were to make it to the waiting site before night fell. Dusk had fallen while they were recovering from the attack, and the remaining light of day was fading fast.

If they had one thing going for them, it was that they hadn't seen anyone else.

The sounds and cries of battle were the first clues that they had arrived.

Anna held up an arm, slowing them to a crawl.

"Get ready to let her out," Zack whispered to his sister.

It was not a smart decision, they both understood that. Revealing Zelda's presence to the Major would accelerate his plans for them. However, they owed the man a debt. Regardless of his reasons for rescuing them, he had rescued them. Now they had the opportunity to pay him back and wipe off some of the red from the scoreboard.

It wouldn't make them even, but it would help.

She opened up the top of her uniform and let the bear crawl out. Zelda waited patiently while Zara tightened the dagger belts they both now wore and then climbed onto her shoulder.

The group pressed closer to Anna as they crept the remaining distance. Each one of them crouched down as they began to hear shouts and other people in the forest ahead of them. The noises barely audible above the constant crack of firing Majair's.

"Are they on our side?" Tessa wondered softly. She was having a hard time seeing in the dark forest and was holding onto the soldier in front of her for balance.

The soldiers all made shushing noises, while one moved stealthily ahead to check the situation out for them.

Branches and twigs snapped in the darkness, while ahead of them people screamed and roared in pain. Distantly, they were able to hear the Major shouting out orders, his voice piercing through the whine of charging Majair's.

"It looks like they just started fighting somewhat recently, ma'am. If I had to guess, the noise we made set them off." The soldier informed them all quietly. "I wasn't able to get a good look in the clearing, where the Major is."

"What about the people in the trees near us?" She whispered back.

"Enemies. I don't recognize the uniforms they're wearing. However, I was able to ascertain that our people are for sure the ones inside the clearing."

"Good, I want everyone to work in groups of two. Assign yourselves to whoever you'll work best with and take out everyone you come across. Now go!" She hissed, dismissing them with the simple order. They were trained professionals and knew what to do better than she could direct them. "Zara, time to let Zelda loose. Then I want you to guide us around. We'll work together to get any they miss."

Chapter 27

Zelda jumped from her shoulders, drawing her small daggers as she fell.

"Okay, I guess I'll lead then. Zelda, tell me where to go." The young girl began feeding the bear and the two suit puppets more magic. It was a good thing that she had been able to get so much practice in lately over her energy control. It was about to become very useful if she didn't miss her guess.

Zack felt the suit tighten around him, each twitch he made amplified by the magical material. It was unfortunate it didn't help his eyesight. The only one who could maybe see was Zelda. If they had time and some spare goggles, Zara possibly could have done something about the situation. Both items were in short supply at the moment, and they had neither of them.

Anna hesitated for a moment before deciding to take up the rear. She had the most experience among them and could guard their rear flank the best. It was not the ideal position for her. Nothing about the night had been. Why should this be any different?

"Put your hand on my belt and keep it there," Zack told Tessa, while he did the same to Zara. It would be the only way they could stay together in the darkness.

If they got separated, it would be impossible to find each other until after everything ended. Hopefully, they would all still be fine if that was the case. It was better to just stay together and not risk it, if possible.

Zack set the Majair to charge so it would be ready when he needed it, and then tapped his sister on the side.

Ahead of them, Majair fired bullets crashed through the trees as the Major's people blindly fought back. The attackers were hidden among the dark trees and held the advantage in this fight.

The small group ducked down even further, as Zara sent Zelda out ahead.

Behind them, Anna forced Tessa to the ground with a grimace. Their place inside the trees was incredibly dangerous, and they could be hit by their own people or even discovered by the enemy.

Zack agreed wholeheartedly with Zara's decision. Depending on the stab-by bear was their best choice going forward. Without their ability to see, anything could happen to them.

"Interesting," He heard his sister mutter, shortly before there was a cry of pain from somewhere in front of them. There was another shout and then a scream that was abruptly cut short.

Zara hissed and sent more energy to Zelda. She was relieved to find that despite being grazed by a stray shot, Zelda was undamaged. Whatever the purple mana crystal had done to her before had made her incredibly durable. If anything, she was missing some fur, and that was it.

Zelda returned with her dagger's back in their sheathes and holding two pairs of bulky goggles.

She passed them off to Zara and Zack, before running off to find her next target.

"What are these?" He asked, unable to see them in the dark.

"I'm not sure what to call them, but the people attacking the Major's troops seem to be able to use them to see in the dark. From what Zelda says she saw, there aren't many people, but they all seem to have variations of tech like this. In the dark, it's enough to keep the Major on the defensive."

He pushed them against his eyes while listening to her. The darkness fled from his sight and was replaced with a black and white view of the surroundings. Everything was outlined perfectly, ensuring that he lost no depth perception. At least that was the case up close. He noticed that trees farther away lost their outlines and melted into a more image-like quality that had no depth to it.

That was probably another reason right there that the attackers hadn't managed to kill everyone already.

Looking at the pair his sister was holding, he saw a small button on the side of the goggles. He pushed the button on his pair, and everything went dark. He pushed it again to turn them back on.

"Hold on," He unstrapped and loosened his helmet. Removing it was not a necessity if he wanted to wear the goggles. It would just be hard, since he was unfamiliar with them. The bulky pack on the back of the goggle hit his helmet and slid under it to press against his neck. It might be uncomfortable, but it was better than nothing. He re-tightened the straps on his helmet and looked around again.

"These are incredible! How come I didn't see any of Grieves' squad carrying these things?" Zara had followed his example and put her pair on as well.

"I have no idea what you are talking about," Anna hissed in annoyance, frustratingly blind under the circumstances. "We don't have that kind of mana-tech. Our last efforts to develop something like that ended a few years ago in failure. The king and queen-"

"Quiet!" Zack raised his Majair as a group of soldiers crept into view. It was impossible to determine how far away they were, which made correcting his aim difficult, to say the least. "We have incoming. I'm not sure if they've seen us yet."

The soldiers swept through the area. Each of them was wearing a pair of goggles different from his and Zara's. They were less bulky, and judging by how the soldiers were searching the area, less effective as well.

Zack passed his pistol to Zara with one hand. "Can I have you and Tessa charge your Majair's and have them ready for me to use if something happens? Zara, can you pass your goggles to Anna as well?" He would need the extra help if the four soldiers came their way.

She got close to the older woman before taking them off and handing them to her.

"Someone is going to pay!" Anna snarled once she had the goggles strapped to her head. "I recognize this setup! It's our design. Whoever made these stole Albion's initial work to make them."

Her voice was too loud and alerted the soldiers to their presence. Their weapons snapped up and began charging as they spread out to search for the voices they had heard.

Zack pressed Zara and Tessa to the ground while mentally cursing Anna. She knew better than that, yet she was the first to make a mistake. It only went to prove that it could happen to anyone.

The sounds of battle continued to ring through the air as they waited. The soldiers came closer with each passing moment. The sight of them walking, but not getting any closer, was honestly rather creepy, in Zack's opinion.

Then one of them crossed over the invisible line and gained all the depth of a normal person. The sudden difference may have startled him, but that wasn't the case for Anna. She raised her modified Majair pistol, aimed, and fired, all in one smooth motion. There was no hesitation in her movements. She knew exactly what she was doing and why. She was protecting her daughter... along with Zack and Zara.

The loud crack of the bullet speeding through the air drew the other soldiers to them. The one Anna had shot dropped without a sound, a large hole where his chest used to be. A high-pitched whine immediately filled the air as her pistol charged for another shot. A second later, it had already finished and was ready for use.

Apparently, one of the modifications she had done to it was a fast charge setup. She would get fewer shots with each processed magi-crystal she used to power the process. However, in a fight where speed mattered, the energy waste could save her life. It was a trade-off she was clearly prepared to pay the money for.

Knowing they were entirely dependent on his ability to aim and shoot the enemy soldiers helped to calm Zack somewhat. He had killed yes, there was no denying that. That disgusting noble Dorn wasn't even his first. That dubious honor belonged to a researcher who had dared to touch Zara in front of him. They had been at the facility for maybe a month at that point, and the man had wanted to take a knife to her arm.

It was a move that publicly disregarded the agreement they had in place. Zack had put the scalpel through his eye, and that was the last time they touched Zara in front of him.

A second soldier sprang into focus, and Zack swiveled, bringing the rifle into position. He aimed and fired. The large Majair rifle bucked as it sent a burst of compressed air out of the muzzle, firing the bullet at supersonic speeds.

The bullet hit the shoulder of the man he was aiming for, nearly tearing his arm off. He screamed and fell to his knees. Anna fired a second time and a large hole appeared in his chest, silencing him forever.

"What are you firing? Why is it so different from the rifle?" He asked her, dropping the rifle and taking the charged pistol from Zara.

"Rifles fire bullets. They're great for when you need accuracy over any sort of distance. The pistols typically fire metal balls or slightly flattened slugs. They are far more destructive, but way less accurate. So, you can only use them at close range. My pistols use shaped slugs, still highly destructive as you saw but also a little more accurate as well. For now, I have to have them all specially made, but maybe someday they'll become the standard instead of the balls."

The remaining two enemy soldiers had begun to shout and panic at the second and third shots. Curses flew from their mouths as they realized that their numbers had been diminished without them ever seeing who did it. They met back up, not daring to separate again.

Zack got distracted as he noticed movement in a tree. As he watched, Zelda toddled out onto a tree branch with her daggers extended. At some point, she had added a few more daggers to her belt, increasing her weight slightly. She crouched and waited for them to pass beneath her branch. The two soldiers were both frantically studying the ground area and never bothered to look up once.

Above them, Zelda stepped off her branch and came down between the two. Her daggers flashed, digging into an arm on each side of her.

Seeing that they were otherwise occupied, Zack lowered his weapon and went to retrieve the goggles from the two they had already eliminated. The pairs they were wearing may not be as powerful as the initial ones Zelda had gotten, but that didn't mean they weren't useful. Anything that let them all see and stay together was valuable at the moment.

Zelda slid down between them, her blades slipping through the gaps in their armor. She went from ruined arms, skipping their protected thighs to jabbing in deep at the meat of their calf. Both men dropped like stones, their legs unable to hold them upright. A second later, she finished them and retrieved their goggles and daggers, adding them to her growing collection.

Zack glanced down at the pair of goggles in his hand and shrugged. He hadn't done a lot, but at least he had tried. No-one normal could compare with a magical bear. That was just silly to even think it was possible.

However, Zara was working with diminished stats since they were in Aperra. Her *'Second to Second'* title should have raised her regular magic stat, offsetting that particular weakness some.

It had for him, which meant that no one should be able to stand up to her, regardless.

Either way, the immediate danger had been taken care of, and now they needed to figure out what to do next.

Zack helped Zara put on the new goggles, while Anna helped Tessa with her own pair.

"What now?" He asked once they could all see. "Do we keep moving, or hang back and hope for the best?"

Zelda searched the bodies for any other goodies while they debated the two choices.

"I..." Anna was hesitant to continue putting them in danger. At the same time, there were people who needed their help.

"I'm fine with continuing on now that we can see," Tessa told her mother. "No matter what we decide, we need to stick together."

"She's right," Zara agreed. "Zelda says the Major needs all the help he can get, and in the stories separating is never a good idea."

"Do you think Zelda can lead us from group to group? If we concentrate on taking enough of them out, then we hopefully shouldn't need to worry about any sneaking up behind us." If his sister was fine with them staying to help, then he wasn't going to say otherwise.

Anna nodded. "That's mostly true, and it would certainly help to ease the pressure on both us and the Major."

Zelda looked up from her scrounging, slipping a small pocketknife onto her increasingly crowded belt.

"She's not a hound dog, Zack!" Zara protested.

He rolled his eyes behind the goggles. "I meant she'll go and scout out for the next group while we take care of the last people she found. That way, we can always stay on the move. Her small size and ability to move through the trees would make her ideal for the role."

"What do you think? Is that something you want to do?" Zara asked her treasured bear and friend.

Zelda spun a full circle with her paw against her chin and then nodded.

"Thanks, and don't worry, we'll make sure to save the best of the knives we find for you."

The bear raised her arms in a silent cheer.

Anna unconsciously reached for her, the desire to hold the cute bear almost too strong. The streaks of blood that would need to be washed from her did little to reduce the effect on the older woman.

Tessa smacked her hands down and shook her head.

Anna coughed and scratched at the scar on her cheek. "Well then, shall we get going? The sooner we get this over with, the sooner we can all be safe again."

"Well, Zelda, show us to the first group if you would, please?" Zack asked the bear politely.

Now that they could mostly see again, their lineup changed. Zack took the lead, charged pistol in hand and the rifle on his back. Zara and Tessa were behind him since they had the lighter, less effective goggles. Anna had the rear and kept her eyes open for any enemies behind them.

It was not the best formation, and they all knew that. Standard logic dictated that the most experienced person, in this case, Anna, take the lead. That worked fine against monsters and other beasts. When it came to humans and their tactics, it was another matter. They rarely attacked head-on if given the opportunity. Which meant guarding the rear could hold equal-or-more importance than the front.

Or at least that was the assumption they were working under.

In a perfect world, they would be the attackers and not the victims. Of course, in a perfect world, they would be rescuing the kidnapped teens right now, not stuck in the forest fighting an unknown enemy.

Zack slowed as ahead of them, Zelda jumped onto a tree and began climbing it with the use of her daggers.

"She says that a group of soldiers found the bodies she left there. The uniforms look like those we're wearing. She's just making sure for us." Zara told them quietly, as they hunkered down and listened to the screams of pained and dying people.

The bear returned a minute later, leaping through the air to land beside them. Her blades were tucked safely away, and within moments, she was safely ensconced in Zara's arms.

"Zelda says that they are the Major's soldiers who managed to sneak up after the enemies in this area stopped firing. I'm guessing that was caused by her and the soldiers that came with us, eliminating enough of them."

"Were they wearing any of these night vision goggles?" Anna asked her.

Zara shook her head.

"It could be dangerous to approach them then. Any light they are using to examine the bodies must be extremely focused, so it doesn't leak out and give away their position. If we just approach them recklessly, they might just shoot us and ask questions later." Anna carefully explained the situation to them, making sure they understood.

They had taken two extra pairs of the goggles from the bodies earlier they could give the soldiers. Not to mention the bodies they were currently examining also likely had some. It was simply a matter of whether they dared to take them off and try them out. Hopefully, it would be enough, because she was not letting any of the ones they were wearing go.

"Can you just call out to them if we get close enough?" Zack asked, going for the simplest solution he could think of.

She rubbed her scar thoughtfully. The tip of her nail dragged across the old, slightly recessed groove. "It's simple, but it might just work. I'll want everyone pressed against the ground regardless, when I call out to them, just in case. Are we clear?"

Each of them nodded.

With that decided, Zelda wiggled out of Zara's arms and onto the ground to lead them. Not that it was a long journey. They had already been close when she climbed the tree. Even at their slow pace, it was a matter of walking for another minute before Zack could see them.

Shortly after that, they decided they were close enough to call out to them. Zelda rejoined Zara, and everyone but Anna hugged the ground. She moved behind a nearby tree and called out to them.

"Are you soldiers with the Major and Albion or the enemy?"

Surprisingly, her question didn't result in them shooting wildly into the dark. Or at least, it was surprising to the kids.

The soldiers immediately crouched and brought their weapons to the ready. Their eyes were narrowed as though they alone could pierce through the pitch darkness of the forest.

"Show yourself!" One of them barked.

"Not until you answer the question," Anna demanded.

"We're under the Major and Albion."

"Is the Major alright?" She probed.

"He was still standing when we were told to come and check this area."

The back and forth continued until they were both satisfied that the other party was on the level.

"Do you see those goggles the enemy are all wearing? Take them off the bodies and put them on. They're a form of limited night vision. We have a couple of extra pairs you can have. I warn you not to try anything. You won't live to regret it if you do." Anna trained both her charged pistols on them just in case.

It never hurt to be cautious.

Chapter 28

Three of the soldiers got their hands on night vision goggles, while the other two were left wanting. That was fine. Like she had told them, they had two extras. There was enough for everyone to have a pair.

"This isn't Albion magitech, the Major would have told us if we had something like this." The first soldier to try them on growled.

"You're partly right. They're based on an abandoned project of ours, but the finished project is indeed not ours. Someone stole the information from us and then finished it." Anna was still enraged at the idea.

She slowly stepped out from behind the tree, weapons at the ready.

The three soldiers who could see snapped to attention. "Ma'am, we apologize for not recognizing your voice earlier. If we had realized we were talking to the crown's advisor, we would have been more polite."

"Ex-advisor, I stepped away from the role. Don't forget." She corrected them, lowering the pistols. "I came up here with Sergeant Grieves and his squad. Unfortunately, the path was lined with explosives around the halfway mark. The group I brought the rest of the way are working to eliminate any enemy they find in the woods."

The soldiers relaxed. "That sounds like an excellent idea, ma'am, and one that will be made easier now that we can see."

"Don't forget, they can see as well. The only thing we have going for us is that they don't seem to be expecting us to come from behind." Anna motioned for the kids to stand. "Here are the other goggles I mentioned."

Zack walked them over and then retreated without saying anything to them.

They accepted them with a nod and helped the last two members of their team put them on.

"We'll be heading out to search for more of the enemy, ma'am. Your group has the right of it in this situation. We are the best chance of ending this as quickly as possible." They saluted and disappeared into the trees.

"They're not wrong," Anna muttered, watching them vanish.

"What do we do now?" Tessa wondered. "We'll just get in their way if we go in that direction, and Grieves' soldiers went the other way."

Zack looked around before choosing a tree to put his back against and sitting down. "Let's stay out of the way, then. We're not trained for this kind of operation. While it might sound like a cop-out, I'm glad to be away from it. This isn't like inside the portals, where I have superhuman powers. Here, I'm just an untrained kid, who can die in an instant like anyone else. I don't have the courage to put myself in danger like those soldiers if I don't need to."

Zara nodded. It was better to let the professionals handle something of this magnitude. The odds of them getting in the way and making everything worse were greater than them actually helping. They had given those soldiers the night vision goggles, which put them on an even playing field with the enemy. Having to worry about untrained kids as well would only hinder their efforts.

Anna put away one of her pistols and agreed with a nod. "He's right. Now that there is another option, I'm not willing to keep risking all of your lives for this." She chose a tree across from Zack where she could see everything he couldn't. Between the two of them, they could see enough of the forest to spot anyone trying to approach.

"I know that. It just feels wrong to do nothing." Tessa sat beside Zara and promptly began playing with her and Zelda.

Zack listened to the crack of projectiles going supersonic, and the distant bark of orders and cries of pain. Something was bothering him about this entire night. They were here to rescue a bunch of kidnapped traveler teens. Why would anyone with this kind of magitech get involved in the mess?

It made no sense. What made Cooper and the gang leaders worth all this trouble? Had they discovered something, or were they part of some experiment?

"Something is wrong about all of this," He finally spoke up, unable to hold in his thoughts any longer. "I know why we're here. But why are they here? Is it really to take out the Major, or does it have to do with whatever Cooper and the others are doing up there? It makes no sense to me!"

The girls looked up, interested in what Anna would say.

"I've been wondering that myself, and make no mistake, whatever the reason is, it's related to those kidnapped travelers. That's the only reason we are here in the first place. How strong the connection between the two is, I can't say just yet, but there is one, to be sure."

"Who do you think is behind the attack and this tech, then?" Zara was curious as to who could have stolen them from Albion.

Anna was slow to respond. "I suspect Shouvain." Was her eventual answer. "After their attack on the airship, and suspected involvement in the research institute, I wouldn't put this past them. Stealing classified project information to then claim as their own certainly seems like something they might do.

"I will admit that they did a good job finishing the project and moving past the hurdles we had with it. However, they still stole it from us, and I will find out how and who facilitated the betrayal."

"Why steal the airship, though? That seems rather high profile compared to how they did the night vision goggles. Which was apparently so quiet you didn't even know it had happened until now. Everyone knows that Fittrel made the airship. Even if Shouvain steals it, they can't pass it off as their own tech." Tessa mused aloud, tossing a small stick to the side.

"It doesn't matter. The airship is just that valuable! If Shouvain was able to make their own version and was willing to sell it where Fittrel isn't... They would win. As for why they didn't go after the plans, my guess is they tried but had no luck. Going after the ship was their last effort until Fittrel starts to actively sell them.

"Of course, now that they know Shouvain is willing to steal one, I doubt they'll sell one to them anytime soon, if at all. Orlo told them to prepare for war, and that is exactly what they are going to do. Selling any of those would go against their own interests until after everything, including the coming Change, has been settled. Albion will be lucky to get one of our own before then, and only then, because we are the ones who warned them."

"If it is Shouvain, then I, for one, would love to know what their interest in keeping the Major from rescuing those teens is." Zack cursed as soon as his brain caught up with his mouth. "Anna, they knew we were coming, right?"

She nodded at the obvious question.

"So, they're not going to just keep everybody at the portal like good little idiots. They're either going to kill them all or stuff them into a troop carrier and haul them away to another location. Probably while we're all busy trying not to die here."

"Ahh," She mouthed, understanding where he was going with this. She cursed under her breath in agreement with his unspoken thoughts. "I thought you said you don't have the courage to put yourself in danger."

He stood, brushing off the leaves and other detritus from his butt and back. "I said when it wasn't needed. If we're right, then it's needed."

Zara and Tessa nodded wholeheartedly, agreeing with the sentiment.

"Quick question. Do we know how to get there from here? Preferably without running into enemy soldiers constantly, as that would slow us down." Zara picked up Zelda and brushed her off.

"I should be able to get us to the road they made. We blocked off the entrance from the main road earlier today, but didn't want to use it and risk alerting them." She laughed dryly. "What a wasted effort this has turned out to be. Going through the woods means that we'll likely run into enemies and friendly soldiers alike, unfortunately. It's been long enough already that any further delays could make us miss them entirely."

"We'll have to run the entire kilometer." That's what they had mentioned before was the distance between the waiting area and the site of the operation.

Anna checked her pistols over and then slid them into their holsters. "That's the distance for a straight run. We're going to the road and then up, so it will probably be closer to a kilometer and a half. Keep your pistol holstered and the rifle at the ready, just in case."

Zack glanced at its charged state and then at hers, which were in a similar condition. "Is it safe to leave them like this?"

"It's a weapon. Of course it's not safe." She answered with a snort of derision. "But we need them at the ready in case we run into the enemy. Nothing will touch the trigger while it's in the holster, so they *should* be safe. It'll be safer than the old gunpowder-based ones, in any case. The rifle you'll be carrying in your arms will be the bigger danger."

Somehow, that wasn't making him feel better. His definition of safe, and hers, could be wildly different. Not that it mattered. This was something that needed to be done. Everyone else was busy fighting for their lives. It was a battle where all of them, but Anna would only get in the way.

Their entire purpose of coming out to the backend of nowhere that night was to rescue those kidnapped teens. It didn't matter that they weren't originally meant to get involved. They had brought this mess to Anna's initial attention. Now it was time to follow through.

"Zelda can act as our scout again as long as she knows the direction we're heading. I'll have her stay fairly close, maybe just outside the range of your night vision goggles." Zara volunteered, anxious for them to get moving.

She hadn't particularly cared about those kidnapped teens before this. Now that there might be a connection to the institute, however, everything had changed. It was personal.

Tessa cracked her neck and holstered the pistol. "Come on, we're wasting time they might not have." She was trying to act tough, but the tremor in her voice at the end gave her away.

"She's right." Zack shook his head, wondering why he was suddenly worrying about such unimportant details. "I guess I'll be taking the spot at the back?"

"Keep your eyes open and stay close. I would prefer it if we all stayed bunched up just in case something does happen." Anna instructed them. "Now, Zelda, if you would? I believe we are going... That way." She had to take a moment to orient herself, using the sound of screams and weapon fire as her main plotting points.

The bear jumped from Zara's arms and took off.

"I'll warn you if she sees anything." The girl informed Tessa's mother.

She nodded, and they settled into an initial light jog, avoiding branches and fallen logs as they ran. Their pace continued to pick up as they left the battle behind them. They only needed to slow once, while Zelda took care of a pair of enemy scouts and retrieved their goggles. After that, they didn't run into anyone else.

Calling it a road instead of a glorified multi-kilometer driveway was being generous. It was a washboard and pit-ridden mess that would have destroyed any vehicle that tried to drive over it at anything faster than a crawl.

At least that was the case when the military had last inspected it hours before the operation was set to begin. Now it was in the process of being freshly graded and made smooth so they could escape.

A retrofitted tractor with a grading blade attachment was slowly making its way to the main road.

Anna grabbed the rifle from Zack and ran after it. She needed to get close enough before the goggles would put the tractor into focus. She dropped to a knee, brought the stock of the rifle up to her shoulder, aimed and fired.

There was the crack of displaced air, and then the tractor sagged as a rear-wheel burst. Without delaying, she charged another shot, watching as the driver pushed the tractor to keep moving.

The wheel she had shot began to shred and was little more than ribbons before the slow-charging rifle was done. It was an older model, which she thought was odd. They could afford to give their people night vision goggles, but not the newer fast charging rifles? What a thing to skimp on.

Anna retreated to the kids and handed the rifle back to Zack. "Come on, let's head up. If they're still making the road passable, then they haven't left yet."

They made good time running up the cleared road and within minutes had reached their destination.

After confirming that there was no one outside, Zelda set about slashing a tire on each of the vehicles there while they had a quick breather.

"I thought you said the entrance had been blocked?" Zack hissed when they saw the four large, modified Hilden vehicles. Hilden was a popular work carriage brand around the construction scene. They were cheaper than either Vortex or Alberitas and had fit themselves neatly into the demanding profession. Everything they made tended to be over-engineered so it wouldn't easily break.

"Well, obviously it's not anymore!" Anna hissed back. Nothing about this night had gone right so far. Why would she expect the military's blockade to have worked?

A door opened on the wooden deck above them, and someone stepped out with a flashlight. "How long are we going to wait for that idiot to finish with the driveway? We could have just crawled our way back to the main road by now and been out of here."

"Would you SHUT UP ALREADY! You know some of that weird equipment we're transporting back with the kids is sensitive and can't be shaken too much. If you want to carry them by hand, then get walking already."

The man above them grumbled under his breath and flicked off the light.

"How are we going to do this, mom?" Tessa whispered after he had gone back inside.

"Hold on," She investigated the back of each vehicle, finding carefully packaged bundles already placed inside each of them. She hoped they would be able to retrieve them later. For now, their goal was still rescuing the kids. "Okay, first thing. We need to lock each of these vehicles. I want that equipment, on the off chance it is something we don't have yet.

"After that, we need to find a way to sneak in. The kids were always kept in an adjacent building, right next to where we believed the portal is. I doubt they would still be there now when they are planning to move them. So, let's keep our focus on this one building for the moment."

"Do we go in the front, back, or through a window, then?" Zara was looking at a set of fresh graves off to the side that Zelda had spotted.

"Back would probably be easiest, whereas going through the front would give us a decent shock factor that would help." Anna was deep in thought and mostly talking to herself by this point. "They can hear the battle from here, so they obviously know there is the possibility soldiers might be around.

"Then again, the man from before had the mannerisms of a gangster. He might not be able to use his mind properly. Which means they could be complacent... Ugh, I need more information. This is all just guesswork for now."

Anna shook her head and faced the three teens. "Has Zelda finished locking the vehicles?"

Zara nodded. "She even stuffed dirt into each of the holes so they can't unlock them."

"Good girl, I was just looking to delay them some more, but that works even better. Now let's make our way around the side. Look for anything that we can use to get inside, a window, or vent that Zelda would fit in."

A direct confrontation was not what she wanted. The goal was to rescue the kidnapped travelers, not get them killed. Zara wasn't the only one who had noticed the graves.

The location of the house was somewhat deep in the mountains and surrounded by forest, as Grieves said. For all that, though, it was well built and had been there for some time. This was once someone's private residence. Judging from the general state of disrepair, however, it had been some time since the original owner had been there.

It was yet another case of someone hiding the location of a portal and keeping it for themselves. Anna hoped they had died inside it for their folly.

The group carefully walked around the side of the house. Each kept their goggles trained on their surroundings, not letting their guards drop in the slightest.

The lower windows had all been boarded over from the inside, and there were no vents, either. After making a full circle of the house, they had confirmed that the front and back doors were their only viable entry points. All the windows they saw were either out of reach or boarded over.

They had even taken a quick stop while they were in the back to look inside the other building where the kids were kept. Just as they had feared, there was no one inside it. They were keeping them close at hand for the quick getaway. Spread throughout the perimeter hidden in the trees were a series of smaller cabins where everyone else involved in the operation had slept.

"Do you hear something?" Tessa asked as they were about to decide between the two door options.

Everyone looked at her and then cocked their heads, searching for whatever she was hearing.

The tractor driver was blindly stumbling his way up the road towards the house, cursing the entire way.

"Front door it is," Anna decided on the spot. "As soon as they let him inside the door, we all crowd in and take them down. Use knives if you can. The noise from the pistols will damage your hearing otherwise, if you fire them inside. Besides, with their power, they'd go right through the target and into whoever is behind them. Just be careful if you have to fire them."

They crept onto the deck and then hid on the far side away from the stairs and the door. It was a terrible hiding spot, but it was better than coming up the stairs behind the driver. They would just have to risk the gangsters being oblivious to them in the dark.

Chapter 29

The driver stomped up the wooden stairs, cursing up a storm. All the while blaming everything from the maker of the tire to the road itself. With everything else going on, he hadn't noticed the extra close shot Anna had fired at it.

Heavy moisture-laden clouds covered the moon and stars as a late autumn storm rolled in. A cold wind blew, whistling through the trees in a mournful howl that mixed with the distant thunder of weapon fire.

The man took a moment to shiver and steel his nerves and then pounded on the door. He was so preoccupied with what he was about to tell them that he never even looked around the dark deck area.

"It's me, open up!"

"Did you finish smoothing it out finally?" The same man from before asked as he yanked the door open. "Get the kids. We're leaving!"

"Not so fast!" The driver shouted, pushing him back. "One of the tires on the tractor shredded not far from here. I couldn't even make a full pass and it's blocking the road. I'll need some help just to move it so we can get the vehicles past it."

"Son of-" There was the sound of a fist hitting flesh, and the driver stumbled back out onto the deck.

"What was that for? I told you I didn't know how to operate it and to choose one of the other guys!" He was screaming in indignation by that point, with the veins of his neck showing in sharp relief.

"Would you both shut up?" A third man hissed. Shoving the one who had punched the driver out the door.

Anna held her long curved blades at the ready, her entire body coiled and ready to spring. Beside her, Zara held Zelda in the ready-to-throw position, aimed at the door.

"Now you said the tire is shredded, right?"

The driver nodded.

"That means we'll need to use the Hilden's to move it out of the way then. Even with all of us together, we wouldn't be able to move that thing without a functioning tire on it." One of the gang leaders they had seen Cooper eating with before stepped into view. On cue, Zara threw Zelda at him.

He managed to look up in time to receive the bear's dagger to his eye and fall back into the house., taking his scream with him. Anna and Tessa burst from their hiding place, weapons at the ready. It was a side of the girl they had never seen before but had always suspected was there. She was Anna's daughter after all, it only made sense for her to have some bloodthirsty skills.

Anna swung her blade at the driver in passing, her curved dagger nearly disemboweling him in one blow. She left him to her daughter to finish off and moved on to the other man.

Behind them, Zack and Zara watched with opened mouths as the mother-daughter duo dismantled the two men together. The siblings were strong inside the portals, with Zara being somewhat strong inside the normal world now as well. Anna and Tessa, however, were what they had always wished to be. They were powerful in both realms.

Their fighting styles were similar, yet wildly different in their aims. Every move Anna made was oriented towards maximum pain and debilitating damage. In comparison, Tessa's strikes with her borrowed blade from Zara's belt were purely aimed at killing the man. The mother was showing her rage, while the daughter was still unspoiled by the ways of the world.

Zack missed his more familiar staff as they waded into the fray. He could use a knife as well as the next untrained person, but he was by no means skilled in their handling.

The siblings chose to ignore the people on the deck and went straight for those inside the house. They didn't have an accurate number of kidnappers that were supposed to be there, but they could easily guess it was more than three.

The doorway had turned into a slippery mess in the few seconds Zelda had taken to go about her grisly work. After stabbing the man in the eye, she had sliced the carotid artery in his neck. Her proficiency was already far above that of Anna and Tessa.

Zack handed Zara back her knife. Her belt had only come with two and grabbed the large hunting knife from the corpse. He even took a moment to retrieve the sheathe that went with it. Since he was untrained in the particulars of their use, one knife was as good as another to him. It was more important that Zara had something to protect herself with.

They were joined by the mother and daughter a moment later. Anna was completely calm. Tessa, on the other hand, was breathing rapidly and beginning to shake. Zack was pretty sure it was her first time killing someone. She had merely reacted to whatever training her mother had put her through. Now she had to deal with the consequences of what she had just done.

"Don't think about it, not yet. Wait until we've rescued everyone. Only think about it then, after you've witnessed what they have done." Her mother whispered to her, pulling the girl in tight. "I know this is hard, but push it to the side. These were bad men who have done some very bad things."

Tessa sniffed and lifted her goggles up to wipe her eyes. "I know. I just reacted; I didn't even think. My training took over and then it was... over."

"That's good. Hesitating will get you killed. That's why I trained you so hard, so the training would take over in times like this." Anna remarked, lowering the goggles.

"No one else is coming," Zack pointed out, seeing that they were done with their conversation.

The brief fight hadn't been exactly quiet. Zelda's fellow alone had created quite the racket on the way down, along with a loud scream. Yet no one else had come running to confront them.

His sixth sense was screaming at him that something was wrong. Knowing that did him no good at the moment. It could mean anything from there was a trap, to everyone was already dead. The sense didn't always work, but when it did, he listened to it.

"Something's wrong," He stepped back uncertainly. "My sixth sense is screaming at me right now."

Anna frowned in thought and looked at the closed door to the rest of the house. "Pile the bodies in front of that door, and then let's go around to the back." She whispered.

The door opened away from the corpses. They wouldn't block the door from opening, only delay whoever might come after them.

As quietly as they could, they moved them into place and then ran around to the back of the house.

Zack sighed in relief as his feeling of dread began to ease. "It's still there, but not as bad. They definitely know we're here and are prepared for us."

"Well, let's not keep them waiting then. They might start going after the kids if we take too long." Anna drew both of her curved knives and gave them a quick, satisfying twirl.

Zack checked the door and found it locked, the same as before. He placed the rifle on the side and cracked his neck. Stepping back, he lowered his head and gave Zara the signal to go ahead. The suit tightened around him as her energy flooded into it. The fibers stiffened around his chest and back in preparation for what he was about to do.

This time, she was leaving control up to him. She was enhancing the suit, but not taking control. The last time she had done that, it had messed up his shoulder. They couldn't afford to have his legs out of commission right then.

He shot forward with supernatural strength and crashed through the door. The wooden obstruction was blown off its hinges and smashed into the wall opposite him. Zack took a quick glance around the empty room and sped into the next. He wanted to make the most of the enhanced strength and speed while it lasted. Zara wouldn't be able to keep it up for long.

The room was filled with armed goons waiting for them to burst through the far door. It was the one they had stacked the bodies in front of. Unlike his group, which had restrained themselves to knives, each of them was wielding a charged knockoff Majair pistol.

He bowled into them, the hardened suit layer on his back and chest helping to dissipate the force. Bones snapped under the impact as grown men were thrown into each other at crushing speeds. Fingers unconsciously tightened on triggers, and the room was instantly turned into a charnel house.

Destructive balls, meant for maximum destruction and little more, did exactly as they were designed to do. The room seemed to explode all at once as the balls went every which way but down.

Zack was no exception and took one to the hardened front section of his suit. It blasted him back out of the room and straight through the wall behind him. The wall ripped the unsecured goggles from his head, snapping them from off his neck beneath the helmet, and sent him tumbling out into the night beyond.

Zara screamed and ran over to him, feeling her energy drain to a dangerous degree. Before being reinforced by the purple crystal and her magic, that close of a shot would have killed him. It might not have made it through the suit, she wasn't sure. They hadn't really tested how everything performed with and without the various enhancements.

What she did know, is that the focused point of impact would have destroyed his body. The unenhanced suit could only dissipate so much force before it too failed. Even if the ball failed to make it through the suit, he still would have been dead.

Zack coughed, struggling to find air while his ribs protested the sudden abuse. He didn't think any of them were broken, a nice change of pace in his opinion. The impact had spread across his entire chest. So, while everything was sore, and he would have the mother of all bruises soon. He would also live.

Assuming he could get some oxygen into his lungs soon.

He rolled onto his side and felt soundlessly at his throat. His mouth flapping about like a dying fish, while his ears rang with their own muffled symphony.

Zara slid to his side, glad to see he was alive, yet unsure of what to do next. This was something she had never seen before. Bleeding wounds she could handle, they had experience with them. This was new. What did someone do when the person they were taking care of couldn't breathe?

"What do I do?" She screamed at Anna and Tessa.

Tessa arrived first and rolled Zack onto his back again. She pinched his nose shut and sealed her lips to his, breathing gently into his mouth. The single-time was all his lungs needed to jumpstart themselves and recover from impact shock.

He inhaled deeply and coughed again. His bruised chest did not like the excessive movement one bit. It took his lungs a minute to calm down and before he could talk to them. "Thanks for that. They were all bunched up together behind the door inside." He coughed again, and groaned as his chest ached.

"If we had gone through it, they would have mowed us down and not cared about the damage to themselves. When I came in behind them, I hit them at full speed." He laughed weakly, remembering the sight. "They all pulled their triggers at the same time. It's a mess in there, and I doubt any of them survived."

Anna nodded. "You two stay out here with Zelda. Tessa and I'll go inside and finish this." She handed him one of the extra pairs of goggles, that Zelda had retrieved on their way over. It wasn't as good as his original pair, but it was better than being blind.

"Be careful, there may be more guarding the travelers still," He couldn't help but remind them.

"Who do you think you're talking to? Of course, we're going to be careful. You just lay there like a lump until we get back." Tessa waved and then followed after her mother.

Zack felt the ringing in his ears dim as his healing went to work on them and his chest. Previously, it had been focused solely on getting his lungs back into operation. Now that they were working again, it could focus on other things. Not that the mana crystal he was using was giving him enough mana for extensive healing.

It was going to be a slow process, just like always. Regardless, it was better than being laid out for weeks or even months like a normal person.

"I thought..." Zara grabbed Zelda and pulled her onto her lap, putting her chin on the blood-encrusted bear's head. "I don't know, it was scary. I felt the impacts and how much they drained my energy. Then you couldn't breathe..." She fell silent as a cold drop of rain hit the top of her helmet. "It was close Zack. Even with the suit, that crystal reinforcing it, and me reinforcing it again, it was close."

"There have been a few of those lately." He stared up at the dark sky, not having bothered to put on the replacement pair of goggles yet. He groaned and blinked as a drop of rain nearly hit him in the eye. "That's cold. Can you help me get these goggles on?"

They got them into place just as the clouds fully opened up and began to dump their frigid contents on them.

"I don't think we're going anywhere tonight," Zara remarked, as Zelda wiggled off her lap and began to slip and slide on the wet grass. "Not with that tractor in the way, and with it raining like this. Anything that tried to move it would simply get stuck."

"No, I don't think we will be either." The temperature continued to drop as the mountainous rain poured down. "Come on, help me inside."

Zack bit back a groan as he stood with her help. His entire body felt like it had just been thrown through the side of a house. Either that, or he was already approaching middle age. Every step sent a shock wave up his sore muscles, while each breath pushed against his bruised ribs.

Tessa met them just inside, obviously on her way out to get them. "Where's Zelda?" She asked, noticing the absence of the little bear. The rifle Zack had left beside the door was slung over her shoulder, where she could reach it if needed.

"She's keeping an eye out for intruders while playing in the rain and hopefully getting somewhat clean." Zara looked back outside, no longer able to see her with the limited range of the goggles. She could feel and hear her through the connection of her magic, and that was enough for now.

"Did you find the travelers?"

She stilled and slowly nodded. "These people were animals! They were starving them, forcing them to go inside a portal without supervision and no healing. They're not in a good state. It's amazing there are as many of them left for us to rescue as it is. I just hope the reason for that isn't because they too turned into animals. If they resorted to sacrificing each other while in there..." She didn't bother finishing her sentence.

They agreed with her, but neither held any hope of learning the truth either. People who did something like that together wouldn't turn on each other, and any weak links would have already been eliminated. They could only hope they were overthinking everything and then move on.

"How many of the kidnappers did you find still alive?"

"Upstairs? There were a couple that were still in the midst of bleeding out when we arrived. You weren't joking when you said it was a mess. Downstairs, however, there were only three people left to guard everyone. They had left them chained together in groups of four, one for each of the Hilden's."

"Was one of the guards, Cooper?" Zack couldn't remember seeing the man earlier. Admittedly, he hadn't gotten a good look at anyone before getting launched back out of the room.

She shrugged and shivered. "It's getting cold up here. Mom is still down there if you want to look. We just disabled them, but left them alive for questioning."

Zack took a moment to retrieve his original goggles from the floor as they walked past them. He was lucky the wall hadn't ripped his head off along with them. As it was, he didn't think the goggles would be working anytime soon.

Zara held onto his uniform as they clomped down the stairs into the increasingly chilly basement. Their wet boots squelched with every step, while their uniforms swished irritatingly with every step.

Anna was standing over three begging forms, two women and a thin but still recognizable Cooper. One of her curved blades had been stored, while the other glinted dangerously in her hand.

"Cooper," Zara hissed, recognizing the man at the same time as her brother.

He looked up at the new voice, despite being unable to see them in the dark. "Who's there? Why do you know me?"

"We're here because of you. You wanted to invite me here, didn't you?" Zack couldn't help enjoying the small amount of theatrics.

"I don't know what you mean-"

"Of course you do. You came to our apartment a while ago to try to make me join your little gang. Too bad you couldn't even make it through the front door."

A look of confusion bled away to dawning realization and then anger as Cooper began to understand what had happened. "This is your fault! All of this is because of you!"

"No, it's because of you! You came after me, which put you on my radar. If you hadn't done that, I never would have known that you took over the gang. Which means that I never would have found it odd to see you eating at a restaurant in the capital. If you want to blame someone, then blame yourself. I guarantee that whoever put all of this together is going to. We'll make sure of that!"

Understanding horror flickered into being in his eyes. He knew what Zack said was true. He would get blamed for this fiasco. His only escape was death, or with them. If he was ever captured by the people who had funded this operation... Death would look like an escape.

"What do you want?"

Anna nodded appreciatively at him. That had been most effective.

Chapter 30

Zack walked to the first of the shivering teens and began inspecting him. He was looking for any signs that they might have been experimented on.

The boy pulled back. "Who's there? What do you want?"

"Calm down. I'm just looking to see if they did anything besides not feeding you."

Predictably, the teenager did not calm down. "You could just ask." He snapped hostilely.

"I could, however, would you answer honestly? Even if you did, how would I know if you had?"

"Just ask your questions and get back, would you? It's cold enough down here, without you standing near me like this."

Zack glanced down at his sopping uniform and took a step back. With his suit on, the only parts of himself that were even a little cold were his hands and parts of his head. Everything else was perfectly warm. It made it easy to forget how the wet clothes would affect the already cold captives.

"Is that better?"

"A little more, please." His teeth had started to chatter lightly.

Zack took another couple of steps back. "My first question is simple. Were they experimenting on you?"

A few of the closest teens who could hear them nodded.

"They injected us with something every time we'd go into the portal. Does that count?"

"It does. Is that all they did, nothing else?"

The boy hesitated for a long moment before replying. "Nothing else to any of us still standing. Every once in a while, some doctors would come up here though. Whenever they did, they would take whoever had been here the longest, and we would never hear from them again. A fresh grave would appear a couple of days later."

He had so many questions, but had to push them back against the rising fury. "Did the injections do anything to you that you noticed?"

"In the beginning, no, they never did anything. Near the end, though, I started to notice that the experience I got from battles increased some for a couple of hours afterward. It was like my compatibility rating with the portals was artificially changed or something."

Tessa's head snapped to attention, her entire body going taut. "Say that again." She enunciated each word carefully and to the fullest extent possible.

Zack remembered the research her father was conducting. "Your mother would know if he was involved. This just means that they found some way to steal his research."

"I have no idea what you all are talking about, but their stuff isn't perfect yet. As I was saying, it increases my experience gains for a couple of hours after the injection, however, right after that, it reverses the process. My experience dips below normal to compensate. Still, it works great on the miners. They get a few hours of better experience, then when it wears off, they go to work on the crystals."

Tessa crossed her arms. "I don't think that is how dad's version works. He's never mentioned his version as being temporary before, but maybe it is. I just don't know." She growled softly and gradually unclenched her teeth.

"One last question. What were they having you do inside the portal?"

The boy snorted with dead eyes. "Do? It was all we could do to not die. The inside of that place was a nightmare with things that could take control of us. It was only because we were all so weak that we survived. Working together, we could subdue each other and drive out the monsters." He laughed weakly. "Thankfully, that gave us experience because we certainly never got any from killing anything in there. Even with that, they still expected us to mine mana crystals for them."

"It sounds like it was a literal nightmare-type zone," Zara whispered as they moved away from the chained captives. "Either that or it's some kind of specialized fiend area."

"Come on, let's go to the other building and get them all the blankets we can carry." Zack offered; his mind occupied with something else.

Both girls looked at him suspiciously before nodding.

Tessa informed her mother first, who had had everything well in hand. The two women and Cooper had been tied up with a cord that she had found somewhere in the basement. Her interrogation of them was proceeding without a problem so far.

"Oh, it looks like they arrived," Zara muttered as they climbed the steps.

A sopping wet Zelda was sitting on the back steps pointing to some trees they weren't able to see with the goggles.

"We're over here Jean!" Zara called out. "You could have just brought her over, you know."

Zelda shook her head.

"It's fine if you don't know the other people with her. Everyone will find out about you soon enough, and I won't allow anyone to take you from me."

"I think you have that backward," Zack nudged her, picking up the water-logged bear. "She's worried about you being taken, not her. It's the same fear I've always had."

A flashlight beam cut through the darkness as Specialist Jean McCleary and three other soldiers appeared from the darkness.

"How's the battle?" Zack asked as they drew near.

"Ended." It was only then that they noticed the distinct lack of booming rifle fire in the distance. "The people you brought with you really made the difference. They were able to open up a hole in their offensive that the Major was then able to send our people through. As soon as more people started going into the forest after them, it was pretty much over."

"Has anyone gone after Sergeant Grieves yet?"

She shook her head. "All our remotely qualified people are busy patching up the injured here. The four of us were all that could be spared to even scout out the objective. The Major wanted to know if everyone here had done a runner yet."

"That was their goal, but the crappy road kept them here for long enough for us to arrive," Tessa told her. "Why don't you come inside out of the rain and then go down into the basement? Mom is down there talking to the three that are still alive. I'm sure she'd enjoy hearing how everything went."

"We need to go get some blankets for the captives they have down there as well." Zack was quick to tell her, not wanting to get waylaid. "It's getting cold, in case you haven't noticed."

They ran past the soldiers on a beeline for the other building. A thick lock lay discarded in the mud as they burst inside and quickly gathered all the blankets together into a pile on the bed closest to the door.

"Okay, so are you going to tell us why we really came out here now?" Tessa demanded after they had finished gathering them up. "There is no way you would voluntarily think of getting blankets for them like that."

"I would... yeah, fine." Zack knew it wasn't even worth denying. He had spent too long taking care of Zara and himself first, without even having the time or ability to think about others. Strangers didn't even factor into that equation. People like Tessa, who he would consider a friend, did when he managed to remember them. "I wanted to look at the portal really quick and I figured this would be our only chance. Once everyone shows up, they might not let us near it."

The portal was supposed to be in a shed right next to the building they were currently in.

Zelda opened the door for them and slipped back out into the rain, intent on scouting the area some more. The Major had brought a full platoon's worth of soldiers, a number that was beyond overkill for the number of people they encountered in the house. However, the man never did anything without a reason, which meant there had been more people hiding somewhere.

Either that or he had been expecting trouble from the get-go.

Zack found that second option harder to believe. If the Major had been expecting trouble, then they would have been better prepared for it.

"Zelda says it's clear," Zara informed them, with an almost visible roll of her eyes. The teddy bear was taking her job seriously, it seemed.

With Zara's help, Zack broke the lock on the shed and opened the door, revealing the shimmering portal inside. He removed the goggles and let his eyes adjust to look at it normally. The power marking rings around its edge were completely black. If the siblings were to enter that portal, it would begin its *Change* without a doubt.

It was exactly as he had been expecting. From everything they had been hearing lately, it made sense for the portal to be in this state. Which made it perfect for what he wanted to try. It was an idea that had been trickling around ever since they had gotten back from Fittrel.

How to trigger that same effect without them going through the portal?

If they could manage that, then they might not need to go through the portal at the research institute. They could hopefully reverse whatever was going on there without getting trapped inside. It was a terrible plan; he admitted. There were so many holes, it looked like one of his old socks. But it was the best he could do with the limited information they had.

It wasn't as though anyone really knew what was going on with the portal there.

Zack reached out and touched the surface of the portal, his hand skimming its rippling face. A droplet clung to his finger as he pulled away before snapping back into the portal. Something told him this wasn't the way to go about it. This was too obvious, and he and Zara had already used them too many times to count without noticing anything.

They needed something out of the way that neither of them had ever touched before.

His eyes drifted over to the power marking rings. Those were a possibility, and they seemed to have something to do with what he wanted. He didn't think he had ever touched them, and certainly not since coming back from the snow elf world.

He stepped to the side and touched the dark ring. His finger sank into the ethereal substance, welcoming him and asking to be let loose. He could tell that it was a request that needed two keys, just as it had when they were inside.

Normally, the portals would continue building in strength until they broke through on their own. With him and Zara there, they didn't need to do that. It was also, unless he missed his guess, the precursor to the Aperran Change. Most, if not all, of the portals, would need to go through their own Change first.

Speeding up, one would also speed up the other.

"Zara, come here and help me with this." He directed her to the opposite side of the portal and had her put her hand inside the dark ring. "Can you feel that?"

Her eyes closed as she focused. "I can. Are we going to do this now?"

He nodded. "We might as well."

As if it had been waiting for their decision to continue, a prompt appeared in front of him.

Presence of Dimensional Children detected. Prerequisites for Dimensional Fragment Change activation under special class access for activation completed.
Would you like to initiate the Change for this Dimensional Fragment?

The siblings shared a glance, nodded, and accepted the Change. In exchange, a tiny portion of the energy entered their bodies before pushing their hands out of the dark rings first. The surface of the portal slowed next and darkened, gradually hardening. No one would be able to enter it until it had finished its Change.

Above the portal, a large dodecahedron dice flickered into being, with a countdown showing on each of its faces.

A new message flickered into being, for their eyes only.

Congratulations, due to absorbing a portion of energy from a portal beginning its Change, your title 'Child of the Portals+' has the potential to evolve. Continue to absorb the energy of Change to evolve this title.

"What did you just do?" Tessa gasped, her eyes twitching from the slowly revolving dice to the now dark portal.

"We, uh," Zack knocked his hand into his helmet as he tried to run his hand through his covered hair. "We just initiated the portals Change, without having to go through it and get stuck this time."

Zelda drew one of her daggers and poked the surface of the hardened portal repeatedly.

Zara picked her up with a roll of her eyes. "Why are you trying to stab the portal?"

"If that is all you wanted to check, we should leave before someone comes to look for us." Tessa had pulled her goggles back on and was staring at the door nervously.

"Yeah, this was mainly it. Let's go back and grab those blankets. Put the dirtiest ones on top. That way, they get wet first."

The group closed the shed, hiding the portal behind them, and retrieved the blankets they had stored by the door. Picking them up in bundles, it was quickly apparent that there was no *'dirtiest'* one among them. They were all filthy, lice and other bug-ridden messes.

Tessa held back a scream as she felt the bugs leap from the blankets onto her uniform and then into her hair. She could feel them crawling over her skin, nipping at her scalp, and slowly driving her insane.

"Why are the two of you so calm?" She hissed as they ran back out into the rain.

Zara waited until they were inside the house before answering. "This isn't the first time we've had lice or other bugs. They were fairly common in the orphanage. Then, when we were rescued and on our own, we had to figure out how to be clean on our own. Everything was so regimented at the institute that the first chance we got, we relaxed on everything.

"Our apartment was a disgusting mess for about a month after that. Then the bugs came. Money was always tight, yet we had to clean the place from top to bottom to get rid of them. We figured out then that it was cheaper to just be clean. We had to figure out things as we went along, or from the occasional advice of our transient neighbors. None of them ever stuck around for long."

Zack spat to the side as a bug tried to crawl inside his mouth. "Although even I have to admit that this is disgusting. Oh, by the way, Zara, Zelda?" He smiled evilly at them. "I call first dibs on the shower when we get back."

"Not fair. It's too early to start calling dibs on the shower!"

"It doesn't matter, anyway. There is no way mom is letting us inside her car in this condition. That military waystation had better have lice and bug shampoo by the barrel!"

They lugged the blankets down into the basement and found Jean un-chaining everyone. She had found the key to their locks while they were outside.

Anna had moved Cooper and the two women to the side and was still talking to them. Her face had settled into a stressed scowl that none of them liked seeing on her.

"Here we brought your blankets. Sorry that some of them are wet, but it's pouring outside." Zack and the others began passing them out to everyone, eager to get rid of their disgusting cargo.

"I'm going to go back upstairs," Zack muttered, as all the teens huddled together for warmth.

He avoided the bedrooms, not wanting to spread the lice and fleas to everything else. He briefly glanced inside what he now saw had been the kitchen. It currently resembled the inside of a trainee butcher's workplace. The Majair pistols had done their jobs well, and few of the kidnappers had even remained in one piece.

With all of them firing at once in such a confined space, he was amazed that any of them had survived it at all.

Zack went out to the back step and sat down in the rain. His mind was going over the second message they had gotten for activating the portal's change. It had given them some of its energy, the same way they had gotten some when they left the portal for the snow elf world.

Only this time, it hadn't been enough to fully evolve the title again. Which made sense if he thought of it as experience. Each level always required more. It worked that way with his spells, abilities, and actual level. Why not his titles as well?

That wasn't why he was outside in the cold rain, however. There was another reason for that. His *'Child of the Portals'* title had always mentioned undiscovered effects. He had just discovered one when that energy entered him.

He was now regenerating a small amount of his magical energy. It wasn't a lot less than what he was getting from the mana crystal for sure. The fact remained, though, that it was there. Now he just needed to learn if he could do anything with it.

Zack wasn't looking to use magic like his little sister could. That could come later. No, he was wanting something simpler, something that would be of far more immediate use in his opinion. He wanted to begin practicing his magical energy control. Of course, if he could use spells, then all the better, but he didn't want to be greedy. That way led to disappointment.

The Shouvain suit kept him warm as he sat there in the freezing rain. Timidly, afraid that he might be wrong, Zack reached for the energy inside his body. Everything was currently being used by his healing ability, but he could touch it, feel it. He knew that once his body healed enough, he would be able to separate his body's natural energy from that of the mana crystals.

Once he did that, then he could begin practicing his control. It wasn't a pipe dream. It would just have to wait until the morning if he was lucky. That shot to his chest had gotten him good.

He sat there for a while longer, a smile on his face despite the growing irritation from the bugs.

Specialist McCleary tapped him on the shoulder after he had been sitting there for maybe fifteen minutes. "How are you doing? You're just kind of sitting out here alone."

He shook his head and stood, cracking his back with a quick twist in both directions. "I was just thinking that it might be time for Zara and me to visit that portal at the institute after all."

Chapter 31

Jean unclipped her helmet and ran her hand through her hair once, clipping it back on afterward. "Tessa filled me in on your suspicions of who might be involved with this. Unfortunately, I couldn't talk with her mother, Mrs. Ricerca. Anna was busy interrogating the prisoners still. If your suspicions are correct, however, then I agree. Bringing the two of you to that portal would force them to act again."

"It's a bit different from what the Major originally intended, I know. Something tells me that he won't be willing to let what happened today stand unpunished." Zack turned to face her. "I know this might be a sensitive question, but how many people did you lose?"

Her face hardened beneath the goggles. "It's too soon to say for certain. I know the Major was expecting something to happen, just not when it did. I think he was expecting it here, not before we had even begun the operation."

"We were out in the open there... if they had waited even just a little longer to attack. A few minutes more and we wouldn't have been able to see them approaching. Instead, they were stuck in the trees, and that distance saved us, I think. Any closer and they would have been able to use these night vision goggles to their full effect."

"You should see their other version of them. They're slightly bulkier, but they show everything beyond what those ones do." Zack held up the battered pair he had retrieved from the ground. "You can't do precise aiming with these either, but they were probably helping everyone else know where to generally aim their fire."

Jean gave a short, terse nod in agreement. "Come on, I actually came out here to get your help with something." She nudged him to the side and walked down the steps. "We are going to get those Hildens back into working order. If we can. It was a good idea to disable them, but now with all the injured, we'll need them."

He followed her around to the front of the old mountain house. "And how are we going to do that?"

"Well, hopefully, they come with spare tires and the equipment to change a tire. Otherwise, we'll have to take the needed tires from one of them and hope for the best."

"Not to complain, but why am I helping you instead of the other soldiers that came with you?"

She shrugged. "I have them about to start searching the perimeter for anyone, or thing we might have missed. Besides, you looked like you needed something to do."

"Do you even have a way of getting in these? Zelda shoved dirt in the keyholes after locking them."

"Sure, I do, just watch." She dropped to a crouch, brought her rifle into position, and fired. The air-powered bullet punched through the lock, ripping a hole in both driver and passenger side doors.

"There must have been another way of doing that," He muttered, opening the door.

"Probably, but they wouldn't have been nearly as much fun or quick."

"Or loud!"

"Meh, you get used to it. Now hit the button to unlock the back. That's where we'll probably find the equipment."

Zack was dead on his feet by the time they had finished changing the four tires. Thankfully, Jean only had to break that first door. Once they had the equipment, the rest was easy. The spare tires hung below the back of each vehicle and could be retrieved with minimal difficulty.

He trudged back into the house, his boots sloshing with each step. Even with the protective suit on, he felt wet. He made it into the back room of the house and began peeling off his sopping clothes. They could dry on the floor of the bedroom for a few hours beside him while he slept.

The girls were already occupying one of the beds. While Anna was in another. So, he grabbed a spare blanket, rolled himself up, and fell asleep.

***

The dim light of an overcast and dreary dawn was creeping into the room when Zack was shaken awake.

The Major was standing above him, with his chest wrapped in a tight bloody bandage. "What happened to the portal?"

"Good morning to you too," He grumbled, shaking his head. "What do you mean? What's wrong with it?"

"I'm not in the mood, Zack! Tell me what you and your sister did to the portal here!" His shout woke the others in the room.

"Calm down Major. I know this has been stressful on everyone involved, but that is not a reason to yell at the boy." Anna commanded him sternly, her hair mussed and tangled. There were pillow creases lining her cheek, and one eye drooped sleepily.

Zack had to bite his lips to keep from laughing. It was such a departure from her normal appearance that it was shocking to him.

The Major breathed in sharply and held it, his teeth grinding, while he glared at her. Finally, he released it and tried again. "Fine, I can understand that. Now, would you please tell me what you did to that portal, and how?"

Zack spotting Zara biting the corner of her lip, from her place on the bed. She shrugged, leaving the choice up to him.

"If you're fine with me talking in a public place like this..." He waited a beat for the Major to say something before continuing. "The portal began its Change, same as the one the Albright's hid from everyone."

"I have someone guarding the stairs. The kidnapped teens won't hear anything. And I figured that much! I want to know if the two of you had anything to do with it? This makes it the second one that has begun its Change with you two nearby."

"Going by that math, it makes it the second one that Specialist McCleary has been near as well."

"True, but I already know that you both are odd. You two did something to that portal at the institute, and then you did something to the Albright's portal!"

Zack unrolled himself from the blanket and grabbed his damp uniform pants. "We did not do anything to the portal at the institute! We weren't even close to it when it stopped working. More over, even if we could do something to the portals, and I'm not saying that we can, what does it matter?"

Going around to each of the portals and inducing their Change was good for the siblings. It would help their title evolve and possibly give them other benefits, as he had seen the night before. That said, it was delicate information, and the Albion government had a leak somewhere inside it. He wasn't willing to trust them with it just yet.

He grabbed the uniform top and pulled it on, beginning to button it without looking at the Major or Anna. "Besides, it's obvious after yesterday that the Albright's weren't the only bad apples among Albion's nobles. Someone gave away information about your operation. No offense, but I'm no longer telling anyone anything about my sister and me. I would rather not be targeted by someone who got the wrong idea, from some half-baked document they stole."

The Major frowned, his brows drawing together. "If we agree that none of this ever gets written down anywhere, and only stays between us, Amar, and the king and queen. Would that be agreeable?"

Zara gave a short nod.

"That is... agreeable." Zack hesitated for a moment, unsure of how much to tell them. "Apparently we can begin the Change for portals that are ready for it. They'll do it themselves normally as well, though I imagine it will take a lot longer. That's how we got trapped inside the Albright's portal. It began its Change.

"Everyone had mentioned that seldom-used portals, such as this one, would have full power marking rings. So, when we came up here, I thought it would be a nice chance to experiment and see if we could do it again. Only this time without getting stuck inside the portal. We succeeded." He began pulling on his boots.

"Do you know how long it is going to take?" Anna had thrown off her blanket and was putting on her own boots.

Zack shrugged. "No idea. Has the first one finished yet?"

"No, the countdown finished, and then that odd dice hanging above it changed colors. No new countdown has yet to appear on it." The Major ran a rough hand over his face, grunting as the motion pulled at his injured side.

"We can't help you then. All we know is that the original countdown is there, so everyone inside can evacuate. I would guess that it takes a different amount of time for each portal, depending on how advanced each one is." Zara spoke up, recalling a conversation she'd had with the Oracle. "Each Change makes them larger, closer to a world fragment. I would imagine the more advanced they are, the longer the time they would need to complete their Change."

The military man grunted thoughtfully. "What about that portal at the institute? How is it related to all of this? All of our portals started getting stronger, closer to their Change, once that first one went dark. Are you telling me that's a coincidence?"

"I'm telling you, I have no idea on that one." Zack shook his head and stood. "We've never been back there, remember? And we only barely learned we could even do this. Maybe us touching that portal will start Aperra's Change, or maybe it'll blow up the world. We have no idea. To us, it's just the first portal they forced us through, that's all."

The Major blew out a breath and nodded. "I appreciate the help you provided last night. Without your intervention, and the arrival of Sergeant Grieves' team that you brought, I would have lost a lot more people. In light of that, I'm going to put our plans of using you, both of you, as a key at the institute portal on hold for now. We need more information before determining our next move."

Zack felt a sense of relief mixed with annoyance at having avoided that place once again. He had just resigned himself to going back there, and then this happened. He breathed in deep and collected the rest of his items from the floor.

"You should talk with Jean, Specialist McCleary, on the matter first. She had an idea about using us as a trap of sorts at the institute. If everything here was really put together by the same organization that was behind the institute, then having us show up there would force them to act.

"You already know someone, whether it's a noble or a person in the military, is dirty. Use them to release the information. Meanwhile, you can be creating a trap for them this time. You've been wanting to have us go to that portal for a while now. We might as well just get it over with and use this to our advantage."

Anna shook her head. "Zara is a princess, Zack. There is no way an operation like that would get approved. Not one that involved both of you being there in any case. The only reason I was allowed to bring you here this time was that we were only going to be watching, nothing more. Her normal royal guards were replaced with a military squad, and this still happened. The king and queen will not be happy when they learn of everything that went wrong with this operation."

He had forgotten about the guards since they weren't around when they were on school grounds. The last time they had gone out with Tessa, the few guards Zara had at the time joined together with the Ricerca's. The number assigned to Zara had been expanded after that whole fiasco.

"It is a good idea, one that may have even worked with some changes to it." The Major began tiredly, resting his hand against the bandage on his side. "But she is right. I'll mention it to the king as a possibility since you volunteered. However, the likelihood of him or the queen agreeing is slim."

"Would you be willing to begin the Change on our other portals? The ones that are primed for it already, and everyone refuses to enter anyway?" Anna asked them, stomping her boots twice to make sure they were tight.

"I don't have a problem with that, as long as it doesn't interfere with what we have going on during the week," Zara answered for them. "We have classes, our tutoring with Edith, and our therapy sessions with her. Speaking of which, didn't you mention that we would get tutoring? I'm fine with Edith, but I hope she's getting paid for all the extra effort she's doing." As always with her, it came down to money.

"I did say that, didn't I?" Anna tied her hair back while speaking. "Originally, it was meant to be a more formal royal tutor. However. if she works for you, then I see no reason to change that. As long as you get good grades, of course, everything depends on that."

Jean knocked on the doorframe. The deep purple bags under her eyes hinting that she had been up all night working. "We are ready to load the rescued teens into the four Hildens and move out as soon as you give us the order, sir. We'll need everyone's help to move the tractor farther down the road. I went to take a look earlier, and it is firmly wedged in place."

"Let's go. I want all of our people out of here as soon as possible and brought to the nearest portal or hospital."

It was only then that Zack realized they had cut off a potential way for the Major to have his people healed. No wonder he had woken him the way he had.

"Has anyone checked on Sergeant Grieves and the others with him?" Tessa asked as she quickly started pulling on her boots as well. Across the bed from her, Zara did the same, with Zelda crawling out from beneath the covers.

"I checked on them and removed the remaining bomb traps from the path that Anna had spotted, along with a few more that were farther up. The sergeant and the rest all survived the night, though unfortunately, I'm afraid that some of their military careers may be over from the injuries they sustained." Jean truly had been busy after he went to bed exhausted.

"Did that tree get removed from the road behind our troop transports?" The Major inquired tiredly.

Jean yawned. "I believe so sir, there was a team working on it last I heard. They brought the sergeant and his team down to the vehicles with them as well after my team and I finished clearing the path of traps."

The Major nodded. "I'm going back to ensure the rest of my people make it back safely. I'll see you all later. Zack, Zara, next time wait to begin the portal's Change. It didn't matter this time, since we didn't bring any healers. If we had though, they could have made a real difference and you would have just cut off their only way of helping us. And don't think we aren't going to talk about *that* later as well!" He pointed at the moving Zelda.

With those parting words, he stalked from the room and left them alone with a very tired Jean.

She rested her head against the doorjamb and muttered a brief curse. "I forgot I hadn't mentioned her to him yet. He is never going to let me live that down."

"Just use me as an excuse. Tell him I wanted it to remain a secret for as long as possible, even from him. A few people saw her last night, which is why I decided he could know now." Anna cracked her back with a sigh.

Jean straightened. "I doubt he'll believe it, besides I only found out about her last night myself. The omission on my part is fine. He'll just be annoying to deal with, is all."

"Uncles can be like that."

Each of the kid's heads snapped around to look at Anna, and then swiveled to Jean.

"Wait, you're the Major's niece? The Major's name is Major McCleary?" Zack felt like his entire worldview had expanded with that single piece of information. Suddenly everything he had never thought to question began making more sense. Like how a specialist always seemed to be able to get in touch with the Major.

"He's from my mother's side of the family, so he has a different last name. Besides, he prefers to just be addressed as the Major, even among family. His military rank has kind of become his entire identity." Jean glared at Anna. "That is something that no one is supposed to know, so keep it to yourselves. We've worked hard to ensure that there are no rumors of him favoring me or giving me extra special treatment."

It was clear she put in the effort for everything she did. It was no wonder she didn't want people thinking that she had been given special treatment.

Each of them nodded, while Anna smirked.

A minute later, they were outside and piling into the sole driverless Hilden. There were also only a couple of the kidnapped teens waiting in the back. Which meant that there was plenty of room for their entire group.

Jean climbed behind the wheel, while Anna and the rest took up positions in the back. Carefully, she began navigating the large vehicle's way down the muddy road. She kept her speed down as the tire treads filled with mud and began to slip and slide.

The last thing they needed was for one of the vehicles to go off the road and into the ditch, where they couldn't rescue them.

Even with all her caution, the vehicle still slid in the mud when they reached the tractor. The wheels inched towards the edge, before dropping into a pothole that hadn't been filled and stopping. Everyone breathed a sigh of relief and turned around to look at the other Hildens as they too, came to sliding stops.

Zack hopped out first, then helped Zara, with Zelda clutching to her upper arm, and then Tessa and Anna. It was going to require everyone helping to move the tractor out of the way.

"Can you just turn the front wheels and then use the remaining back one to pivot it mostly out of the way?" Zara asked Jean, after making sure the key was still inside the machine.

"You mean to simply angle it away, using the busted wheel as the pivot point?"

Zara nodded.

Jean climbed into the driver's seat of the tractor and looked down, while the other drivers joined them. "It would have worked better on dry ground, but it might still work if I can get everyone to push on the front bucket."

She started up the tractor, twisted the wheel, and put the large machine into gear while they all got into position.

Chapter 32

Z ack flicked a clump of rapidly drying mud onto the floor of the vehicle and glared at his sister. Her stupid plan had worked, sure, but it had also coated everyone in mud. Only two people had escaped the rather explosive mud bath. Jean since she was driving the tractor at the time, and Zelda, who had hidden behind Zara at the last moment.

At least the mud was helping to calm the bug bites.

"Hold on!" Jean called out.

She braked softly, as they crossed over from the muddy back road and onto the proper paved road without stopping. The Hilden sped up, as Jean floored it for the military waystation.

"Do you want to switch out now, Jean? I got some sleep while you have been up all night."

The tired driver thought the offer over for a few moments before nodding slowly, a yawn escaping from her mouth. "Thanks, Anna, I would appreciate that."

Anna took the opportunity to scrape some more mud from her body and then slid behind the wheel with a grin. "Shower here I come."

The wheels chirped and spun as she floored it and ignored the speed limit like always. With her behind the wheel, they would reach the waystation much sooner than the rest. Guaranteeing them plenty of hot water and de-licing shampoo.

Jean stretched out in the passenger seat beside her and fell asleep within moments.

Zara looked at the two up front and then motioned to her brother and Tessa. "I have something to tell you from last night."

Zack leaned across the space while Tessa, who was sitting next to her, simply tilted her head.

"I got some experience last night when Zelda killed those soldiers. It wasn't much, since they were people, and it wasn't from all of them either." Zara's hand shot up and clamped over Tessa's mouth, which had already widened into what would have been a loud gasp.

"You said it wasn't everyone?" Zack asked, wanting to make sure he had heard her correctly.

Zara nodded.

"I wonder if maybe those could have been travelers... Still, the fact that we can get experience now on this side of the portals-" He broke off sinking into thought.

"At least it seems like the kills have to be done from your spells for it to work," Tessa said, pulling Zara's dirt-covered hand from her lips. She briefly blew away some grit before continuing. "Everyone would have noticed otherwise, and Zack, for sure, would have noticed last night if that wasn't the case."

He frowned. "Were none of the men in that room last night travelers, or did me barging in with the enhanced suit, not count as a portal spell?"

Tessa shook her head. "I don't think you killed anyone doing that move. Their own shots are what eliminated them. You might have gotten some experience for helping normally, but not the bulk of the amount." She paused. "Maybe, I don't know. I've never come across a situation like that before. It could count as a trap of sorts, I guess? We should pose it as a question to Quinn later."

"Either way, she's right. I didn't notice getting any experience from them last night." The three quietly tossed a few more ideas back and forth and then fell into silence as their thoughts consumed them.

Zack went back to practicing his control, while Zara and Tessa played with Zelda across from him.

The kidnapped teens, though they were all around the same age, stayed in their own corner and didn't say anything. That was how the trip back to the waystation passed, without the two groups ever interacting more than needed.

The siblings could still remember parts of their own rescue vividly even years later. One of the major things that stuck out to them was the soldiers giving them time to process everything. They had needed time to understand that they were safe, that they weren't being taken somewhere worse. All of that and more was best done in their own time.

So, they kept Tessa from saying anything, explained what had worked for them to her, and simply let them process.

A while later, as they were nearing the military waystation, the first of the teens broke down and began to cry. It was the sign that opened the proverbial floodgates, and within moments; the others had begun to sob as well. Some of them had been in those mountains for longer than others. All to feed the greed of people like Cooper, and whoever had set their operation in motion.

Everyone piled out as the large vehicle came to a stop and stretched.

Zack plucked his helmet from the floor and grinned. The pair of night vision goggles he had been using was still attached to it. They were his now. He hid them beneath the Ricerca car as he walked past and continued on to the showers.

A couple of soldiers that were stationed there on a revolving basis were already handing out fresh uniforms and the de-licing shampoo when he arrived. Everyone was eager to shower and get changed. All their old clothes would get burned, and who knew what would happen to the uniforms?

Thankfully, that wasn't something that Zack needed to worry about. All he needed to think about was stripping out of his suit, washing it down with the shampoo a couple of times, and then doing the same to himself.

Despite all of that, he still beat the girls outside by several minutes.

Anna had clearly explained the situation to the soldiers further, as they were in the midst of taking statements from each of the rescued teens.

Jean stumbled out first. The small amount of sleep she had just gotten had done her a world of good. Anna and the other two appeared a second later, wisps of steam still curling up from their red faces.

"I'm taking them back with me. They'll be at school tomorrow," Anna informed the soldier slash teacher and then pushed them towards her waiting car.

Zack picked up his goggles, while Zelda gave herself one last shake, flinging a few water droplets from her body.

"What's going on, mom? I'm not complaining about skipping classes, but it seems like something more." Tessa asked her mother once they were safely inside the vehicle and speeding down the road.

"We are going to speak to your father, and I thought it was better to do it ourselves before everyone else showed up." Anna forced some more speed from the Alberitas made car.

"You think the injections they were being given are based on his work?" Zara asked softly, clutching Zelda tight. Her voice carried to the front seat without an issue in the whisper-silent vehicle. There was absolutely no road or wind noise inside the cabin.

"Yes, I do. I would rather not believe he is involved, however. Shouvain has demonstrated that they are not only willing but also rather adept at stealing secrets." Anna blew a long tuft of hair from her eyes in frustration, her hands refusing to leave the steering wheel.

"Mathew is not perfect, honestly he is kind of a dull man, and that is what I love about him. I have all the excitement I can handle with my own affairs. I don't need my husband or partner adding to them."

Tessa groaned. "I don't need to be hearing this."

"Yes, you do, dear. It pertains to why I chose your father. He fit me, and what I wanted in a man. You're young yet, but it is something you will eventually need to think about. Sooner rather than later, if you decide to follow the traditions of most nobles."

Anna let that hang in the air for several seconds before continuing. "My point is that over the years, I have learned many things about the man. He is obsessive with his work, careless with his words on occasion, and absolutely brilliant. The two things that I have never believed him to be are malicious or a traitor to Albion."

"I have a question somewhat related to that, actually. It's been bothering me ever since last night when we talked about Shouvain being willing to steal tech from everyone. I can understand that it makes sense in the way you explained it. What I don't get is why would they do all of these experiments anywhere but over there?

"I would think that they or their research organization would want to be able to control everything more. Surely, they could better manage all these projects in their home territory in front of one of their own portals. Right?" It was a question that Zack desperately wanted answered.

"Oh, I can explain that one for you!" Tessa turned around to grin at him. "I looked up everything about Shouvain after what happened with the car and Ben. First off, they call themselves a country, though it is more proper to refer to them as a small kingdom. Second, from what I was able to learn, they got extremely unlucky when it came to portals. They are publicly known to only have a few portals."

Anna nodded along with her daughter. "They do have a couple more than are reported, ones that have been found over the years. Unlike Albion, which contains a rather diverse amount of geography, Shouvain is almost completely flat. Before the portals appeared, they were devoted to farming and other food related endeavors. There are few places for the portals to hide from view."

She slowed as they neared the city limits and the turnoff for their house.

"In other words, they got screwed. The few portals they do have are needed for mana crystal mining. So, they have little choice but to go elsewhere for their experiments. I doubt Albion is the only country either that they have done this kind of thing in. We were probably just the easiest for a while, but that will be changing soon enough."

The car slid to a stop in front of the large mansion she and Tessa called home.

"Mom, dad will be in his lab right now. Are you sure it's fine to disturb him?" Tessa wondered hesitantly as a maid rushed to open the door for them.

"No, but these questions need to be asked and answered, and it would be better if it was done by me, rather than Amar or someone else." Anna glanced at Zack and Zara. "Not a word to anyone of what you see beyond this point, is that clear?"

"Yes, ma'am." They both answered, meeting her eyes. Neither thought about turning down the chance to visit the man's laboratory.

A smile ghosted across her lips as she faced forward and led them to the back of the house. Leading them near the room where they had overheard Tessa's conversation with her father before. It was there that Anna opened a locked door to reveal a small lift going down.

"There is a set of stairs for emergencies, also locked, of course, but I would suggest we all crowd into this. It's not a long way down. He just prefers his privacy when he works from home is all." Anna gently pushed them all inside and then entered last.

The lift took them down maybe two or three floors before slowing and opening the doors with a ding.

"I thought you said it wasn't far?" Zack complained in wonder. He had been on enough construction sites to know how much of a pain it was to set something like this up. "How did you all even manage to dig this out?"

"It was easier than you would expect, actually," Mathew answered for his wife, wheeling over to them on his chair. "All of this is what remains of a now dry well. The shaft for it was originally dug when my ancestors first built the house years and years ago. It went unused for a long time after it dried up, then I had the idea of turning it into my lab. Brilliant right? The hard part was actually the stairs, as those needed to be dug fresh. Everything down here we simply reinforced with concrete and dug out as needed."

He blinked and twitched his nose, scratching lightly at it. "Why are you down here, dear? And what is that smell? You said you were going into the mountains..." He scooted closer to them and took a deeper sniff, eventually zeroing on Zelda. "This teddy bear smells especially strong, of whatever it is."

Zelda smacked his hand away and hid behind Zara.

Mathew's mouth flopped open and refused to close as he looked agog at his wife.

"We have no time for this, Matt. The military might be on their way already, so focus, please!" Anna's sharp tone had him focusing solely on her and his daughter.

"What happened? Tell me."

"Your research on raising the compatibility of travelers. How does it work exactly?"

He pulled back, clearly not having been expecting that question. "What's going on? You rarely ask about the specifics of my work unless it's concerning a project for the king or queen. That's my own personal one though…" He frowned. "I don't mind explaining it to you, Anna, you know that. Can you tell me why you suddenly want to know though, first? Please?"

Anna studied her husband for a tense minute, the man paling under her scrutiny.

"What do you want to know?" He whispered weakly.

"Have you sold any of your research data to anyone? Or has any of it been leaked or stolen to your knowledge?" Anna ignored the large room filled with equipment and filing cabinets full of his research. She had seen it all before many times. All she wanted was the truth.

Mathew slowly nodded. "I didn't sell anything, but after Tessa mentioned the Albrights knowing about my personal research project, I started going through everything related to it. I noticed some discrepancies in the files from two years ago when I first started human testing.

"If you remember, I did all those tests off-site and hired a couple of assistants. They shouldn't have had access to the files, but it looks like some of the information had been changed. The handwriting wasn't mine, and the data didn't match what I remembered."

Anna relaxed a fraction, though her scowl deepened. "And why didn't you say anything about it to me?"

He shrugged weakly. "I don't know. I guess I figured it didn't matter. All the research from back then was outdated. I've refined and changed all of the formulas I used in the experiments. My current work barely resembles the material from back then." He swallowed and looked his wife in the eye. "Anna, you're scaring me. Please, tell me what happened?"

"It looks like the country Shouvain is the one who stole your work, and they managed to create their own version."

"Oh," He said blankly. "Oh," He repeated again, his eyes widening. "What did they do with it?"

"They were using it as a temporary compatibility booster on already awakened travelers."

"That's not how it's supposed to work." He stood and began to pace in front of them. His fingers rubbed together constantly as he muttered to himself. A minute went by, and then another before Anna suddenly clapped, shocking him from his mental quandary.

"Could it be based on your work or not?" She demanded.

"It's possible. I've always focused on using it on people before they awaken because I believed that would ensure it would have the greatest effect. If you messed with the formula and gave it to a proper awakened traveler, however, it's possible that is could work as a temporary booster."

Anna closed her eyes. "We need to head back up to the house. Shut down anything you have going on; we need to go talk to the king and queen. NOW!" She yelled when he failed to move right away.

She pushed them back towards the lift while they waited for him.

"Mom, why are we suddenly going to the castle?"

"There are a few different reasons, of which this is just the least compelling. No, the real reason we are leaving is that I still think someone is going to come for him soon. It is better for him to not be here when that happens."

Mathew shuffled over to them and turned off the lights as they climbed into the lift. He shut and locked the door behind them as his wife hit the button that would take them back up.

Zara looked around as they all hurried outside to the waiting car. In the distance she could see Ricerca family guards walking the grounds. "Do you know what happened to my guards? I haven't heard anything specific about them after that attack on the way back from our shopping trip."

"Your original two were injured and have been swapped out for another pair." Anna told her distractedly, looking at them in the mirror as she sat behind the wheel. "How much do the two of you know about Cooper?"

"That's kind of an odd segue," Zack joked. "Um, he was someone I always tried to avoid, so most of what I know about him comes from rumors. From firsthand experience, I can tell you, he is someone who is ambitious and wants to stay alive. Nothing is more important to him than himself. I've heard rumors that he also used to be a halfway decent sneak back in the day. Until he got caught one too many times and it almost cost him his life."

Her fingers drummed on the steering wheel in thought, the roads flashing past them. "So, if I was to tell you, he had overheard something concerning Zara's guards, not knowing they were talking about her. Would you believe he was telling the truth?"

Zack thought back to how scared the man had seemed after he explained the situation to him the night before. "I would say that there is a fair chance it was mostly all true, with some lies woven in. What did he say about her guards?"

"It would seem that they used the attack on you three that night for several different reasons. You already know it was supposed to act as a diversion of sorts while they went after the airship. Thankfully, that failed for a multitude of reasons. One of the things Cooper mentioned, however, was that they also used the opportunity to replace a certain princess's royal guards. The Albion noble that has been helping them ensured the new ones were loyal to them instead of the crown."

"Why would they do something like that? If they had wanted Zara or me, there have been plenty of chances for them to just grab us. There is no need to make everything so complicated!"

"That is what we are going to find in just a while. Sometimes people just like to make things complicated. It doesn't have to make sense. Once we get to the castle, I'll have the noble in question brought there for questioning." Everyone in the car could hear her teeth grinding.

Chapter 33

They were waved through the gates to the castle and brought to a room deep inside with no windows. The Queen, Caroline, arrived a few minutes later with Amar and Nivean in tow. A line of staff brought in some hastily prepared food behind them.

"Orlo will be a few minutes. He's finishing up some paperwork and then he'll join us." The queen told them once they were alone. "Why did you come over so suddenly? I wasn't expecting you until later, and even then, I was only expecting your report, or you alone."

"You haven't heard then? We were ambushed up there. The plan was exposed, and they attacked us." Anna carefully explained everything that had happened, only pausing when the king entered the room halfway through her tale. "When we got back, I stopped to question Mathew, and then brought everyone here." She finished, reaching for a glass of water.

"We need to confirm whether it was Shouvain or not first. Then we need to learn who betrayed us and released the plans to rescue those kids! There were only a few of us who knew of the plan." The King was furious as he began to shout. "And then we are going to talk about you taking a princess into such a zone without her guards!"

Caroline rolled her eyes. "You approved the plan to let her go without them, agreeing that a platoon of trained soldiers should be plenty. She only has two guards dispatched on her, to begin with, and even then only when she leaves the academy grounds. Every time she has left so far has been with the Ricerca's and they just end up combining with their own guard detail."

Anna coughed, bringing their attention back to her. "Sorry, I forgot to mention that I interrogated the three prisoners while I was up there. The one known as Cooper confirmed a few other things during our time together. It seems that his ears are as large as his mouth. Her guard detail was actually bought off anyway. It happened right after the ambush that injured her original guards. That was another reason behind the attack on them and not just the distraction we thought it was."

"Did he happen to mention who the noble is that did all of this?" Orlo ground out

Zack sat to the side, listening in while eating a sandwich with his sister and Tessa. They were all hungry after having skipped a couple of meals. Even Zelda was behaving and not exploring the room. He was, however, taking the opportunity to train his magical energy control. Now that he had the chance and knowledge to do so, he wasn't going to waste a second if he could help it.

"He did," Anna answered hesitantly. "However, I am on the fence somewhat as to whether I believe who he said could do something like this."

"Just say the name already, Anna," Caroline snapped. "This is a matter of security for our entire country."

"I know, and that's the problem. He mentioned two names. One was my husband, Mathew Ricerca. I personally believe that they are trying to shift some of the blame for the formula onto him. I understand if you think I am too close to this matter and don't believe my opinion. The second name he mentioned, and the far more dangerous one by far, is George Trask."

The adults all inhaled sharply, while Zack took a moment to remember who the man was. "Isn't that the man who you gave the piece of suit to?" He was also the man who had spoken at the commencement ceremony for the academy.

"He is," Amar agreed softly. "George Trask also happens to be a minor noble through his own efforts and has access to most of the country's mana-tech and magitech related research."

"Oh, so he's the one who stole the night vision goggles research for them then," Zara stated casually, more concerned with the food than the conversation.

"More than likely, along with everything else we have, I would guess." Anna sank back into the couch tiredly.

Beside her, Mathew was as still as a statue, his eyes filled with fear.

"Relax Mathew, we don't think you were really involved in any of this," Amar said, taking pity on the man. "We'll still need to ask you some questions, of course, but we've known you for years..." He sighed. "Then again, we've also known George for years."

Mathew inched closer to his wife, who grasped his hand in a reassuring grip.

Zack imagined that Trask had replaced his sister's guards under someone else's orders. While the man was a mana-tech researcher, he worked with the more physical aspects of items. He was an engineer of sorts. The people who had experimented on them years ago were more like Mathew. They were more interested in the biology side of things.

Which meant that even within the unknown organization, there were potentially multiple factions. Either that or George Trask wasn't a member and was simply working with them. He hoped that wasn't the case. It would make everything far more complicated.

"How much does Trask know about the coming Change?" Zack asked suddenly, remembering their promise to keep Shouvain in a total information block out.

"Nothing, we haven't told anyone anything about it yet, outside of Fittrel." The king nodded to Nivean, who hadn't said a word the entire time. "We've been having a difficult time deciding the best way to break the news to everyone, without risking it leaking out."

"What we need is a plan to deal with them, once and for all. Inside our country, at the very least." Caroline's eyes were spitting fire, but her voice was deathly calm. "If we simply bring in Trask now, then we lose everyone else involved. However, if he catches wind that we know he is guilty, then he'll escape, and we'll get nothing."

"There should be little chance of that happening. I haven't told anyone but those here of his involvement and the prisoners won't be talking to anyone either." A cold wind blew through the room at the casual proclamation.

"You could still use us," Zara said between bites of her sandwich. "Tell them of our plan and what we did to the portal."

Anna slowly nodded and explained to them what she had heard that morning.

"No, absolutely not! She is still a princess. I have been lenient so far with her protection, apparently far too much so, if the troubles that have befallen her are anything to go by. What you are suggesting would be beyond negligent on my behalf and would send them both into danger. Not to-"

"I am not a real princess!" Zara interrupted the king. "We have to go back to that place at some point. It might as well be now when it can make a difference."

"You certainly act like a princess, daring to interrupt me like that." Orlo grinned, looking over his nose at her.

Amar sighed and rolled his eyes.

"She does have a point, as unfortunate as it is. The Major has been wanting to bring them back to that site for a while now, and this would be effective." Caroline grabbed her glass of water and took a sip. Immediately afterward, her finger began running along the wet rim, producing a dull sound.

The queen's face went through a variety of comical expressions as she thought. Everyone in the room was careful to remain silent, lest they interrupt her. It was well known how fiery her temper could be to anyone who interrupted her when she was thinking.

"The idea has merit," She said at last. "It will require a few days, minimum, to set everything up and to make a proper plan out of it. But it does present a decent opportunity to get rid of them all. We can even get rid of those filthy, traitorous guards at the same time."

"Are you sure?" Orlo asked her.

The queen nodded. "I'll explain my thought process to you later and you can see if you agree with me."

He smiled; it was how they had always done things. He was the king by birthright and traditionally held most of the power associated with the throne. Truthfully, however, he and Caroline were equals, just as his parents had been. Besides, she had an eye for details that he simply didn't. He was broad strokes and vision.

"Fine, but if we are going to do this, then we are bringing the kids back right away. I don't want to risk them being held hostage should anything go wrong."

"Of course," The queen smiled wholeheartedly. "We had been planning on bringing them back before the Change. This will just bump up the timetable." She glanced at Zara. "In fact, why don't we use her as the excuse, so no one gets suspicious. We can tell them that they are coming back to meet their adopted sister?"

Orlo laughed, "Oh, I like that. It's perfect, and nobody will suspect anything with a reason like that, even if it is a tad late."

Caroline waved the complaint away. "We can just mention that the delay was due to all the excitement lately. After all, she was attacked while on the way back to school from a shopping trip, and the field with the airship was also attacked. The delay is completely understandable. We all want our children to feel safe when they come home."

"These people are weird," Zack muttered, biting into his sandwich.

"You have no idea," Tessa whispered back, pretending to take a drink of water.

"Does that mean we are going to do this, then?" Zara asked, looking for clarification.

416

Orlo rubbed the spot between his eyes for a brief moment, before his wife grabbed his hand and pulled it away. "I can see this being advantageous to us if we spin it properly. This is the second time we have had to move against a noble recently, both times with good cause. We've been trying to restrict their power and authority for some time now, and this might just be the catalyst we need to make that happen."

Amar nodded slowly. "It will be tricky; however, you are right. This could be exactly what you have been looking for."

The queen placed her glass on a nearby table and stood. "Anna, will you and Mathew stay for a while longer? I have some questions regarding his personal research project."

Mathew stood first. "I will be happy to answer any questions you may have, my queen." The meeting had progressed from friendly acquaintances talking to where formalities were now needed.

"As you wish, milady. What about the kids?" Anna wanted to be there when her husband was questioned, to make sure they didn't go overboard. She also needed to ensure that her daughter, along with Zack and Zara, were taken care of.

"Just take us back to our dorm. Tessa can come with us and play some games until you are finished. Or she can spend the night if that's easier?" Zack offered.

"We'll need your help with planning and with setting parts of the plan into motion, Anna." The queen told her softly.

"Tessa, what would you like to do? It sounds like I'm not going to be around much, and your father will be busy with his work like usual."

Mathew had the good grace to blush, though he also didn't try to defend himself or deny it. "Do you want to go with them for the night and then have them come over for the weekend?"

"As long as we can stop by the house so I can pick up my uniform for tomorrow, then I'm fine with spending the night at their dorm." Tessa peeked at the siblings. "What do you both think, want to come over for the weekend?"

They nodded in unison.

Orlo clapped. "Good, now that those matters are all settled, do you three want to stick around or leave?"

"Leave." They all agreed.

None of them wanted to get stuck in any more boring meetings where they had nothing to say or do. Besides, they were all smart enough to understand that there were plenty of things that couldn't be said in their presence. That was his way of politely giving them an out.

The ride back to the Ricerca house was quiet, with the three staring at the guards inside the vehicle with them. There were two additional guard cars as well, one in front and one behind. For a few obvious reasons, for the moment at least, their security had been upgraded.

Tessa hurried inside and retrieved her uniform and bag, needing only a couple of minutes to gather everything together.

"That was so awkward!" Zara complained as she collapsed onto the couch inside their dorm a while later. Nobody had spoken the entire drive, and even Zelda hadn't dared to do anything but act like a stuffed teddy bear.

"Agreed. Now why don't you get the game set up? I'm going to go talk to Edith and get my therapy session out of the way early, if I can." Zack ruffled her hair and decided it wasn't worth it to change his clothes just yet.

Edith was glad to see him and had no problem doing the session early with him. Although she did insist that Tessa sleep at her apartment after he mentioned she would be staying over.

For whatever reason, that session hit him harder than usual, and by the time he left, he was feeling emotionally wrung out and raw. It was good for him, he knew; it was what was allowing him to finally process everything and move on. That didn't make it fun, or even pleasant, just necessary.

Having them over so often was also helping Edith to relax again in her apartment. The readily available wooden bat by the door and the small folding knife she carried in her pocket also seemed to help.

Zack leaned against the closed door of his dorm apartment and sighed. His eyes were red, and the corners were raw from wiping them repeatedly. He unlocked the door and walked inside to find Zelda dancing with George and Aisha.

"You decided to wake them both up as well?" He rasped.

Zara, who was hanging off the back of the couch watching them, turned to look at him. "It seemed like the thing to do after last night. I have a little more mana to spare on upkeep after all."

Both of them were regenerating small amounts of their magical energy naturally now. It had started after they absorbed the energy from the portal the night before when they began its Change. Depending on the excess from mana crystals only got them so far. For Zara, that limit was their suits and Zelda, with a little extra leftover in case something happened. Now that limit had been raised a little higher, and she could comfortably include both of the other bears all the time as well.

"Tessa, before I forget, Edith wants you to sleep at her place tonight instead of here." Zack patted each of the bears on the head and headed into his room. "I'm going to change and then we can start the game or do whatever else you both want."

"We're debating whether we should start a new game, so George and Aisha can play with us, or finish our current one and have them watch while learning how to play," Zara announced as he came back out in a pair of clean clothes.

"How far are we into the current game?"

"A little over halfway, I think," Tessa answered from her spot at the table. She was studying the gameboard.

They could choose either option then without a problem.

"What do they want to do?"

Zara tilted her head as she listened to the bear's talk. "They want to watch us finish this game. Zelda will explain the rules and how to play to them as we go along."

Tessa pulled out some snacks from her bag and spread them across the table as they began playing. It was a sight that had become familiar to the three of them over the last week. Each of them holding it precious for their own reasons.

They were friends, the first each of them could remember having since they were children. Well, outside of Zara and the bears.

"Are you really alright with being used as a pawn in their plan?" Tessa asked suddenly, as their game was drawing to a close.

Zack rolled the dice in his hand, feeling the smooth edges and divots before answering. "If this were any other plan or group they were going up against, then I, or we rather, probably would have a problem with it. As it is, these people have something to do with the organization that experimented on us!" His voice deepened into a growl. "This will be the first time we'll be able to do something to them, to take back the piece of us they stole back then."

"Proving they no longer have a hold over us is an important step to healing Edith says," Zara said as Zack rolled the dice. "This will be our first time going back there as well, so it will give us the opportunity to face several different aspects of our past."

The red-haired girl was fixated on her own thoughts until it was her turn again. She stared down at the dice that Zelda had slid in front of her and then up at the siblings. "I want to help." She announced softly. "When it's time to go to the institute, I want to go with you all. Maybe I can help watch your back while the soldiers are springing their trap."

"Why would you put yourself in that kind of danger for us?" Zara wondered."

Tessa played with the dice, a finger slowly flipping them over instead of picking them up. "Because it is what friends do for each other. You kept me safe during the accident. Now it's my turn to stand by your side and do the same."

"Will your mother even let you come with us?" Zack asked the most important question. Their opinion didn't matter one way or the other if Anna didn't approve.

The dice snapped out from under her finger and flew off the table. "Um, maybe mom can come along as well with some of our guards?"

"Does that woman even need any guards?" Zara muttered quietly.

Chapter 34

C lasses started on an interesting note that next Holztag morning. Quinn was sitting on top of his desk, which was completely normal for him. What was unusual was the rather large smile he was sporting.

He waited for the entire class to trickle in, before zeroing in on his favorite student. "Spencer VanCamp, would you please come to the front of the class?"

The confused boy stood and walked to the front.

Quinn's smile abruptly changed to one that held a distinctly predatory edge. "The headmaster asked me to call you up to the front of the class today to give you a piece of news on his behalf."

Spencer nodded, his confusion dulling his wits. "Alright, tell me."

The teacher smirked. "Spencer VanCamp, for the act of ganging up on and injuring another student of this academy, you and all the other students involved with the act have been expelled from this institution effective immediately. I dearly wanted to paraphrase this next part, but I was forbidden from going too far off-script.

"Just let it be known that you are to be off academy grounds by nightfall. Anything left in your dorm at that time will be thrown out. This school allows voluntary duels for a reason. There is absolutely no reason to bully or injure someone outside of one."

The room was absolutely silent as he finished, with even Spencer not knowing how to react.

"You're joking, right?"

"Thankfully, no. With this, I no longer have to look at you each day and remember what your father did to me and my wife!" All pretense at playing the nice and even remotely civil teacher had vanished in an instant. "I want you out of my classroom this INSTANT!" He roared, startling the boy.

Spencer ran back to his desk and grabbed his bag. "You'll pay for this!" He snarled at Zack.

Behind him, Quinn grabbed an eraser and threw it at him. The lightweight object smacked into the back of his head and sent him stumbling forward, dropping his bag.

"You don't learn, do you? Your own actions are what got you into this mess, while his place on the noble food chain could keep him out of it. His sister is a royal princess of Albion. All she has to do is ask the crown and your head would roll." Quinn snorted in amusement, seeing as a pale Spencer finally began to understand the situation. One he had created for himself and potentially his family. "Now imagine what she could do to every business your family runs. Countless and endless audits, supply chain problems, workers that no longer want to be associated with the companies. All of that and more, all because you gave her a reason."

"I..." Spencer rubbed the back of his head, where the eraser had hit. All signs of his formerly cocky self were gone. Without saying another word, he picked up his bag from where he had dropped it on the floor and left the room.

Quinn sighed happily. "Ahh, that felt good. I know this sounds bad, but I really need to thank you for getting beat by him, Zack." He gave the boy in question a quick thumbs-up and then began their class for real.

Hours later, Anna was waiting for them outside the dorm with Ben. His head had been shaved, and he was leaning weakly against the car beside her.

"Ben," Tessa shouted joyfully, seeing him up and about for the first time in a while. "How are you feeling?"

"Much better miss, still somewhat foggy, and weak, unfortunately. However, I'll be back and performing my duties in no time."

Anna groaned. "He keeps going on like that, saying duty this, and duty that. I'm half tempted to fire him, just so he'll shut up and take some proper time to heal."

Zara chuckled, holding lightly onto George, who had accompanied her that day. Zelda had stayed back to teach Aisha how to better fight and utilize her size.

"Please, don't joke about that, ma'am," Ben said stiffly.

"Alright," Zack interrupted before things got out of hand. "Are we leaving for your house already?"

Anna winked at him and nodded.

"We have everything packed already, just in case you were here right after classes. We just need to grab them and let Edith know."

They left Tessa at Edith's door and hurried on to their own dorm. Where their own bags and the bears were waiting.

Zack gave the dorm a quick once-over as they were leaving and stopped. His gaze snagged on their night vision goggles and Zelda's belt of daggers. His own staff was standing beside the door, and after grabbing the goggles and the belt, he left with the staff in hand. It was better to be prepared and not need them, than to need them and not have them.

He was fairly certain Anna would have said something, but he couldn't be positive. They were out in the open, and it was a sensitive topic that she might not have felt safe mentioning. Either way, he had them in the bag now.

Content that they had everything, he locked the door and picked up Aisha. The other two bears were already in Zara's arms. They met Tessa at Edith's door, and after a brief goodbye, they were on their way.

"Something about this goodbye feels different," Zack muttered uncomfortably. A yawning pit of anxiousness had appeared in the center of his stomach as they hugged Edith.

"Is it your sixth sense?" Zara whispered back.

"I'm not sure. I mean, my normal magic stat is over twenty, but it rarely works over here."

"Yeah, but that was before we had access to our magic again."

He tapped his staff down the stone steps of the dorm building. "Then we might not be seeing her for a while after this." It was a surprisingly painful thing for him to say.

Edith had done a lot for them, and become almost exactly what she wanted, a grandmother. It was a tenuous connection, to be sure. They hadn't known each other long enough for it to be anything but. Just weeks before, they had no connections tying them to Albion or Aperra. Now they had several.

Anna saw the staff in his hands and nodded. Ben was leaning against the open backdoor and was breathing heavily while squeezing his eyes shut every few seconds.

"Are you sure you're feeling alright and should be out of bed?" Tessa inquired worriedly.

"It's just a minor headache, miss," He answered between huffs of breath.

"Take care of yourself, Ben." With that, she slid into the back of the vehicle.

Zack passed her their bags and the bears. "I'm glad to see you back up and about. Tessa's right though, you need to take care of yourself." He angled the staff and climbed inside.

Zara reached up and patted the older man on his head, smiled at him, and then joined the others inside the car.

"Why did you bring the staff?" Tessa wondered as the door closed.

"I'm not sure. It just seemed like a good idea."

Aisha sat up, shook herself, and hurried over to the tinted windows. George followed behind her a second later. Only Zelda, who was more experienced in the ways of the world, remained calm and sitting on Zara's lap.

"How's dad?"

Anna looked back as her door closed with a click. "He's good, sweetie. He answered all their questions and explained everything that he had found, along with what led to him looking in the first place. Not to speak ill of your father, but it's a good thing that he has the personality he does. If it had been anybody else, I have no doubt that they would be held as a potential traitor.

"As it is, his work is going to be more closely monitored from here on out. I did get Caroline to agree to partially fund his personal projects, at least. That way, they can have some claim to everything he does." She turned back around and gripped the steering wheel. "For now, he's still at the castle, going over his research with them. Explaining what had been changed by the assistants, and what he has learned since then."

"I'm sure he's in heaven then." Tessa grinned.

"I don't think he even noticed when I left earlier." Her mother agreed.

"What about all the people we helped rescue? What happened to them?"

Zack and Zara leaned forward, interested in what she had to say.

"They are all still in the process of being extensively debriefed. After we take care of the traitors in a few days, they will be returned to their families and connected with counseling services."

Tessa peered out the window at the passing landscape. "A few days? Is the plan moving ahead that quickly?"

Anna angled the rearview mirror to see her daughter better while she focused on driving. "The Major has had his troops at the institute facility for years at this point. They know the place like the back of their hand. All of its dirty little secrets were revealed to them a long time ago."

Zack jerked, remembering some of those ghost-filled rooms. Not all secrets were created equal, and that place had its fair share of horrors.

"When do they plan on setting it into motion?" He asked, reaching for his sister's hand.

"It has already been confirmed that the royal prince and princess are on their way back here. They'll switch vehicles tonight and then again in the morning, making sure that no one is following them. After they are deemed safe and secure, we'll bring you to the institute.

"From there, it's just a matter of spreading the word that you'll be arriving the next day. That will give us time to ensure you are safe, while also letting you look at the portal. If everything goes according to plan, Shouvain's and Trask's people will attack early the next day before you were scheduled to arrive or at the same time."

"Wow, he really does work quick. The Major will have everything set up by Sonntag?" Zara's voice squeaked in surprise.

Anna chuckled. "Oh honey, that man wants revenge on these people bad! He's been working all the healers ragged to get his people back into fighting shape. He even called up the rest of his soldier company for this. Everyone is going to be there."

"And he managed that without anyone noticing?"

"They've found a few secret ways in and out of the institute over the years. They'll be blocked for the attack, but they're perfect for getting his people inside undetected."

"Are we even certain that Zara and me going to that portal is going to be enough of a draw for them to appear?"

Upfront, Ben pressed against his door, as Anna chuckled darkly.

"About that, your lives are about to get more complicated, I'm afraid. We had the same thought, so all the rumors we'll spread will include some additional information."

"Mother, what did you do?" Tessa groaned.

"Nothing much. I simply made sure to include two extra pieces of useful news. Like, say, a certain portal going mysteriously dark and locking itself while Zack was inside. As well as another portal that has been in a similar state since Zack was removed from its presence."

"You aren't mentioning Zara in the rumors?"

"Of course not. She's a princess, and besides, her age at the time of the institute event is still a factor."

"Well, that should certainly get them interested in what will happen when we go there." Zack leaned back and closed his eyes. Something was bound to go wrong with this plan. They were rushing it-

He opened his eyes and sat up straight. "You're rushing this by at least a week or two. Why? What changed?"

Anna passed the turnoff she would have taken to her house and continued on the main road, heading towards the capital. "George Trask was captured last night trying to leave the country. He had the plans for more of those suits you two are always wearing in his suitcase. He also had a small, fully functioning thinking-box, which is apparently called a *'Workstation',* that was ahead of what we are making. It obviously came from whoever designed the original one from the institute."

"Has he said why he was leaving?"

"I haven't spoken with him yet. He is due to arrive from the border tonight. Needless to say, since he is one of the people we were counting on using, him almost disappearing moved up the timetable. Once they realize he hasn't appeared, they'll grow suspicious, which means we have a limited window to work with."

Tessa fisted her hands. "Mom, I want to help. I want to be there, where I can keep an eye on them and keep them safe!" The words came out in a rush, but there was an energy to them that spoke of her resolve.

"No, absolutely not!"

"Mother!" She shouted, almost deafening them all in the enclosed space. "They are my friends; this is something that I have to do. You taught me that."

Upfront Anna was grumbling and cursing, holding a conversation of one with herself. "We'll talk it over tonight with your father, assuming, of course, that we can pull him away from everyone." She said at last. "And Tessa, do not ever use my own words against me for something like this again. This is going to be dangerous. Luckily for you, I'll be there, and if you are very lucky I'll be able to force Trask to procure you a suit similar to theirs."

With any luck, it would be less dangerous than their foray into the mountains had been. Anna regrettably knew better than to count on something as ephemeral as luck. Rushing any plan was dangerous, and this one had too many moving parts where it could all go wrong. She was loath to bring her daughter into that kind of ticking time bomb of a situation.

Yet she couldn't deny her outright either, no matter how much she wanted to!

What Tessa had said had reminded her of something similar she had promised years ago. A promise that she had failed to keep. She knew it wasn't the same situation. Anna's promise had been to her cousins, not too simple friends, yet it had struck a chord with her. Against her better judgment, she had found herself compromising with her beloved daughter.

The regret came as soon as she uttered the words, and she found herself glaring at the road.

Tessa sat in surprised silence for a few minutes, watching Zara play with her bears. She hadn't thought that would work, and now the reality of what she had possibly signed on for was hitting her.

"You scared?" Zack teased.

Zara glanced up at her and giggled. "I think it just finally hit her. Before this, it wasn't real. Now that her mother has tentatively agreed to let her come, it is, and after what happened in the mountains, she knows what can happen now."

"You're mean," Tessa pouted, and turned away from them.

George hopped over to her and climbed onto her lap, where he began poking at her puffed-up cheeks.

"He says you're too old to pout." Zara translated.

"How would he know? Isn't he mentally like four or five right now?" Tessa shot back, poking at the bear's worn face in return.

"Exactly. All young kids are outspoken and annoying, right? I mean... they were at the orphanage, at least."

George stepped back in shock and grabbed at his chest. He had been betrayed!

Zack chuckled, glad that the serious atmosphere from before had been broken. There would be enough time to think about how stupid they all were as they were facing the portal. He much preferred to spend the time before then, enjoying himself and forgetting about what was to come.

Anna drove them to the castle, and then to a tunnel that led underneath it. It wound around, with paths leading to different areas, but the main one always taking them deeper. At the bottom, or at least what they assumed was the bottom, was the dungeon. It was where all the country's traitors were taken.

It was the place Mathew had nearly ended up spending whatever remained of his life in.

Anna would be meeting George Trask there later that evening when he arrived.

"Why'd you bring us down here?" Tessa asked her mother when the car stopped.

"It's just in case I need the vehicle later after speaking with Trask, plus your father is only a couple of levels above us. I thought we might as well speak with him now while Zack and Zara head on up ahead of us."

Zack shrugged and grabbed their bags. "I don't mind, just point us in the right direction."

"We'll be taking the lift as well, so there's no rush. Ben will ensure you get where you need to go. I believe Caroline wanted to speak with you as well. She hasn't had a chance to talk with either of you alone yet, something that I know she has been wanting to."

Tessa shared a wide-eyed look with the siblings. Her mother pointed them to a lift built into the center of the spiral core she had driven down around. Ben lagged behind, struggling to keep up with their already slow pace. Tessa offered to help him, but the freshly baldheaded man stubbornly refused to consider the offer.

Zara pointed to Aisha, who promptly picked him up and allowed them to speed up.

"I would have been fine," Ben protested, losing his normally proper and contained self.

"Sure, you would have been." Zara winked at the others. "Your slow pace, however, would have resulted in us keeping the queen waiting."

He blanched, losing what little color his face had. "I shall have to prevail upon you and Aisha until we reach the lift then."

"Too easy," The young girl whispered.

The lift dinged as they drew near, opening to reveal one of the butlers that usually accompanied the king and queen.

"Mrs. Ricerca," The butler blinked in surprise at seeing Ben being carried by a giant bear and then continued on without missing a beat. "The King wants to speak with you right away. He is currently in his office."

"Ben, take Tessa to talk with Mathew while I speak with the king."

Aisha gently lowered the man to his feet as they entered the lift.

Chapter 35

The queen took a sip of her tea, her eyes flicking from each sibling to the bears sitting calmly at their sides. "Anna and the Major had mentioned they could move in their reports. Seeing it in person, however, truly drives home how close we are to our world going through its own Change."

Her index finger drifted around the rim of her cup.

"I'm a traveler, you know, and so is Orlo. Not that it matters. We've only been allowed through the portals a few times. The risk was deemed too high for him, and since everyone assumed, rightly I might add, that we would get married. I was placed under similar restrictions. It is one of the few items I miss. All those worlds that I will never get to see." Her eyes took on a dreamy look. "Orlo and my kids are worth such a small sacrifice. I have never doubted that for a moment, despite occasionally missing it."

"Is that why you brought us here, to talk about the portals or the coming Change?" Zara had George in her lap and spoke with only a hint of a quiver in her voice.

Zara had regained much of her confidence over the last two weeks. Having constant access to her magic while others didn't helped tremendously in that regard. A mobile and active Zelda helped even more.

Zack hadn't seen his sister this willing to talk with others since their time in the orphanage. The rapid change in her filled him with hope, and a sense of dread of what would happen should they fail. Would he, or anyone for that matter, be able to pull her out of her shell a second time?

"Not the Change specifically. However, I am interested in discussing that topic at a later time. You are correct in that I want to talk about portals, more specifically the one at the institute." She gently placed her teacup on the small table next to her chair.

Zack shifted uncomfortably. The couch no longer feeling as luxurious as it had when they first entered the room. "We've spoken about the portal a couple of times already with Anna and the Major."

"No, you haven't, not really at least. Believe me, I checked. Each time the subject has come up in the past, you duck their questions in some way, answering one, or maybe two, and then changing the subject. That isn't going to fly this time. I want and need to know what makes that portal different from all the rest? What makes this one so special? Was it chosen for a reason, or did its interaction with the two of you change it?"

The siblings stilled, unable to hide their shock.

"Ah," The queen sighed. "So, it's you two who are special, not necessarily the portal. Interesting. In that case, I understand why you avoid answering so strongly. You might not even know the answers." She ran her finger around the rim of her cup a few times, producing a dull musical note. "We can address that later when we have more time. I'm expecting guests, and I doubt you want them, well, one of them at least walking in on that particular conversation."

There was a brief jingle from the bell to the side of the door, as though her words had summoned them.

Caroline stood and opened the door. The room was soundproofed and necessitated her doing certain things herself. Anna was waiting on the other side, with Jean coming up rapidly behind her.

"Come in," The queen moved to the side for Anna. "Specialist McCleary, I was expecting the Major."

"He sends his apologies, but decided that a friendlier face would be better suited for this conversation." She stopped by the queen's side and whispered something into her ear.

Caroline's face was blank when she invited the soldier inside the room.

"Now, where were we?" She asked, retaking her seat, and picking up her cup of tea.

"You were asking about what made the portal at the institute so special," Zack replied with a resigned sigh.

"It was a rhetorical question, dear." The queen dropped a few darkberries into her tea to steep. "Now, do you have an answer for us?"

"We may," Zack began slowly, unwilling to reveal one of their secrets but also not seeing a way around it. Not without lying, at least. A generally bad idea when it came to the three women in front of him. "You have to understand I don't know why we were able to awaken in the manner that we did, whether it was through their efforts or just plain luck." He chuckled dryly. "I'm pretty sure they never knew either."

Zara reached over and took hold of his hand, gripping it tight as he began to breathe faster.

"We had been at that place for a while. I can't remember now how long it had been, a few months at least. The researchers had tried to force me through the portal what must have been hundreds of times by that point. Obviously, it had never worked. That particular day, they had done something to my neck and then gave me the normal round of injections.

"And then they brought in Zara. Sometimes they would have her watch as they tried to force me through the portal." Zack swallowed around the lump in his throat and blinked repeatedly. He was skimming over the details, but remembering that day was enough to set him off. "Anyway, one of the guards, I guess, thought it would be funny to throw her at me, not sure why. I caught her, thankfully, but the force pushed me back and we both slipped through the portal together."

"Just like that?" Anna asked in surprise.

"Just like that," Zack confirmed. "For whatever reason, it worked that time on both of us. They were experimenting on her as well, of course." He said bitterly, not bothering to hide his resentment. "Not all of them were the same on both of us, which hopelessly muddled the data. Regardless, we made it through and gained a title tied to the portal."

"And?" The queen probed. "What was the title? What were its effects? How does a title have anything to do with a portal pretty much shutting down after the two of you were removed from its vicinity?"

"I was getting there-"

"Get there faster, Zack," Anna cut in, leaning forward. Her interest had been peaked as well.

Standing behind her, Jean was taking notes of everything he said.

"The title is called *'Child of the Portals'* and the description reads, *'a person who has taken a piece of the portal energy and made it a part of themselves.'* If I had to guess, then the reason the portal shutdown as you said, after we left is because we are tied to it. How it is related to all the other portals and their power markers, however, I can't say."

"Interesting. So what you are saying is that it might be a proximity issue? We only need to get you close, and then the portal will open again." Jean continued taking notes as she spoke.

"Maybe, I don't know. We haven't seen it, and it depends on your goal. If that is the case, then as soon as we leave the area, it will probably shut down again. In order to keep the portal open permanently without us there, Zara and I will likely have to begin its Change."

"That will shut it down anyway," The soldier remarked dryly, with a discreet wink.

"Maybe, but we should take the opportunity to do it while they are there, regardless. After everything is safe and the fighting has ended." Anna clarified. "We can hide them near the portal. If he's right, then it will make a good emergency exit in case something unexpected happens."

Jean winced and lowered her notebook. "Why did you have to say that? Now, something will happen!"

"Always plan for the worst, and hope for the best," Anna told her. "That adage has saved my life more than a few times."

The soldier and temporary teacher grumbled a few times and then went silent.

The queen, meanwhile, was running her finger around the rim of her cup. "You won't be able to take them there early. Everyone has to see them arriving. The enemy won't walk into the trap without knowing for sure that they are there."

"Our original plan had been to parade them out the door for some fresh air when the time was right," Jean explained.

Anna coughed lightly. "I tried to protest for a similar reason, your majesty. Unfortunately, I don't believe that the Major is currently in the right frame of mind for outside opinions. He wants revenge, plain and simple."

"Why wasn't I informed of this?"

"It was something we were going to discuss with you together later," Jean answered, sinking wearily into the spot beside Anna. "Sergeant Grieves is struggling to hold him at bay, despite also wanting revenge for what happened to everyone. There is only so much he can do and the Major, frankly, is being a pain. Bringing in one of the other company commanders, however, is not the answer."

"That was one of the first things we thought of asking you to do," Anna told the queen. "However, we both agreed that such a move would be the wrong one for the Major's future."

"I am inclined to agree as well," Caroline said slowly. "We'll discuss that matter further later and come up with an alternative. Zack and Zara will go when I allow them to, and not before."

The siblings were excused a few minutes later now that their part in the meeting had been finished. A maid who had been waiting nearby took them to a different part of the castle filled with rooms.

They were led to a suite that contained several rooms and allowed to pick whichever they wanted. She left after informing them that a snack would be brought over shortly.

The bears ran from room to room, exploring the accommodations. Their bags and weapons had all been placed in the main sitting area of the suite.

"There are four rooms in here, and each of them is mostly the same," Zara told her brother as the bears returned.

"Four, huh? You think that means Tessa and her parents will also be staying here as well?"

"Maybe it's also possible that this castle has no suites smaller than this."

Zack cracked his neck and pointed to a room. "Well, there is something we need to do before anyone else gets here. The crystal has been in my suit for a few days longer than it was yours, or Zelda. I think it's time we moved it to George or Aisha. I'll go in there and take it out now."

His sister nodded. "That's fine. I'm glad you've had it a few extra days, in any case. It really helped up in the mountains. Your suit needed the extra support it gave."

He nodded, remembering how close he had come up there. She canceled her puppet spell, and Zack went into the room with a knife to cut out the crystal.

Aisha was the one who received it a few minutes later. She and George had played a game of their own devising and she had won. It was a given, really, considering her size and the benefits that came with it.

Since it was his second time, Zack quickly cut the threads down her back and thrust the crystal into her back. He took a moment to make sure it was secure and then held the pieces of her back together for his sister. Under the guidance of Zara's magic, the bear was quickly repaired and fixed.

Aisha bounced away from him as quickly as she could, her fluffy arms reaching around to her healed back. It took Zara several minutes of coaxing to get her to calm down.

"I take it she didn't fully understand what I was going to do?" He asked, collapsing onto the couch next to her.

"No, she didn't. I had to take control of her while you were working, otherwise, she would have made a mess of it." Zara closed her eyes and leaned against him. "I know it would have been easier, and maybe even better, to just cut the animation spell to her... But I can't do that. It feels too much like killing them."

"I know. Don't worry too much. I'm sure Zelda will explain what the crystal will do to her."

A plateful of small crème sandwiches, too sugary for Zack's taste but perfect for Zara, arrived as the promised snack a little later.

"Is that what you're wearing for dinner with the king and queen?" Tessa asked after walking silently into the main room. Her bag was held in her arms and a pale, trembling Ben was behind her.

"We didn't even know we were eating with them," Zack replied, looking down at his clothes. "I'm not sure either of us brought anything fancy enough for something like that."

"Are you staying in this suite, too?" Zara wondered.

"Yeah, mom will probably grab the last room, along with dad if he remembers to sleep in time." Tessa gently guided Ben over to a chair and pushed him down. "You're not well enough to be out of bed yet. You really should have stayed at home."

He nodded mutely; his head beaded in a cold sweat.

"What did your father say? Did he agree to you coming with us to the institute?" Zack hoped the man had enough sense to say no. Even if George Trask was able to procure or even create a suit for Tessa in time, it would be a dangerous place for all involved.

"He said he would talk it over with mother," She sniffed, her shoulders sagging. "Sorry, it looks like I won't be able to go with you after all."

"It's probably for the best this time. The plan seems to involve us being seen and little else. If it got to the point where we had to fight, something would have gone seriously wrong." Zack dusted a few sandwich crumbs from his shirt and stood. "Now, you mentioned dinner and clothes. Why don't you help us pick out something decent then from what we brought?"

Zara ran into the room she had picked and brought out her bag. Zack didn't bother. He knew what he had packed. The outfit he was wearing now was about as formal as any of his clothes got. It turned out to be the same for Zara. Neither of them had been expecting to be taken to the royal castle instead of the Ricerca mansion.

"I'd say I was in the same situation as you, except I think mom or one of the maids packed me a dress," Tessa told them looking over Zara's nice new clothes, that were nowhere near formal enough for a dinner with the king and queen.

"They did. I'll go down and retrieve it shortly, milady," Ben answered, looking absolutely wiped on the chair.

"Mom or I can get it. You just stay there and don't move."

He nodded weakly after a moment, his posture collapsing. It was a sign of just how tiring moving about had proven to be for the injured man.

Dinner turned out to be a relaxed affair, with the king and queen treating the siblings almost as family the entire time. Not like their own son and daughter, but more like cousins. People that were family, but you weren't sure where you stood with them. The dinner helped everyone to understand where the boundaries were.

Later that night, George Trask arrived, and Anna went down to interrogate him with Amar. Neither mentioned what they learned, but whatever it was had them both on edge afterward.

The next morning, it was confirmed that the royal prince and princess had switched vehicles and had been deemed safe for the moment. It would be some time yet before they were secure, however, they were on their way. Driving their way across the country of Albion was slower than flying, more so when you had to keep making stops to switch out vehicles. The crown was taking no risks with their safety, not after everything that had happened recently.

Meanwhile, at the castle, Zack and Zara had been invited to tea with the queen twice more that day. Once to talk about school and the second time to talk about their life after the institute. She was appalled to learn about how bad the quality of their food had been and interested in what else they had to say.

In many ways, they had been lucky, their housing had been taken care of, and with it, their minimum energy needs. So, they told her stories of the people around them who hadn't been so lucky. Those who had to pinch and scrape for every coin to keep their apartments warm and food on their table. The rising cost of mana crystals and the energy they provided trickled down in an ever-increasing balloon.

It was a problem she was naturally aware of. How could she not be? It was, however, the first time she had heard how bad it was getting for the poor. They were often the most overlooked and forgotten about demographic of any country, and Albion was no different. The poor were simply too poor to have a voice anywhere it mattered.

Caroline and Orlo were doing the best they could to make a difference. Unfortunately, they were pushing against the nobles that liked the way things currently were. This was just another project that had been turned into a long-term goal. One that was then unknowingly to her at least filled with corruption and people who didn't share their goals.

"Do you think she really had no idea about how bad everything was?" Zara asked later that night. She had crept into his room, with all her bears in tow.

They would be heading off to the institute in the morning, and she didn't want to spend the night alone. Even having Zelda, George, and Aisha awake and ready by her side wasn't enough to offset the fear that place brought to her. It was deep-seated in her bones, a core part of herself. Something that had become an integral part of her identity over the years.

The thought of going back there again filled them both with an unspeakable amount of dread and anxiety. They were mentally stronger than back then, and the circumstances were different. Yet the conditioned emotions refused to leave them alone. Only facing the place of their fear could have a hope of doing that.

"I'm not sure. She's smarter than I thought she would be, so normally I would say she must have known. Then again, taking care of a country isn't easy. Did you see the paperwork on the table earlier? She was reviewing the rising crime in a city near one of the borders. Caroline is spreading herself so thin, trying to do everything. I think both her and the king are going to burn themselves out if they're not careful."

"That's what I was thinking as well. I think they are both good people who are simply trying to do too much. I wonder why they aren't delegating more?" Zara yawned and snuggled up to Aisha, using her as a pillow.

Zack rolled over and closed his eyes. "Who knows? I'm sure they have their reasons, and a lack of trust in their nobles is probably a big one."

Chapter 36

Three separate large, armored vehicles left the castle in the early hours the next morning. In the back of one of them sat Zack, Zara, and the bears, along with their chosen weapons. Anna and a few armed and armored soldiers took up the rest of the room.

Anna inspected her pistols and blades, setting each item in her lap as she finished with it. "You might as well stop hiding, Tessa. You need to check your equipment as well." She said in a resigned tone after they had been driving for a few minutes.

A soldier near the rear doors pulled off their helmet, revealing Tessa's vibrant, slightly sweaty red hair. "How did you know?"

"I knew you would try something when you didn't fight us more on our decision to not let you come."

"You could have stopped me then," Tessa said as she opened a bag sitting on the floor between her feet. A pair of curved blades with sheathes identical to her mother's were inside.

Anna ejected the ammo magazine from the Majair pistol in her hand and shook her head. "Your father convinced me it would be a bad idea if I did. We don't want you to end up like me, someone who is on a quest for revenge for years. I doubt their deaths, if it ever came to that, would cause such a drastic change in you.

"Mathew felt otherwise, and after arguing about it repeatedly, we decided that if you cared enough to sneak onto the mission, I would let you come." She double-checked the magazine was full before pushing it back into place with a satisfying click. "Of course, that comes with the caveat that you stick with them and don't do anything stupid."

Her fists clenched tight, popping her knuckles in a rare show of stress.

"Of course, mom. I know this isn't a game, just like I know that I'm better trained than either of them. You've made sure of that, ever since I was a kid, in fact." Tessa studiously ignored the soldiers in the back with them and concentrated solely on her mother.

"We'll talk more when we get there. After we parade the three of you around, I want you by the portal with the door to the room locked tight. No one gets in until this is all over. Is that clear?" She glared at the three teens.

"Yes, ma'am," Zack replied, holding tight to his staff with one hand, and his sister with the other. His sixth sense had been screaming at him ever since he entered the vehicle earlier. Something, possibly everything, was going to go wrong with this mission. The only thing he could do was hold his sister and then sit back for the ride. The uncomfortable, gnawing feeling in the pit of his stomach growing with every passing second.

Zara nodded and pulled Zelda and George firmly onto her lap. Aisha was sitting next to her, the big bear timidly playing with her paws.

The rest of the soldiers began checking their equipment. It was done more as something to pass the time than something they needed to do. Each of them had thoroughly checked each item back at base before ever putting it on.

The drive to the institute dragged on for hours, the armored vehicles passing one city after another.

Zack had never known the exact location of the institute, only that it was in some remote location. He hadn't realized it was also so far away from the capital, though now that he thought about it, that made sense. Who would take the extra risk of operating so close to a country's capital when they didn't need to?

Food was passed around for breakfast and later for lunch from a cooler in the front. There was even a small bathroom built-in for long trips such as this when they couldn't afford to stop.

Finally, sometime early in the afternoon, the vehicle slowed and turned onto a road leading up into the hills. They had nearly arrived at their destination.

It was a good thing too. Zack felt as though his stomach was trying to eat itself. It was intensely unpleasant and not something he was used to dealing with for such a long period of time before.

The first chance he got when they stopped, he was going to warn Anna of what was to come. He had held off up till that point, for fear of the soldiers overhearing. Zack hoped it wouldn't be too late to warn her when he finally got the chance.

"You can calm down. They won't attack us until they know for sure you've arrived." Anna stood and strapped on her knives. The sheathes came with an easy attaching mechanism that also let her move it up and down the sides of the belt. With them shifted above her hips, nearly on top of her pistol holsters, she was able to sit back down comfortably.

"That helps, but only a little. I know the Major has prepared as best as he could, but you do realize that we are still about to walk into some form of a trap. Right?" Zack felt his sister's hand tighten in his own, while the bears shifted slightly to better comfort her. They had remained mostly still the entire ride, to not unnerve the mostly unknowing soldiers.

"I do, we all do. Every soldier in these three vehicles specially volunteered for this mission. They knew it would be more dangerous than just waiting at the institute and the various ambush sites. But they believe in what we are trying to do. With the goal of ridding our country of these people and getting revenge for what they did in the mountains." Anna answered, ensuring the three teens understood.

Zack squeezed his eyes shut and swallowed with a nod. "Alright. It's just my sixth sense has been going crazy ever since we left the castle. That's not normal, usually, it just pings to let me know something is wrong and then goes away. This has been a non-stop feeling of building dread. Something is going to happen, and it's going to be significantly worse than you are expecting."

She cursed and rushed to the front. "I wish you would have said something sooner than when we were a few minutes away from the site." Anna thumped on the back panel of the driver's section. "Give me the radio and pipe me through to the other vehicles and everyone else if you can!" She ordered when it opened with a snap.

A big blocky black rectangle the size of a small brick and attached to a cord was passed through the hole to her a moment later. Anna needed to use both hands to hold and operate the unwieldy tech. Pressing a button on the upper topside of the item, she began speaking into it.

Everyone in the back burst into motion as they secured their armor and equipment. Doing everything they could think of to make sure they were fully ready when the time came.

Zack tightened the laces on his boots and picked up his bag. His and Zara's role in whatever was to come was simple. They were to be seen, and then they needed to run inside the institute. Nothing more. They weren't combatants, at least not yet.

The large vehicle shuddered and skidded to the side, jostling everyone inside as behind them a bomb went off, narrowly missing the last personnel carrier.

Anna whipped her head around and violently cursed. The road behind them was destroyed and completely impassable. "Why don't these people learn some new moves? They did the exact same thing in the mountains."

"It worked there too," A soldier muttered, as trees fell across the destroyed road further blocking their way back. "They must have buried them at night when no one was watching this stretch of road."

"Change of plans! Get us as close to the doors of the facility as you possibly can." Anna commanded the driver. She spoke quietly into the transmitter and then passed it back to the communications officer in the front passenger seat.

The armored metal on the side deformed and bulged inward as a bullet hit it with a loud pinging thump. One after another, new bulges appeared. Up front, the driver-side window cracked and spiderwebbed, threatening to break at any moment.

The driver spun the wheel and pushed the pedal to the floor. The heavy, armored vehicle went off the road, bounced, and then jumped over a small ditch, landing with a bone-jarring thud, bottoming out the shocks. Zack held onto Zara and Tessa as their loose seatbelts barely kept them in place. The back end began to grind and scream as they pushed forward for a few more seconds before stopping with a squeal of newly misaligned brakes.

Everyone held their breath and looked at Anna for guidance. Everything had gone sideways so quickly they were still processing what had even happened.

"As soon as the doors are open, I want Zack, Zara, and Tessa surrounded. We're parked as close to the doors as we possibly can now, far closer than originally intended or designed. They're only going to get a brief look at the kids, and then we are going to have everyone inside. Understood?"

"Ma'am, yes ma'am!" They shouted.

"You two stand in front of me. I'll be in the back. Now that we can use our magic here, I can cast my *'Arcane Armor'* spell as we rush out."

"Don't forget, my bracelet also has a shield in it." Zara protested.

"Have you charged it yet?"

She hesitated. "No, I forgot that I needed to. I've been so excited about having the bears back, that it even having a shield has slipped my mind until now."

He nodded. "Mine too, which is why we are going with my spell." He would only be able to maintain it for a little while, but it would be enough to hopefully save their lives if something happened.

His magical energy control over the last couple of days had improved some, with his constant practice. The major difference was the amount of energy that had slowly filled his body as it regenerated naturally. He couldn't afford to waste it, and he also couldn't afford to save it at a time such as this.

Aisha stood up, startling the soldiers, and moved into position by the door. George hopped off Zara's lap and joined her a moment later. Zelda would remain with Zara as her primary protector.

Zara and Tessa nodded at each other and knelt behind the bears with their packs. Zack was ready just behind them, with his bag already strapped to his front.

The soldiers lined up alongside them in a tense silence.

There was a single knuckle rap on the outside panel of the cargo doors, and then they swung open, letting in the evening light. The sun was low and to their side, highlighting the waiting soldiers profiles as they urged everyone into motion.

The soldiers worked together like the thoroughly trained teams they were and had everyone out and running within heartbeats of the doors opening.

The expected attacks failed to materialize on their bodies, instead continuing to pepper the sides of the armored vehicle. The driver and communications officer abandoned it through the passenger door as the backend had been destroyed by the jump.

That particular vehicle wasn't going anywhere. Even the thick tires they used had their limits. The armor, on the other hand, seemed to be holding up to the distant Majair fire much better.

Zack risked a single, confused glance back. His eyes raked over the tree line that had been pushed farther back, recently if the countless tree stumps were anything to go by. The open space needed for the large leafy multi-colored trees made it hard for any large group of people to effectively hide.

It was making more sense to him now why the Major dared to walk everyone into such an obvious trap here. They should be able to see anyone who got close well before they could do anything. Outside of the usually rare snipers that were currently destroying the vehicle they had been in.

Still, that didn't explain why his anxiety was growing as they ran towards the building entrance. Was he confusing his sixth sense with simple fear and apprehension for returning to this place?

He stumbled and was forced to turn around as the soldier behind him caught the collar of his shirt.

"Pay attention!"

He grimaced and kept his head down. Every step he took felt as though it took an eternity, with his gut screaming at him to activate his armor, that an attack must be close at hand.

Step after step they raced, with nothing hitting them. Then they were through. They had made it inside the foyer of the institute building. The soldiers spun around and brought their weapons to bear, searching for any target that might appear.

"Meet up with Specialist McCleary or Sergeant Graves and the rest of your squads! Our original mission has changed. I'll get them to the portal and then come back." Anna yelled at the soldiers, already pushing the kids and bears deeper into the structure.

Zack began to hyperventilate as the familiar walls brought back long-repressed memories. Things that even he had forgotten.

Zara slowed, pulling Zelda into her arms. The whites of her eyes were showing as they darted from place to place. The corridors they were making their way down were the same ones they had seen only twice before. The day they had first been brought to this accursed place, and then again when they had been rescued.

Only once going the direction, however, that they were currently going. It was easily one of the worst days of their lives.

It was memory overload, and neither was dealing with the sudden resurgence well.

In front of Zack's eyes, the color of everything shifted to a slightly different hue as memories from the past overlayed his vision of the current. Behind him, the exact same thing was happening to Zara. Ghostly forms of captors long-dead walked past, laughing as they tormented him and his sister. The white coats, kept immaculately clean in life, had turned to grey as he rushed past them.

Unbidden, his hands came up to his neck, protecting the spot they seemed to cut most often. His staff clattered to the floor, forgotten, and was then summarily kicked to the side.

"Zack, Zara, where are you going?" Anna called out to them as the duo rushed ahead.

Zara was seeing similar visions from the past as well and was looking to escape them with him. An impossible task, in a facility riddled with so many terrible ghosts, all wanting to haunt them.

It didn't matter. In their increasingly panicked minds, they both ran to the only place they could think of that might provide even an ounce of safety. Their old room. A prison cell where they had been able to escape the daily tortures of their existence, if only for a while each day.

They ran through the halls, desperately ignoring the questing hands of the researchers that wanted to pull them in for more experiments. They flinched and cried, each time anyone came too close, mentally regressing to the scared kids they had been all those years ago.

Behind them, mother and daughter ran alongside a panicked Aisha and George. The bears could feel the terror Zara was experiencing and were helpless against it. This was a portion of her life they knew nothing about, only Zelda did.

Errant soldiers still in the halls turned into guards with physical form, further terrifying Zack and Zara. It was as though they had never left. Every memory from their time after being rescued was suddenly locked behind an impenetrable vault door.

Anna cursed and put on a burst of speed. "We don't have time for this." She reached for Zara and was tackled to the ground by Aisha.

The large bear was doing what she was supposed to do and guarding Zara. Which in her panicked and confused state meant everyone but her brother was a possible enemy. Aisha, however, was smart enough to know that Anna wasn't a true enemy and only took her to the ground.

Tessa and George ran around them, intent on not losing sight of the terrified siblings. The interior of the building was a veritable maze of corridors and rooms that would make it easy to lose them in.

Zack gripped his sister's hand tighter as they dodged the ephemeral fingers of one cruel, laughing researcher after another. At last, they were close to their room. He could see the door. They would be safe there. He knew they would, though he couldn't say why.

Together, the duo burst through the unlocked door and slammed it shut behind them. Holding tight to each other, they huddled in a corner and watched the door with bated breath. Waiting for it to open and praying that it wouldn't.

Zelda wiggled out of Zara's arms and onto the floor of the room. She remembered this place as well; it had changed from back then, if only a little. The bunk beds were gone, replaced with a single bed in the corner and a desk next to it. The same open toilet in the corner across from the beds was still there, though someone had put some short walls around it now. Other than that, it looked remarkably unchanged by time or people.

"Zack, Zara, can I open the door?" Tessa called out through the closed door.

Zara whimpered and squeezed her eyes shut, clinging tighter to her brother.

Zack, for his part, shook his head, some of the panic beginning to fade with the imagined safety of the familiar space. For all that, he had thought he would be fine on their return. The truth was he had buried too much of what had been done to them, to him. He was never going to be fine returning to this place, not while those memories still lurked unknown beneath the surface.

Zack felt his shoulders begin to shake as soul-wrenching sobs were torn from his throat. He wanted nothing more than to forget again, and yet he doubted he would be so lucky a second time. He could thank whatever divine being that ruler class existence had spoken of before, that his sister had been so young. She had been spared many of the indignities and tortures because of that.

The door opened a crack as no one responded to Tessa's pleas. Zelda took it upon herself to amble over to the door and swing it open the rest of the way for her. Unofficially inviting her in, while simultaneously revealing the pitiful sight of the sobbing Zack and shaking Zara.

George ran past her and settled into the crook of Zara's arm.

"Oh, I'm so sorry..." Tessa walked slowly into the room with downcast eyes and sat down next to them, with her back against the wall. "I don't think anyone even considered what being back here might be like for you two. Everyone thought you had moved on, at least somewhat, and had made so much progress..." She trailed off, knowing that nothing she could say would be enough.

"We were never going to be alright returning here." He gasped out between sobs. A hint of clarity returning to his eyes. "Too much happened here, with too many repressed memories."

Zara convulsed and screamed into his chest while gripping tightly to him, letting out all her frustration and fear. She went limp afterward and called softly for Zelda.

The bear ran over and picked up her hand.

Over the course of the next few minutes, Zack let out all his bottled-up emotions. While Zara worked on rebuilding her mental walls.

At some point Anna and Aisha showed up. However, only the bear entered the room. The mother instead remained outside, looking in with compassionate eyes. This was something that the kids needed to work their way through. If she interfered now, it would do more harm than good.

The mission would have to wait until they were ready. Who cared that she could hear the distant sound of weapon fire? Despite what had happened to them outside, it wasn't enough. The boy had been right. Something was wrong with their trap.

Zack inhaled sharply with a shudder, bringing himself under control. "Come on," He muttered to his sister, his voice rough from the emotions he was barely holding back. "Let's do this."

She nodded once, pulling Zelda and George up to her face. Aisha crept closer and wrapped her arms around the siblings, hugging them as best she could.

Tessa stood first, her normally bright eyes shadowed in shared pain for what her friends had once gone through in this place. She extended her hand to Zack. "Let's go. Our place is by the portal, not here, hiding in a room. You two are better than that. You're both stronger than that, especially now.

Don't forget, you have access to your magic here, something that no one else does. They can't hurt you, not again."

Zack closed his eyes, and breathed in deep, letting her words trickle through him. Sometimes all it took was someone else saying something that you already knew.

"Yeah, it's time." He took hold of her hand and pulled himself, Zara, and Aisha, into standing positions.

Zara opened her eyes, grinning as George used his soft paws to dab away her tears. "Yeah, we can't expect them to wait forever to spring their trap on us all. Let's go."

They could both still see the ghostly forms of the researchers and guards from their past haunting the halls. With a clearer, less frantic mind, those apparitions no longer held any power over them as they walked through them towards the room that housed the portal.

They would never come back to this place after this mission. There were too many memories, and literal ghosts from their pasts, haunting the place for either to even consider it. For the moment, at least they could look past them.

Chapter 37

The large doors to the room with the portal opened into the walls as Anna entered a code at the side. It was a pointless precaution for a portal that no one could use, but that was the military and their secrets for you.

"I want you three to stay in here until I return and give the all-clear. Zack, Zara, see if you can get the portal working again in case we need it, but do not begin its change! Am I clear? That could be our escape route if everything goes sideways like you think it will."

They nodded, glancing around the mostly bare room. All the equipment that had once filled the room had been taken away, leaving it open and empty save for a few pallets of stored food.

She pushed a button on the pad and the doors began to close, just as the entire facility trembled. The large doors groaned as something thumped loudly against the ceiling above them, the sound echoing through the reinforced concrete layers.

"Move," Anna screamed, punting Aisha further into the room with them while she ran in the other direction.

The ceiling above the doors cracked and bulged outward as an explosion punctured through the levels above and sent it crashing to the floor.

Everyone rushed farther into the room, hiding in the far corner behind the portal with the bears as pieces of the ceiling and walls continued to destabilize and crumble. It soon became clear that whoever had designed this bomb wasn't trying to destroy the room but to merely bury the opening and prevent access to it.

In a flash of insight and guesswork, Zack knew why their trap had failed. It was because there had never been a reason for the other people to ever show up at all. He and Zara were interesting, and what they could do with the portals could even be considered important. But how did that measure up to potentially eliminating the Major and however many soldiers they had inside the facility and the opportunity to destroy some of Albion's forces?

Besides, who said that there was no other way into this room? With what the *'leaked secret'* revealed about them, the most logical place for them to be taken was the portal.

The Major's people believed they had discovered the secrets of the facility, and maybe they mostly had. But they hadn't torn it down, and why would they? They had made use of the facility, not destroyed it. There could still be an undiscovered passage into the room, or they could simply be planning on making their own entrance.

The entire facility continued to tremble, sending plumes of concrete dust into the air. Thankfully, for them at least, no more of the room collapsed. They were left with a horseshoe-shaped wedge around the portal, leaving the back of the room completely unharmed.

"Well," Zack cursed, and coughed around the sudden influx of thick dust that coated the inside of his mouth and tongue. The light flickered above them and dimmed before returning to normal.

"Mom!" Tessa screamed, running to the pile of rubble and shifting what she could aside.

"Stop her," Zara order the bears, who quickly restrained the hysterical girl. "If you aren't careful, that entire mound could fall on you! Give Zack and I, a minute to start on the portal and then we can help clear the way to the door."

"Yeah, the bears can move everything to the back without destabilizing everything and bringing it down on our heads. And I can also just blast a hole through it all with my magic. Trust in your mom, she knew something was coming and ran. She's smart. I mean, she could have run in here with us, but she didn't."

Tessa growled and sniffed, shaking off the bears with a nod. "She told the soldiers she would return and probably thought that we would be safest in here alone with a collapsed entrance."

Zack walked over to the dark portal, while Zara began directing the bears on what pieces to grab first. For all intents, the portal looked as though it was undergoing its Change, only there was no dice floating above it. Not one that had changed colors and was lacking a countdown, nothing.

It was just a dark and unresponsive portal until he touched it.

The dark surface beneath rippled with a faint show of life as his fingers probed at its hardened crust. The outer layer cracked and flaked, the crumbs sinking into the portal proper beneath.

"Zara!" He called out. "Come, check this out."

She gave one last hurried instruction to the bears and then ran over to her brother. Standing by his side, it was easy to see why he had called for her.

"I guess the Major was right all along. We really were the keys to this portal." She muttered, reaching out to it with him.

The ripples underneath the surface grew more violent, licking away the underside of the crust in places. The cracks widened and broke, each piece pulled inexorably into the stormy portal beneath.

They moved their hands as the pieces of crust broke. Unsure of whether they should touch the portal itself or continue with the crust. They decided to play it safe. The roiling surface of the portal did not look like something they wanted to touch right then.

Piece after piece of the outer layer broke free, revealing the true portal beneath. Finally, only those they couldn't reach remained. It was time to either touch the portal or spend time they might not have waiting for the remaining pieces to fall in.

It looked different now. Each piece of the crust that had fallen back into it had seemingly brought it back to life, restoring its color.

"Do we wait, or risk touching the portal?" Zack asked, pulling his sister back with him. The violent, choppy surface of the portal unnerved him. It was different from the normal calm and welcoming one he was used to seeing. This portal felt dangerous.

"Let's wait. Something feels off about the portal right now. Let's focus on clearing the debris and reaching the door while we wait for it to get the remaining pieces and then calm down."

Zack turned around and raised his hand. "Everyone, move aside!" He yelled as a telltale purple glow appeared around his fingers. He waited for everyone to be out of his way and then fired.

The bolt tinged with black ate through the rubble, drilling a hole straight to the thick bent doors. To the side of them, crushed pieces of concrete and metal rained down from the ceiling. His space element had randomly chosen that location to disgorge everything it had eaten with the spell.

Unfortunately, with his lower stats on this side of the portal, the arcane bolt didn't have enough power to go any farther than the door. Not to mention that the only ones who could fit through the hole it had made were Zelda and George. He would have to exhaust his energy to widen it enough for the rest of them.

First, they needed to know if that was even a viable possibility. Which they could do by sending the two bears through the narrow passage. If everything beyond was also blocked, then they would need to think of another plan.

Zelda crawled into the hole he had created and made her way to the end. Where she proceeded to press her glass eye against every opening, she could find.

"She says she can see a few flickering lights from the hallway in the cracks, but that the doorway is completely blocked." Zara translated for them as the dusty bear returned. "And no, she didn't see any sign of your mother. It looks like she got away."

Tessa sighed in relief, her shoulders sagging from the weight that had been lifted from them. "What are we going to do, then? It sounds like we are trapped and cut off from everyone else."

"Don't forget, we are also stuck in a facility, that is, I'm guessing, being bombed from above."

Tessa's eyes tightened as she turned to glare at Zack. "Of course, how silly of me to forget that!"

"I'm just saying-"

"Guys," Zara called out, looking behind them. "Zack, Tessa, look!" She pointed at the madly fluctuating portal. Its undulating surface was reaching farther and farther out. All in a desperate bid to reach those last elusive shards at the top.

Everywhere the violent portal surface touched disappeared as it was sucked away. Concrete blocks vanished, along with pieces of the floor.

Everyone crowded together and moved to the side just as a long tongue of energy extended from it. The thick whip of energy lashed at the ground, digging a deep groove before lifting into the air and finally reaching the last pieces of hardened crust.

The surface of the portal calmed like a lake after a storm, with the ripples and waves slowing and growing smaller by the second. With the last of the ripples fading, the color of the portal finished returning to normal.

"That was different," Zack muttered, skirting around the new groove in the floor.

"Yeah, and so is that." Tessa pointed to the side of the portal where the power markers were. Only now, instead of being black, they had turned silver and combined into one ring.

He reached out to touch the portal, feeling the familiar and welcoming surface it had returned to at last. A message appeared as his fingers grazed the thick liquid syrup-like face, strands of it clinging to his fingers before snapping back to rejoin the rest of the portal.

Congratulations, you have received half ownership of a portal and all lands inside due to a title and your race interacting with each other. The other holder of this unique combination has received the other half of the portal's ownership. Once this dimensional fragment has been upgraded to a world fragment or beyond, ownership is still retained.

As owners' all time limits related to the portal can be adjusted, limited access to the dimensional fragment inside the portal may also be granted, restricting certain people from entering. More options will become available once it has upgraded to a world fragment and beyond.

This portal is ready to begin its Change, would you like to begin it now?

(Note: Due to the excessive length of time that the portal has been collecting energy and been unable to begin its Change all portals in the vicinity will undergo their Change as well. It is unknown as to the exact number that this will affect.)

Zack stepped back and glanced at his sister, the other holder of the unique combination it had mentioned. Her eyes were wide and staring into the air. She blinked and looked at him. That message was big, too big! And none of it mattered if they died or were captured again.

"Ookkaaayyy…" Zack drew out the word, his mind scrambling for something to say. "The portal works if we need to escape that way. Just know that we'll be trapped inside, probably, since it'll likely start its Change."

Tessa growled and threw her hands up in the air. "That's great, but let's think of a proper way out of here first, please. Can you just blast a hole through the wall into the next room?"

Zara shook her head. "The mountain is right behind this room, and what rooms there were are near the front. Where the walls already collapsed."

"So, what it really does come down to is Zack widening that hole, or going through the portal?" Tessa demanded, slowly giving in to panic. "WOULD YOU QUIT BOMBING US!" She screamed.

The facility shuddered again, a crack appearing overhead as the remaining concrete ceiling groaned.

Zara pulled off her pack and dropped it next to the portal. "Pretty much, and whichever one we go with needs to be quick. I don't think this place is going to last much longer."

Zack dropped his pack next to hers, having forgotten he even had it strapped to his chest. They would need them if they went through the portal. On the other hand, they would only get in the way if they needed to fight.

"Tessa." He walked over to the stressed-out girl and took her hands in his. "Calm down, we've got this, and so does your mother. Wherever she is, she's safe. She is scarier than these explosions. She'll just glare at them, and they'll stop until she passes. She could walk on a live mine and order it not to explode until she had walked away, and it would obey her. The woman is terrifying and no matter what, she'll be fine."

Tessa snorted and then laughed at his ridiculous impression of her mother. "She's not that bad."

"Yes, she is," Zara called out from her position near the debris. She was already back to directing the bears on which pieces to move.

The dusty redhead breathed in with a flutter of her lashes. "Thanks, I needed to hear that. Let's just worry about ourselves for now. You're right, mom will be fine. She knows what she's doing. What are the odds that there is another way out of this room?"

Zack shrugged. "I have no idea. Probably not good. I imagine that the Major's people would have found it if there was one. However, I figure it makes sense that they would think we would be brought here and since they didn't destroy the entire room..." He let the thought dangle.

"You're right, with the info mom released about the two of you, they would definitely assume you were brought here." Her eyes trailed down to where his hands were still holding hers, and a blush crept up her neck.

He released them and stepped back. "Exactly, it really just depends on how much thought they put into this place when they built it."

"I'm more curious as to what's going on with all the soldiers right now?" Zara looked away from the blocked door. "Did the Major have them all in the facility waiting or were they outside?"

Zack winced. "I was thinking about that earlier, and it's possible that the organization and Shouvain could have just dealt a decent blow to Albion.

I'm not sure how high up in the military the Major actually is, but he does seem to have the king and queen's ear, so he's at least trusted."

The facility shuddered again, and a chunk fell from the ceiling with a crash.

Zara spun and pointed at Tessa. "You! What did you scream about earlier?"

"Um?" It took Tessa a moment to remember. "I think it was something about, stop bombing us?"

The young girl paled and collapsed onto a chunk of fallen concrete.

"Zara!" Zack raced over to her. "What's wrong? Talk to me."

"I think Shouvain just declared war on Albion, and either Fittrel joined them or is now at war with them as well."

It took Zack a second to understand what she was saying. "The airship, of course. They're bombing us from above, which means they must have some means of doing so. And only Fittrel has that capability right now."

"How did they get it? It left here after the attack and returned to Fittrel, where it should have been safe." Tessa interjected.

"Maybe they were expecting them to do that, and the attack here was actually a feint to get them to play into their hands." Zack guessed, throwing up his hands. "Or maybe the ship made a pit-stop somewhere and was hijacked there by a lucky idiot. Does it really matter?"

"No, you're right, they have it either way. How they got it doesn't matter for now."

Zack scratched at his head, displacing a plume of concrete dust. "Okay, so that's bad, especially for the soldiers, but we're still trapped, so let's focus on that for now. Zara, do you know what was above us? If I was to shoot it in the right spot, we might be able to climb up and escape that way."

Her face screwed up in thought. "I think it was the floor where most of them lived, but I'm not sure. It could be completely blocked off from whatever they used to destroy the ceiling though. Actually, it likely is in worse shape than down here, assuming, of course, they were aiming to lock us in this room. If it was merely a lucky shot, then anything is possible."

Zack felt at his magical energy level and made a rough guess. "I have enough for another two, maybe three shots. What do you both think? Should we try it?" He had no idea if his *Life Burner* ability worked on this side of the portal yet. There was no reason to believe it didn't, since the healing was a side effect of that ability.

"Could you clear a path to the hall for us with those?" Tessa asked.

"For Zelda and George, probably. It wouldn't be wide enough for any of us though."

There was a squeal of noise and dozens of long dust lines suddenly slowly drifted down from the ceiling between them. Apprehensively, the three looked up. Dozens of holes were in the process of being drilled into the ceiling while they had been arguing in a roughly circular pattern.

"I don't think we need to worry about a way out anymore," Zack muttered, grabbing his sister and Tessa. "Get ready for some uninvited guests instead. We need to stop them before they can touch the ground and draw their weapons."

"That's going to be a problem. I only have my knives!" Tessa hissed as they backed away and into a corner near the door.

The bears ran towards them and quickly began stacking the chunks of concrete they had been moving into a barrier. Every little bit would help in whatever was to come. If they were lucky, they might even be able to get them high enough and convince the soldiers that there was no one in the room.

The circular outline in the ceiling shuddered and cracked as new holes were made around its perimeter.

"Hurry," Zack urged the bears, helping them to stack the pieces higher. It wouldn't fool anyone unfortunately, there wasn't enough time for that. It would give them a place to stage their eventual fight back from, and that would need to be enough.

The bears climbed inside with them and clung to Zara, just as the cutout cracked and fell from the ceiling. A rope was thrown down from the gloom above, the angle keeping Zack from seeing anything. If he had been able to see up there, he could have blinked into their midst with Tessa's knife. It was a bad plan, and he would have died quickly, in all probability.

Still, he couldn't keep the thought from running through his head. He hated waiting in these situations.

"Do you see them?" Came from above.

"Not yet. The ship is holding position. We have time."

The first of the soldiers slid down the rope, followed quickly by the second and then a third.

Chapter 38

Zack felt his heart calm. They could handle three soldiers. He had at least two shots left and there were also the bears and Tessa. They would be fine.

A fourth, much larger and by far uglier soldier rappelled down, and he grew a little worried again. How many soldiers were they going to send down simply to look for and detain them? Had they been expecting soldiers in the room with him and Zara?

A fifth soldier began to rappel down.

"I don't see anyone." One of the soldiers said.

"I do," The big soldier was looking straight at their hastily constructed hiding place. "Come out, or we'll have to hurt you!" An evil grin was spread across the brute's ugly face.

"Just try it!" Zack yelled back, huddling behind the rubble. "You all came here for us, so you can't kill us, and we can handle some pain." He was trying to goad some of the soldiers into moving closer to them. "Get your knives ready, in case more than one comes over." He whispered to Zelda and Tessa.

The big guy laughed. "Good, so you are the brats we're looking for."

Zack was half-tempted to wave his hand in front of the guy's face and say, *'We are not the brats you are looking for'*, just to mess with him. Luckily, he had come a long way in gaining control of his tongue recently. Besides, he didn't want to get that close to someone that big and ugly. He might get eaten or grow warts; anything was possible when you looked like that.

"What gave it away, the fact that we're in here with a fully functioning and glowing portal? Or simply that there is no one else in here?" Then again, maybe he hadn't made as much progress as he had thought.

"He's got you there Georgy!" A couple of the soldiers laughed and stepped closer.

Zara stilled and hissed out, "That thing! Is an affront to the name George. He's not cute or cuddly at all!"

The teddy bear George preened.

Zack rolled his eyes, while Tessa twitched a brow in temporary amusement. These siblings were odd in a lot of ways, but she liked them. They were her first real friends, and that meant something to her she couldn't quite explain. Not yet, at least.

The now named Georgy grunted and stomped towards them. The five soldiers were confident that they could overpower a couple of young teenagers and weren't bothering to even pretend they were worried.

Zack's hand began to glow as he prepared an arcane bolt. "Tessa, grab his pistol or rifle as quickly as you can. Zara, toss Zelda towards the soldiers as soon as I fire. Then I want you both to huddle behind me and the big oaf's body. I'll bring up my armor spell, which should be good for blocking a shot or two." He rattled off instructions to them quickly, as the big guy crunched his way over.

"You might be right in that we can't kill you, but that doesn't mean I can't break each of your bones for annoying me." Georgy roared, jumping onto the pile of broken concrete they were hiding behind.

"Man, you have a very short fuse." Zack quipped, pointing his finger and taking as much energy from the bolt as he could. A slightly smaller than normal arcane bolt shot from his hand and destroyed the man's head, erasing it from existence. The bolt sped on past, skimming the rope they had rappelled down and then slamming into the ceiling.

Above them, Zelda sailed through the air; daggers held at the ready in both paws.

A spurt of blood fountained up from Georgy's empty neck, as his heart beat for a few more seconds before figuring out the meat sack was dead. Tessa reached around Zack and pulled the pistol from the dead fellow's holster and set it to charge for a shot. She would need to wait for his lifeless body to fall over before she could grab the rifle from his hands.

Zara chucked George through the air, aiming him in a different direction from Zelda. Unlike the other bear, his paws were empty of weapons. He would only be able to punch the enemy and serve as a distraction. Taking her own initiative, Aisha bounced over the concrete barrier and sprinted towards the rope. She planned on climbing up it and taking care of those above them before anyone else could come down.

Everything happened within seconds of Zack taking his shot. The arcane bolt shocked the soldiers, who hadn't been expecting him to use any kind of magic. Tessa and Zara spun around to line up behind Zack as he used his arcane armor spell for the first time since getting it this time around.

A transparent purple armor appeared over his clothes instantly, a split second before the soldiers opened fire on them. The bullets hit the misshapen concrete blocks and bit into them, disgorging clouds of cement dust everywhere.

The explosive noise temporarily deafened them all as the sound waves bounced around in the confined space.

Tessa waited for them to stop firing before unsteadily popping up and taking her first shot with the pistol. Narrowly avoiding shooting the same person that Zelda was in the process of working over with her knives. Pained screams filled the air as the sharp blades dug into him. Her shot was slightly off the mark but no less effective as it winged a soldier in the hipbone. The ball the pistol fired destroyed the man's hip completely and ensured that he would bleed out within minutes, if not sooner.

Aisha started to swing her way up the rope, only to have it snap where Zack's bolt had skimmed it earlier. From there, everything descended into madness as George climbed onto one soldier and began punching them.

Zelda abandoned her lump of meat and threw a dagger at the last free soldier running towards where the others were hiding. The knife arced through the air and bounced, hilt-first, uselessly off the man's helmet. If they survived, she was determined to practice throwing her blades mores. The Shouvain traveler working with Dorn before had made it look so easy and useful.

It might be useful, but certainly wasn't easy to do correctly.

Zack spotted the incoming soldier and stood up, intent on making himself the focus of any attack. Tessa still needed another second or two for the pistol to recharge for its next shot.

All thoughts of taking Zack and Zara alive had seemingly fled from the man's mind as he raised his rifle and fired.

Zack felt his magical energy reserves plummet as his armor absorbed the impact and damage. Without delaying a second longer, Tessa raised the pistol and fired, praying that it had enough of a charge to kill or disable the man. Unlike the people in the mountain, these soldiers had gotten proper weapons that were capable of half-charges.

The soldier flew backward, a hole appearing in his chest where his stomach had been moments before.

Seeing that the last soldier was busy with George and Aisha, Zack wearily let his spell drop. Using arcane armor was great in a pinch, but maintaining it all the time was impossible, as it continuously used up his limited energy.

Zack ripped the rifle from Georgy's fingers and climbed over their hastily constructed barricade. It had performed better than he thought it would. Honestly, he hadn't been sure how the material would hold up to Majair fire, especially in its semi-weakened state.

Tessa dully shot the last surviving soldier while Zack went underneath the hole with the charged rifle at the ready. From beneath, he could see where explosive charges had been used to pierce through the other floors to reach their room quickly. Only their ceiling had been drilled through with care, while the others looked like gaping holes of ruin.

He wasn't sure what kind of explosive they had been using, but he was glad they hadn't used it on them. Unfortunately, there were no other soldiers in the room above. The few that had been there escaped when everything had gone sideways for the team below. Most people were smart enough to know they couldn't compete with magic, and a giant teddy bear climbing up the rope was a clear sign of magic.

Zack propped the butt of the stock against his shoulder and aimed the rifle straight up at the hovering airship above them. From his vantage point below it, he could see sparks flying off its surface as soldiers fired on it. He had to admit, despite not really working inside the portals, the Majair's had proven their worth to him.

From below like this, it would take more skill to miss than it would to hit the giant target. With a defiant roar of frustration, Zack squeezed the trigger and fired.

His ears were ringing from the constant loud noises in the confined space as he stepped away from the hole.

"What do we do now?" Zara shouted, wincing as her eardrums throbbed.

Zack stared at the hole in the ceiling and the blocked door. "We keep moving what we can, and hopefully we'll unblock the door or create a path to the next floor."

The need to hurry before the airship dropped another explosive on them went unspoken. This time, they might just cut their losses and decide nobody could have the siblings. After all, nobody knew what they could and couldn't actually do. To them, it was all rumors, even the portals going dark in relation to him.

Without confirmation of any kind, there was only so much effort they would put towards capturing them. After a certain point, it simply made more sense to just bomb the entire facility into oblivion.

Tessa was standing over the soldier she had shot. The one that was being pummeled by George and Aisha. "He was helpless, no longer a threat to us, and yet I still shot him." She muttered, unable to reconcile with what she had done in the heat of the moment.

"Does it really matter if he was helpless or not?" Zack asked, coming up beside her. "He knew what he was doing when he came down here. Besides, if you hadn't done it, then the bears would have killed him, eventually. There's no point in feeling guilty over someone like him. He wasn't innocent in this. He wasn't a civilian or a bystander, but someone who actively chose to attack us."

"Is it really that easy for you?" Tessa turned to look into his eyes. Unconsciously dropping the pistol onto the man's body.

Zack looked away and nodded. "It's been me and Zara against the world for so long, we didn't have the luxury to develop normal morals or values. These soldiers wanted to attack people that I hold close, so my conscience is clear."

A grinding noise from behind them disturbed their conversation. Aisha and the others had managed to dig out one of the pallets of packaged military food and were dragging it over to the hole. Most of the packages on top had been crushed and broken open, but the ones beneath them were still good.

The entire pile of concrete groaned at the sudden void they had created.

Zack shot forward and pulled his sister back just as it shifted and began tumbling down. In moments, all the progress they had made was undone. On the bright side, however, a path had now opened to the ceiling above the door.

Scrambling up the ramp of broken concrete pieces, they were able to reach the floor above easily. Not that it helped much. Whatever bomb or explosive the airship had dropped on them had done a real number on that entire area. Everything had collapsed, blocking their way forward.

It did give them a nice view, however, of the smoking ship as it sank towards them. One of the many shots the soldiers had fired must have gotten lucky.

"Push the pallet through the portal. We'll need the food!" Zack screamed at Aisha and George, breaking the other two from their shock. "Grab your pack and let's go jump through it before that thing lands on us."

Zelda, meanwhile, had retrieved the dagger she had thrown and picked up both of their packs from the groove in the floor. George and Aisha pushed the pallet through the portal in a show of magic-induced strength and then ran over to Zelda.

Zack skidded to a stop beside the groove and retrieved his pack from his sister and Aisha, hoisting the large bear into his arms. "Everyone, link up arms with me. Something tells me we don't want to go through this portal alone."

Zelda leaped into Zara's arms with her pack, while Tessa retrieved George.

"I have no idea what is going on outside this room, but mom had better be safe when we return!" The fiery red-haired girl told them, placing her arm in Zack's.

Zara did the same with his other side, and together, they stepped through the portal. Moments later, the airship crashed down onto the facility and exploded, setting off every bomb it still had on board.

In an instant, the back half of the institute had been erased, turned into a smoking ruin that would take months to dig through before they could reach the portal. A portal that was now dark with a slowly spinning twelve-sided dice hanging above it.

***

Zack felt as though he had been punched in the gut as he collapsed on the ground and hurled. Tears pricked his eyes as he gasped for breath. Beside him, he could hear two other people doing the exact same thing he was.

"What was that?" Tessa gasped out.

"That-" Zara spit out some chunks from lunch and retrieved a bottle of water from her pack to swish out her mouth. "Was us not going where we were supposed to. This isn't where that portal is supposed to connect."

Zack finished spitting out the gunk in his mouth and looked up. She was right. Wherever they were, was nothing like where that portal had always taken them before. What was worse, the pallet full of military food hadn't made it through to wherever they were.

"Did it move?" He wondered.

"Not likely," Zara flopped onto her back beside a motionless Zelda. The bear was looking up at the sky. "Look at..." She trailed off.

Above them was a completely normal moon and sun in the sky, not something you usually saw inside a portal. They had seen them when they were on the snow elf world, but they were on a world then, not inside a portal. Right now, they were supposed to be inside a portal.

"What?" Zack followed her gaze. "Oh."

A message appeared in front of the three as they were taking in the alien sky.

> *Excess of portal energy required for Change detected – Beginning transfer to all portals in the vicinity and beginning their respective Changes. Energy is still in excess of safety limits, expanding transfer reach to global parameters.*
> *Shunting incoming transfer to -ERROR- no incoming transfer detected -LOCATION LOST-.*
> *All access to world parallel fragment code-named -Aperra- locked.*
> *Current location is under -Gaia's Control- all time limits have been erased in this location.*

Abruptly, the message flickered and closed, leaving the three stunned.

"Did it just say that we got shunted off into an unknown space?" Tessa screeched.

"There are no time limits," Zara muttered. "That means we won't get taken back automatically either since this is a world."

George waddled over and held a paw up to his mouth.

Behind him, Aisha was staring at some nearby trees with her fists at the ready.

"We can worry about where we are and everything else later." Zack cracked his neck and surged to his feet. "It looks like we're not alone."

The trees trembled as something crashed through them. Each second bringing the sound closer to them.

"It's a world, so maybe they're friendly." Zara held up the Majair pistol that she had retrieved when Tessa had dropped it. Since they were on a world instead of inside a portal, maybe it would work and not blow up in her hand after a few seconds.

A large ogre stomped into view, the remains of a tree dragging behind it.

Zelda glanced down at her small daggers and then the large tree it was using as a club. It was as though a whole new world had been opened to her eyes. One where she wasn't limited to just small blades. Why wasn't she carrying around swords as tall or even taller than herself? They were all pointy and sharp, after all.

The three teenagers shivered and looked around, wondering why it had gotten cold all of the sudden.

Zack grinned at Tessa, "You know wood burns, right? Why don't you start us off this time?"

Tessa felt for her magic and smiled when she found it ready and at her disposal. "Yes, why don't I?"

Epilogue

"I can't believe you stole that monster's knife!" Zara grumped, glaring at a filthy Zelda. "It's not even made of anything good. I know you have been wanting something bigger lately, but couldn't you have gone for something sharper and less rusty?"

Zack swallowed some water and passed the bottle to Tessa. "I think she was desperate at this point. We've been here for what, a week and a half without seeing anyone or anything besides monsters wanting to kill us? She took what she could get, and she wasn't the only one."

George, who had already gone through the crystal's strengthening process inside him, after Aisha was done with it, had also picked up some weapons of choice. With the help of Zara's modification spell, a pair of deadly punching gloves had been shaped to his paws.

Aisha had it easier since she just picked up a random bow and decided she liked it. Not that she could hit anything with it in the beginning, but after a week of practice, she was getting better.

The main problem lay with where they were. The group had been following a stream of water they had found in the woods that first day. Yet despite seeing monsters and animals aplenty, they hadn't seen any other intelligent beings.

There was another problem as well, though it had taken them a while to understand it. The amount of experience they were getting here was odd. It was almost as though it suddenly had no idea how much each kill was actually worth. Sometimes, they would get a lot, and other times, nothing.

It was infuriating, and more than a little disturbing.

So, while their physical levels weren't progressing like they should have been. The same couldn't be said for their spell and ability levels. Those depended more on use, not experience. Each of their spells and abilities had gained at least one level, while some, like their attack spells, had gotten two.

Zelda strutted forward with the giant, to her, knife in tow. Imagining all the things, she would be able to poke and stab more efficiently with the larger, if somewhat dull and rusty blade. She pushed past a few trees beside the stream and then broke into a run.

Zara's breath hitched in surprise. "Hurry up, Zelda says she can see a clearing with buildings ahead!"

The group broke into a tired run, winding their way past the trees and coming to an abrupt stop once they reached the clearing. It was true that there were buildings ahead of them, but they all looked broken and had been left to the elements. Tufts of grass and trees could be seen poking through the cracked brickwork.

Whatever the place might have once been, it was abandoned now.

They sat there for a few minutes, feeling helpless and alone. When abruptly Zara stood up and pointed at the abandoned town.

"Come on, we've finally found signs of people... We can't give up now! We just have to follow the roads out of this place once we find it and go to the next one. Surely, they can't all be deserted!"

Zack came to his knees as the ground appeared to ripple out from the middle of the town and extended towards them. Everywhere the ripple touched vanished into particles of light and was replaced with verdant green grass.

In a second, before any of them could react, the ripple had eaten everything in sight, revealing a single dark building. There were easily dozens or more people surrounding it during the brief glance they got. Where the ripples ended, a wall grew from the ground and extended high into the air.

"Let's look for the gate," Tessa said, coming out of her shocked state first. "Whoever has the power to do something like this might be able to help us!"

The gate was easy enough to find and thankfully open when they ran through it a few minutes later.

They pushed their way through the gathered people and stopped in front of the building everyone was looking at. The closed-door opened a moment later, revealing a woman with purple streaks in her hair and a man with glowing golden eyes and silver runes on the back of one hand by her side.

The man opened his mouth to speak, and then stopped when he saw the bears and the three newcomers. "Well, this isn't what we were expecting when we stopped here today. Then again, I doubt anyone ever expects to meet otherworlders. At least not down here, this isn't Roswell, or Ohio."

He tilted his head and smiled at them. "I wonder who could have brought you here... No, I guess that doesn't matter. Welcome to Earth, other-worlders. My name is Charles, and this is my fiancé, Kira. What might your names be?"

End Book 2

Acknowledgements

I would like to thank my alpha readers, my family, who spend endless hours reading and re-reading everything I write, as well as seeking out any plot holes and typos. It has taken me a long time to get to the point in my life where I can actually sit down and write like I have wanted to for so very long, to all the people that have encouraged me over the years and helped make this possible, I thank you!

About the Author

J oshua Kern was born in a little town situated somewhere in Ohio and raised in an even smaller town someplace in Colorado. He attended University for a time, where he discovered that while he enjoyed Electrical Engineering and Computer Science his true passion lay in writing. He lives primarily in Colorado but has been known to move around as the need arises. When not writing, Joshua enjoys riding motorcycles, reading anything he can get his hands on, and anime.

Other Books by Joshua Kern

Refton & Thomas

Forgotten Spies

Forgotten Child

The Game of Gods

Arc 1 – Human

The Beginning

The Death of Champions

Arc 2 – Demi-God

Fragments

A Tower Novella

Pieces of Divinity

Arc 3 – God

Everything Ends

The Dungeon Alaria

Arc 1 – Integration

The Dungeon Alaria

The Creator's Daughter

Arc 2 – ??

The Nameless Chronicles

Portals of Albion

Portals of Change

Realms & Runes

Runic Cultivator

The Well Within

The Well Within

Stand Alone

The Ridden

Duologies & Box Sets

The Game of Gods: Arc 1 Duology Box Set

The Dungeon Alaria: The World of Alaria Arc 1 Duology Box Set

www.ingramcontent.com/pod-product-compliance
Lightning Source LLC
Chambersburg PA
CBHW031024030726
47497CB00004B/998